Readers love DAMON SUEDE'S

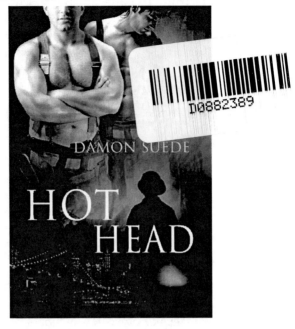

Named by Goodreads as one of the
"Top 100 Romance Novels of All Time" in 2014

A *Romantic Times* "Favorite Firefighters in romance" on 9/11/2012
A Band of Thebes Best LGBT Book of 2012

"Up front, this is one of the best M/M romances I have read lately … The story is simple but hot as hell … It had that level of romanticism that makes your heart ache good … I strongly recommend this novel to all romance lovers."
—Elisa's Reviews and Ramblings

"Magical and beautiful even when it gets down and dirty. Not only is there hot sex, but it is hot, emotional sex …The one thing this book has that no other does is Mr. Damon Suede and his unique and authentic voice … A raw, emotional, very hot, worth-every-penny read! Awarded the Golden Nib: for books that knock our socks off!"
—Miss Love Loves Books

"Grip-you-by-the-gut angst … and Mr. Suede's unique, fascinating voice … Wildly entertaining and fresh … I just could not put this book down."
5 Gold Crowns and a Recommended Read
—Laurel, Readers' Roundtable

PENT UP

DAMON SUEDE

Published by

DREAMSPINNER PRESS

5032 Capital Circle SW, Suite 2, PMB# 279, Tallahassee, FL 32305-7886 USA
www.dreamspinnerpress.com

This is a work of fiction. Names, characters, places, and incidents either are the product of author imagination or are used fictitiously, and any resemblance to actual persons, living or dead, business establishments, events, or locales is entirely coincidental.

ISBN: 978-1-62798-050-0
Digital ISBN: 978-1-62798-464-5
Library of Congress Control Number: 2015950525
First Edition November 2015

Printed in the United States of America
∞

This paper meets the requirements of
ANSI/NISO Z39.48-1992 (Permanence of Paper).

For all the secrets that break us and the promises that make us.

CHAPTER ONE

SOME GUYS are born with a target for a face.

At 8:17 on a Monday morning, Ruben was stomping up Broadway through rush-hour pedestrians when an elbow jabbed him in the ribs and shoved him sideways. Hot coffee sloshed onto his belly and pants and splattered onto the sidewalk along with the lid.

Really? His blocky knuckles dripped caffeine. Some asshole had knocked it all over him.

His free fist tightened. He spun to spot the guilty son of a bitch. "Hey!"

Ruben's face got him into plenty of scuffles. Stony scowl, dark skin, proud nose. Strangers swung at him often enough that he didn't mind anymore and took advantage of their fear whenever he could.

Step up. Ruben crushed the cup and what was left of the coffee gushed up and out. He said nothing as he scanned the nervous faces, allowing the menace to bake off him. *Step to me, junior.*

But the elbow's owner had vanished, and the commuters around him jostled away like Ruben was radioactive. No one said a word.

He had stopped for real java to wake him up for his first day. Not that syrupy Starbucks shit, but hand-roasted perfection from a tiny Peruvian lady he'd found around the corner from his brother's office. She always had a line and he didn't care.

"Jeez." He stopped and swatted at his soaked belly. He'd already removed his borrowed jacket on the 6 train and sweated through his shirt crossing Central Park South. The windy day was hot enough that it might dry before he reached the office.

His bull's-eye face had gotten him in trouble again.

Ruben eyed numbers on the buildings. He looked at the map on his phone again. He hadn't figured out the streets and the avenues yet. He had been in New York three weeks, ditching Miami as soon as his divorce was final. Fuck Marisa and fuck the Sunshine State.

Ten months of not drinking and living in a motel had kicked his ass all the way to Manhattan. He'd found an AA meeting in the neighborhood and started to look for a sponsor in the city.

New start, new life.

He'd caught a jetBlue flight right onto his kid brother's doorstep. He arrived with all his hair, two changes of clothes, and plenty of experience beating the shit out of people. Anything was possible.

Half a block from the office, pounding footsteps on the concrete made him turn to look over his shoulder. Someone yelped in surprise back at Ninth Avenue.

"Stop!"

Twenty feet up on the crowded sidewalk, a skinny man in a windbreaker sprinted right at him, knocking angry New Yorkers out of the way. He sported a thick walrus mustache and clutched something black. *Gun?*

"Stop him!" A thirtyish dude in a suit sprinted hard, catching up in the cleared wake. "Hey!"

Both men were running directly toward Ruben, and the rush-hour mob gave him no room to maneuver. When he tried to step clear, an old man on his right pushed back with a glare.

Skinny walrus plowed into the commuter crowds, elbowing suits and secretaries out of his way. No one interfered. Typical.

Hard to tell who the bad guy was, but to be truthful, Ruben had no shits to give.

None of my fucking business.

He could see the door and all he wanted to do was get off the street. Already, Ruben was late for work and had no intention of sticking his beak in. He'd bounced and brawled enough to know trouble when he saw it chugging at him on rails. He was hemmed in by shuffling commuters and too big to slip between them.

The red-faced pursuer kept chasing, slower but steady, the tie flapping over his shoulder. He barked again breathlessly, "Wallet. Hey!" A picked pocket, then.

No time to react. Ten feet now, Walrus looked up, right at Ruben, then lowered his head to rush like a bull. On purpose most likely 'cause Ruben hadn't moved back.

Fuck you.

As Walrus rammed into him, Ruben shifted left and twisted, extending his arm, and caught his waist. Instead of releasing him, Ruben hoisted the narrow body into the air on his shoulder and flipped him sideways into the newsstand at the curb. Candy bars and magazines smacked the pavement.

"Asshole." Ruben stood and wiped his cheek, and the crowd pulled back, gawking. He stepped on the skinny arm and clawed the wallet from the scrabbling hand. He tugged, the wallet gaped, and without warning a sheaf of $100 bills whipped loose into the hot breeze churned by the traffic. *Good job, Oso.*

The crowd went berserk. Pedestrians knelt and scrambled to scrape the cash off the sidewalk and street as Walrus tried to get to his feet, slipping on shredded newspapers.

Ruben was so broke that even one of those hundreds would've made a difference, but he couldn't make himself crouch. "I can't believe these—"

"Hey!" Footsteps. The suit in pursuit had reached him, red faced and out of breath, running right over the money. "Thank—"

Ruben pushed through the pandemonium. "Where's a cop? Huh?" He looked at the shameless crowd stealing in plain sight. One girl was holding her phone up, taking pictures or video of folks scraping and squabbling over the crisp bills. "Where's a goddamn cop?"

Movement and growls behind Ruben made him turn. Walrus had staggered to his feet, knocking over a pile of *New York Post*s that slid across the sidewalk as he loped away, kicking the other thieves aside. So fast everything almost felt staged.

"Thank you." Closer now, the wallet's owner didn't sound upset. "Thanks."

Ruben looked up as the other guy pushed in front of him: handsome with a square Anglo face like a goddamn bull's-eye.

Talk about a target.

Ruben had always thought his resting thug face picked fights for him, but this one? *Shit.* Practically begged to be mugged or popped.

"Beautiful, man. Amazing." He smiled at Ruben, still shaking his hand.

Jesus, he's good-looking.

"You're a life saver."

"Uh. I didn't save shit." Ruben gestured at the bold thieves around them.

"I don't care about the money. No." He shrugged and riffled through the wallet, checking for something besides the cash, maybe? "Doesn't matter."

Ruben was too late and annoyed to pay much attention.

"Yeah. Great." The coffee stiffened Ruben's shirt in the sultry June air. He had zero interest in sticking around to explain to cops. The way he looked, he needed to tread careful here. "Whatever."

A faraway siren scattered the rest of the commuters. Back at the newsstand, a paunchy vendor salvaged the papers he could still sell, cursing at no one and everyone.

Ruben swiped at his chest again. The spill didn't show too much on his brother's suit but the shirt was a goner. "Damn it, damn it." His brother could bitch him out later for screwing up his first day. *Like always.* He pushed through bodies toward the office's front doors.

Empire Security had an itty-bitty suite Charles had leased next to a nail salon far west of Columbus Circle, over near the river. A ten-minute walk from any subway station. Ruben knew nothing about Manhattan, but from the battered grates and overflowing garbage cans he figured the rents were lower in this area for a reason. Charles loved to cut corners, so his firm was called "Empire" because that was the name painted on the door when he moved in: Empire Salvage. Charles had replaced "alvage" with "ecurity."

As Ruben reached for the elevator button, he sensed someone in his blind spot. *Company.*

"Hold up." Wallet dude stood right behind him, shifting his weight in a two-thousand-dollar suit with his gold tie still crooked from running. Handsome but a little goofy. Late thirties, couple years younger than Ruben. Not skinny or thick, more of a medium build. Glossy ash-brown hair and a jaw too square to take seriously, like a corny dad in a minivan commercial.

Is he following me?

"Uh. I didn't take your money." Ruben's skin tightened. *Go away.* He looked back in the direction of the scuffle. "You shoulda stayed out there to talk to the cops."

"Same." The man smiled, flushed but not sweaty. His eyes were a strange blue-gray, soft as felt.

For the first time, Ruben clocked the expensive clues he'd missed outside: the razor-cut hair and four-hundred-dollar dress shirt. Manicured hands, buffed and pink. On his wrist, he sported a seven thousand dollar Ebel watch. Handmade loafers. "Look, I gotta—" He nodded at the Empire Security sign.

"We're going the same way, then." He let Ruben step through. "Allow me."

Allow you what?

Ruben scowled as he poked the button for his floor. "Empire?"

"Appointment." He eyed Ruben's arms and shoulders. "You got some fucking moves, huh. Soldier? Fed?"

Ruben shook his head. He'd dropped out of boot camp so long ago it didn't count. "Not really."

"Gotcha." The guy seemed to be waiting for a signal. "But security now." He nodded sagely as if that explained everything.

Ruben stared at the numbers overhead, his inner freak detector blaring. He plucked at his drying crotch and wished for a swallow of the coffee he was wearing. "I'm late already."

"Me too." His stalker didn't move. Just that intense scrutiny which made his skin prickle. "Sorry about before, the—" The guy snapped his mouth shut, biting down on whatever he'd almost shared.

Off-balance, Ruben swiped at the cooling splotch of coffee on his slacks. *Terrific.*

"I'm Andy." He didn't blink. "Bauer." *Huh.* The exaggerated jaw practically begged for a left hook, such an obvious target it made his square face seem familiar. He smiled crookedly, revealing one deep dimple.

Ruben snuck another skeptical glance. "Do I know you?"

"No. I owe you, man." Like Ruben, he stood a couple of inches under six feet, but he seemed glued together out of felt scraps. *Raggedy Andy.* Ruben had twenty pounds on him easy.

Ruben looked down at the greasy linoleum. This is what he got for giving a shit. He was gonna show up for his first day at work late, wet, and ignorant, followed by some Anglo weirdo who looked like a handsome punching bag. *Could this elevator be slower?* He'd bet money this loaf of white bread had never thrown a punch or held a gun in his life.

That face.

Ten bucks said Andy Bauer didn't curse. Twenty bucks said he played Frisbee with an Irish setter.

He seemed to be holding his breath, so Ruben did too. *Freaky.* The elevator arrived and they both stepped inside.

Fifty bucks said he'd never talked to an alcoholic greaseball. A hundred, all Bauer's friends were as uptight and lily white as he was.

Nobody can be as honest as this guy looks.

And so, Ruben ducked into his brother's office ten minutes late with a good-looking lunatic in tow, ready to be bitched out.

The trim receptionist turned back to wave him toward the office, her ass like a plum, high and sweet. They'd met a couple days ago, and she only knew him as her boss's loser brother. She barely looked at him. "Mr. Oso? *Le esperan.*"

He nodded at the Spanish and pretended he understood so she'd smile and stop talking. He was Colombian, so people assumed, but he only spoke about ten words of español. "Good morning," "Thank you," and "Fuck off, I don't speak Spanish" marked the outer limits of his conversational abilities thanks to poor, snobbish grandparents who'd given up everything to come north to the Land of the Free-range Idiots.

Behind him Bauer said something to her and she made friendly chatty sounds.

Charles poked his head out and knocked on the door frame. "Wanna introduce me to your buddy?"

Bauer chuckled.

"We don't know each other." Ruben nodded a silent apology at his brother. He could feel Bauer approaching him from behind but didn't turn. "I think he's yours."

Charles sported one of his Hawaiian shirts: hibiscuses and starfish on teal. He collected the ugly things and wore nothing else, even under suits. Back in Florida, everyone made fun of the habit, but Charles dug the comfort and the color, still pretending to be a mobster when he could get away with it.

"Andy Bauer. I'm your nine o'clock."

"Charles Oso."

Handshakes. They stepped into the cramped office.

Bauer turned back to Ruben. "And you are?"

"Ruben."

Charles sat down. "How—?"

For the first time, Ruben looked Bauer straight in the eye and was a little startled to find him staring back with unblinking intensity. Baffled blue-gray eyes, soft and hidden as dust bunnies. Bauer spoke without turning. "He tossed a mugger for me downstairs."

"Ruben is joining us from Florida." Charles rummaged in the heap of files composting on his desk.

Bauer looked between them. "You look like brothers." Uptight little nod.

They did: same square build, same Colombian beak, same crappy clothes… except Charles had gotten tubby and wasn't sleeping on anyone's couch. Ruben had wrestled in high school and had his father's barrel chest; he couldn't touch his toes, but his knuckles could crack a windshield.

Besides, Empire wasn't exactly the Secret Service. In lieu of a loan, Charles had thrown Ruben a job, paying him to get his shit together.

Charles nailed Ruben with a don't-fuck-it-up glare, but he spoke to the handsome stranger. "Point is, I'm giving you my best, here."

Bauer looked to be loaded and paranoid. "I've considered hiring a private investigator, except security is the real issue." He kept fidgeting and combing Ruben with those weird light eyes, as if trying to place his face.

Ruben cracked his knuckles quietly. Something didn't fit. "Private investigation isn't something Empire offers."

"But security is." Charles waved Ruben's objections away.

"I appreciate it." Bauer spoke with a lowish voice, not deep but hushed… like he needed extra air to get words out. "I know the whole thing sounds crazy."

Charles turned to Ruben and they shared a glance that felt like an eye roll. This job sounded like bullshit. Charles knew he needed the money, and maybe this was some kinda bone, beginner-friendly and screw-up-proof. A favor for a client?

If Ruben hadn't been late he could've gotten the 411 from his brother, but that was his own fault. Long as someone paid him, he'd guard an outhouse.

"We're going to need details." Charles flapped a sheaf of paper onto his cluttered desk. "I got a contract here. Formality, but still."

Ruben stole another glance at their new client, which gave him a funny feeling he couldn't name.

Charles's mobile rang and he held up a finger to answer it. He looked to Bauer. "Why don't you fill Rube in?" That quickly, Charles had ducked out and Ruben was low man on the pole. *So much for felt scraps.*

Taking his brother's chair, Ruben let his wide shoulders brush Sir Whitebread anyways, just to let him know who'd be in charge. Well, as in charge as you can be when you're surviving on Burger King and your little brother's pullout. Ruben had the indigestion and the crick in his neck to prove it. He wasn't twenty. Hell, he wasn't thirty anymore. He'd turned forty-one in January and his body didn't bounce back the way it had.

"What's the situation, exactly?"

Bauer stared right at him. "Precarious."

The unblinking scrutiny made Ruben squirm. Was this guy a bigot? A queer? No, just… odd. Ruben flipped open his pad, a leather journal that fit in his hip pocket. *Time for a list.* Plus it gave him somewhere to look that felt less intense. "For example?"

"Well, it's an office in a residence. A few employees and most of them work from home. But I have clients in and out at all hours."

And you chase muggers in broad daylight. Right.

"Look, way you nailed that guy, I figured you for an off-duty cop."
Again that intense stare.

"I dropped out of the army." Ruben had ditched boot when Marisa had
her first miscarriage. "But I can fight and I take orders fine."

"My situation is.... What's needed here is something a little more...."
His mouth couldn't make the word. He plucked at his pants.

"Off the record." Ruben nodded. Tighty-whitey wanted some brown
hands to do his dirty work.

Sure enough, Bauer gave a sigh of relief. "Nothing crooked, you
understand, but I don't want to run the risk of compromising any of my
clients because I've got Dudley Do-Right riding shotgun."

Ruben squinted and then forced his face to relax. "So you're
looking for...?"

"More of a Dudley Do-Wrong?" Money to burn, then. A whale had
floated into Empire's little lagoon. "A bodyguard."

Ruben looked up at that. "Executive protection." Why did he have a
bad feeling about this? He throttled the thought and focused on landing as
much cash as possible. Hell, maybe a place to crash. "Twenty-four hour?"

"Work hours, I think."

Lucky me. Ruben could imagine how Raggedy Andy's fancy guest
room compared to a Spanish Harlem walkup. Privacy mattered enough that
his current digs won there. He had enough headaches without a head case
down the hall.

"Of course."

"Incidents." He fell silent and did the goofy dad-smile again with his
deep dimple.

Ruben held his tongue. Obviously this dude had sat in first class reading
too many airport novels. When Ruben looked back up, Bauer was eying him
critically, and that funny feeling returned. "What type of business?"

"Finance. A trader, really. Apex Securities. I run a hedge fund." Bauer
bounced his knee. "I work from home." He kept eying Ruben with blank
hero worship, as if casting him in some super-spy bullshit studded with
dry martinis and wet pussy. "As a precaution. I've got a lot of sensitive
documents in the office right now, and I'd feel better with someone on hand
to make sure there are no—"

Ruben raised his eyebrows, patient.

"Up on Seventy-Eighth and Park. I live in the Iris."

Which meant exactly nothing to Ruben. He'd ask his brother.
"Sure. Okay."

Why would someone this loaded hire Charles's little company, which
mainly rented bouncers and backup security for parties? Bauer could have

gone to Citadel or Stone Security. They had tech departments and goons who'd fought in the Israeli army. By comparison, Charles had a gut and a divorced drunk on the payroll. *Something odd there.*

When he looked up from the pad, Bauer still hadn't moved or blinked, apparently... his dashing face still as stone. Hell, maybe Bauer was only pretending to like him.

"I mean, it's a secure building. Co-op bachelor pad. They did the renovations three months after 9/11, so the board went a little nutso with the cameras and alarms."

"Who has access? Besides you."

"To the Iris? Uhh...."

Ruben flipped to a blank page. "Your apartment. You gotta wife, girlfriend?"

The guy looked married, the kind of walking Sears ad: as if any second a ranch house, a chirpy wife, and giggly blond toddlers would spring out of the ground around him.

Headshake. "A couple girls I get with. Nothing serious. I travel a lot." Bauer blinked and looked away. "For work, y'know."

Not queer, then. With a stray flicker of jealousy, Ruben tried to imagine any woman who'd wanna fake a climax with someone this bland. Then again, who could figure women? Maybe he had a cock the size of a pint glass.

Bauer's eyes came up, soft as flannel. "Marriage doesn't agree with me."

Ruben's gaze flicked to Bauer's lap. No sleeping anaconda there; maybe he fucked 'em with his wallet. Batshit Bauer had capital to spare.

Note to self: get rich ASAP.

"You got angry employees? Clients with a beef?"

"Hardly. I got an assistant that stops in a couple times a day, for schedule and research." He looked at his nails. "Housekeeper comes in three times a week. My IT kid when the computers need pruning or weeding."

"Which tends to be?"

"Weekly, at a minimum. Has to be. My biggest expense." Shrug. "My computers never stop upgrading."

The emphasis made Ruben pause and raise his eyebrows. He didn't ask the question, but he left space for an explanation. Curious played better than stupid, in most situations.

Bauer's lips scrubbed his teeth before he explained. "For investors, a quarter-second lag can mean millions of dollars. Finance drives all technology. We're the reason chip upgrades happen. Even more than gaming or medicine."

Ruben perused his brother's tiny, cluttered office. *A thousand security places in Manhattan and he comes to us? Sketchy.* "Anyone else who drops in with any regularity, then?"

"A couple international clients I'm friendly with. My assistant. Cook. The gardener comes up twice a month."

Gardener? How big was this bachelor pad? The knot of irritation tightened in Ruben's belly.

Bauer must've caught the reaction because he added, "I'm in the penthouse, so I have a couple terraces with trees. Pool downstairs. Y'know."

Oh yeah, genius. I know all about penthouse pools on Park Avenue. "Right." This jerk was so loaded he'd forgotten that most people wanted shit they couldn't afford.

Ruben kept his face blank, the expression Marisa called "Aztec asshole." A sharp pang of missing her took him by surprise. He hoped that new guy treated her better than he had. "And you suspect some kinda theft?"

"A security breach, more like. The Apex Fund handles some players."

"We're not equipped for tech breaches, let alone a full executive protection detail." Charles had trouble checking his e-mail.

"This isn't hackers." Bauer held up a hand, right on the edge of rude. "These people have been in my house."

Paranoia much?

"Look, I know how it sounds. I'm not a nutjob. High-risk investment creates some pretty weird bedfellows."

"And enemies." *Invisible enemies who leave no proof.* Right.

Bauer bobbed his head and exhaled loudly. "You see my problem?" The way he said "my" made it sound like the problem was something he owned.

Only a saint would turn away a client like this. Charles would shit nickels, but Ruben smelled a rat.

Ruben squinted, trying to provoke a real reaction. "Well, not really." *Too easy, too easy.* The words slipped out of his mouth. "Why us?"

"'Scuse me?" Condescending and jittery, both. Maybe he wasn't a nutjob, but Mr. Bauer definitely wasn't telling the whole truth.

"Empire is hardly a triple-A outfit, Mr. Bauer." He looked around at his brother's shabby office, the coffee-ringed desk and dusty cabinets. "We're not exactly at home on red carpet. We do event security mostly for people who don't make the papers."

"Exactly." Bauer blinked. "I'm sitting here because of what you did this morning." Boy Scout bullshit.

Ruben trusted his instincts. He wondered if he could convince Charles to give this gig a pass. He crossed his arms, giving his best bouncer glare.

"I don't want the NYPD involved. On white-collar crime they suck, and I don't need feds digging up the bones in my closets." He obviously hadn't heard "no" or "why" too often. "I need an experienced pair of eyes on me while I close a deal, but I need to steer clear of the standard bullet catchers."

"Still, why slum it with us if you're really worried?"

His calm brow clouded. "That's a bit tricky."

"Yeah?" Ruben held his unsettling gaze. "Meaning?"

"A high-end firm may be the... problem. I'd like a fresh pair of eyes from a new angle. Tighter security. Nothing flashy or complicated. And so I came to you." The goofy smile returned, almost desperately casual and cheerful.

"Right." Ruben ignored his gut and thought about the money. "Executive protection. Daytime only."

"A few nights. I hit a lot of black tie events. Partying with clients and grooming accounts. I'd present you as a friend, an associate."

"Again, I feel like we're a bad fit, Mr. Bauer." Ruben sat back. Those investors would take one look at his dark complexion and crappy clothes and peg him for a blue-collar bruiser, a middle-aged drunk who cashed checks at the bodega. Everything about this gig raised his hackles. "We don't exactly look like buddies."

"Why not?" Bauer eyeballed Ruben's clothes, the scuffed oxfords, the crooked tie. "A haircut. Wardrobe. Incidentals. Expensed, obviously." He looked serious.

"'Cause you're pretty prepped out and I'm a big ugly spic?" Ruben scowled a second. "Just a hunch." Ruben dropped the pen on the pad. "All due respect, don't shit a shitter."

"Fair enough. My family has accounts with Kroll, and I don't want to worry them unnecessarily."

"Mr. Bauer, you're not being straight with me."

Bauer blinked, for the first time, it seemed. "Straight?"

"Pretty sketchy logic there. Espionage? Sabotage? Your family of superspies and stock market ninjas."

"Now you're not being straight." Bauer's eyes hardened. "Let's just say I have reason to *distrust* my family and their friends." For the first time, the predatory edge sliced through all Bauer's folksy charm, calculated and forceful. "So I'm hiring you."

There he was. *Nice to meet you, motherfucker.*

The silence felt like embarrassment, but whose? Without waiting for an answer, Bauer opened his briefcase and began writing a check. He glanced up. "Retainer." All balls and no sense. Scribble, scribble.

Ruben could hear Charles bellowing in his head: *Take the fucking job.* Empire needed the money. He did as well. He'd go nuts sleeping on a couch all summer with a busted A/C. The red flag wasn't Bauer or his bull's-eye face; it was the cushiness of the deal.

"Two, three weeks at the outside. Twelve hundred a day plus expenses."

Even though Empire only would have charged him seven.

Ruben knew exactly what things cost—one of the side effects of growing up broke and scrimping his whole life. He probably knew the prices on Bauer's clothes better than the man who'd paid for them. Too easy.

"I've seen you handle trouble, and money's not an issue for me. I'm faced with a sticky situation. The risk is minimal and the pay is not."

Who on earth had steered this crazy whale his way?

Charles. Ruben sighed. *Thanks, little brother.*

"Excellent. I'll meet you at the Iris then to go over particulars." Bauer gave a victor's smile and stood. "Tomorrow morning, say?" He rubbed his hands together as if they were sweaty. "I'll leave your name with the building staff. Ruben…?"

"Oso." He waited for the joke. In Spanish, the name meant a couple things, all silly.

Not even a smile. "Oso. Right." Just the square-square jaw and the flannel eyes looking back out of a handsome face that said *Punch me.*

Ruben stayed in the chair, feeling like he'd had his pocket picked.

Mr. Bauer gave a sharp nod from the doorway. "Perfect."

Not even close.

Five minutes later, Ruben was still considering that door when Charles came back, eating a greasy bacon sandwich, and shuffled through the paperwork. "You all set with the Apex guy?"

"I guess."

"Cakewalk. That Bauer is hiring a wingman to impress someone." Another swallow. A drip spattered on his hibiscus shirt. "Ten bucks he's some Wall Street gonk who's seen too many thrillers. Scariest thing he deals with is silicone titties and erectile dysfunction."

"Carlos…." Charles had been christened Carlos, but their parents refused to speak Spanish on principle. No immigrant bullshit for them. Their grandparents had moved to Florida from Soledad after the Second World War. The Osos were American through and through. Roots, nothing. Charles had learned Spanish during his pretend-to-be-mob phase.

"Tsssh. Yeah. You watch." Charles took a drippy bite. "He just likes your scary mug."

My bull's-eye.

"Whatsamatter? You said you were doing good."

"Yeah." Ruben lifted a shoulder noncommittally. "Yeah, sure. I'm doing great." Even if he couldn't put his finger on the feeling that nagged him.

Charles narrowed his eyes.

"No. No way. It's not that. I'm great. I just woke up late." Ruben hoped that was the truth.

"I don't wanna come home to you punching holes in my wall."

"I promise." None of that here. Ruben had patched plenty of walls on plenty of mornings.

"Something funny there."

"Ha ha." Charles balled up the sandwich shrapnel and tossed it. "What's funny?"

Ruben squinted. "He is."

"He is"—Charles overlapped his words—"a spruce goose laying golden eggs, baby. You better sit on that motherfucker till all of 'em hatch."

Ruben tapped the desk, then slid the check across the clutter toward his brother. Something Bauer had said, but what? It stuck in his teeth like gristle he couldn't stop worrying with his tongue. "He's all balls and fulla shit."

"So much the better. It's all in his head, then, and he wants to put on a big fancy show. Paranoid on Park Avenue." Charles rubbed his hibiscus gut and sat. "I think the problem is you're looking for a problem where there ain't none." He plucked the retainer check off the desk. "Good gig. Easy money and no headaches. Fancy clientele. This is a milkbone. You chew on it all summer. Scare up business from his, uh, associates."

Ruben nodded.

Charles held the check over his face and closed his smiling eyes like the zeros were sunshine. "Give him his show. Ya needta get laid. You need some new threads. Place of your own. Bauer's your ticket. He does anything funny, you laugh." A look.

"Sure. I promise."

"And Rube." He pointed, fake stern. "Up that penthouse, you better be passing out my cards like crabs." Charles tried to sell it. "I'm taking care of you, man. You needed work and this deal's a cinch."

As in, boring as hell. Ruben tried not to feel insulted.

"You just got divorced. Off the bottle. And it'll get you outta the apartment."

"So it's bullshit."

"The check'll clear."

"Fuck off. I mean that he's in no danger."

"Psssh. Danger! I'm in danger, you're in danger. Life is danger, bro." Charles wiped his jowly chops. "Might as well get paid."

CHAPTER TWO

THERE'S ONLY one way to find out if a man is honest: ask him. If he says yes, he's a crook.

Ruben fidgeted in his brother's little offices through a lunch he didn't take and calls he didn't answer. Something about Bauer's flannel stare kept right on bugging him. "I'm gonna go to church."

Charles looked up at him and nodded. Church was Ruben's code for an AA meeting, and Charles probably didn't want to ask questions. "Sure." He thumped Ruben's back, man-to-manly.

In the hall, Ruben pulled up the AA app and found a *Big Book* meeting at the Jan Hus Church on East Seventy-Fourth. He headed down the hot stairs.

He skirted Central Park, nervous about navigating his way through the trees. Even at its margins, the air felt cooler than he'd expected, but then he was wearing an outsize cotton suit without a tie. He'd seen pictures of ponds and castles hidden in there, and hot girls running in their goddamn underwears practically.

Nature was about the only thing he missed living in the city. He'd definitely be coming back to these trees when he felt braver.

A half hour later, he reached a red brick church wrapped in gingerbread arches. He grabbed a folding chair with five to spare. Maybe fifteen people, mostly white and mostly older. Not surprising given what Charles had told him about the Upper East Side. Still, no one blinked at him. Mostly Ruben kept his head ducked, surprised to feel a sunburn on his neck.

The meeting didn't help: a roomful of wealthy retirees who treated it like a gabby social club. Their problems were not his. He sat in the back, and though he stood up to introduce himself at the open, he didn't share and he only half listened. Peach would have smacked him and snapped him out of it; she was always after him to *share*. In her absence, he'd have to man up.

The group talked through Step Four, the Step he was still hung up on: "We made a searching and fearless moral inventory of ourselves."

Good times.

They broke after an hour. He thanked the old man who'd run the meeting and dialed his sponsor before he'd gotten outside. His feet headed back toward the park. On the third ring, Peach picked up.

"Hey." She sounded raspy and out of breath. "There you are." She always answered like she expected his call, which he found weirdly comforting. As a guy, Ruben knew he should have had a male sponsor, but no one cut to the bone like her.

He smiled. "You working in the garden?"

"Kid, I'm too old to work. I'm having sex with the pool boy." Peach lived alone in a retirement community in Aventura, fifteen miles outside downtown Miami. "Of course, he's fifty, so it takes a while."

"So you're on a break."

She cackled and coughed. "What's up? You sound like shit."

"Meeting. Fourth Step, still."

"Inventory is rough." The sound changed, like she'd moved outside onto her little balcony. "Ruben, here's a thing. You don't have to love the process, but you gotta live with it. Shame puts the glass in your hand."

He nodded and then realized she couldn't see him. "Yeah. It's good. New York is good."

The *tcchk-tcchk* rasp of a lighter. She was all of five feet tall and chain-smoked menthols. He could imagine the smell exactly, and the smoke curling around her knobby knuckles.

She sighed. "Lonely, I bet."

He pressed his lips tight before he spoke. "Oh, man. Like you wouldn't fucking believe."

"Tell me. I'm a seventy-eight-year-old floozy from Boca." Peach breathed loudly for a few seconds. "See any great shows?" As a former hoofer, Peach loved musicals.

"C'mon. I don't even watch TV these days. I work and I sleep."

"Kiddo, lonely sucks, but other things suck more. Work your Steps. Pay attention to what matters, huh?"

"Mmmh."

"And call your damn parents." She was right, of course. "They're old and they worry." In other words, Peach was older and worried more about him. She gave the best guilt.

"I will."

"Ruben, lonely isn't always such a bad gig. Stay focused. Howzat job?"

Little by little his shoulders relaxed. As he walked west he told her about Charles, about his sofa bed, about the office, even the mugger that morning and the money tornado, but not Bauer. For whatever dumb reason, Andy Bauer and his paranoia didn't come up.

Before he realized it, he'd reached Park Avenue and Seventy-Fourth. Peach asked, "And have you met anybody?"

"Not like that." He looked uptown. Bauer's building had to be right there.

"Good. Take your time. Remember: The elevator is always broken. Use the Steps."

Again he bobbed his head at the slogan like she could see him. She probably could.

Peach coughed. "Go home, rub one out and relax, Ruben."

"Fuck off. G'bye. You know I don't do that." He hung up laughing with her.

He didn't. Not jerking off had been a point of honor for him all his life, almost a competition.

At eleven his dad had explained the man/woman/baby deal and what his two-by was for. The Osos weren't Catholic enough for Ruben to get horny-guilt, but he'd taken his dad's lecture as a kind of challenge. A real man kept shit under control. His coaches said the same: game first, pussy after.

Easy enough. Ruben didn't need to masturbate as long as he had a girlfriend to tap the sap. He always did.

He looked down at the map on his phone. *You are here.*

Why did Andy Bauer bother him so much?

According to the blue dot on his GPS, Bauer's building was on the corner of Seventy-Eighth and Park, so he headed north for a looksee.

Much quieter, this neighborhood. Boutiques and townhouses. Expensive cars even on the street. The buildings all had doormen, and the pedestrians dressed for show, not comfort. He spotted his destination from over a block away, a digital icicle rising ten stories higher than anything nearby.

880 Park Avenue turned out to be a white stone sliver with exaggerated windows above the twenty-fourth floor. The lower half definitely blended in with the surrounding Park Avenue buildings, but the upper floors resembled a space-age dildo. The glass cap kept it from sore-thumbing the block by angling the windows to reflect the sky. Out front, a zigzag row of chestnut trees bloomed in creamy pyramids. The gray awning said "The Iris," so maybe the whole thing was supposed to look like a flower bud.

As a test, Ruben decided to bluff his way past the door staff. *Just to see.* Look like you know where you're going, most staff steers clear.

He crossed Seventy-Eighth and approached a plate glass door held by a young doorman in a suit the building had probably hired for his smile, not his smarts. He was listening to a leggy blonde in a sundress holding a leash with a ball of peach fluff at one end.

Bauer had to be many times a millionaire to live here.

Ruben passed the door boy and the blonde, not even grunting a greeting as he strode across the white marble. *Bright.* Somehow brighter inside here than the June afternoon outside. Almost blinding.

He tucked his chin, squinted, and ambled inside as if mulling his millions. His pupils started to adjust. Maybe *that* was why it was called the Iris.

Another thirty feet.

On his left, a green wall of living vegetation and three tall silver birches in a line growing out of containers set into the floor. Sort of a deconstructed indoor garden. The leafy wall muffled half of the sound. Polished limestone slabs covered the other walls.

Twenty feet.

A lacquered desk to the right. Two doormen? One seated, one bent over a ledger talking on a phone. Both kids and too groomed to take seriously. He sauntered past and gave an absent nod to the youngsters. No response; geniuses obviously. A short hallway hooked to the right behind the doormen. Mailboxes, looked like.

Ten feet. *Secure building, my ass.*

Past the spindly trees, a rigid semicircle of brown leather armchairs on a spotless ecru rug. Hell to keep clean, but maybe the residents wore new shoes every day. The chairs faced a blown-glass coffee table that cost upward of nine grand. Ruben pretended to dig for his keys as he neared the elevator bank at the back.

Five feet.

He pressed the button. According to the posted fire escape floorplan, the dogleg hallway ahead hooked back toward the stairwell and a service elevator opening into the garage.

These kids seriously weren't going to stop him. Feeling brave, he swiveled to check the lush, hushed space behind him. Not a peep.

The vaulted elevator slid open without a sound. He stepped in and pressed PH. No key, no code required.

Digital numbers flicked by up top, even though the car didn't seem to be moving. The interior was paneled in cherry burl with a narrow bench running the length of the back. Maybe rich idiots got tired if they stood too long.

See? He knew what he was doing. Charles owed him a raise. Bauer owed him a debt of thanks. Ruben had just stuck his fingers into a fancy fortress built of Swiss cheese.

The digital display above the buttons slowed, although he still couldn't feel any shift in momentum. For a moment, he thought he was about to walk back out into the lobby, but he had indeed reached the PH without a single hiccup.

The cherry doors slid open directly into the penthouse to reveal Bauer two feet away, big dumb grin on that square face. Dress shirt, slacks, but he'd ditched the jacket. "Oso! You're about fourteen hours early, my man." He held out a glass of white wine.

Ruben opened and closed his mouth. His face and neck prickled with a blush. "Uh."

Bauer's lips flickered with a suppressed smile, dimples framing it like apostrophes.

Lunkhead. Ruben hadn't snuck past anything. His new boss had poured him a goddamn drink.

"Didn't we say eight?" The elevator started to close until Bauer waved his hand in the beam. "A.M.?"

Ruben had to step off right into the man's personal space.

Instead of backing away, Bauer put the glass in Ruben's hand. "This is yours. I left mine out on the terrace." Without waiting or explaining, he headed right toward brightness. He was barefoot.

Ruben followed him toward a blinding double-height living room. Floor to ceiling glass faced south over a hot sky and high-rises. The windows were kept so clean they were invisible. It was uncomfortable, actually, as if they were standing on an open platform; wander off and you might fall five hundred feet and end up Park Avenue pudding. He had to turn away and his eyes took a second to adjust. Total showplace.

"Sorry." Bauer pointed a remote at the gigantic wall of glass and the ambient glare *dimmed*. "Smart glass." The sheet windows darkened the day to what looked like early evening.

Ruben nodded stupidly at the glass walls and massive wrap terrace. "Nice."

"That's tinting, it can also—" The windows frosted over until they were almost opaque. "Privacy."

With all that glass, Ruben figured these digital shades cost upward of a quarter million. *Some toy.* "Uh. Yeah. Cool."

To his right a wide spiral staircase with glass treads led up to the mezzanine. Not just a penthouse, a *duplex* penthouse. Bauer had to be worth two hundred million at least. Standing there barefoot on a thirty-two thousand dollar silk rug over a ninety grand square of fruitwood floor.

The toxic sticker shock only raised more flags. Ruben's breath rose high and cold in his chest. *All this fucking luxe.* Who was this Bauer guy? What the hell was Ruben doing up here?

Off-kilter, Ruben finally looked at the wineglass in his hand. "I don't drink." Why had he admitted that?

The cocky grin faltered.

Fuck anonymity. "Not anymore." Ruben set the glass on a Lucite trunk serving as an end table. *Four grand, easy.* Inside the trunk was a polished bear skull. He had no fucking idea what a bear skull cost. He blinked. "Sober."

"Sorry. Good for you." Bauer picked up the glass. "Water? Soda?"

"No, I'm fine." Ruben shuffled in place and squared his shoulders. His eye kept resting on objects and pricing them as best he could. "Look, I'm sorry. I came to case the setup."

"I got that impression." Bauer tapped the side of his nose and chuckled. *Jerk.*

Giant abstract canvas on the west wall over a celery green vase deep enough to hide a four year old.

Ruben had no idea what the artwork was worth, but he could imagine. "Because that's what you're supposed to do. To see what happened. Buildings talk about cameras and logbooks, but all that matters is what's on the ground."

Bauer took a sip. "The elevator has to be cleared for every single person headed upstairs. It won't leave the lobby if the doormen don't release it. Hell, they can lock people in it if there's a breach."

Ruben blinked. "I had to check."

"I know. The staff notified me when you reached the block. Cameras."

Ruben scowled. "What, 'cause I'm brown?"

"Jeez." Bauer put a hand on his arm. Again. "No. I gave them your picture. I snapped you this morning at your brother's office."

When? Another huge red flag right there. "You shoulda said." He dug his little leather journal from his breast pocket.

"Oso, I wasn't being a dick. I had to run a check. I took your picture because that's what I'm supposed to do." Bauer ran a hand through his floppy hair, releasing a cowlick at his crown. "Believe me, the guys hassling me won't worry about doormen. Just relax."

Why would I do that? Ruben frowned.

Every fiber told him to get the hell out of there, just punch for the elevator and cancel the job. His experience was nil and his qualifications minimal: basic CPR and a concealed carry permit. In April, his brother had sent him to a three-day workshop with the Executive Protection Institute just to get him up to speed, with the understanding he'd fly down to Virginia for the full seminar when he could afford it.

No harm in a surreptitious photo, but it felt weird. First day and he felt stupid and outclassed. "I wish you'd said something, Mr. Bauer."

"Andy. Call me Andy." *Fat chance.* "You did right." Back slap. "Just, this is a weird situation. Let me give you the five-dollar tour."

Bauer looked ready to drape an arm around his shoulders so Ruben walked back toward the hall.

"Living room, obviously. The big silver spiral thing heads up to the bedrooms. Powder room and access to one set of fire stairs." Bauer turned too fast and a slosh of white wine spattered the couch. "Shit." He righted the glass. "Again. Liliana will kill me." He touched it absently.

Ruben glowered at the stain. "Girlfriend?"

"Housekeeper. Serbian. She's very house-proud."

Ruben added her name to the journal, and started counting entry points. "Lotta nice things."

"I just sign the checks." Bauer shrugged. "I hired my mom's decorator. I want things comfortable."

Ruben couldn't imagine being comfortable in a place where a slip or a spill cost the average annual income. Everything here was for show. Instead of dwelling on his irritation, he pivoted and advanced along the main hallway.

Bauer spoke from behind him, explaining the chain of rooms on the right. "Den. Dining room. Kitchen's around there with breakfast area." A hallway branched east toward the terrace. "Guest suite down there. And this is the office."

Ruben stepped into a double-height office at the far north end of the duplex, directly opposite the living room. Two desks. Shelved walls. Three plasma screens on cantilevered arms displayed a stock market crawl.

"Library really, but it's just me and Hope in here so I can spread out." Bauer paused to turn. "My assistant."

"Lotta TVs." He added Hope to his list. Charles could run checks on the staff.

"Sorry. Broker's delight." Bauer pushed the floating screens back against the walls before perching on the messier of the desks.

Ruben smiled in spite of himself. "Not what I expected." It wasn't. A low couch and a scatter of chairs. Reading nook with a lamp. Unpretentious even with eighteen-foot ceilings. Sliding doors opened onto the terrace from another wall of windows. *Wow.* "Great room, man." Without meaning to, he smiled right at Bauer for the first time.

Bauer's blue-gray eyes gleamed. "Oh. Oh! Thanks." His grin spread and set.

He wants to be liked.

Bauer bobbed his head. "Spa out that way. And shower." He pointed at the staircase folded upward on the right wall. "And then upstairs, my bedroom, dressing room, and two guest rooms. Laundry. I spend most of my time down here though. I love this room."

"I can see why." Ruben ran a calloused hand over the desk's satiny wood. Even though they were equally high, the north-facing windows let in a soft platinum light.

"And this right here is my total favorite thing." Bauer grasped one shelf on the west wall and tugged. "This is the only feature I asked for. Panic shelf!" To Ruben's surprise, the lower half of the bookcase swung back, books and all, to reveal another service door hidden behind. "That one leads to the service access and the other stairwell too."

"Awful lot of doors." Ruben frowned. "Front elevator opens right into your foyer. Besides that, you got two separate stairwells and a secondary elevator that all feed into the apartment. Doors, doors, doors."

"Upstairs too. Fire safety, right? But the doormen control the elevator."

"The main one. Not the service. And you got those staircases. This is nuts." Ruben put his hands in his pockets, watching Bauer look over his office with undisguised pride. "Mr. Bauer, I think you should consider having a full team in here. An alternate, at least. Empire is not equipped to handle—"

"Andy, please." He turned. "Have to disagree with you there."

"Okay. I just wanted to be clear. Any direct access from the terrace?"

Bauer shook his head then stepped close to Ruben and sniffed.

Uhh. Ruben froze. *Freaky.*

"I smell tobacco. You don't smoke?" He didn't move back.

Embarrassing. "Very occasionally. Socially, I guess. Y'know, clubs or whatever. My rule is, I don't buy them, I just light 'em." Ruben followed Bauer down the office stairs and into the hall.

Bauer frowned a little as he punched for the elevator. "Outside only, okay?"

"Sure! Of course. That smell never comes out. This jacket is my brother's, like I said—"

"Or you could quit. Don't even need twelve Steps." Bauer flashed the dimple. "Cheaper and healthier besides." Bauer rubbed his shoulder with a surprisingly strong grip until Ruben shifted away.

Jerk. And why did his new boss keep touching him like a carpet salesman?

Bauer grinned and patted at his cowlick. "I think that's everything. Let's go down and get you logged in with the staff. Photo, fingerprint."

Only half joking, Ruben countered with, "DNA sample?"

"If you want to leave a specimen, I'm sure a couple guys'd be willing." Bauer's small dimple made an appearance.

"I probably look weird to them."

"Everyone looks weird to them. All the doormen are models. Literally. The building hired its guys from Elite and Ford. At least you're handsome; I look like a slipcover."

"C'mon." Ruben scoffed. "A couch, maybe." *A guy with a face that says welcome, which assholes use to wipe their feet.*

"Nice. Fuck you." But Bauer laughed. The sound made him seem likeable. "We just need some clothes. That jacket is doing you no favors."

"Fair 'nough." He tried not to feel insulted. *It's a job.*

"Oso, what you look like doesn't matter to me."

Ouch. Ruben's vanity reared its ugly head. "'Cause all your friends dress like shit?"

Bauer blanched. "That sounded crappy. It's not—" Swallow, grimace. "More like Upper East Side camouflage."

Ruben blinked and kept his face impassive. What did he care what this rich ragdoll thought? Being broke sucked, but there were worse options. All of this was for show. If Bauer wanted to buy him a few costumes, why not?

"This morning you said blending would make things easier. I'd rather you feel comfortable around the office."

Office, nothing. Ruben had always been snobby about clothes. Women appreciated a man who took care of himself: Gym. Tan. Threads. Even the smallest effort could land the ugliest idiot knee-deep in C-cups and enthusiastic anal sex with ladies who tried on dick like shoes.

Slick temptation coiled around him and squeezed.

Ruben always knew the price tag, always had a plan, but he'd never been able to afford the stuff he saw in magazines. He wasn't a label whore, but given the means he'd be happy to learn. Bauer could afford all that noise and didn't give a what-what. Ruben never got a credit card bill without worrying about how he'd cover it.

Even now, he had loans out the ass, credit card payments, a Kendall storage unit full of shit he'd already forgotten, and no bed to call his own. He couldn't imagine a life when he wasn't thinking about covering his rent and beating the bank. Andy Bauer *was* a bank.

Ruben scrubbed his teeth with his lips. "Better clothes will probably keep me out of fights."

Bauer laughed. "Y'don't seem like the kind of guy who picks fights."

"I got a face picks fights for me. Fucking bull's-eye."

"How do you figure?"

Ruben favored his boss with a skeptical glance. "I look like every drug lord on every show."

"C'mon."

"I'm not kidding."

"You do scowl a lot." Bauer smiled. "You're scowling now."

"I'm not scowling." *Fuck you.* He stopped scowling.

"Well, optical illusion, then. Black eyebrows, Roman nose. Five o'clock shadow. Probably good for this security gig, huh? Nobody messes with you."

"Everybody messes with me. My whole life. Teachers. Cops. Guys take a swing 'cause I'm drinking from the same kinda glass as their girls."

"Nah." Bauer clenched his square jaw in that Sears-dad smile he'd worn this morning at Empire Security. "You look like a badass. I look like the neighbor who drops in to borrow a rake."

"Right." Ruben shook his head. He didn't say anything about Bauer's face picking a different kinda fight. They weren't friends.

"Just, people in this neighborhood pay a lot of attention to the, uhh, externals."

Ruben tried not to feel self-conscious in his baggy jacket. "A lot of my stuff is still on the way."

"S'not a problem." Bauer leaned over his desk to make a note. "Don't sweat it. *Cómo se dice* expense account?"

"Yeah." Ruben knew he was trying to seem friendly and chill. "Just so's you know, I don't speak Spanish. At all."

"Oh?"

"Yeah. My parents were big on the American Dream thing when they got to Florida. My mother only fights in Spanish and my pops won't speak it at all."

"We say that you're in real estate, maybe, visiting from Sao Paolo but you were raised in Miami."

"We're Colombian."

"Medellín, then." Bauer squinted, his make-believe motor warming up. "Banking family, but you're a prodigal. Cars and women. Our parents know each other from Grand Cayman. Offshore confrères."

"I don't know anything about that." They were alone in the apartment but he couldn't shake the sense that even now Bauer was using him to put on a show for someone.

"You shouldn't. You're a black sheep. Relax!"

"Not likely if you want me protecting anything."

"Let's say you're a new investor who's on the fence. Best if they think you're a potential client, someone I'm planning to do business with rather than an existing partner. That way you're on their side, not mine."

"Makes sense. I don't have to play dumb, just be dumb. Keep an eye."

"But scary." Bauer brushed something off Ruben's shoulder and squeezed it. "A little *loco*. Good suit, they'll piss their pants."

Ruben wondered who "they" were. Who was this show for precisely? He wondered if Bauer had even made that part up yet. Still, as long as the check wasn't make-believe, he could play along.

Bauer walked them back down toward the elevator.

Talk about a meal ticket. Bauer didn't care what he spent to make Ruben blend in. Maybe this made some kinda sense. Summer job, nest egg. Get a place, a girlfriend.

In AA there was a rule about not dating in your first year of sobriety because it stole focus from your recovery. Wisdom in that, definitely. Ruben had struggled with it, but going to meetings and dealing with the divorce hadn't left him time for much in the way of social intercourse. Hell, any intercourse, if you got down to it, but at eleven months he saw the wisdom. Who wanted to date an addict? No one healthy, no one sane.

Dating as a drunk had been hard enough. Now he'd need to unlearn all his dodges and learn how to get a chick while sober. Still, a new city and a new job seemed like a solid start. *Price tag, plan.* Maybe he was finally ready to dip his toe.

At the door, Bauer asked offhand, "You wanna grab dinner, maybe?" His voice sounded casual, but his eyes flashed like teeth in deep water.

A free meal sounded terrific, actually. Eating at his brother's meant takeout and keeping the cat from rolling around in his mu-shu pork. And free always meant delicious. Yet the impromptu invitation hit him funny and made him feel irrationally powerful. "Nah, you got somewhere to be, I'll bet."

"Oh." Bauer blinked at him, hand locked in midair. "Well, I'll see you in the morning."

"Eight still okay?"

"Your call, man. We're right here waiting." Dimple again.

"I'm an early riser." Ruben ignored the hinky feeling.

"I figured. Shopping first thing, then. Beat the crowds." Bauer nodded. "You're here."

As Ruben stepped onto the elevator, the gleaming box felt even more claustrophobic and precarious, as if his new boss had trapped him in a coffin balanced on a radio tower. Any second the doors would close and he'd be stuck, suffocating in midair.

Finger hovering over the button, he had the sudden urge to quit, call the whole thing off.

When he turned to say the words, Bauer extended his arm and shook hands once, sealing the bargain.

All the way down, Ruben wondered exactly what he'd bought and what he'd sold.

CHAPTER THREE

TIGERS EARN their stripes and keep them by choice.

The next morning, Ruben woke up before the alarm, tangled in the sweaty sheet. He could hear Charles sawing logs in the next room. Next stop: sleep apnea if his brother wasn't careful.

Ruben drank a big glass of lukewarm water. Instead of coffee, he did his mini-circuit of push-ups, crunches, and pull-ups on the bar he'd hung in the bathroom doorway. A hundred each and he needed to piss at the finish. He rinsed quickly, forgetting to shave but not remembering till he dried off. Bauer didn't care about his stubble.

Instead of breakfast, he grabbed a cup of crappy java from a bodega and took an empty bus down Park around seven thirty. Ruben had never had reason to travel this way before. As he watched, botánicas gave way to boutiques, dumpsters to daffodils. He considered his borrowed clothes and tried to see them through these eyes. Bauer's building was only thirty blocks south, a mile and a half away, but it might as well have been on the other side of the moon. He hopped off the bus two blocks early, wondering exactly when the Iris surveillance spotted him.

"Mr. Oso." At the awning, a towheaded doorman he hadn't seen before waved him straight into the building and handed him a package to carry up. *Creepy.* In the elevator, he stared front and refused to look up at the camera.

Upstairs, he expected Bauer to be waiting, but nothing. He heard a woman's sharp voice to the left, in the office maybe.

Ruben found the lady on the phone: blue-black skin, high cheekbones, and a ballerina's poise. *Ballbuster, that one.* Not what he would have expected of Bauer's staff, but up in this penthouse expectations kept getting kicked over. She touched a glowing earpiece and nodded. "You see?"

He set the box on the table, and she frowned and ran her hand along one edge as she talked to the air. Leaning in, Ruben realized the package had been sliced and resealed. She held up a finger at him and nodded impatiently. Impeccable suit, heart-shaped face that looked much sweeter than she sounded. "And that's all we're asking you to do, Mrs. Blantin. *Mmph.* Now, my eight o'clock is here, so I'm going to have to let you go. We'll talk next week." She hung up and held out her hand to shake as she walked over to him. "Anxious divorcee. Apologies.... I'm Hope, and you're Mr. Oso."

"Ruben, yeah. Hi. I'm—"

"I'm glad he took this situation by the horns." Journal on the desk. Files in the cabinet. She never stopped moving. A gorgeous tornado.

"You're the—"

"Assistant. Yes. I would've met you yesterday but you weren't expected and I had classes. Columbia Business. I transferred from library science, and the goddamn professor never lets me forget it." She rolled her eyes like he understood.

He didn't, but he nodded anyway. "Great." Ruben shifted his weight, unsure if he should sit or find his new boss.

She leaned in, conspiratorially. "Andy's upstairs in the shower. Bad night." She said it as if Ruben knew the full dossier on her boss's history and psychological profile.

Ruben stood very still for fear the tornado would scoop him up and tear something off.

She shifted one of the big floating screens and tapped on the laptop. "Can I get you a coffee? Juice? No? I'm hoping you can help me keep him on his schedule."

"Sure. If I can, I'm—"

"Happy to hear it." She glanced at her watch. "Now, I've got to get down to his lawyer by ten, and the car's already downstairs. You're going shopping this morning."

Ruben shrugged. "Whatever he needs."

"What you need. I've set you up with Joysann as your shopper. I didn't know your sizes, but I sent over the photos at six to get her started."

"Umm. Sure. I'm...."

"Me too, Mr. Oso." She shook his hand, one firm pump with her slim hand. "It's terrific to meet you. Back by twelve."

He wondered if that meant she would be back or he should be, but decided Bauer would clue him in.

Instead of going upstairs, he retreated to the kitchen, found a skinny man slicing leeks. The chef? Another employee, whoever it was. They raised hands at each other but said nothing.

Uncomfortable, he drifted back to the office but didn't sit down. He leaned over the resealed package he'd delivered. The cut was razor clean, and someone had glued—

"There you are." Strong hands gripped his shoulders and squeezed, sending a jolt of electricity all the way to his knees.

Ruben turned.

Bauer's hair was still damp from the shower, with that stubborn cowlick wrestled into submission. He looked down the hall but asked Ruben, "Breakfast?" He stood there buttoning a pale blue dress shirt over his muscular chest.

"I'm good. I met Hope."

"Great. I meant to introduce you, but I overslept." Bauer rolled up the sleeves as they climbed the stairs. "The financial markets operate in every time zone, so I keep odd hours. Sleep is for amateurs." He tucked the shirt into his jeans. "Hope keeps me in one piece, for the most part."

"She is something."

"Victoria's Secret model for two years till she got bored. A dancer for like two seconds. Exotic, not ballet. We met at Jaded. Now she's with me while she works on her MBA."

Ruben assumed Jaded was some bar, maybe a disco. Hope didn't act like any stripper he'd met. He nodded. "She said we're meeting someone named Joysann."

"Barney's menswear. Excellent. She used to dance with Hope. Great gal. You're not carrying, are you?"

"To go clothes shopping? No." Ruben didn't add that he saw no need for a gun to prevent imaginary stalking.

Bauer snapped his fingers. "Shoes." He headed up the spiral staircase and Ruben trailed after him.

When he caught up, Bauer was kneeling in a giant closet tying his laces. *Even zillionaires tie their shoes.* "This should only take us an hour.

One sec." He turned right into a bathroom bigger than Charles's entire apartment, its walls lined in slate and the granite tub deep enough to hide a cheerleading squad. Without comment he unzipped his fly, flipped the toilet lid, and took a piss.

Fuck's sake. Ruben turned his back before he had to look at any whiteboy peen.

Bauer sighed and coughed. "Sorry, man. I'm not private about most things. And we gotta get used to each other, right?"

"Sure. No worries. Still finding my feet." He could hear Bauer finish and put himself away.

Bauer paused to rinse his hands and dry them before heading down to the elevator on the main floor. Waiting, he poked at his iPhone, muttering to himself.

Ruben scrubbed a hand over his shadowed chin. His black stubble made him look like a gangster. "I should have shaved this morning."

"No, it's good." Bauer laughed. "I'm not offended. Actually it's more believable that you wouldn't shave every day. You look meaner this way."

"What's 'mean' mean?"

Bauer thumped his shoulders and kneaded them. "Scary. Powerful. I don't want you to look like a cop."

The elevator slid open silently and they stepped on. Again the car descended in such quiet Ruben felt like an actor standing in a silver box while God changed the set outside.

"You think I look like a cop?" Better than robber, at least.

As they crossed the lobby, one of the young doormen nodded at them amiably. "Your car, Mr. Bauer?"

"A cab's fine. We could almost walk, but it's freakin' hot. Right?" That last question was aimed at Ruben, who didn't feel like he had any say.

By the time they reached the curb, the younger Asian doorman was holding open a taxi door.

When you're loaded, the world just falls into line.

Bauer slid across and Ruben followed. The doorman shut the door with a quiet *thock* and rapped it to signal the driver.

"It's only twenty blocks, but this time of day the sidewalks are more crowded than the street."

"My first New York taxi." He hadn't the money to waste.

"Yeah? Cool." Bauer smiled and raised his voice toward the driver. "Barney's. Madison and Sixty-First."

Ruben had heard of Macy's and Bloomingdale's but apparently this was the classier option. On the way, he couldn't stop thinking of the goddamn purple dinosaur.

When the cab stopped, Bauer passed a twenty dollar bill for a seven dollar fare without waiting for change. He stepped through the department store door Ruben swung open for him.

No dinosaurs. A smattering of white, groomed shoppers like a music video. Most department stores in New York were for working people, but this place was a plush safari.

Ruben caught a couple people staring at them. Either he really stuck out or Bauer had pissed off a few of his neighbors.

Oblivious and laser-focused, Bauer navigated the cosmetic counters and hooked left to a bank of elevators. He pressed the button and Ruben stood next to a table of neckties, trying not to feel like his parents were buying him clothes. He picked up a lustrous tangerine tie, cut wide with a thin gold diagonal. Alexander McQueen.

Bauer gave a nervous laugh and relaxed. "I never know what to buy." Spoiled rotten.

Ruben knew plenty about clothes. *A hundred, maybe? Hundred-thirty?* He paused to lift the tie and flip its tag: one hundred and eighty-five American dollars and no sense. *For real.* To purchase a seamed strip of tangerine silk that might get worn a half-dozen times. He'd lived in apartments where that was a week's rent. Keeping his face neutral, he dropped the tie quickly and carefully back to the table.

"Why not?" Bauer plucked the tie off the table. "You're gonna need a couple anyways." What the hell was happening? He grinned. "Sixth floor, I think."

The elevator doors glided open and Ruben pressed 6. "What exactly are we buying, here?"

"Hmm. Hope suggested three suits to start. A blazer. Couple pairs of pants. Some casuals. A tux is overkill, but dress shirts that fit you."

Tux?

"You got an amazing build under there." Bauer jabbed the 6 button again till the doors closed on them.

The praise pleased Ruben in an uncomfortable way. "My brother's packed it on the last year." He tugged at his collar. "But a lot of my stuff is being shipped from Florida."

"Deductible." For a moment, Ruben could see the number cruncher hidden under all the expensive grooming. Bauer watched the digits climbing on the elevator panel, elaborately polite for no reason. "These boys'll get you hooked up."

Ruben gulped. *Boys?* Right. 'Cause this was a New York department store; he'd seen makeovers on Bravo. He was embarrassed enough without a bunch of homos scoping his crank in front of his new boss.

For about two weeks after dropping out of boot, he'd danced in a queer bar, and he knew how aggressive dudes could get when they got a whiff of a ripped straight guy down on his luck. He'd grown up Catholic and, though he didn't have a problem with gays in theory, the macho worship gave him the heebs. In his experience, queers were either clueless kids afraid of football or creepy geezers who wore too much Drakkar... or at least that's how it had felt in the bar. The hot homos he saw on TV had never showed up to grope him and call him *papi*. Not that he wanted them to, of course, but getting sexually harassed by friendly jocks would have made the stripping easier to laugh off. No such luck. The first time some grampa licked his knee, he quit.

As they reached the sixth floor, a willowy carrot-topped boy with a mustache caught his eye, all of twenty-four and prettier than Ruben's ex-wife. He squinted and moved in for the kill. *Great.* Bravo makeover in five... four... three—

"If you dressed differently." Bauer eyed the pleated pants, also Charles's.

"Man, you put me in whatever the hell you need. I am at your service. I'm like: free threads?" Ruben shrugged. "Done."

Checking the other side of the menswear aisle, Ruben clocked a girl with a short cap of streaky blonde hair and a mouth like split berries. *Yes, please.*

The ginger kid had vanished. Her eyes glittered at Ruben and a saucy grin flickered at the corners of her mouth.

Thank you, baby Jesus. His cock swelled; he fought the urge to shift it and hoped he didn't get an embarrassing poky in front of the client. Was this hot slice gonna take his measurements? He hadn't been with anyone in so long.

He squared his shoulders and tightened his abs under his belt. Would it be sleazy to cop her number while his boss paid a couple grand for his clothes? Ruben hadn't gotten his ashes hauled in so long that he'd almost forgotten what it was like to get off beyond sex dreams and ninety seconds of salty midnight fireworks.

Then she saw Bauer and the smile caught fire. "Mr. Bauer!" Ruben and his sticky candle winked into invisibility, as if someone had pinched his wick.

What did that mean? Was his boss some kind of celebrity?

"Joysann." Bauer raised a hand at her.

She crooked her pretty finger and they ended up in a large dressing room with a three-way mirror and a row of leather Ralph Lauren armchairs facing a dais. On one wall hung a rack of understated clothes on hangers.

Joysann's eyes, smile, hands sparkled at them. Her lips were very pink.

Bauer flicked through the hangers, nodding at them. "This is my friend, Ruben Oso. He just flew in from Orlando, but his luggage is on its way to Cartagena."

Instead of sitting to give them space as Ruben expected, Bauer hovered, which only made his arousal more awkward.

Joysann looked at Ruben. "Lose the pants, but keep the shirt and shoes so things hang right." She was teasing him.

Really? In front of his boss. He sighed. Ruben draped his jacket over a chair arm, and started to kick off the shoes. He shucked out of his slacks and returned to her wearing the button-down, his red boxer briefs, black socks, and a pair of weather-beaten loafers. Unsexy as hell. Oh well.

Bauer considered Ruben in the mirror. "Shoes too, I think."

Joysann didn't blink, ready to stroke his ego till he squirted cash. "Hope didn't know sizes, but she sent your photos." She nodded at Bauer like she smelled fresh credit cards. She squinted at the rack and pulled a couple of hangers before she asked Ruben, "Forty-eight regular?"

"Uh, sure." Ruben gave her a shy smile and stepped onto the dais with his back to the mirrors. He had his pop's square build and sharp nose: pure Colombiano. "You think you can hook me up?"

"Any friend of Mr. Bauer." She snapped a measuring tape and— *srip-swip-thit*—swiftly checked his shoulders, chest, arm, waist, neck, even squatted and slid her hand straight up his fucking inseam, just barely jogging his nutpouch.

He flinched and coughed.

"Sorry." She giggled from her knees. "No hernia."

Ruben swallowed and turned. In the mirror he could see Bauer's blush.

"Broad in the back. Arms too. Serious rugby legs, *papá.*" Joysann stood and jotted numbers in her little journal. She blinked at Ruben. "I'm impressed you got him outta the house."

In the mirror Bauer blinked, and a strange expression locked his oversquare jaw for a minute.

Huh. File that away.

She tipped her head and scanned Ruben's physique. "Definitely no Italians and no Japanese. Hugo Boss, I'll bet. *Maybe* Paul Smith." She bit her slick lower lip.

Ruben let her slide a double-breasted navy blazer onto him. He'd never even touched clothes this expensive. Light and crisp on his shoulders. He looked taller in the mirror.

Apparently Joysann disagreed, squenching her face like a cat's butthole. "Ugh. Those buttons. I knew the double breasted would suck."

Bauer agreed with her. "Slicko. Sleazo."

Ruben stayed mum. *The fuck do I know?* Florida wasn't known for its elegance. And bodyguards didn't wear double-breasted 'cause they made drawing a weapon near impossible. Single breasted you could get to a shoulder or hip holster. Either way, Joysann nixed it.

She tugged the offending garment off him and rehung it, returning with another: gray polished cotton with three buttons.

Even pushing his arms into the sleeves and letting Joysann settle the lapel, Ruben could feel the difference. "Oh my God." The words slipped out on an exhale of the jittery splurge excitement fizzing in him. "That feels fantastic." This one looked so good that his dick seemed bigger.

"You like?" Joysann returned with a clacking handful of hangers and let Bauer fuss at Ruben's back.

He tugged at the vents; his fingers brushed over Ruben's ass but Ruben pretended not to notice. "Color's great, but it's a little, I dunno, real estate agent."

"You must be a good friend." She explained to Ruben, "He's being an asshole, trying to impress you."

"I'm impressed."

"I'm crushed." Bauer covered his heart. "Ruben is one of my oldest friends, and he doesn't want to spend a week in New York naked."

Ruben grinned at her as she peeled the gray off him. "Not the whole weekend."

Joysann tapped her teeth with the pen, taking another look at the rack. "And this is the Boss."

Another summer wool, this one with a tonal pinstripe, black on black. Bauer nodded.

On the hanger, Ruben thought it looked kind of *meh*. Expensive, sure, but he wasn't going to a funeral. And then Joysann settled it on him.

Wings. The jacket held him aloft.

In the mirror, Ruben saw a warrior, a hitman, an archangel. He didn't hesitate. "We'll take it."

Bauer laughed loud, his white teeth glinting as he ran a firm hand down Ruben's back right to the top of the boxer briefs. "Okay, then." He turned to Joysann with his dimples carved hard. "We have a winner."

The jacket exuded the kind of calm sophistication Ruben had envied his whole life. "Joysann, I think I just died. You're an angel," Ruben gabbled like a teenager. He couldn't help it. He turned to preen and gloat.

"I wouldn't say angel, Mr. Oso." Joysann stared at his bunching thighs and calves.

Oops. Yeah. Underpants. Embarrassing.

Again, Bauer smoothed the back of the coat over Ruben's spine slowly, brushing hard with his hand from neck to the curve of Ruben's butt.

She shrugged. "Hugo Boss. I had a hunch." She made him try on two more with the same label: a slate gray and a three-piece olive check. A phone rang on the wall and she answered it.

Bauer tugged at the vent and brushed the back. "Boss."

Feeling awkward, Ruben watched his own muscular legs in the mirror. "I never understood why people get so weird about clothes. Till now." He tightened his quads and pretended he couldn't feel the shopgirl's frank appraisal. Pushy broads always turned his crank.

Bauer lifted one lapel and thrust his hand around the side almost to Ruben's armpit. It slid cool and firm across Ruben's pec and ribs.

Ruben flinched, not ticklish, but conscious of being touched by a stranger. *He's petting me.* In public.

"S'good." Bauer grunted. His fingers pulled the shirt tighter across Ruben's chest. His ash-brown hair smelled like fresh bread.

This was what every suit wanted to be. He would have committed crimes to buy this suit, and it came at no cost as part of this crazy job he still didn't want.

Joysann put her hand over the mouthpiece. "Would you gentlemen like a beverage?"

Gentlemen.

"Uh." Bauer looked up distractedly as he came back with the suit trousers and handed them over.

"Water would be great." Ruben made the decision, feeling powerful because for the next hour his needs were her prime concern. It wasn't love, but it felt damn close. The sense of numb power coursed through him like vodka.

Joysann nodded as if she'd read his mind. "Sparkling?"

"Mmh." Ruben slipped into the trousers, zipped, and stepped back into his crummy loafers. The pants felt as sexy as the jacket. Sexier, maybe. The flat-front showed his goods in a great way.

Bauer nodded. "They can tailor everything while we do incidentals. Socks, ties. Casuals, maybe." He spoke tentatively to the air as if expecting Ruben to be offended. He turned to check. "Okay by you, Oso?"

"Of course." Ruben's ridiculous pleasure spilled over. "I could get used to this, man." They smiled at each other for some reason. Raggedy Andy wanted permission to spend a few grand to GQ the shit out of him for babysitting duty.

The carroty mustache kid ducked in to put two fizzy glasses on the table, then vanished again. The power of money at work.

Ruben snuck a look at Joysann, but her eyes were hidden. He moistened his lips and sighed. He usually hated shopping, but now he'd be happy to stand on pedestals all day spending Bauer's money in front of a juicy audience. In the mirror, Ruben could only see Joysann's creamy ankles. He imagined holding them together and pressing them back while he drilled for sweet oil.

Joysann pretended to crack her knuckles. "Let's get him fitted, boys."

Bauer pinched the shoulders of the jacket and shifted the yoke. He licked his lips and murmured, "Better, yeah?"

"A little snug." Ruben glanced at the girl. "But I like that."

He flexed and stared front, drunk with the indulgent attention. The pressure stretched the worsted wool over his wide lats and the shelf of his glutes. Thank Christ for the push-ups this morning. He'd been tempted to slack, but chin-ups and crunches before the sun came up had gotten his blood flowing in his brother's dusty apartment.

She brushed his chest and shoulder, running a hand under the lapel up to his armpit, right over a stiff nipple.

Ruben flirted back, making the word a growl. "Yeah."

She pulled out an oblong of grease marker and stepped behind him. He could feel her hands pinching and swiping the fabric.

Standing on the block in front of the mirror with Joysann perusing his assets turned him into a victorious gladiator being offered spoils and slave girls. He'd lost track of Bauer and that was just fine with him. *A little privacy.*

The grease marker dragged across his back as Joysann measured him like a side of beef with a feathery tickle that gave him gooseflesh and made his balls draw up.

Poor thing, trapped up here with all these uptight nimrods. Day in day out, she got twitchy head cases who fucked with the lights off. He'd seen the way she looked at him. She probably had a thing for rough dudes, dark skin, sloppy uncut dick… wrecking her, wrecking her good. He'd be happy to oblige.

Bauer handed him another jacket, another pair of pants, and Ruben stripped down without batting an eye.

Who cares? He was in charge. He wanted an audience. Standing in his underwears felt like showing off. He just wanted to stand on this pedestal in this jacket for the rest of time while people brought him expensive shit he didn't have to pay for. *Guh.* Now Ruben did have a tilted stiffy hidden under the tails of his shirt. Thank Christ for his fucking shorts holding it up against his belly or he'd be dripping on the dais. But maybe that was okay too. Maybe Joysann would get down and clean the mess he made.

Another suit, shuck, and swap. Ruben wanted to shop all day. This was better than booze.

Somewhere to his left, Joysann crossed her arms under her small high tits and made a soft surrendering sound. "Fuh." She marked and plucked behind him, the sides, the waist, the hem. Through half-lidded eyes he could see slices of her tight body.

Usually he went for Spanish chicks 'cause they were so much more sensible: unfazed by sex and serious about family. Plus they didn't automatically treat him like a mechanic or a pimp. White girls could get so uptight and judgmental about the little shit. But not all... every once in a while, he found one that wanted a ride on the wild side. Joysann seemed to have a fever for the flavor. She kept groping him hard.

Ruben calculated his options. Maybe he could send Bauer to pick out socks and drag this piece off to the john or a maintenance closet.

Suddenly, Joysann reappeared beside the mirror but the hands were still on him. She hadn't been measuring him at all.

My boss.

Bauer's touch, a man's hands. Everything else had been in his head. Pathetic, is what. Worse, the rough, impersonal groping had gotten him so boned up his oblong knob showed through his shorts.

You needta get laid, boy. And his boss obviously had serious boundary issues.

Now Ruben felt exposed in the mirrors. He tried to forget the intensity and pressure in his groin and focus on the new clothes.

The swishy ginger salesman came back and Bauer popped to his feet, pleased with himself. Joysann winked as she watched Bauer touching him. "Nice."

Shit. She thought they were together, as in, boner-buddies. *Why?* She knew Bauer, and he had hot chicks in and out of his place, chicks that ended up in the paper. Ruben had seen the Page Six clippings online.

"You boys need anything else from me?" Her smile was genuine, like she dug the thought of big dudes together doing things. She tasted her lower lip. *Jesus.* She thought they were fucking, that Ruben was a butt hustler getting spruced up on whitebread's dime.

Bauer signed something without looking at it. He was looking at Ruben's eyes in the mirror. "I think you should do it, Rube."

"What?" Ruben twisted in surprise.

"The fourth suit. Can't hurt to have options." Bauer held up a shoebox. "Footwear?" He hadn't finished the overhaul. Without waiting for an answer, he knelt again like a servant before the dais and removed Ruben's old loafers carefully.

Joysann looked at Bauer kneeling and those smooth hands on Ruben's body. "Listen to your man, there."

"We're not— He's my—" Ruben dug around trying to find an explanation that wouldn't blow his cover. He grimaced. "We work together."

"You sure do, *papá*." She gathered clacking hangers. "Oof. You two work together like—pow. I totally get it."

Jesus.

"Let me get these alterations started." Joysann handed half the hangers to the ginger kid, who reflected her knowing grin. "You boys take your time."

She gave her fantasy a thumbs-up as she walked away… probably to give them privacy to wrestle and make out. *Fuck.*

As soon as the salespeople were gone, Bauer laughed and dug in the shoe boxes. "That was awesome."

"Dude." Ruben raised his eyebrows and shook his head. He wanted to grab his pants, but didn't.

"How you did that. Got her juicy, huh?" His voice had a predatory edge. He liked conning her.

Ruben pretended to laugh. "Sure."

"Man! I love screwing with people like that. "

Did he mean the girl or Ruben or both?

"Yeah, uhh, Bauer. She thought we were—" Ruben spread his fingers and made a fist. "Together."

"I dunno. Maybe. Who cares?"

Ruben shrugged. "Great. I'm some dick-lick shopping on your dime." He could feel Bauer's body heat against his shins. He needed to hit a meeting, talk to Peach, take a step back.

"Dude, you don't look like anyone pays for you. Relax."

"Uh huh." He *wanted* to step back, but he could sense the dais edge under his heels.

"Our cards work. She's bored and we're two loaded guys."

Well, no. "One."

"Big deal. People see what they want. She just saw two rich jerks who fuck whoever, however we want. You totally sold it." Bauer patted his bare calf. "This is gonna work."

"What is?" The undercover just-buddies ruse. "Oh."

Bauer held up a glossy oxblood shoe. "So?"

"Uh. No. Laces, if that's okay." Off Bauer's look, he explained. "Safety. If I gotta move fast, I don't wanna sprint up Park Avenue in my socks." He didn't look down, and prayed his borrowed socks had no holes.

Bauer fished in the tissue of another box on the floor. He guided one foot and then the other into buttery black wingtips and then tied them.

Like I'm a science project.

"Good team." Bauer squeezed his foot through the shoe. "I'm a leaper, you're a looker."

Ruben scowled at the compliment. "I'm no looker."

"Before you leap, I mean. You check things out. Gonna keep me outta trouble."

Ruben hadn't thought this excursion through. Being broke sucked, and he knew that the clothes would make a difference, but some part of him resented that hot shopgirl misreading the situation so completely. *Deal with the devil, deal with the devil.* Part of him wanted to go out there and flash a weapon or punch a paparazzo so she wouldn't think—

Even with the shirt and briefs, somehow those glossy shoes made him feel even more exposed. The new soles were slippery as oily glass.

Bauer crouched closer. "Those'll work." His shark eyes glittered in the mirror as he stood straight up right in Ruben's personal space, all of eight inches between them.

"No." Ruben shifted back in the slick-soled wingtips and almost pitched off the back of the dais. "Whoa!"

Bauer grabbed and gripped his arm.

"Sorry." Ruben looked down at the gleaming wingtips his boss wanted to buy him.

"Y'good?" Bauer let go and wiped his hands on his jeans. "Okay?"

Ruben stepped down onto the floor with a fake smile. "Fingers crossed." But whether those twisted digits meant he was hopeful or lying, he couldn't have said.

SOMEHOW IN the course of that first day, Ruben got tricked into a sleepover.

After they got back from Barney's, he spent the afternoon watching his new boss make phone calls and standing outside shut doors when Bauer ejected him. The cook made a mango shrimp salad for lunch, which he ate by himself.

Apex Securities didn't seem like any business he'd seen. Phone calls, yes. A couple visitors in eight hundred dollar loafers. The stock market stream on the monitors. But nothing that looked like 9-to-5 grind.

At sundown, he could hear raised voices: Bauer speaking harshly and Hope countering, and silences from what he assumed were someone on the other end of the phone. Without thinking he drifted closer, eavesdropping by default.

Suddenly, his boss emerged from the office, flushed pink and tie askew. "There you are." As if Ruben had been hiding. He took off his jacket.

Ruben started making exit noises. "It's late...." He shifted his weight awkwardly. "Sorry."

"Don't go, man. You should just eat here. Crash if you want." His voice sounded casual, but the way he said it, Ruben knew how planned it was. Bauer was angling for something.

But what and why?

"And I'm off." Hope walked out of the office in a trench, flipping her hair out of the collar. She held a small gunmetal attaché case. She looked between them. "You boys good here?"

Ruben nodded, unsure what she meant.

"Thanks, doll." Bauer saluted her. "You'll have a bite, then."

The hell? Ruben waited two breaths before he looked up at his boss.

"I mean, it's not like I don't have space up here."

Ruben nodded. Two guest rooms upstairs and one down the hall. The idea scared the shit out of him. He wanted to stay and needed to run.

Bauer pointed. "Stop panicking. I don't believe in the wrong side of the tracks, Rube."

Ruben shrugged. "I grew up in South Miami. Both sides of the tracks were wrong."

His boss didn't elaborate. His waist buzzed and then he was talking to the air again, holding up a wait-a-sec finger at Ruben and speaking loudly in French.

Without waiting for a reply, Bauer walked back toward the office. The door shut behind him.

Ruben knew he didn't need to stay. Better that he go home and try to get some rest. He already felt off-kilter, and a vague thirsty pressure rose in him that he recognized. Insidious and powerful, the itch for one drink to take the edge off. *What could it hurt?* The idiot urge to medicate his anxiety was a golden oldie by this point.

Stop right there, kiddo. Peach in his head.

Ruben drifted into the dining room, where the flame teak table was set for two with sterling utensils and minimalist bone china, $750 a place setting, easy. Three glasses at each chair, for water, white, and red respectively, and each light as a tulip.

He spun the glass like a blossom in his blunt fingers.

"All the way from Prague." Bauer spoke right behind him. His breath smelled like orange peel.

Caught. How does he materialize like that? Ruben tried not to tense and put a couple feet between them. "Nice."

"Handblown, but Czech crystal is the best." Bauer considered him with those relentless blue-gray eyes. "You can stay for dinner." Not asking anymore.

Ruben dodged. "I bet these cost a hundred-fifty, two hundred bucks apiece, right?"

"I dunno." Bauer scratched his head absently, and a muscle ticked at the angle of his oversquare jaw. "I had brandy out of a snifter at the Boscolo in Old Town." He picked up a glass with his long, loose fingers. "I'd never felt anything so right in my hand. Y'know?"

"Bauer, I wasn't giving you grief. It's a nice glass."

"I used to be an asshole to my parents for buying expensive shit, and my mom said you have to pay for art or else artists starve. And this is art." The glass glittered in his grip.

"True."

"The man who made that probably lived for six months off what I spent at his little shop. He didn't grow up in Scarsdale with a triple trust fund, but I did, so I feel like I can throw a bone. Even the shit I do for fun makes money." He swept a hand at his bear skull and the silk rug and the zillion-dollar view of Manhattan laid out like a willing sinner. "Plus for an added bonus, it drove my stepfather *crazy*." A manic smile.

Ruben nodded like the family drama meant anything to him.

"Not like I don't know how lucky I am, Ruben. I know I won that lottery." He sounded lonely.

"I know. It's cool. I know you do." Why did his new employer feel the need to make a case? Ruben drifted back toward him.

"Anybody can rip people off. If you make serious money you have to leave the world better. Charity. Art. Anything."

Ruben snorted. The belly of the glass filled his palm perfectly. "See what you mean. And you can afford it."

Bauer grinned. The shark had vanished and the ragdoll returned. "I mix business with pleasure whenever I can."

"No shit." Ruben shook his head in disbelief.

"So... dinner. Food's already prepped if you want to grab a chair. Chef's gone. It's just us, so we're gonna rough it."

"I bet." And just like that, Bauer made the decision, which pleased and terrified him. *He's keeping me here.*

Whistling, he returned with a pork thing with parsnips that smelled good and tasted better. For whatever reason, once Ruben sat down here, the price of everything stopped bothering him. This was the first time he'd spent in this penthouse without money on his mind. Instead of boss and hire or bodyguard and principal, they turned into two guys who needed to eat and sleep.

Bauer acted more relaxed than he'd ever been. They ate hungrily and though his boss had wine, Ruben felt no temptation. *Huh.*

Peach always said alcoholics reach for a drink when they're Hungry, Angry, Lonely, or Tired. *HALT, the acronym was.* Whenever the urge emerged, he'd tell himself to "Halt" and it usually worked. Except, in this penthouse, Ruben didn't feel any of those things. Anything but. More like the opposite of "halt." *Full steam ahead.*

After food and coffee, Bauer seemed intent on entertaining him, and they both wound down. Just as at Barney's, the stream of flattery and charm gave Ruben the hypnotic feeling of being in absolute control. Something seductive about his wishes holding sway and Bauer's eagerness to please him. Made no sense, but made Ruben drunk with luxe and borrowed power.

He likes having you on the premises, Ruben's brain offered, but he ignored the thought.

Courtesy of ESPN, the projection TV spewed a baseball game across the whited-out windows. Bauer had a lot to say about the scoring and stats that went right over his head. Ruben didn't particularly like baseball, he preferred the pace of soccer or basketball, but a game was a game.

Eventually Ruben caught himself staying awake out of politeness, hoping his boss wasn't doing the same. *I like him too.*

Gradually the commentary dwindled and Ruben turned to check. Bauer's face was cuddled hard against the white cushions. His eyes were closed and his chest rose and fell smoothly. The cowlick in his hair had sprung loose.

His boss had fallen asleep on the couch with the news blaring, a vague smile on his lips, his breath steady. Not nervous for once.

'Cause I'm here.

Even weirder, Ruben could have dozed if he stopped fighting. Again he stole more than a glance. A narrow strip of abdomen revealed the line of springy fuzz pointing south from his navel. Even now, at the end of the day, Andy smelled fresh baked.

"Bed," Ruben whispered to himself, and as he bent to wake the man, he thought better of disturbing him when he'd finally found some peace.

Let sleeping dogs lie.

Instead, Ruben tiptoed down the main hall to the guest room next to the office and stripped to his boxers.

As soon as the door shut, he questioned the decision to sleep over, even with Bauer forty feet away, even for a night. This room made him feel like an impostor, underlining everything he hadn't figured out and all the things he needed to change still.

Not that his brother's couch was so comfy, but without Bauer's coaxing he knew he didn't belong.

His brown toes sank into the sixteen thousand dollar Agra rug. His jeans hung like seaweed from the Philippe Starck valet. His stubble scraped the eight-hundred-dollar pillowcase. No part of him belonged in this place. He put a glass of water on the nightstand.

He shouldn't have stayed.

Sleep steered clear.

If he'd had a book, he'd have read. Instead he opted to play Scrabble on his phone for an hour before he gave up and turned off the lights.

For the first time in his life, he lay awake staring at the ceiling with no cracks to count. Bauer's ceilings looked as seamless as the rest of his life.

Around two thirty he heard someone moving in the library and then his door opened. He shut his eyes.

A whisper? "Rube?" His boss going to bed, checking on him. The door closed again.

He opened his eyes when he heard Bauer climbing the stairs and moving around directly overhead.

Something still bugged him here that kept him from settling. The unnatural stillness, maybe. Bauer's climate control kept the air exactly ten degrees below body temperature. The mattress held him like a gentle hand. The triple-glazed windows overlooking the park kept the room goldfish quiet, but Ruben couldn't keep his brain from scurrying on its wheel and his thick dick from slithering against the mattress.

Princess and the Peabrain.

Despite the spacious quarters, Ruben wrestled with the surge of claustrophobia and closed his eyes. If he'd been at home in Miami, he'd have bumped Marisa's ass with his joint to wake her and get it wet. At his brother's he'd take a cold shower. His cock wasn't fully hard yet, but the sore tingle telegraphed how long it had been. Since coming to the city, he hadn't gotten laid. *Weeks*, come to think of it.

As he hunched against the warm bedding, his juicy foreskin slipped smoothly back and forth a quarter inch inside his boxers. He imagined trying on the suits with Joysann. The wet pout of her mouth. The hypnotic rush of power that came from taking whatever he wanted, no price tag. The firm clutch and drag of those hands tugging and smoothing his body through the wool.

Andy's hands.

He froze, horny and ashamed. His cock vibrated beneath his belly. Bauer's hands. His *employer's* hands had felt too good and he remembered them exactly.

"Halt," he whispered to the dark room. It even smelled expensive.

He sat up to take the final swallow of the water, warm by now. Time for a refill. He tried not to think about the liquor in the library, living room, kitchen, and more. He was only thirsty for water.

Starved for contact is all. And he could not afford a wet dream in this bed.

Self-conscious about his bare brown legs and his stiff boner, he pulled on his trousers over his straining boxers but didn't bother with anything over his wife-beater. Barefoot on the wool rug, he padded out into the hall. The over-the-top security made the entire building feel like safe space.

At three thirty in the morning, the silent apartment held its breath. The wide plank floors didn't even creak as he made his way back to the kitchen to refill the glass of water instead of using the bathroom sink. He opened the Sub-Zero refrigerator and stared at the shelves loaded with kumquats, lamb chops, and fresh cilantro bagged with its roots still attached for maximum organic whatever-the-hell.

Crazy. He'd let Bauer's paranoia seep into him until it metastasized into insomnia and blue balls. For the millionth time, he understood why guys jerked off out of boredom just to numb their brains.

He drifted to the dining room where the dishes waited for cleanup by Bauer's staff. Resisting the urge to put everything in the sink, he tugged open the terrace door and stepped outside into the quiet, sultry air.

His skin started to ooze sweat, but at least he could breathe out here. His back prickled with the sensation of being watched. Bullshit, of course. He and his boss were alone up here, and he was the only one awake. *Right?*

Hating himself, he looked up at the blank black of Bauer's windows.

For reasons he didn't examine, he stood looking up at them for a full two minutes, for a sign, for a clue.

Nothing and no one looked back, but his prickling unease did not subside.

Stupid. His cock bobbed and finally sagged inside his creased boxers.

In other circumstances he'd have said his instincts had him on alert, but in this bullshit situation he knew better. Andy Bauer was more likely to be struck by lightning or abducted by aliens than fall prey to any kind of Tom Clancy scenario.

Bullshit.

Bauer had to be running a con, with him as window dressing. Maybe that was it. Maybe he wasn't telling Ruben the whole truth after all. Maybe he did want a rough wingman to crack the ladies. And maybe the reason

Ruben was earning so much for so little was to allow Bauer to act out some egomaniac kink. Exhibitionism, voyeurism. Best to stay dumb.

Sleeping dogs lie.

Two puzzle pieces snicked together in his mind, and in that moment, sweet certainty gripped him: his boss had duped someone.

Watching the dark glass above, he hoped it wasn't him.

CHAPTER FOUR

FEAR IS the cheapest weapon and the hardest to hold.

"Think fast." A blue racquetball bounced off the window and smacked into Ruben's chest hard enough to sting. He spun. "Ow."

It was day three, 2:19 p.m., and Bauer glared from the other side of the living room with his hands extended to catch.

Ruben squeezed the little ball, collapsing it in his hand. Why was Bauer pissed? And why the ball?

"Think. Faster. Dumbass." Bauer sounded angry and looked straight at him. "Well, then you tell him to sell or we destroy his family and sell them off for parts to the Swiss."

Ruben straightened. "The hell?"

"I *want* him to shit his pants!" Bauer shook his head and pointed at his earpiece and laughed without smiling. "Lowball him."

Oh. Phone call on the headset. Until today, Bauer had kept his business behind closed doors. What was this call, anyways, and why did he want Ruben to hear it? Or did he? Had he just come out to play?

Andy ground his teeth. His jaw flexed. "This close? He *should* shit his pants, man. And then he sells or you're going to come give him a colostomy with a chainsaw." He beckoned for the ball.

Speechless, Ruben gently tossed the blue ball back underhanded. He didn't want to break anything. Fuck knows, he couldn't afford replacements. Was this jagoff playing catch?

"Bullshit." Bauer sighed, either at him or the call. "If not fast, at least you can fucking *think*, Joe. We got him pinned down." With a snarl, Bauer pitched the ball hard at the window so that it smacked into Ruben's chest again.

A game.

Ruben goggled and muttered, "Nuts," but finally he threw the ball back at the glass. *Following orders.*

It bounced wild but his boss caught it, giving Ruben a thumbs-up and that goofy clean-cut grin. Raggedy Andy wanted to play.

For the next half hour, they played fake handball against the window in a million-dollar room, grinning like idiots while Andy brokered some kind of takeover. Happily, nothing got broken.

By the end of the call, Ruben had learned fuck-all about international finance or the Apex Fund, but at least he'd started to think of Bauer as Andy. Dude was too nutty to be called "Mr." Anything.

As predicted, Ruben's security duties just peddled make-believe, but they sure as hell paid well. Every time Ruben felt like grumbling, he looked at those new suits hanging in his brother's closet and bit his tongue. None of his business how Andy wasted his money or anyone else's.

A couple of clients came to the apartment for meetings while Hope served drinks and research reports. Ruben shook their hands, laughed on cue, and saw nothing to endanger Andy's money or safety. The clients were bland and blank, mostly old white dudes dressed like soap opera villains in handmade shoes, but not an eyepatch among them. Boring, actually. As he'd suspected, any black ops Wall Street mercs were strictly no-show.

Sure enough, the man spent most of his time on phone calls piped through a Bluetooth earpiece, shouting financial advice into the air like a schizophrenic with an MBA.

By the weekend, Ruben felt pretty certain the biggest threat to Andy Bauer... was Andy Bauer. The security gig ended up feeling funny but harmless. As long as Ruben stuck around, Andy could pretend he was in danger, but protected at the same time. Ruben could track Andy's paranoid logic: he wanted an invisible goon, so he'd bought one.

Gradually Andy monitoring him and his lack of boundaries started seeming pitiful, unnerving, but unfreaky. He seemed as lonely as Ruben felt. Maybe he was.

Let sleeping dogs lie.

Funny thing: he dug Andy's company. The occasional predatory flashes showed calculation and financial know-how, but he wasn't a prick, exactly. He took an interest in Ruben, which automatically made him interesting. Not a bad guy, just lonely, rich, and too brainy to be normal. Personally, Ruben thought Andy had suffered from too much education and not enough life. Boarding school, fancy college, all kinds of shit that obviously kept him rich but made him no friends that Ruben could see. He sympathized; they were both private people, holding cards close.

A leaper and a looker. They made a good team.

Maybe loneliness and boredom did strange things to his imagination, but Andy began to live rent-free in his head.

The long shifts with Andy left Ruben no time for a life. His best window for meeting some rich nymphomaniac was in the twenty-two minutes it took him to walk down Park Avenue in the morning, but Park Avenue at dawn proved to be sadly nympho-free.

Ruben got in the habit of taking a scalding shower every night before crashing on his couch. The hot water wore him out, and he'd struggle toward sleep while the cat glared at him, waiting to be overfed. At least he managed to hit a couple AA meetings, but in this neighborhood, most were packed with old-timers and in Spanish.

Still, tonight was Saturday and he'd hoped he might be able to go out, maybe a movie or dancing. Anyplace where he might be able to hook up, because these days his balls throbbed like a fucking root canal.

As soon as Ruben got downstairs at the Iris, he texted his brother that he was homebound, and a few blocks later he got a reply. "GIMME THIRTY" which meant Daria was over and Charles was getting busy.

Whenever his brother entertained the girlfriend, Ruben took a walk around the block for a couple hours. Stations of the cross for losers. *Here is the pizza parlor, here is the free clinic.* Wasn't Charles's fault. Tonight Ruben opted to hit the grocery.

On the way he dug out his phone. "Peach?"

All the way to Ninety-Sixth Street, she golfed and he griped. She kept asking about his social life and he shrugged it off. He was grateful for the friendly ear but conscious of the lonely box he'd built around himself. His weird fixation on Andy didn't come up and he was too ashamed to spill the beans. Him, as a guy, having a female sponsor was really unorthodox, and for once he understood why. Her Sondheim quotes didn't teach him anything, but they calmed him down even as he was surprised by how tired Peach sounded.

Finally, Ruben hung up and wandered into Associated Supermarket. Paying rent, he couldn't afford, but since moving in four weeks ago, he'd helped his little brother out by covering groceries and meals.

Charles lived up on 109th in Spanish Harlem, so a lot of the locals and signs used language Ruben couldn't understand. He tended to nod and glower so no one asked him questions. Scary mug to the rescue, again.

The grocery store still seemed like an alien planet to him. Marisa had done the shopping, always. He cooked sometimes, but mostly she'd been a housewife and happy about it. Standing by the baskets, Ruben fished the list out of his pocket: Fanta, Wheaties, pasta, chips. Nothing green, nothing fresh. Charles still ate like a teenager because Daria did most of the cooking. For the past month, Ruben had fought his gut with crunches and push-ups.

Ruben headed down the first uncrowded aisle and realized he was standing in a narrow aisle of wine and beer. What motherfucker had decreed that supermarkets could legally sell booze? He nodded to himself and avoided that landmine, knocking out the whole list in about twenty minutes.

The air conditioning inside the store chilled him so much that the swelter outside felt refreshing when he emerged. Taking his time to waste another ten minutes, he trudged back to the apartment, balancing the bags, praying the stretched plastic would survive the journey and that his brother had put on pants.

He took the stairs slowly and made noise with his key in the lock just to be safe. "S'me." He ducked into the tiny kitchen.

The cat showed up expecting a snack, but settled for dry kibble, crunching at him with bored resignation.

Ruben scratched its head. "At least you didn't have to walk around the block."

Charles swore otherwise, but Ruben needed to find a place of his own ASAP.

"Rube?" His brother came out of the bathroom, hair damp and wrapped in a towel. "We're good."

Ruben put the groceries on one of the stools in front of the tiny counter to put away later. No way could they both fit in the kitchen.

"Nice threads. My jackets looked like shit on you. Jesus."

"You got fat, man."

"Fuck you." His brother rubbed his hard gut.

Charles was tubby, had no kinda chin, and lived on maxed out credit cards, but he got way more pussy because he was without shame. He'd lie, beg, and whine to get inside a girl's ass. Daria had managed to hang on to him for seven months, which was some kinda record. "Bauer's right about the suit, though. He dressed you up sharp."

"Yeah. I guess."

"Job still kosher?"

"I guess? He's buying." Ruben nodded. "But I still can't figure why Empire." *Why me?*

For a moment he imagined Andy's shark smile. He realized it didn't scare him anymore, which scared him.

"Bauer wants to feel like a badass with some pit bull on a leash, so let him." Charles shrugged. "It's all in his head, and he wants you to put on a show."

"He thinks the pigeons are spying on us. Rich people don't cheap out on safety."

"Then who fucking knows, Rube? Slumming? I say thank God for paranoid cheapskates." Charles took a swallow of milk and wiped his mouth. "He a homo, y'think? Crushing on your mean *pinga*."

Ruben snorted. "Bauer? No way. Uptight is all." He didn't add that he'd probably spent more time scoping Andy than vice versa. "That dude uses the Playboy channel like the home shopping network."

An odd look, clenched eyebrows. "You should get with some ladies, mingle. Get your ashes hauled."

"Yeah." Ruben pressed his lips together and looked at the mottled floor. For five seconds he considered braving the hot night to hit a meeting then crapped out. *Tomorrow.*

"Socialize. Everything you got's been taken. I get it, Rube. You're not a kid, and you're gonna have to get your feet under you again. Man up."

"I'm not a charity case, Chucky."

"No. No, you're not. A charity case would say thank you and get off my back. No, you gotta bust my balls and bitch that I'm not sending you into something crazy and dangerous."

Ruben exhaled. "I gotta feeling."

"A feeling. You're thinking about Marisa."

Ruben shrugged. Actually he hadn't obsessed about Marisa in three months, but it made more sense than what he had been obsessing over.

"Ruben, all that's past. Almost a year, huh? She's done. Moved on. You do the same."

"Sure." Eyes up. "No. I'm good."

"I thought you dug Bauer's assistant. Hot and smart."

"Hope? Yeah. No. Engaged." Every time Ruben flirted she held up a diamond the size of a throat lozenge, but she seemed unoffended by his attention.

"How engaged can she be?" Charles always assumed they could talk their way into any panties. Maybe he was right. Down the hall, Daria's plaintive voice asked something.

Charles raised his voice to answer. "Almost, *cariño*. M'talking to my brother, huh?"

No reply from the bedroom, but Charles nodded toward Daria anyway.

How did they talk about Ruben when he wasn't here? Did he even want to know? Shame choked him.

I'm intruding here. Irrationally, Ruben wanted to be back at the penthouse spying on a life he'd never be able to afford. Plenty of room there. At least Andy listened. He swatted that thought away.

Peach's voice in his head: *Analysis is paralysis.*

He needed to make himself scarce somehow. The apartment was tiny, but it had an old, footed tub in there big enough for three people. Charles hated to sweat so he liked to sit and soak. Ruben tried to keep his showers short 'cause this wasn't his place and never would be.

Ruben pointed at the john. "Okay if I rinse off?"

"Please! You stink, *papá*." Charles wiped his face again and ducked back toward the safety of his girlfriend.

After making up the sofa, Ruben washed fast and went to bed wet and wobbly. If he slept at all, he didn't remember it in the morning.

SOMETIMES A plan is just a list of things that don't happen.

Ruben talked Andy into working out and some basic self-defense training. In exchange, Ruben consented to hit the paths in Central Park three mornings a week at dawn. He refused to sleep over, but the tradeoff seemed fair.

Ruben made it downtown half-awake, freshly rinsed and wearing old soccer shorts and duct-taped Nikes. The Iris doormen watched them leave with undisguised pity. What did they know about staying in shape at forty? *Madness.*

The first time they met in the Iris lobby at 6:00 a.m., Andy chided, "The early bird catches the worm."

"Sure." Ruben raised one grumpy brow. "But the early worm gets eaten by the bird."

What he learned is that jogging is legalized suicide.

Ruben, a few steps behind for much of the trek to the park, watched the sweat spread across Andy's back like faint wings and then creep toward his waistband before they'd even started in earnest. He'd forgotten that it was almost *July.*

They ran.

Andy, for his part, led the way silently, allowing Ruben to follow the subtle cues of his body. No need to speak really. Together, they fell into a lope that Ruben hoped he could sustain without puking, pissing his shorts, or passing out.

Central Park was shaded, but the morning sun still drizzled over them like hot grease. Humidity made breathing slow and arduous as they pounded the concrete paths under the trees. His quads burned, and after ten minutes he could feel sweat glinting off him with every step.

Andy obviously knew how to pace himself, matching Ruben tread for tread. He was slippery with perspiration but looked relaxed and happy for some horrible reason. His corded legs took the terrain effortlessly.

Ruben focused on keeping his breath steady. He'd been cooped up indoors for too many weeks. He hadn't realized just how much he missed sun, trees, sky. On the other hand, his thighs and calves felt flayed raw.

Without thinking Ruben took off his T-shirt and wrapped it around his fist. Too hot to feel self-conscious. Besides, he'd been in New York long enough to start losing the Florida color, his brown skin dulling to a fishbelly-beige. Sunlight slid over his shoulders like a heavy robe.

Andy looked him up and down but said nothing.

Suddenly jogging seemed like a great idea.

After fifteen minutes, the air didn't even feel hot anymore, and Ruben could feel his thirsty skin drinking the crazy green light that snuck through the trees. Sweat slid down his ribs, staining his waistband dark.

Andy gave what sounded like a big, satisfied sigh, and Ruben realized he could hear it as if Andy had exhaled right into his ear because the city was so far away.

Quiet.

Aside from the scuff of their shoes on the path, the noises of Manhattan waking up had all but vanished. No cars yet. A dozy scent of bark and fresh grass hung in the air, and the skyscrapers rose like geometric cliffs too distant to deserve caution. He snuck a look at Andy and caught him looking back.

Andy nodded and raised his eyebrows, some secret arcing between them.

Not that Central Park was a secret, but that it hid one: this mild dappled glow that filtered out the city. Strange, but somehow familiar.

When have I been in the park before? That first day he'd come to break into Andy's place. He looked again to his right.

"Good?" Andy's hushed voice sounded loud suddenly.

Ruben nodded. "I think so. I guess. You're strong." He glanced at the perfect legs.

"Habit. I ran at Columbia. Fencing team."

"You don't even stretch."

"Massage later."

In other words, someone else was scheduled to stretch him. Them?

"Fuh." Ruben clamped his jaw, unsure how he felt about that. "You do this every morning?"

"Clears your head. Builds the appetite. Charlotte's making brioche."

"Fuck you." But Ruben smiled, his lungs sluggish from the cigarettes and his blocky frame not built for speed. He tried to breathe through his nose. Maybe he wasn't built for running. "I'm too thick."

Andy looked down at Ruben's churning legs. "Bullshit. Those calves? Sprinter, probably." He was still looking as he thudded along in sync.

"Wrestled. High school. No running." The unblinking attention made him feel funny. The burn in his lower body was excruciating.

Andy spun and ran backward, jabbing at Ruben's slick midsection. "Candy ass." How did this nutjob stay so chipper? He turned and pulled ahead of Ruben to let a cyclist pass.

"Easy for you." A little smile of sweat on the top of Andy's shorts drew Ruben's eye. "To say." He exhaled raggedly. "Asshole."

Grin. "You'll get the hang, *vato*." Andy fell back into judding sync with Ruben, at his right elbow. "One mile and we're done. How else am I gonna keep my ass in shape?"

No comment. Andy's ass needed no help. Ruben looked down to the pavement as he jogged. "Too fucking old."

"Bullshit. At forty-whatever?" Andy swallowed and his big jaw flexed, what Ruben had come to think of as his concentration muscle.

"One. Almost two."

"C'mon, Rube."

Ruben stopped in his tracks, drip-dripping on the asphalt. "That's what my family calls me." Except, for once he didn't mind it. He tried to throttle the cool rush of inappropriate affection that surged over him.

Andy jogged in place till Ruben started running again. He shook his head. "What?"

"No. Nothing." Ruben ran easy after that, not even feeling his legs till he stopped moving.

Even jogging slow, they eventually reached the edge of the bubble and emerged onto Fifth Avenue next to a big white building with columns that looked like a wedding-cake courthouse bank.

Andy caught him goggling. "The Met. Big museum."

The façade stretched up several blocks of Fifth Avenue on its park side. "Cool."

"I used to love it. My parents brought me all the time as a kid." Andy watched him, unblinking. "We'll be back. Promise."

Ruben thought it was weird that this gigantic museum should be tucked away up here in such a quiet neighborhood, but then realized the Upper East Side gazillionaires had probably built this mausoleum and then filled it with whatever Picassos and sarcophagi they couldn't fit in their condos: a very fancy storage unit, not designed to keep the commoners out, but to keep all the valuables in.

He was getting a feel for New York, finally. In a way, the entire island of Manhattan had been designed for the convenience of the people living in this zip code. Upper East Siders could order anything to be delivered. He could imagine a couple of these rich buzzards who only descended when it was time to scoop up the millions that paid the bills on their swank perches.

They made it back to the Iris in no time. The doorman saluted them as they passed. After the park, the lobby's groomed green wall seemed tame and lame. Ruben's legs throbbed if he didn't keep moving, so he did.

Inside the elevator, Andy eyed him. "You lift, right?"

Ruben nodded. "When I can."

"Thought so. I got a surprise."

"Is it alive? Do I have to walk it?"

Big laugh. Dimple. "Private gym, if you ever wanted one. All ours," Andy said, pressing the button for the thirty-third floor. His white tee was translucent with sweat.

"You're gonna work out now?"

Andy regarded him from the other side of the elevator. "I just wanna cool down." He rested his hands at the waistband of his shorts so that his fingertips dipped inside the elastic, grazing the tops of where his pubes had to be.

Glass double doors rose opposite the elevator, with a bunch of fancy exercise equipment on the other side.

Andy pressed the pad with his damp thumb and the door popped open, revealing a plush gymnasium about twenty-five feet square. "Building already has your prints."

Ruben could see an elliptical trainer, a couple treadmills. A basic weight circuit. All the machines looked untouched. *Creepy.* "Brand new."

"Been here seven-plus years, but I'm the only tenant who uses it."

To the east, a wall of sheet glass looked down on a tiled terrace: polished teak furniture and sculptured trees ringed a shimmering rectangle the color of a Miami sky.

Beside him, Andy peeled off his sopping shirt, revealing the sun-kissed torso.

"No one at all?" Ruben walked into the spotless corner room. Sheet glass windows. Shrubbery beyond. Turquoise water.

On the fucking thirty-third floor.

"When Equinox was remodeling, Lisa on seventeen came here with her trainer." He shrugged at Ruben. "She does the morning weather for Fox." He made a face.

"Nobody uses the deck even?"

"Mmmh. Some of the kids come splash around in the winter because it's heated and has a wave machine. Teenagers sneak out to smoke weed and make out. But I'm the only tenant that doesn't summer out of town. Like, *summer* as a verb. I hate that scene. I get enough during the week."

Ruben looked at the sparkling equipment and through the sheet glass at the impeccably landscaped terrace. Low trees grew in teak boxes filled with white quartz gravel. Their dense leaves were clipped and sculpted into mod blobs. "Looks... clean, I guess."

Andy folded his shirt and wrung the dripping cotton out. His blocky muscles were pinked and pumped. His arms bunched and his drips polka-dotted the deck.

Unaccountably, the sight relaxed Ruben at a primitive level. Maybe because they were both guys, both sweated, both had worked hard. Maybe.

"All the plants are leased seasonally. So much for nature, huh?" His pecs looked even more square than his dumb jaw.

Ruben smiled to himself.

Andy twisted his shoulders to crack his back. He had a relatively smooth chest and thighs and then this springy golden fluff on his calves and forearms that caught the light. Ruben couldn't take his eyes off it, partly because it was so unexpected and partly because he'd never seen body hair that looked so soft.

Andy walked straight down the stairs into the water.

Ruben wanted to join him, but felt strange splashing around with his boss with the possibility of other tenants spying on them from some window.

Except, they think I'm his buddy.

"Wanna cool off?" Andy turned back. "Feels great."

Headshake. "Needta stretch." But he didn't.

Instead, Ruben stood and watched while Andy dove in: a single hard line of sinew that made no splash. On the swim team at his prep school. He popped back up, scraping his hair out of his face and squeezing the water from his scalp. Powerful arms, snub nose, peachy skin. The prince of Park Avenue rinsing the dust of the commoners from his perfect body before returning to his cage above the city.

Ruben flashed on the crowded neighborhood pool he'd gone to growing up, cracked tile and cloudy water. Now he faced a forty-foot heated bathtub hovering above Park Avenue that didn't get used because the tenants forgot it was here.

He gritted his teeth in loose envy and frustration.

Andy had no fucking idea how the world worked. He lived in an imaginary bubble of spare houses, ignored pools, decorative gyms... wine that needed to breathe and dresses worn once.

For a good thirty seconds he spent watching Andy bob and surface, Ruben wished that his brother had given him the stupid bouncer job on the West Side. Nowhere near the pay but way easier on his ego and libido.

"You don't know what you're missing." Andy stood on the little run of steps facing him. His running shorts stuck to his muscular legs and his hair darkened by the dip. "Grab me a towel?" The sheen of water made his muscles look even more perfect.

Ruben nodded, wondering if Bauer expected him to run up three floors, and then saw the fluffy white pile on a pedestal just inside the door.

Andy's wet feet slapped toward him until his broad shoulders filled the doorway, so Ruben tossed the folded terrycloth rather than carrying it like a fucking Key West cabana boy. *There are limits.* He drifted toward the hall door.

Andy grinned dimple-deep and muttered in a teasing voice, "Se siente cachondo, Oso."

"What?" The word "cachondo" sounded dirty and slightly familiar.

Andy looked at his face, shoulders, chest, legs. "You're all jacked up. Sun did you good."

"Thanks." Ruben rubbed his hot skin. He'd be darker as a result, is that what Andy wanted? *Cachondo.*

Andy scrubbed his ear, squinting. "You can use it whenever. Pool, I mean."

"Sure." Ruben was here to do a job, not get a tan.

Inside again, Andy scraped himself semidry before following Ruben back to the elevator. "Seriously. Nobody ever uses this deck in summer."

Ruben grunted noncommittally. He pressed the UP button and turned to nod thanks to his boss.

Except Andy faced the other way and his thin blue shorts were plastered to his flushed skin, and wedged between the high cheeks of his ass.

Freeballing?

Ruben swallowed and aimed his gaze at the elevator ahead. *What the hell?*

Andy scrubbed his thick hair with the towel. "Most of the tenants vanish. The wives move out to the Hamptons or the Hudson Valley in May with the kids and the staff. A couple of the artsy types take the Jitney on Thursdays. Stays pretty dead up here." His eyes hardened a moment.

"I'll bring a pair of shorts."

Andy shrugged. "Or you can borrow—" *Yeah, no.*

Bing. The silent doors slid open, and Andy gestured Ruben inside first, swimsuit loaners forgotten.

Keeping his eyes low, Ruben could just make out the faint dimples above the waistband and the white straps of the jock Andy was wearing. Nothing but creamy skin under the pale blue shorts, so Andy must shave fore and aft. The sight made Ruben's dick feel funny—hollow and somehow heavy—to creep on a dude that way. He glanced back up into that intense gray-blue stare again.

Andy had caught him looking. He winked and coughed.

They both looked up at the big numbers climbing and nobody said a damn thing, which worked out fine. His arm brushed Ruben's, tickling for a millisecond.

Ruben would never wear a jockstrap. Just an open ass? Straight guys didn't wear jocks. Gay guys wore jocks for, like, porn fashion, but what the hell did it do for you at the gym?

Inside the apartment, Ruben hooked left toward the guest room. "Gonna rinse." His hands shook, so he flexed them to cover.

Behind him he could hear Andy grunt and pour a tall glass of something in the kitchen.

In the bathroom he stared at himself in the mirror. *Thlip.* A salty drip from his chin reminded him of the shower he needed to take.

An ugly, small part of him wanted to go back to the pool to swim in that hot water. Or to let his boss paw and praise him so he could have more of that numbing, in-control feeling he'd started to crave.

Drunk on just being there.

Ruben needed to hit a meeting, ASAP. He wasn't drinking, but he was acting exactly like an alcoholic. The choices he was making seemed destructive and selfish. This is what AA was for. Like every ex-boozer on earth, he'd transferred his addiction to something convenient, in this case the job, the money, and his boss.

He texted Peach but got no reply. *No.* Before the party tonight, he'd duck out and hit a meeting. Any fucking meeting. He needed to get away. Take a break. Just an hour outside of this place talking with other alcoholics would help him get his head back on straight.

Straight.

Ruben peeled the sweaty shorts off, and they hit the tiled wall with a grim slap. He needed to look up *cachondo*. He hated feeling ignorant, especially when he was.

A flicker made his head jerk. Was someone watching him? His skin prickled as he poked back out into the bedroom's uncanny silence. Nothing and no one.

He stood there a moment, goosefleshed and straining to hear. Finally he locked the door. Stupid, maybe, but at least nobody was gonna sneak up on him.

When he stepped into the shower, Ruben thought the steaming water was cold until he realized that it was pinking his brown skin. He rolled his shoulders and let his head hang forward. The water pelted his shoulders and neck but did nothing for the tension. After all his bitching at Andy about stretching he hadn't done jack to limber up. He'd stretch after the shower. No way could he stretch with Andy in those wet shorts watching him. *Freaky.*

What the hell did *cachondo* mean?

Ruben soaped his skin roughly, kneading his quads hard enough to force a gasp.

Andy's strength had surprised the hell out of him. The guy sat at a desk all day but kept ripped up, wide lats and the small, high butt of a soccer player. *Go know.* Maybe some kinda personal trainer came and made him do squats in that blinding white jockstrap.

Help.

As if summoned, his cock plumped and pushed away from his scrubby pubes. Again that heavy pleasure weighed his genitals and made his stomach tighten. Ruben watched the water sluice down his legs and kept his hands above his waist. This was why people jerked off: to keep a lid on these kinds of weird feelings so they didn't leak out into your life.

Boner bad. He needed a night off and a night out. Standing in this room made all Andy's nonsense seem real.

Again that sense of being watched slithered over him from behind. Instinct? Paranoia?

He dried off, his stubborn erection not cooperating. For a moment he considered combing the room for a cam or a microphone before he got hold of himself.

"I'm crazy. This is crazy," Ruben muttered.

As soon as he unlocked the door and left the guest room, he checked the office.

"Are you on the clock?" Hope looked up from her laptop. "Good. I'm about to split."

"How bad'll this party be tonight?"

She flashed her eyes in mock horror, but kept mum. "S'fundraiser at the American Museum of Natural History. His mother is on the board. At least it's not a dancing for a disease." She closed the laptop and tucked it into her briefcase.

"I'll prep the car." Working tonight meant he technically wasn't on duty until 1:00 p.m.

She nodded. "Museum gala." She looked sympathetic. *Cold comfort.* "Tux on your door." She flapped her hand. "Guest room... door. You know what I mean."

He did know, but he ignored the implication. They'd bought him a tux. He hadn't worn a tux at his damn wedding. Had Joysann used his measurements? Thinking of the personal shopper made him think about her perving on him with Andy. *Not good.*

"What?" She sounded impatient.

"Are there...?" How to ask. "Does he have cameras and all in the apartment?"

"*Hfft.* Y'kidding. In this place? Course he does." Off his surprise. "Not in the bathrooms, of course, but most the rooms have surveillance. For security—"

His word overlapped hers. "—security." *Not paranoia.* Being proven right didn't kill the cold prickly feeling that Andy was watching him.

Hope snapped her fingers. "Look. Andy's got the Citigroup guys this afternoon. Highline project. I'm out most of the day."

"Yeah." Ruben blinked. "Oh. Sure."

"Andy, I'm headed to class. I'm on my phone. Forget the cameras." She rolled her eyes.

"Yes ma'am." Andy came into the kitchen looking fresh pressed. *Asshole.* "Good shower?"

"Great," Ruben lied.

"Tuxedo okay?" He gave Hope a thumbs up as she left. "Museum does a dance every spring, but I don't dance."

"Everybody can dance, Bauer."

Andy even made the clumsiness seem charming. "Really. Ever. I dance like a white guy. Actually, more like a couple white guys in a dryer."

Ruben remembered his parents dancing in the kitchen. His father had a collection of *cumbia* records that they broke out on Friday nights. As much as they pretended to be American-born, his mother still baked the best *pandebono* he'd ever eaten.

"What?" Andy was staring at him gently.

Ruben shook the memory loose. "Nothing. No. I was thinking about my folks." *And you dancing.*

Andy smiled. "I hope that's a good thing."

"Why go if you don't dance? I mean, what's the point?"

"There's more involved. Schmoozing. Rubber chicken. Adulterous supermodels who fantasize about brooding bodyguards who can't speak Spanish." Andy bumped their shoulders together.

The friendly teasing plinked into his heart like pennies in a piggybank.

No need to ask Andy about the surveillance equipment. Better to do a proper sweep later on his own.

That afternoon, while Andy was hustling Citigroup, Ruben stopped in the garage to prep the town car with his kit. He felt stupid for checking; he knew this was all for show. If nothing else, it was practice for a real job.

If something's worth doing....

First he squatted and did a grid sweep inside and out, using an inspection mirror on an arm to check from concrete up to carriage to make sure that nothing hung down, that no suspicious packages, bulbs, or cans lurked underneath. No tracker or bomb on board. *No surprises there.*

Feeling stupid, he shimmied under on his back and drilled the tailpipe. He inserted a bolt across its diameter to make sure nobody would insert anything or pack the pipe with fabric. From his bullshit training weekend, he knew that more VIPs got killed with bombs than bullets because they were easier to control and the perp didn't have to stick around.

Finally, using a small portable vac, he cleaned gravel and dirt underneath the car. Ditto wiping down the interior. He'd do the same at the museum. If he spotted any shifted grit or scuffs, someone had interfered.

As soon as he was done, he headed upstairs to check on his boss, who was on the phone. Andy nodded at him and rolled his eyes at whoever was on the line.

Ruben whispered, "Bauer, I'm gonna grab lunch and hit, uh, church. Back in an hour." He'd be back before noon, but he didn't want to be anywhere else really. Truth was, he liked hanging around this place. Even if he didn't understand Andy all the time, he wanted to. "Want anything?"

Andy shook his head and gave a wink that made them both smile.

Time to go.

Ruben couldn't remember the last time he'd wanted anyone to like him, let alone watched it unfold. Here in this penthouse, Andy had changed that. The easy warmth between them freaked him out some but pleased him more. He felt loyal to Andy because Andy seemed loyal in kind. Kinda wonderful and surprising.

For a minute, Ruben considered blowing off AA and just eating something from the fridge, but knew that was a trap. Giving in to the urge to trust Andy could only be a mistake.

Andy was safe. Ruben's real job was to keep his distance. The real danger in this place was to *him*.

In the elevator, he pulled up the Twelve-Step app and found a Big Book meeting on Eighty-Fifth Street that started in twenty minutes. Just as he hit the lobby, he finally used his phone to find out what *cachondo* meant.

There it was: "Funny. Rowdy. Sexy. In heat." *Jesus.* He swallowed. "Horny."

Whatever secrets he had, that wasn't one of them.

CHAPTER FIVE

A HUNDRED million dollars rubbing together never makes any sparks you can see.

That night, the car took them through the park to the west side and deposited them on Seventy-Seventh in front of a massive building that looked like a haunted college decorated for a prom.

Ruben got the town car squared away in the parking lanes and then joined Andy on the steps where they both pretended he knew people he'd never seen before. His tux blended with every other, so who could say?

Inside, he found a weird jumble of expensive clothes and kid-friendly dioramas.

Instead of trailing Andy over to his waving friends, Ruben went to the bar for a seltzer and lime. It was easy to find reasons not to drink; he just pretended to be on antibiotics. Before he could check on his boss, Andy stood at his shoulder.

"All good?"

"All good." Ruben put his hands in his pockets, conscious of the holster against his ribs.

"I figure if we're efficient, we can swing through and be out in… My mother can't make it because of some fake crisis, so an hour tops."

"I'm at your service, man." Literally. *Because you are my boss and not my friend.* Ruben felt like the world's luckiest stalker.

"Thing is, events like these are some of the best hunting grounds for new investors. Chatty. Relaxed." Andy nodded at a stout man with a stout wife eating some type of dim sum with red sauce. "These people can afford to gamble their money. Plus, we all grew up together. Dalton, Loyola, Exeter, Brearley, Beekman."

Headshake. "Are those friends of yours?"

"Those are prep schools." Andy didn't grin. "Dairy farms for cash cows."

"Jesus." Ruben kept forgetting Andy was a rich dick, but Andy kept reminding him.

"First lesson of investment: money is personal."

Yeah, yeah. "You hustle them," Ruben teased him.

"You gotta show up at their weddings. Cards at the holidays. Stroke their pet charities." Why did Andy need to rationalize his lifestyle to him? "Hey: I'm a single, straight male with the right pedigree and a waist smaller than my shoulders."

Again the word "straight" gave Ruben a hollow feeling because there was no reason for Andy to make such a big deal about it. Either he was saying it to prove something or to make something clear. Invitation or warning? Was he interested? Did he think Ruben was interested?

Worse, Ruben couldn't say for sure what he was. Andy confused the hell out of him.

Andy misunderstood his silence. "You'll be fine." Nudge.

"Yeah. Ha ha. It's fucking funny." Ruben didn't smile. "How do you rub elbows?"

"They're gonna eat you up." Andy laughed, flirting out of habit.

"I don't belong with those people. Just let me wear an earpiece and a shoulder holster and stand against the drapes."

"You're a funny one. You probably think about status more than anyone here does. People don't notice much, if you don't make them."

"Still sucks."

"That's not—" Andy looked down. "Sorry."

Ruben pointed at himself. "Mean face I got. Stopped at the airport because I look like a 'filthy' Arab. Pulled over if I glance at a traffic cop because they figure I'm a Dominican gangbanger. Shitty bar service because Sicilians never tip. I spent more days in jail during Spring Break than a drug dealer because Miami security knows how a Cuban pimp looks or mobster, junkie, wife-beater. You fucking name it." His voice heated there at the end, so he pinned Andy with his eyes to make him listen.

Andy didn't say anything, but he seemed to be fishing nonetheless. Again he stood too close.

"Has its uses. I make a great thug."

Andy eyed his shoulders and hands. "And you musta been a helluva jock."

"I'm not an idiot, Bauer." Ruben scowled. Was Andy yanking his rope on purpose?

"It was a compliment. I was on the swim team, but mainly because my stepfather forced me."

Ruben nodded, irrationally pleased he'd guessed right. "I wrestled some. Too big for soccer. And football was mostly the black kids."

"Huh."

Ruben nodded.

"If I coulda, I woulda stayed locked in my room yanking off till I graduated. At least swimming I met a few people and got a little exercise." Andy slapped his abdomen.

Ruben remembered Andy in the shower. He could imagine. He did. He covered with a gulp of seltzer.

"And my butterfly is killer." Andy winked.

Ruben stopped imagining, but kept his eyes on the crowd. He kept waiting for Andy to go about his business, to talk to the other guests, or the museum director, but Andy stuck to him as if they really were buddies prowling the town together. He didn't seem willing to abandon Ruben. "So how does this work?"

"See and be seen. Press the flesh and smile a lot. I try to turn up in about ten photos for the magazines. Spend Fifty-K or so."

"On what?"

"Auction. Donated crap. People wander around to the bid sheets and agree to buy it." Andy shrugged. "Usually I pick up a couple of the stinkers just to help out."

Ruben laughed. "Wine from Detroit."

"Yeah. Tour of Bulgaria. That kinda thing."

Easy enough to spot the desirable items. Clusters of upscale partiers chattered in clumps around the electronics and tropical travel posters.

"Why not just write a check?"

"Trick I learned from my dad. These receptions make great press, and it's always easier to explain a donation to the IRS when you can point to an exact time and date. I just let the museum keep the prize to reauction. Spin classes and baseball tickets? No thanks." He made a sour face. "Wanna play?"

Ruben turned in surprise. "Me?" Was he serious?

"Why not? It's all charity. Many hands make light work. Plus we can escape faster." Andy winked. "You take that wall and I'll take this. Try to blow twenty-five grand, and I'll do the same." Without waiting for an answer, he waved at a painfully skinny brunette wearing some kind of shredded dinner napkin and hared off.

And so Ruben spent the next half hour buying twenty-five thousand dollars of crap no one needed: a football signed by the Giants, a spa weekend in Kentucky, a snowboard airbrushed in colors so ugly that no one would stand next to it. A few people made eye contact and so he smiled back, but he kept quiet.

The disguise Andy had given him sat a little too comfortably on his shoulders. He ignored the champagne circling on trays.

Instead, he took a break to grab another club soda and scanned the sea of white faces, looking for Andy. A couple Asians scattered in, but these folks were adamantly young, Anglo upper crusties. Without question, he was the darkest person in the room, even counting cater-waiters. Didn't look any different to Ruben. Bunch of middle-aged people standing around a museum talking. The men looked bored, the women looked anxious. The only person having any kind of good time was an old guy with a horseshoe of silver hair who kept stopping in the knots of guests to chatter excitedly and point at the air.

Finally he spotted Andy laughing with a polished group about twenty yards away. Their eyes met for a split second and held till Ruben looked away from Andy's satisfied grin. Man knew how to work a room.

He's your boss, not your friend. He's the principal.

Later, shrill shouting made him turn. A whip-thin socialite in vintage Balenciaga flailed and wailed at Andy, purple faced. A short, chubby man tugged one of her elbows forcibly, but she wouldn't budge. *The hell?* Andy seemed amused.

Frowning, Ruben started to walk toward the fracas. He couldn't make sense of her ranting. Thick veins were standing out in the angry woman's throat. *A mistress? A rival? A lawyer?*

He began pushing through people faster, until Andy caught his eye.

Headshake at Ruben: stay put. Whatever was happening he didn't want his bodyguard in the middle of it. He wanted Ruben undercover.

Ruben froze, watching the Balenciaga hysterics with the boozy crowd. Protective rage rose in him, but he needed to stay put.

Suddenly she swung her hand and slashed Andy with champagne across his face and chest. People yelped and jumped back. More shrillness from her. Splintered crash of the flute breaking, but between the bodies Ruben couldn't see where and he wasn't supposed to move closer. *Stupid.*

Andy grinned big and made a show of scraping the wet off his goofy face. He shook his hands, scattering drops. Big joke. The room laughing with him.

She clawed at her own throat, grabbed the neckline of her dress and ripped it, exposing one high breast. Her chubby date tried to cover it. Scandalized gasps. The crowd edged away and gabbled excitedly.

The hell?

Over the fascinated partygoers and echoing space, Ruben couldn't really hear her. Two words only crossed the room and only because she kept shrieking them: "Trust" and "Apex." The whites of her eyes blazed. Again he looked to Andy, but all he got was a headshake that held him in place across the room.

Security guards joined the socialite tug of war now and herded the angry couple out the side door. The Balenciaga woman cursed Andy over her shoulder all the way out, not bothering to cooperate or cover herself.

What did I just see? He couldn't ask.

Instead of joining his slicko boss, Ruben stood to one side, watching the meandering guests with the dead-eyed concentration of a snake. He put crazy bids on a few more crappy prizes that guests had wisely avoided. He kinda loved the idea of getting Andy stuck with that fuck-ugly snowboard or a romantic safari to a miniature emu ranch. *Ha-ha, twenty five grand.*

Eventually Andy spotted him and drifted over, joining him under a sign for the "African Mammals Room." Some kind of temporary disco throbbed inside.

Ruben peered through the arch and started to investigate, but stopped when he saw Andy's grimace.

"White prep schoolers dancing. Abort, abort." He shook his head and took Ruben's bicep. His warm breath smelled like whiskey. His fingers didn't let go of Ruben's arm.

"Yes, sir." Ruben chuckled. "You done all your hustling?" *And who in hell was that dame?* Ruben was dying for some kind of explanation, but obviously they were going to ignore the Balenciaga chick and her champagne freak-out.

"Mostly. I pledged a sum of money to them, but Stanley insists that donors come to these receptions. Publicity and all. Those balls aren't gonna lick themselves."

Ruben nodded. "Most these people look like they'd pay money to not come."

"Yes and no." Andy stepped closer to whisper, his chest brushing Ruben's shoulder blade through the jackets. "Donors show up looking for other things: favors, husbands, dodgy attorneys. All the crap that requires face-to-face."

"People." Ruben smiled. Somehow he'd expected the upper crusties to live on a rarefied plane. Noble and strong. Cheaper clothes and sketchier locale and this could have been a tailgate party. "Everything's the same all over. Everybody wants shit that isn't theirs."

Andy grunted and didn't move back. His torso felt warm against Ruben's back. "Monkeys with manners."

"Bauer—" Ruben opened his mouth to say, *You took the words*—and stopped himself. The tickle of air at his ear made the hairs on his neck stand on end. Without thinking he asked his real question. "—you ever had a job-job? Like, working for someone else who's not related."

Andy looked startled and pleased. "My stepfather made me get a summer job after sophomore year in college. To keep me away from the house." He peered up at his own eyebrows. "Mmmm. I worked in a bank for two months. Ugh."

"Poor kid."

"Yeah I know. But hey, I escaped the stepfucker. Short days and all the free pens I wanted."

Ruben laughed, although it didn't seem really funny. He knew Andy was joking for his benefit.

"Having serious money made everything tricky. You can't talk to people. Everyone wants stuff." Andy leaned even closer, his mouth an inch or two from Ruben's ear. "Wealthy people think of themselves as a different species, though a lot have forgotten they do it."

Ruben tried not to feel insulted. "And poor people are chimps."

Andy frowned. "Other way round."

"Howzat?"

"The rich are the damn monkeys. Only, we burned the jungle down, so we live in a glass box so *homo sapiens* can watch us dying out. We're so slow and inbred, we're practically extinct." Andy scratched his scalp hard, setting his cowlick free.

Ruben refused to smooth it. He thrust his hands in his pockets. "You're a nut."

"Helped me survive fourteen years of prep school. And Columbia." He didn't sound happy about it.

"Everyone's got their own shit sandwich to eat." Ruben's schooling had been public and sloppy. He'd scraped by with a C average, coasting on athletic ability and the piss-poor Florida standards. When he was growing up, the superintendents got indicted and replaced almost annually due to corruption. Education was something they'd survived.

"That's the key thing." Andy swung his arm toward the main doors and the street beyond. "The sweaty masses are way more clever and evolved. Opposable thumbs and hyoid bones. They adapt. They aren't as inbred and stubborn. Like *Clan of the Cave Bear*. The Neanderthals all know they're on the verge of extinction. So they set up these little enclaves and lure Daryl Hannah inside to nanny the brats and fix the air conditioning."

"Bauer, just for the record: you're one of them." The shrieking champagne woman flashed before his eyes, bare breast and Balenciaga.

Andy blinked his big felt eyes. "You only assume that 'cause of my camouflage."

"Okay. Yeah." Ruben's brow felt stern but he nodded. "A tribe. I get it."

"That's dying out. With all these rules. A hundred bucks says the lunatics harassing and attacking me were classmates, because they know the system from the inside. There's nothing random here. They could be in this room."

That seemed like a leap, but Ruben could see the logic. He eyed a pair of blonde debutantes drifting by with several thousand dollars' worth of hand-tailored silk draped over bony magazine bodies.

"Which is why I wanted you here. Well, partly." Andy shook his head firmly. "All I'm saying is, the Upper East Died thinks of the rest of the world as outsiders and tradition is everything. S'why they form clubs and committees and co-op boards. S'why they marry each other and buy the government. They huddle together and communicate in grunts and clicks while the Ice Age settles in around them and Daryl Hannah dates John-John then puts on her eyepatch to go *Kill Bill*."

Ruben chuckled. "You're such a fucking hypocrite."

"Why? I didn't say that I'm one of them; you did." Andy's blush caused two high, hard points of pink on his cheeks, like rouge spots on a marionette. "My father is sterile."

That stopped Ruben cold.

"Radiation in college for testicular cancer. I found out by accident. I didn't look anything like him anyways, so it wasn't a complete shocker. He's French and German, pretty dark." He looked at Ruben's skin, hair, eyes, but didn't elaborate.

Noted.

"Then who was your real dad?"

"One of his partners? Chauffeur? Bodyguard? Who knows? Turns out Mom was a bit of a swinger back in the day. Coulda been the plumber. Or her plastic surgeon."

"She told you this?"

"Not like... no. One of her nasty 'friends' said something to me in high school because I was dating her daughter at Exeter. Turned out everyone in Scarsdale knew I was the cuckoo's egg. Worse, my stepfucker sold insurance. Kids acted like I was a convict."

Ruben frowned. "Sucks."

"Hardly! I'm grateful. All those inbred dickheads. I have a real chin, thick dick, and both my nuts still. I'm way smarter than Dad is. Besides, his name was on the certificate and all the checks, so... I got all kinds of shortcuts."

"Lucky you."

"I watched these inbred idiots my whole life. The guys squat in dark rooms looking for a tribe who speaks the same language. The wives barter for status, venture out to hunt, and gather shiny shit. But when they get robbed or conned, it's terrifying to them because the earth isn't flat and the sun doesn't live in a cave." Andy snorted. "Hell, that's how Bernie Madoff happened."

"Well, some of them think you're one of them."

"A few. I learned how to blend in. My parents taught me. Dorky cuckoo grows up to be an apex predator."

Hence the company name. Ruben nodded. "Did you ever ask your mom?"

"Cilla?" Andy gave him a funny look and then busted out laughing. "Oh man. Oh Rube." He snickered loudly. "You're awesome. I love that."

Other partygoers turned to look at them with gormless expressions. Ruben smiled uncomfortably, waiting for Andy to straighten up and pipe down.

Andy calmed down mostly, though a few stifled snorts slipped out. "My mother doesn't like to refer to my birth in any way if she can help it. Cilla's never put her hands in cold water. She hired caterers for dinner parties so the cook could go home."

Ruben left for another soda water and pointedly did not refill Andy's glass.

Gradually Andy grew more incautious. The drunker he got, the warmer and more expansive he became: loosening his tie, laughing too loud, and greeting the other party guests with a hug instead of shaking hands. He kept an arm draped over Ruben's shoulder like they were brothers.

Ruben couldn't tell what Andy was thinking, but caught himself staring at the handsome face as if it was a code that could be cracked.

"We should make an appearance at dinner." Then Andy caught sight of a pretty, animated redhead wearing a dress with so many patterns she seemed to be drifting toward them. "Other way."

Maybe another champagne assassin. "Ex-girlfriend?"

Andy grimaced. "Eesh. No. Her husband is on the board of Princeton. They want me to endow a chair."

Ruben shrugged.

"Math Department, except Princeton and Columbia are rivals so fuck 'em." Andy made his embarrassed face. "Colleges, not countries."

Ruben said, "Yeah. Thanks." Andy didn't know he was being condescending, so taking offense seemed pointless.

The dinner was a sit-down snore under a life-size blue whale suspended from the ceiling. *Taxidermy?* No one looked up at the gigantic model but him.

Each table had place cards, but Ruben ignored that and took the seat against the wall. Dinner looked to be some type of creamy chicken with about three green beans angled across it. It looked fancy. It tasted like socks.

"I shoulda warned you. The food is usually Natural History too." Andy considered his own plate of artful glop skeptically. "We'll eat properly once we leave. Sushi. Steak. Tapas. Whatever you want."

The other diners ate like it was delicious, chatting and clinking in the echoing hall. In a nearby wing, nineties dance music pumped dully.

Ruben caught a couple young bucks eying Andy like poison, but maybe that was payback for the shrieking champagne woman or even snobbery about his parentage. Everyone knew everyone in this room.

A murmur in his ear and the scent of fresh bread. "You spend your twenty-five?" Andy smelled better than the food.

He stiffened. "You mean your twenty-five. Yeah. I think so. Near enough."

"Good man." Andy patted his back then rubbed it in slow circles through the jacket. *Petting me again.*

To make space, Ruben stood and dropped his napkin, scanning the crowd. "I think maybe we ought to make an exit."

Andy stood slowly. "Why?"

"We spent your fifty K, right? You saw your tribe and they saw you."

"Boring, huh."

"Not how I'd spend a Thursday night, no."

Coming back into the gallery he put his face right at the nape of Ruben's neck to whisper, "Le's go, *niño.*"

Ruben rolled his shoulders as goosebumps crawled across him. The warm boozy exhale and the butterfly scrape of Andy's dragged knuckles stood Ruben's hair on end. He told himself it was just the sweet tang of alcohol calling to the drunk in him, but it was something more insidious; the intrusive chumminess didn't make him feel lonely, but more as if Andy had noticed him out in the cold and wanted to help. Ruben's grinding loneliness had gained a rich, handsome, drunken witness.

What did the other guests see in the corner? Two members of the same asshole club? Two unclaimed bachelors with fuck-you money? Two tame wolves circling a garden of sheep?

Ruben didn't move away or tip closer. His face burned and his heartbeat seemed slow. And yes, that was wood in his fancy new trousers.

Jesus. What was wrong with him?

"S'matter?" Bauer squinted unsteadily at him, drunker than he'd seemed a few minutes ago. He stroked the side of Ruben's neck with his fist.

Ruben frowned. To his credit, he didn't step back. "'Cause I'm starving and you're loaded. We stick around, you're gonna end up married to one of these bony dames."

"You wish."

No, I don't. That's not what I wish at all.

OUTSIDE THE museum, Andy tried to send the car away. "Night's too nice." He thumped on the hood. The Israeli driver wavered, gripping the door's handle with loose fingers.

Ruben caught up. "You're sloshed."

As soon as he said it, he heard Peach's menthol drawl in his head. *It's a mug's game, kiddo. He'll get high before you'll get him sober.*

Arguing with a happy drunk made Ruben feel like apologizing to all of South Florida for forcing them to put up with him for four decades. How was he supposed to force his drunken boss into the car without making a scene? He liked Andy a lot, respected him and trusted him. They weren't friends but they were friend-*ly*, right? Too friendly, then. Ruben could no longer control the situation adequately. *Time to quit this shit.*

Ruben nodded to the driver, who popped open the sedan door with a polite, "Mr. Bauer." One advantage of their cover story: a public bodyguard couldn't give orders, but if they were "friends" then Ruben didn't have to get mugged in the park if he didn't feel like it.

Andy rubbed at his nose with numb roughness. "S'right across the park. We can walk."

Peach was right, he did know this song. *By heart.* "I can't."

"Trees." Whatever that meant. Andy obviously disagreed.

"Yeah."

"Shhh'p." The sound didn't seem like a word, and Andy didn't clarify.

"Wallet's at home, bub. What'll I give the muggers?" Ruben shrugged out of his jacket and tossed it on the seat. If he had to lift his boss into the car he would.

Exiting couples waved at them, but Andy, shifting unsteadily in the gutter, paid no attention to them. He stared at Ruben, asking a silent, inscrutable question with his thick eyebrows. The chauffeur pretended to be deaf.

If Andy was one of his friends in Miami, Ruben would have smacked his head and left him there on the corner to find his own way across the park. If Andy had been some insulting drunk tourist, Ruben could've decked him and slung him across the seat, ladling "Aww, man" apologies over him. If Andy was family, he'd have machoed his way through, crossed his arms and growled till he got his way. If Andy had been a chick, Ruben could've flirted and wheedled him into the vehicle, charm-bullying him into submission and manhandling him to keep the peace.

None of the above.

Andy laughed at something and teetered on the curb. His tousled hair gleamed like brandy under the sodium street lamps.

Makes no sense.

Ruben regarded his boss carefully, from a yard away. "Tell you what, buddy. You still feel like walking once you're home, we can stroll down Park Avenue." Never happen, but whatever treacherous hope lived in him wished they could stretch their legs under the shadowy trees where no one would see.

Andy screwed up his face like a teenager, about to bitch and groan no doubt, but something stopped him before he could. He straightened. "Right." He unleashed a lottery-winner smile.

"What? It's a date."

"It's a deal. You sold me, Oso."

Ruben caught the driver looking at him and flicked his eyes skyward as if to commiserate: *rich assholes.* Then he stopped himself. This Israeli kid didn't know Ruben was in on the joke because he saw Ruben *as* another rich asshole.

Without further protest, Andy slid smoothly into the town car and dropped his head back on the leather seat. "Well?"

"Well." Ruben walked around the car, not waiting for Eli to trot over and open the door, and climbed inside.

The driver started the engine and pulled into traffic, headed for Eighty-First. "The club?"

"No, Eli." Andy raised his voice to speak through the partition. "The Seventy-Ninth transverse. Early night, I guess." He pressed something and the privacy glass slid up, hiding them from the front seat. The shark-Andy had swum away, again leaving the ragdoll.

The traffic sliced into the trees, black and pewter through the tinted glass.

When Ruben rolled his head on the seat, he caught Andy grinning crookedly at him.

"Thanks for all the song and dance in there, my man. You were great tonight."

"Yeah. I dunno." He stared through the windows at nothing, anything.

"Hunnerd percent. They all loved you." Andy grunted. "Good job, Oso."

Ruben wished for a cigarette. He wished he didn't want one. "You're hammered."

"Not even close. Just relaxed." His eyes drooped happily.

What Ruben needed was a shower and about thirty feet and steel beams between him and Andy Bauer.

"But—"

"Relax." Andy flicked his arm with a finger. "You've got it covered."

"I do. Says you." Instead of retaliating or reacting, Ruben laced his fingers together in his lap, conscious of Andy's splayed legs bumping against his as the car curved through the dark trees.

How could it only have been a week? Joking and bickering like this, smiling and snapping at each other, they sounded like… something else.

I like this guy way too much.

Central Park watched them through the tinted glass.

"Suit looks great, Señor Oso." Andy coughed. "Me parece increíblemente guapo."

Whatever that meant, it sounded positive. Ruben blinked and turned, drunk on the attention. Greedy for it. "Yeah, okay. I don't *habla español.*"

Andy checked out Ruben's shoulder, the legs, the glossy loosened tie. "Means handsome." It came out a whisper and Andy looked away out the windows.

Uh. "Thanks." His heart thumped blindly in his chest. Any second it would stumble and knock something breakable over and smash it to pieces. "You got good taste, Bauer." Too fast, too fast.

Andy closed his eyes. The rhythm of the car rocked his skull against the leather upholstery. "You ought to learn, one of these days."

"To dress?"

"Spanish. Might come in handsome." He snorted in slow motion and looked back. "Handy. That is."

"Sure. Right after I finish medical school and my MBA, before I start my talk show on the space station."

Andy smiled and sighed, square jaw clamped. "It's not that hard. Beautiful language besides. *Claro.*"

Clearly. *He's teaching me.*

The town car veered to the left, and Ruben had to grip the door to keep from being shifted against his boss's strong legs. They passed under some kind of bridge and then slowed to a stop. They inched along in the Park's crosstown traffic.

He could imagine himself on Andy's terrace, staring down at Central Park. He looked out the window at the passing trees: nature boxed in so a few penthouses had something to look at.

Andy rolled his head to watch Ruben watching him.

Buddies. Yeah, right.

Andy pushed himself back, shifting his weight. His hand scraped Ruben's and... remained on the seat, separated by a millimeter or two. The light hair on his wrist brush-brushed the wisps on Ruben's, rocked by the car's motion.

Ruben swallowed. He wanted to slide the hand away from the delicious feathery scrape, and at the same time wondered how long Andy would leave it there. He wondered what would happen if he closed his dark square paw over Andy's, laced their fingers and squeezed. He could imagine the way their knuckles would intersect and the exact pressure of Andy's smooth palm against his. *That skin.*

Occasionally the car jostled them as it navigated potholes and pedestrians, gently rocking their shoulders, but their two hands stayed nailed to the firm, soft leather, barely touching, but touching nonetheless. That warm strip of Andy's hand made it hard to breathe.

Why didn't Andy move his arm back? Then again, why wouldn't Ruben? As the car glided under the black trees, Ruben's whole being, all his attention, tightened around the half inch of faint contact between their skin. Ruben imagined he could feel Andy's pulse, then realized he was hearing his own as it jarred his skull.

If the brushing contact wasn't an accident, removing his hand first would send a clear message. Easier to leave it there in case.

In case of what?

In case he was a queer? In case his boss was another? In case they needed to go out together to spend another fifty thousand American dollars to buy nothing in particular in a room full of strangers? The money and the man had gotten all jumbled in his head.

Maybe that was it. Ruben had gotten sucked in by all the sloppy luxury and forgotten whose it was. He wasn't gay, just broke, sober, and lonely. Even if Andy was some kind of closeted homo, he had no interest in playing house with some middle-aged macho he'd known for a few days and rescued from a couch. Ruben had clocked the predator in him. If Andy wanted a dude, he'd lease some Calvin Klein model with a trust fund and a degree in corporate espionage.

And still, and still.... The butterfly stroke of Andy's wrist hairs dried his mouth and pricked his eyes, and Andy had no clue. *I want him.*

All too suddenly, the car sliced out of the trees across Fifth, headed east. *I'll quit in the morning.*

The unwelcome thought landed cold and jagged inside his head. He needed to find an apartment and a real job. Andy needed a high-end security service protecting him. And they did not need to be hanging out together under any circumstance, at least till he'd gotten himself sorted. Ruben would do what needed to be done.

When they turned south onto Park Avenue, Andy blinked... handsome, lazy, and expensive. "I really could use a walk; clear my head." His biscuity skin looked warm under the tux shirt where he'd unbuttoned. "C'mon. We gotta date, huh?"

"I don't think so." Ruben tugged at his collar. "I'd like to ditch the suit."

Andy smiled strangely.

"No. I mean put on some jeans. If you're trying to go get mugged, I don't want to mess up my new rags."

"You'll come?" A smile lit up Andy's square face.

Sirens ahead. Flashing emergency lights strobed the inside of the limo as it glided to a stop. They both craned to see.

Two firetrucks in front of the Iris. A crowd of annoyed rich people squawking, the older ones in robes.

Ruben didn't wait for the driver to open the door. "We'll hop out, Eli." He climbed out and Andy followed.

"No date." Andy looked annoyed and petulant.

A black Irish doorman tried to herd the tenants back inside. "...False alarm. Very sorry.... Yes, ma'am, we have." The other doorman was trying to stem the tide lurching under the lobby's greenwall. "Elevator's broken."

A flash of Peach saying those exact words. *Take the Steps, kiddo.* Ruben didn't smile.

Andy's hand rested against his lower back. "Two secs." He sauntered to the front desk, barging past the oldsters and too drunk to care. He ducked his head and murmured a moment with the porter.

Ruben stared at his boss's handsome profile until he realized he was staring. Deliberately turning 180 degrees, he stepped into the elevator mob. Selfish disappointment simmered in his gut. He'd leave tomorrow and that'd be the end of this insanity, but he'd hoped.

A moment later, Andy joined him, hip to hip. "Break-in upper floor." They shared a look.

Paranoia is catching.

Ruben asked, "Think you can climb thirty-six flights fucked up?"

"No, Rube. You're gonna carry me upstairs." He squeezed Ruben's neck playfully, sending a sharp, sweet jolt down his spine and legs. "Or forget your damn clothes and we could catch that walk."

Seriously?

Anxiety rippled through Ruben. About thirty people remained in the lobby. They could duck out for ten, and by the time they got back....

Ruben lowered his head. "You don't wanna check upstairs?"

Andy leaned against him. Could he be that bombed?

The alarm stopped blaring and the silence rang in his ears. The entire lobby lowered its collective shoulders. The elevator doors opened.

Ruben wavered. *Why not, huh?* Central Park was so close. They'd be back in—

"Mr. Bauer?" Black Irish was back. "We have a situation."

The doorman's face was all guilt and apology. Maybe he could get fired for that kind of breach. "Your assistant surprised an intruder."

"How?" Andy's voice hardened and his tipsiness seemed to evaporate. Ruben's fists tightened. "Hope?"

"She wasn't injured, but she's shaken up." He ushered Andy and Ruben to the front of the line past the undisguised irritation of their neighbors. "The NYPD should be here in the next three minutes." His eyes flicked back to a squabble at the front desk. "'Scuse me, sir."

The other tenants piled on, glaring at them, but said nothing. In the silent elevator, Andy looked green but stone sober.

He fidgeted with Peach's menthol croak in his ear: *Kiddo, you're always exactly where you're supposed to be.*

Once they passed the eighteenth floor, Ruben started to say something, but Andy shook his head. Looking at the muttering gray heads still with them.

And then they were at the top. The door slid open on the little foyer, and Hope stood there with her arms crossed under her breasts, a blue cold pack in one hand. "I fucked up. I fucked up, Mr. B."

"You stop that now." Andy spoke gently, no longer slurring. How had he sobered up so fast?

"Are you hurt?" Ruben scanned her quickly.

She looked seriously rattled. "Asshole smacked me. Knocked my noggin really, but my damn sister hits harder than that. I was more surprised than anything." She sniffed and wiped her nose with the back of one hand. "I heard that stupid fire alarm, but I always ignore it. Thirty-plus flights? Fuck you. I'm too claustro and who the *hell* clogs a staircase during an emergency? Dicks." Grim laughter.

Ruben spoke calmly. "Hey, it doesn't matter. The cops will be here to take your statement."

Hope and Andy looked at each other for a beat. She took a shuddery breath. "So the alarm's bleeping and I was in the office finishing up the spreadsheet for Brussels, and I heard something crash in your bedroom, y'know? I thought you'd ditched the museum early, so I climb the stairs to check. Big guy came out of your room and popped me cold." She pressed the ice pack to her left eye. Her skin was so dark Ruben couldn't see the bruise yet.

"Jerk! I didn't even think. I swung back and he goes over the rail—*bam*—Hit the floor like a sack of onions. Bastard. I didn't even go down, just called the police from my cell. Alarm was going off already so I couldn't hit the panic—" She started to shake.

"You oughtta go to the hospital anyways." Ruben looked at her for permission and cautiously checked her cheekbone and temple.

"I don't break easy." She sniffed. "I ran to the other side of the apartment in case he popped up. Then when I looked down the hall he'd split. He musta split."

Andy thrust his hands in his pockets, looking guilty as hell. "So sorry, Hope. This is my fault."

After weeks of thinking the threat to Andy was imaginary and taking the paycheck anyway, Ruben felt like an asshole.

A knock on the wall, and Hope flinched.

Two cops walked into the apartment and badged. "Hope Stanford?"

Ruben waited for the assumptions, but to their credit, they didn't leap to any conclusions about the weepy black girl and the scary Hispanic guy wearing a shoulder holster. For once, his bull's-eye face didn't drop him in shit with the police. Must've been the tuxes. Money makes everyone so polite.

Andy led them to the dining room to sit down and left Ruben to his thoughts. How had the intruder escaped? Hope had had time to make half a call before he'd vanished.

Ruben doubled back to the elevator to check the waste closet that maintenance cleared twice a day. A low door at the back opened into the back stairs and service elevator the porters used. No signs of entry, and the bags blocked it besides.

Think.

In the dining room, Andy was asking the cops something in a guilty undertone. He sounded shakier than Hope, actually.

Ruben doubled back toward the living room. Next to the powder room, a narrow door opened onto the B stairs. Again, probably designed for exit during a fire.

The alarm was a decoy. The intruder had cleared the building so he could make his way upstairs with no one watching the monitors.

Except this exit hadn't been jimmied or cracked either. Ruben looked around at the apartment's layout.

Behind him the cops asked the boilerplate incident-interview questions.

Ruben walked to the cavernous living room with Manhattan stretched out in sequins to the south. Had some intruder actually scaled the building? Yesterday he'd have laughed at the paranoia.

Where was the rathole?

On a hunch he slid the terrace door open and moved out into the sultry air. The traffic below was muffled by distance. Following the guardrail, he skirted the whole apartment. No furniture or plants out of place. Inside Hope mimed the encounter again.

Ruben reached the outside of the guest room underneath Andy's and around to the office without finding so much as a dead bug. Then he saw.

Jimmied door. Bloody streaks.

"Motherfucker." He spun and jogged all the way back to the living room. He raised his voice. "He broke the lock on the service door by the Jacuzzi." This place had too many bolt-holes.

The cops blinked at him.

How could he make them understand what was happening up here?

Andy stood up. "He's back there?"

"No. Long gone. But the bolt's cracked and there's blood."

Hope smiled at that. "Good. I knocked him hard."

"Not a lot, but enough to test. I didn't want to disturb anything."

The younger officer stayed with Hope while she called her fiancé, and the elder let Ruben show him. When Ruben returned Andy was pacing in the living room.

"And you said I was paranoid." Andy looked white. "Thank Christ you're here, man."

Yeah, about that.

"Some help I was."

"You were. You are."

By the bar, Hope cleared her throat. She had her purse over her shoulder. "Mr. Bauer, I'm gonna go to the hospital with the officers. Get checked out."

Andy nodded. "Good. Great. You want me to call your fiancé, your sister? We could come with you?"

She shook her head. "John's coming to meet me. Oso, you keep an eye on him. I need this job."

When she'd gone, Ruben plucked at his lip. "You gotta hire a real outfit that can keep this place secure. I'm not sure—"

"I am." Andy's voice dropped and he stepped close enough to grip Ruben's elbow, his eyes hard and cold. A muscle ticked in his angular jaw. "Look, they sent one guy. Far as anyone knows, you're just some client. You're my secret weapon."

"Fine. Great. Bang bang. But you may wanna trade me in for a scarier model."

Andy's flannel eyes looked baffled. "Why?"

"Because I give a shit. Seriously. Andy? You're not safe."

"I been saying."

"Well, I finally believe you." Ruben nodded.

"Good. All the more reason you should be staying." Andy squared his shoulders. He looked scary and scared, both. "And I'd like you to move in. I've got the room. Whatever room you want. You come up with a quote and I'll pay."

As if. "Andy, I can't. That's not possible."

"Why?"

Ruben closed his mouth. Making sense of his feelings was like trying to eat spaghetti with a spoon. How could he explain something he didn't understand himself?

"Just a couple weeks. Till the deal is done." Andy looked sweaty and pale. "Please, Ruben."

Shit. Voice, eyes, hand on his arm… all pinned him to the spot.

He couldn't leave now, leave Andy in the lurch, at least not till Empire could sort out someone else to come in. Except he knew that Empire Security wasn't up to this job. If he left, some overfed cop who didn't give a shit would be swapped in, and Andy would get hurt for real.

If he really cared, if he wasn't a coward, what choice did he have?

He'd have to move into the Iris temporarily. Just a few days, at least until he could convince Andy of hiring a bigger executive protection outfit for his own safety. After all, another week at the outside in a cushy apartment with a guy he'd started to consider a friend. Friend-*ly*, at least. His feelings shouldn't be a factor.

How bad could it be? How much worse could it get?

Andy watched his face, waiting for the answer.

Oh man.

"Okay."

CHAPTER SIX

THE BEST way to find out if you can trust somebody is to trust them.

The next morning, with his entire life loaded into a duffel over one shoulder, Ruben stepped off the elevator into maniacal shouting.

"I want to die! I hope I die!" Andy was flushed and snarling in the hallway. "No."

The fuck?

To his left, the paunchy Yugoslavian porter opened and closed his mouth a few times. He carried a toolkit and a red and gray box. "Mr. Bauer, all apartments must be outfitted with a carbon monox—"

"And we are. That's great. If there's any problem, you should take it up with the board. Oh wait, I'm *on* the board!"

Andy's exaggerated anger almost seemed like a joke. The porter had no idea how to react. "You've already paid—"

"Thank you, no thank you." As if the penthouse had spat him out, Andy ejected the poor guy without ceremony. "Let me suffocate and die in peace."

The unused detector sat on the hall table.

Ruben moved out of the foyer, waiting for Andy to direct that rage at him. *Nope.*

Andy nodded at it. "Toss that." Ruben picked up the brand-new box and shrugged. Perfectly good CO detector. *Waste.* More paranoid bullshit. "Hope let them in by mistake."

"What the hell was that about?"

"Fucking bug. Fucking surveillance."

"Well, may be. But are you sure, Andy?"

"Test it! You test that shit and see." Andy's waist buzzed and he pressed the earpiece into his skull, spinning away as if Ruben had vanished into the floor.

"Uh." Ruben lowered his duffel. "I guess we're done here."

That evening when Ruben ran down to grid-check the car, he scooped up the box to toss it in the recycling, but when he'd gotten downstairs realized he still had the package in his hands.

"Crazy." He'd take it home and install it at Charles's apartment. His brother would be safer and Andy none the wiser. He carried the detector back to his room and stuffed it in his bag. He'd get rid of it next time he swung by 109th Street.

That second week, Andy took Ruben everywhere, as if they really were college buddies and business partners. The clothing helped Ruben blend, but no further threats materialized. He had to acknowledge that living up here on Park Avenue made New York way easier. He got to sleep in an actual bed, meals were free, and the commute was about twenty yards. They were roommates is all.

Except Ruben caught himself staring at Andy for reasons that had nothing to do with security. Being somewhere else made no difference. He told himself it was procedure, but the lists and sweeps became another way for him to get closer.

Andy had become a sexy puzzle with no solution.

THURSDAY AFTERNOON Ruben got his first three-hundred-dollar haircut and finally got a chance to spy on Andy undetected.

"Haircut." Soon as Ruben got off the elevator, Hope popped her head out of the office and pointed outside to the terrace. "He said you're both looking scruffy."

He ran a hand over his short hair and raised his eyebrows.

Hope shrugged but didn't reply.

He sighed. "Time to polish the goon, I s'pose."

"Drink?"

"I don't."

"Oh. Me neither." Hope's glance caught his as they walked to the living room. A silent question. "I'm a friend of Bill's."

Meaning she was in AA. An old code sober folks used to maintain anonymity out in the world. Anybody could be a drunk.

Ruben smiled and nodded, relieved to find an unexpected friend. "Me too. I've only known Bill about a year, but he saved my ass."

"I met Bill when I was still dancing. Bad habit. Bad boyfriend, crazy debt. Little toot and a fresh bottle, I'd stay on my feet for a week. Then one night I fell off a stage and broke my arm." Hope touched her nose and glanced toward the office. If Andy heard, he wouldn't understand. "You?" Her voice dropped.

Sharing your drunkalogue was almost a handshake in the program. "Well, Miami. Odd jobs in bars, clubs breaking up fake fights. Free drinks. My wife worked the real job, y'know? Then one morning I woke up with a broken collar bone in the drunk tank, only she didn't show to bail me out that time 'cause she'd left. *Left*-left." It was a relief to tell someone up here. He looked at the office, but still no sign of their boss. "I sat there two days in pants I'd pissed and that was it."

"I get that." Nod. "The longer I'm sober, the drunker I was." Shrug. "The program got me into business school. Apex. Life."

"Good for you."

"Likewise." And for the first time since he'd come to work in the Iris, she touched him, placing her hand lightly on his shoulder like a benediction. She might not know his hell, but she'd crawled out of her own.

Peach always said, *Let go or be dragged.* He had admired Hope before, but now he understood her whirlwind intensity.

She left him out on the terrace. Andy was nowhere to be seen, and the sky was hazy with humidity. Ruben considered the extra four or five million it cost to have this kind of outdoor space on Park Avenue. After a minute, he hooked around past the guest room toward the library before he heard the hiss of a shower past the Jacuzzi.

He didn't mean to spy, but somehow his body didn't cooperate. He drifted toward the sound as if he'd gone deaf. He didn't have any reason to spy on Andy, but a strange, hungry curiosity drove him.

Sure enough, Andy stepped out buck naked, toweling his scalp so roughly that his dick bounced. He had no tan lines and his flesh had a beige undertone, as if he'd tan rather than burn. His skin seemed one continuous biscuity length, broken only by the fuzz at his pits, pubes, and the spray between his tiny nipples. His calves were noticeably overdeveloped. The running, probably.

Andy hunched forward, scrubbing his hair and shoulders, dripping diamonds on the tile. His cock and balls seemed plump and vulnerable, although Ruben hadn't seen many circumcised units in his life since boot camp. Then again, he hadn't exactly hung around busy showers. Spying on Andy like this made him feel weird, somehow. As if he was doing his job and not, but at the same time. *Oxymoron.*

Andy turned, scraping water from the blocky muscles. The haircut had tamed his cowlick.

Ruben swallowed. In the short time he'd been working here, he'd never felt free to stare at his boss unobserved, but Andy was doing something he shouldn't want to see. *Huh.* It made him feel powerful but guilty. His skin prickled with stolen excitement.

Andy bothers me.

Ruben knew the signs of envy. Guys in the gym did the same, checking his junk out "just to see" or whatever. A lotta guys checked out adjacent wieners. *Gorilla logic.* They didn't want to seem like fags, but basic primate curiosity forced them to scope any competition in the vicinity. Instinct.

The shadow of Andy's cock bobbed on the terrace stone. He'd watched Andy plenty. And if he hadn't seen Andy's junk, he'd seen enough to get a sense. He'd spent all week looking without ever satisfying that grunting impulse.

Finally, Ruben dropped his eyes. Any second, Andy was bound to sense him across the terrace and look up. Ruben turned and returned to the dining room door, making plenty of noise so it didn't seem obvious that he'd been sneaking.

He pretended to look out over the balcony. He thought about that plump shadow.

A minute later, Andy looped a too-warm arm around his shoulders. "Haircuts."

"Hope said. Why?"

Even rinsed Andy smelled like fresh bread. "We got a client thing tomorrow night, and we both could use a cleanup." Without permission or explanation, he ran a warm hand over Ruben's scalp. "He just finished me."

Ruben had begun to ignore being petted. It didn't feel bad, which probably meant he was just as starved for human contact as his boss.

Pot. Kettle. Black.

Andy herded him to the right. "Terry's on the other side."

Sure enough, somebody had set up a beauty parlor on the terrace outside the living room's doors.

"Terry." Andy introduced him to a trim older man with intense eyebrows. "This is Ruben."

"Terry Foster." His hand was cool and smooth. "Mmh?" Glancing at Andy, he scrutinized Ruben's face and the shaggy buzzcut gone to seed. "I've heard a lot about you."

You have?

Andy said, "Severe, I think."

Terry dried his comb with a towel that he flicked over his shoulder. "How severe?" He directed the question at Ruben, but Andy spoke first:

"Scary and expensive."

Terry looked down at Ruben. "That good by you?"

He shrugged. The fuck did he care about his hair? He usually sprang for a high-and-tight four times a year at Supercuts.

"You're sure?" Terry spritzed Ruben's springy mop with water.

"Yeah. This is grown out 'cause I been busy. Mostly I just buzz it short with clippers in the tub. Cheaper than going to the mall."

"Oso." Andy chuckled and shook his head.

Ruben expected scissors then, but Terry produced an old-fashioned straight razor and unfolded it.

Ruben's eyes widened. "Whoa. Okay. Okay. Wow, man."

"You're perfectly safe, Mr. Oso." Terry smiled. He took a handful of Ruben's shaggy top and hacked at it methodically. He released and ruffled the hair, then gripped another lock.

Ruben blinked, wondering for the first time what Andy wanted to make him into.

Black strands floated onto Ruben's shoulders and the tile of the terrace. Terry tugged at hanks of his hair in what felt like a random pattern that polka-dotted his scalp. He sniffed. He'd never get laid looking like a mangy Dalmatian.

"We'll see what we can do." Terry worked quickly: *tug, snick, flick.* The long fingers yanked and hacked at his hair. *Tug, snick-thwick, ruffle.* He paused to address Ruben. "How are you adjusting to all this?"

"This?"

"Park Avenue. Your first time." Terry gestured at the skyline and the apartment, then took another fingerful of hair, as if Ruben's history was encoded in his follicles. "You cut hair, you learn things. Right, Mr. Bauer?"

Andy chuckled but kept his eyes on Ruben. "Fair enough."

Hope came outside with a stack of papers. She shook her head at Andy, some secret signal.

Andy looked back. "Ruben's visiting for a few weeks from Colombia. We're both Columbians."

Ruben gave him a look. "The country has an O. You're a U."

Andy pointed at his own sternum sheepishly. "Math guy. My spelling sucks."

Hope handed him a file. He crossed his legs to look at it, giving Ruben a quick flash of his bunched junk.

Ruben coughed and looked away.

The hell?

Andy stood, flipping through the file's contents, and Hope followed him back inside.

"How did you end up in New York?" Terry raked his damp scalp.

"Business, I guess."

Terry snipped his hairs at an angle. "Serious or Monkey?"

Ruben grinned but said nothing. Lying to him seemed foolish and Andy trusted him.

Terry snipped and combed.

"I moved up north after my divorce."

"What was her name?" Terry looked at him with gentle intelligence. This nice old barber was the first person he'd met up here who didn't seem to want anything from him. "Your wife."

"Marisa."

Whether he'd really wanted to know, Terry bent forward to flick a few of the clippings off his torso.

Andy barged into the quiet moment. "This is looking sharp, Terry." He leaned in close enough that Ruben could see an eyelash that had fallen to his cheek. Andy didn't seem to realize what he was doing looked odd.

Bzzzzzzz.

Humming from behind him, then Terry's voice. "Sure?"

Ruben blinked, but the barber was talking to his boss. Andy nodded so he did as well.

"Keep still." *Bzzz-bzzzt-bzzzz.* Terry cleaned the back and sides of his head, leaving the top intact. *Bzzzzzt-bzzz.*

Then a knocking sound behind him and the smell of herbal soap. Terry used some kind of fat brush to wet and foam the exposed stubble all the way around, and down to Ruben's neck.

Pausing, Terry held up the gleaming straight razor. "Won't feel a thing." Terry's fingers held his skull firmly as he shaved the sides of Ruben's head right down to the bare skin.

The metal skimmed light and deadly. Ruben held very still, conscious of Andy watching, almost entranced.

Terry dragged the long blade in arcing strokes that chilled his scalp. *Man.* The afternoon air felt cool on the exposed skin. What the hell kind of haircut was this?

Terry stopped and dunked the razor in a glass full of pungent blue solution.

"Rock and roll." Andy clicked his tongue and shook Terry's hand. Whatever the cut looked like, he dug it. Hope reappeared with a portfolio under one arm.

Ruben took the mirror and saw. "Jesus fuck."

Terry had cleaned the sides and left a wide, wavy mohawk down the center of Ruben's skull. The hair remaining up top was long enough to curl, but smoothed to the side, so it looked like a conservative side part but for the bare skin beneath.

All this for a club where he wasn't a member.

"Extreme undercut." Terry squinted. "Easy to keep clean whenever you shave. Safety razors will be fine."

Ruben touched the top. "I look like a villain."

Andy grinned. "No. Not a bad man, a bad boy. Different thing."

"Yeah, uhh...." Ruben wanted to end the discussion.

"Fantasy." Terry dried his hands with a small towel. "Love is messy. Gentlemen like a challenge and ladies love a rake."

"Et al," Hope said. "Same principles apply whatever folk you poke. Human nature."

Ruben looked at her. *The fuck did that mean?* "Uh, yeah."

Andy crossed his arms. "Definite upgrade."

She looked at the air and let go of whatever thought she'd been having.

Why discuss him while he was sitting between them? Why were they discussing him at all?

Terry considered him again. "Most people are too close to even see the circle they're born into. Nobody makes it out."

"A few make it out," Hope added. "But not in one piece."

"You take my point." Terry handed her the towel.

"Yeah, I'm nowhere near this cool." Ruben gulped staring at his new reflection. "I feel like a fraud."

"It's only a haircut, Mr. Oso." Terry started tucking away his razor, scissors, and comb in the pockets of a leather pouch. He caught Ruben's eye.

Right then, Ruben knew that Terry had figured out some version of the truth with his scissors and razor. He knew that Ruben didn't come from wealth or Colombia or anything else Andy had said. What's more, Terry probably could've named his old stomping grounds in Miami just by reading his old haircut.

Terry looked hard into Ruben's eyes, as if telegraphing something critical. A warning? A promise? "Mr. Oso, You have a unique opportunity to be a tourist behind enemy lines. You mustn't squander it." He rolled his case into a tight bundle and straightened, precise as a surgeon.

Andy rose with his salesman grin. "Nobody cuts like you, man."

Ruben ran a hand over his mohawk thing.

As Terry reached the foyer, he held a hand out to Ruben to shake. "Keep your eyes open, Mr. Oso. There is so much to see when you open your eyes." It felt like a warning. Was he afraid of Andy?

Ruben nodded. "Hope so."

BACK IN his room, Ruben took a shower he didn't need so he could hide for ten minutes.

He'd never wanted a roommate. Certainly not one who got under his skin like this.

Living in the Iris tested him daily. The easy camaraderie, the swanky partying, and Andy's dogged kindness would make a drink start to seem safe.

He called Peach and tried to explain. She was less than sympathetic.

Of course, he didn't confess his feelings about his boss.

After a few minutes, Peach coughed. "You make no sense, Ruben. Why is this security thing bugging you so much? Is he a prick, this Bauer?" Her gravelly voice made it sound like a sly compliment.

"No. Not to me, at least. He has money, but he's been cool."

"The checks clear? You're being careful?"

"Sure." Which was a lie, but not for the reasons she thought. He had no way to explain his freaky fixation. Even if she understood, *he* didn't want to understand. Talking to her about Andy would make it real. "This place is…. Living in this environment is tough."

"Cooped up? Of course it is," Peach said, "Spend enough time in a barbershop, you're gonna get a haircut. So talk to him. Don't make it into a new cage."

"I know." If he wanted to stay sober, he needed to set some ground rules with his boss.

"Ruben, look at where you are and whatcha got. If you find a path with no obstacles—" She coughed. "It prob'ly leads nowhere you wanna go."

He nodded. "Maybe I need to get out. Get clear. Get my head on straight." She couldn't know what he meant by *straight*, and he didn't want to tell her.

"Good. Yes. Right," she said distractedly. "Do your job. Finish your Fourth Step." A rough cough. "Lighten up. Remember: it takes time to get your brains out of hock." A bell and a voice. "Hey! That's my soup."

He had zero desire to go back out there and face his boss and his feelings, but he needed to let her eat. "Sure. We'll talk later. Thanks, lady."

"God isn't finished with you yet, kiddo." She hung up.

Ruben sat looking at her picture on the phone, her face like a pink raisin and a loud print because she still liked to draw focus. He missed her more than he missed his parents.

FROM THE office he heard Andy's angry voice. "Do what you're told. Why won't you just do what you're told?"

When Ruben checked the door was locked. Andy sounded pissed at whoever, and his voice had that chilly, tactical bite that set Ruben's teeth on edge. He'd heard that shark snap but never felt it directly. He didn't know this Andy at all.

What if that's the real him?

Resisting the urge to eavesdrop, he retreated to the other side of the apartment. Surely Andy didn't want him overhearing anything personal.

A searching and fearless moral inventory. How long could he do this, live up here with Andy before he broke and started telling uncomfortable truths?

He drank a glass of water and then went out to the terrace, staring back through the window at the imprisoned bear skull. He left a guilty message for his parents so they wouldn't grill Charles about him. He almost called Marisa but thought better of hassling her.

Ruben dug out his wallet and flipped to the last personal photo he still carried in it.

Marisa had gotten knocked up before he headed to boot. They'd gotten married outta high school. He couldn't stand the thought of her living with her ma, but he needed the Army paycheck. Seven weeks in she'd had a bad miscarriage, so he'd ditched the service with an ELS discharge and come back to Miami to set up house. In the first six months of enlistment, anyone can request an administrative separation. *Price tag, plan.*

Truth was, he'd been grateful for the excuse to drop out of the military. His face had made him a target day one; he got pegged as a troublemaker, and hardly a week went by he didn't have a black eye and stitches from twitchy pukes with shit to prove.

Instead he came home to Florida and worked in a paint store and a garden center hauling trees before he started doing pickups and deliveries for a couple clubs on the South Beach strip.

He had the right build and had a knack for intimidation. Plus, free booze tastes the best... and the pussy! He shook that tree and sweet peaches fell all over him. Year by year, he and Marisa fought more while he drove more, cheated more, drank more. The clubs sloshed around him till he got so wet he started to drown while his marriage dried up and blew away.

But his pothead brother Charles? The lazy dumbass who'd jerked off seven times a day and dropped out of school junior year? He jumped at the Big Apple and landed in cake: promoting illegal clubs long enough to make a nest egg and then setting up his security company by hiring a couple cops he'd been bribing.

Down in Florida, Marisa got her divorce. Ruben got sober and dragged his sorry ass to the big city. *Price tag, plan.*

"Oso?" Andy's voice.

Ruben looked up to see Andy looking at him strangely.

Ruben laughed. "I guess I still got her picture hanging on my mind."

"Who's hanging?" The voice sounded closer than it should've. At least Ruben managed not to flinch.

Sure enough, his boss had returned silently and stopped behind him. Andy took the wallet from his hands to inspect the photo.

"Man, she's a dime."

"What?"

"Dime. A dime. A ten. She's a stunner." Andy nodded at the old snap.

Ruben could feel the male bullshit faucet clank. Were they all about to start swapping pussy stories?

Still, for whatever fucked-up reason, the thought of Andy finding her hot seemed sexier somehow. For a breath or two, he imagined what it would be like to have a three-way with them. Just as quickly he kicked that door shut, because he saw the twisted action hidden there once he tugged it open.

Andy flipped the edge of the photo. "You were married how long?" The question sounded calculated.

"Twenty-two years. No. Nineteen. We were together before that. High school."

Overhead, the evening sky swirled clouds low enough to touch. A soupy fog had settled over the hot city, like rain that refused to fall all the way to the hot pavement.

Ruben wondered who he'd been arguing with. It seemed important and pointless at the same time.

Andy pushed a wrapped gift box at him. "I didn't wrap this."

Inside was a thick pile of folded cotton. A sweatshirt? An embarrassing rush of gratitude sloshed inside Ruben.

Andy's face lit up. "Good?" He had just put it on his plutonium card, but a gift was a gift.

Ruben brought it up to his face, irrationally happy about an item that probably cost forty bucks. It was navy blue and had a shield with three crowns under the word COLUMBIA and a ribbon of Latin at the bottom.

Andy leaned on the ledge to nurse a whiskey. "College, not country. Hence the U." He tapped his temple.

"Yeah. Fuck you."

Andy raised his glass in a toast. "Motto: 'In your light we see light.'"

Ruben shrugged. "Which means?"

"Do I know?" Andy laughed until Ruben joined him.

After all the swank clothes, this could've seemed like nothing, but given the past week it seemed like everything. A little secret joke between friends, if they were friends, which they weren't. Well, not exactly. Ruben petted the cotton with his rough hands.

Andy watched him. "Now we're both Ivy Leaguers."

"I don't even know what that means."

"Most of the Ivy League has no fucking idea. People think it means fancy or whatever. The Ivy League is just a group of private colleges that play games against each other."

"Cool." Ruben smiled, ridiculously pleased by the heavy cotton pullover. Even as a joke, it felt like kindness.

"It should fit." Andy flipped the tag to check the size, standing too close as usual, whiskey on his breath.

Extra-large. "It will."

"Not if you keep working out." He gripped Ruben's delts once, in exactly the right place to send a spike of sweet pain down his legs. "Fucking animal, huh." The hand stayed put.

The praise pleased Ruben more than it should. The hand made him fucking uncomfortable, but in a snaky, sexy way that made his dick prickle. He should've brought up AA the moment he walked in, but Andy had distracted him again with the sweatshirt, the squeeze, the bromantic joking.

Ruben shrugged. "I'm Colombian: big arms, fat dick. Girls love that shit." Why act this way around his boss? What did he have to prove?

Andy played along. A grin caught one corner of his mouth and crumpled into a naughty smile. "White boys gotta mop up the leftovers, huh?" Was he trying to make fun?

They both laughed and even the sound felt phony with the sweatshirt in his hands.

At moments like this, Ruben wondered if they were doing a skit for each other, exaggerating stereotypes and feigning ignorance they weren't guilty of. Guys did it all the time, pretending gross things were normal.

Pretending women weren't people. Pretending they didn't have emotions. A trap, all of it.

Ruben had had mancrushes before—not sexual, but intense friendships amplified by chemistry and circumstance. In high school and boot, he'd joked around with his buddies like anyone does, dares and grab-ass. Marisa had a gay cousin who looked like a model and acted like a pimp. *Gross.* When Ruben had stripped, he'd hung out with a couple dudes whose hotness had its own gravitational field, but he'd never actually wanted to get with any of them. He'd felt it, but as an impersonal thing. *Gravity.* If anything he'd prayed their charisma would rub off on him so he'd score with the ladies.

He'd never wanted a man before. Not like this, in his bones and at his core, with a feverish longing that cooked the air every time Andy smiled at him.

Andy smiled at him. "You look so serious." A chuckle.

"I'm so fulla shit." The words slipped out unbidden.

Andy looked up sharply and stopped chuckling.

Ruben spread his blunt fingers. "We both are. Fucking frauds."

Blink. "Sometimes." Andy took a swallow. "I wasn't—I joke to break the ice."

Ruben frowned. "What ice?"

Andy stared at him for a couple heartbeats. For a moment, Ruben wondered if that same cold shark voice he'd heard behind the door would be turned on him, but no.

"Andy, here we are, you and me. What do you expect to break by acting like some generic asshole you're not? That's like drinking to medicate an awful situation."

"I think you make me—" Andy blinked. His face pinked. "—nervous, sometimes."

"How? I'm forty-one. I'm a divorced alcoholic with a crap resume and no options." He didn't want to be anonymous here, now.

"C'mon."

"I'm not fooling anyone, not really." Ruben looked at him in the dim light. Unaccountably, he thought about Marisa, and his eyes misted. "No one fools anyone. Not really."

"Okay. Okay." Andy set the glass down again in slow motion. "No one is as stupid as we pretend."

"Truth?" Ruben pointed at the glass. "You only drink when you want to lie. You ever notice that?"

Andy frowned, looking right into his eyes. "You think I'm a liar?"

"I know you are, white man. I live here behind the curtain, remember? I seen the face you got before you make a face." He gave a mock bow. "Likewise, I'm sure."

This was how he talked to Peach. Hell, he could almost smell the menthols.

Andy tapped the glass. "Everyone lies. But I'm not drinking this because I'm lying to you. It just tastes good."

"And it's anesthetic."

Andy frowned, wary. "I'm not in pain."

"Not you. Anesthesia for the truth." Ruben cracked his knuckles and looked out at the low-hanging fog beyond the terrace.

"You think I'm an alcoholic."

Ruben shook his head. "Not really. I don't think that stuff owns you." He squinted at the glass. "But only you'd know. With me it's like a spark in a dry forest. In an hour, I can go from one drink to national emergency and they're calling the army reserve."

"That why you got divorced?" The question came from right beside him. Andy's face had gotten closer than he expected.

"No. Well, yeah in a way, but not because of Marisa." Ruben looked down at his lap, his brown hands holding the glass of melted cubes. "Alcoholics don't have relationships, we take hostages."

"I'm sorry. I'm sorry, man."

"Dude, I am a professional drunk, currently retired."

Andy picked up the drink slowly, waiting, maybe.

Ruben swallowed and nodded at no one. "Addiction is completely egotistical. No one else, nothing else matters as much as the crazy, fatal shit you want. Before I got sober, I lived like a bulldozer with no brakes."

"You mean AA? Twelve Steps?" The words came out of Andy's mouth like a foreign language. "You go to meetings though. Still, I mean."

"I don't have the Desiderata tattooed on my gut, but yeah. When I say I'm headed to church I mean a meeting."

"AA has church?" Not joking. Andy leaned forward, kind but unsmiling.

"It has God. Or... a power greater than us. Whatever. Some kind of ordering principle bigger than you and your shitty problems." Ruben sighed. "We are powerless over alcohol but we got a Higher Power."

Andy frowned. "Not necessarily God."

"I don't like all the God business. I was raised Catholic, but I don't go. Not for a long time. I don't need all the show biz and guilt. I sure as hell don't want communion."

"Communication instead." A snaky smile slithered across Andy's mouth.

"Well... yeah. I guess. And a lot of meetings are in a church, but Sunday School bullshit wasn't gonna restore me to sanity. Those angry

Jesus people are worse than drunks. I only got sober once I realized how lucky I was. Alla things coulda gone wrong that didn't. Something watched over me, something too big to put a word to. So I let it."

Andy smiled and nodded like he wanted to show he was patient, that he understood, which he couldn't.

"Catching bullets is nothing, man. I gotta full-time job as a drunk, just keeping myself retired." Ruben held up his hand and counted off by tugging at his rough fingers. "I'm trying to work all my Steps, the whole dirty dozen." At least, he meant to. "I call my sponsor from any ledges. I don't pick up any bottle I don't needta." He knew he'd been avoiding his Steps and tried not to think about Peach's advice. *Lighten up.*

"I didn't think. You should've said something." Andy's voice had gone hushed and deliberate again, the voice he used in private.

"Authenticity. You gotta look right at your stupid life and live it true so other people don't get mangled."

Andy looked at the topaz finger of liquor in the glass pointing at him. "I get that."

"Every good thing I said thank you. Every bad one, I said sorry." He swallowed. "Hard."

"I bet. Paying the price."

Ruben looked up at that, in warm surprise. "Yeah. Exactly."

"Twelve Steps." Andy nodded. The fog churned just above them, smearing everything with sky-sweat.

"Every Step is the same Step. You put your foot down."

"Hard," Andy whispered.

"Like you wouldn't believe. 'Stead-a drowning my fuckups in poison, I just started looking, just looking, at my life head on. That sucks, let me tell you. Seeing the people around me instead of being a self-centered prick."

"You don't seem self-centered."

"Then I fooled you. "

"You're like some kinda knight. A paladin. Held in check." Andy laughed. "No."

"I meant it as a compliment. Like you keep everything bottled up and in reserve."

"Then you're not very observant." Ruben shrugged.

Andy shut his mouth—snap—biting the air. His eyes swam with something ugly and sad. "You're a good man, Ruben Oso."

"Dunno." Ruben frowned in a friendly way.

"You know plenty. Best bodyguard I've ever had." Andy sounded serious.

"Anyone who can fog a mirror could do the job."

"I don't think so. You've got hidden talents." He winked.

Ruben scowled. "What's that mean?"

"I'm onto you. You're nothing like you seem at first."

"How do I seem at first?" Ruben knew the answer, but he wanted to hear the lie Andy would tell. "For real."

Andy frowned before he answered, "Angry…. Stupid…. Stoic."

Ruben snorted. "Good."

"But that's not how you are. Even a little."

"Saves me time." Ruben shifted. "Make you a deal: you stop pretending you're a rich asshole, I'll stop playing spic thug. Fair?" He took Andy's hand and shook it, ignoring the smooth slide and how soft the skin felt against his callouses.

"There's dinner." Andy headed for the terrace door and tugged it open without spilling his drink. "Thai."

"Cool." Ruben held the door for him to step through, trying not to feel like a dude on a date.

There were bags on the coffee table, but Andy wandered toward the wet bar. "Florida must've been easier than New York. Growing up, I mean."

"Howzat?"

Andy frowned. "Big Cuban community." His face looked like a blank billboard: he had no idea he'd said something ignorant.

"You mean 'cause we're Hispanic too?" Ruben laughed. "Man, the Cubans don't get along with the Dominicans who don't get along with the Puerto Ricans and everyone shits on the Mexicans. And all of 'em gotta chip on their shoulders about South America. You should hear the Spaniards." Ruben huffed under his breath. "My pops hated all that picking and bitching. English only for us. We were American, period, fuck you."

A muscle in Andy's square jaw ticked. "We're both bastards, then. I grew up camouflaging myself as a blue blood until I could escape to New York so I could look down on them."

"I pretended to be white and so did you. Except there's no such thing as white. Not really. Even you." Ruben grinned.

"Nah. We're all the ghosts of our own childhoods."

"Sorry. People are selfish. Even people who can afford not to be," Ruben said.

"Money's shit. You should ignore what people have. That's luck. Pay attention to what they *want*." Andy took a swallow. "That's what matters. Everything you need to know."

Well, what do you want? "You still beat them."

"Yeah. None of it mattered. They'd gotten theirs. I had to get mine. I was the boy most likely. Brain. Balls." Andy shrugged. "I was the white sheep of the family. Rules. Grades."

"Jesus."

"Tell me about it." Andy seemed about to admit something, but nothing else came.

"So what happened?"

"Reality. My parents got divorced finally. My mom picked up another stodgy white-collar prick while I was in college."

"Why? I mean, what did that change?"

"I'd colored inside the lines my whole life and then there were no lines. My dad was living in Thailand with a girl younger than me. My mom married someone I knew she hated. My dad's former partner, no less. Mr. Tibbitt. Insurance douche with a Lexus and an embezzlement habit."

The confession made Ruben lower his voice. "He still your stepfather?"

"Stepfucker." Andy nodded once. "I kept sticking pins, but he stuck around. Stupid. Me fighting him just made my mother more loyal."

"Sorry."

"I have to pay her an allowance because he keeps going bankrupt." A clinking swallow of booze. "Like a... a habit." A lunatic smile. "My mom won't fight him."

Ruben tried to imagine fighting with his parents over money, even now. He made a sour face.

"I know, right?" Andy stared like a snake at his drink. "I got my revenge. He tried to move into Manhattan 'bout ten years ago. I killed that shit quick."

Ruben loved his folks, but he didn't ask their help for a reason. "He's that bad?"

"Kicked me out of our house, treated me like a maggot till I got my MBA. Fired me from my dad's firm right after, so he could gut it. Now he's trying to rewrite history so I'll let him invest with Apex. My family." He raised the glass in a mock toast, then started to take a sip and stopped.

Ruben chuckled. "Nice. Regret can break a man. Does your mom...? What?"

"I'm a prick." The smile slid off Andy's face. He glanced down at the glass in his hand. "This probably doesn't help. Me sloshing this shit in your face."

"S'fine, Andy."

"Dumb habit, though."

"Just 'cause I'm a drunk doesn't mean anyone else has to be. It's not contagious."

"Still."

"I gotta live in the real world, huh? People drink. People drug. People fuck themselves up all over, anyway they can."

Andy laughed, but his eyes were serious as he rinsed out the glass.

"No one's got a gun at my head, not even you, Mr. Bauer." Ruben pressed his mouth shut. He'd already overshared. Side effect of any Twelve-Step program. If Andy wanted to talk about it more, he'd ask.

"Still, it can't be easy having it in your face alla time. My family drinks."

"Anyone can be a monk in a monastery. I want to live in the world, man."

"I get that." Andy nodded. "I'm not as stupid as you think."

"I don't think you're stupid."

"Naïve, then."

Ruben had no intention of arguing on that score. "Okay."

"Sure. God you're a dick sometimes, Oso. Anybody ever tell you that?" Andy laughed.

Ruben laughed back. "Yeah. Plenty." *I like him too much.*

"Likewise, I'm sure."

"Stubborn, maybe." Ruben sat on the couch and leaned back, then crossed his arms, aware of Andy checking out his guns. "Marisa used to rag me about wanting to be special. Not holding me back, but because I spent so much time telling everyone how special I was gonna be that I forgot to actually do anything worth remembering."

"Oh, man."

"Right?" Ruben laughed at himself, trying to remember being young enough to think the details mattered, that anyone gave a damn. "She's a good woman. And we tried, but we were, I dunno, young and stupid for a long time and then I just stayed stupid while old crept up on me. Same shit as everyone else."

"You think there's such a thing?"

"As shit?"

"As same." Andy pulled a goofy face. "What's the same as anything else really? Not much. I mean, people pretend for the sake of convenience, but expecting life to provide cookie cutter people, problems, whatever...."

"Mmmh." Ruben bobbed his head in agreement, but couldn't find the words.

"Know what I mean?"

Ruben knew exactly.

An expectant silence settled over them.

Andy looked at him and he looked back and everything changed, everything and nothing.

Ruben opened his hands in happy surrender. "Thanks for, y'know."

"What?"

"Talking. Listening."

"Welcome. Not that big a thing." Andy turned, swaying a little on his feet, and sat down next to him, closer than necessary, as usual.

If Andy was a woman, Ruben would've called this flirting.

If Andy was a woman, he would have dropped an arm across those shoulders or slid a hand up the smooth thigh into the cotton boxers or pressed them both into the cushions, onto the rug.

If Andy was a woman, Ruben woulda used his size and strength, taking the reins of sexual tension to steer them into bed.

But Andy wasn't anything like a woman. Whatever excuses Ruben made, he couldn't pretend otherwise. Andy wasn't some pretty boy, and the attraction had plenty to do with him being a strong, successful man.

The thought made Ruben gruff and panicky, but the feeling flowed easily between them. He couldn't control it anymore, and at times he stopped wanting to. His cock was sprung, tenting the cotton.

"And listen." Andy poked him. "Never love anyone who treats you like you're ordinary." He relaxed into the cushions. He only relaxed like this, the two of them together.

Because he trusts you. Ruben sat there amazed and amused.

"So." Andy bumped him, smelling like fresh bread. "I was thinking a dude-movie night." He leaned forward to unload waxy cartons of Thai food onto the large chrome coffee table. "I didn't know what you dug, so Hope ordered the one-of-everything spread."

"Now?" Ruben looked at his watch; the little hand pointed to eleven. Did Andy expect him to go stake out a crowded theater in the middle of the night?

"Maybe *Scarface*. Or *Duplicity*? After today, I'm in the mood to see some fancy assholes taken down."

Ruben looked down at his clothes. "I didn't know you were planning to go—"

"Netflix IMAX, my man." Andy tapped his phone and the digital shades activated.

"There's no such—" The big living room windows blurred into a perfectly white wall. "Thing."

Jesus Christ, the toys.

He ignored Andy's hopeful, lonely smile and shook his head no. "I'm beat." *More like I'm beaten.* Less exhaustion than a swift retreat from Andy's full-frontal charm offensive. Next stop, Andy would break out his porn collection and things would get insane.

"You don't have to go hole up in your room. We're both here."

Was Andy trying to kill him?

Instead, Ruben decided to take a shower and read before the Dolby explosions proved too tempting and short-circuited his logic. If he gave in to his grunting passive man brain, he'd end up on the couch snacking and bullshitting with his boss until 4:00 a.m. watching sequels he'd hated the first time, undirected testosterone choking the air like spermy smog. Ruben didn't doubt for a second they'd have fun. Andy's charm and humor would trick him into lowering his guard and spilling his messy emotions between them.

Ruben declined. "Next time." Meaning never, but telling this truth wasn't an option he had.

And *oh man* did Andy look handsome in his rumpled T-shirt, surrounded by gleaming luxury with a DVD menu projected thirty feet wide behind him. At his feet, the bear skull glowed in its Lucite trunk.

Maybe all Andy wanted was a friend, but Ruben needed something more. He was sober enough to see the potential disaster for both of them and steer the fuck clear.

Back in his room, behind the closed door, Ruben changed into shorts and, after a moment, the new sweatshirt. Even if it was his imagination, the apartment felt cold to him.

Liliana, the invisible maid, had made the bed for him. Worse, she had actually *ironed* his four thousand dollar sheets. He ran a dark hand over them. The pressed cotton felt like something woven out of the eyelashes of angels.

Someone had moved his things. The maid maybe, but the room felt... off. Hangers shifted. Ammo clip on the wrong shelf. The drawers subtly rearranged and his toiletries out of order. *Why?* It had to be the housekeeper. Still, the intrusion seemed too casual, too familiar.

He needed to be vigilant against that weird sleepover vibe that Andy encouraged. The man was lonely, but that didn't make them friends. Ruben was an employee hired to do a job and that was all. They liked each other, and that just made the gig less of a hassle.

No. Doing his job meant avoiding the illusion of intimacy and maintaining clear boundaries. Hell, staying sober was no different. The program had plenty to say about boundaries and respecting them.

And still, and still... he knew that the border between boss and buddy could get blurry in close quarters with the wrong person even if he was the right guy.

One more reason why Ruben hadn't wanted to move into this bachelor pad, eating food he couldn't spell with assistants wiping his ass. This penthouse was too much of a hermetically sealed playpen. Everything just jumbled together in a way that confused him. No real cost for anything.

Free glitz and swapping stories from his days as a hardcore loser. Jogging in the park, ducking into the gym and taking a dip in a pool built in midair and then forgotten.

A quick flash of Andy's wet blue shorts and the blinding strap of his jock at the top of his hamstring. The smell of warm bread.

Ruben blinked it away, but the tenacious image re-formed gradually as if he'd stared too long at the sun and Andy's creamy lower back had burned his eyes. As he plugged in his phone, texted his brother, emptied his suit pockets, he couldn't stop seeing Andy climb out of the hot turquoise square, water sheeting off him. Then the high, square jut of his backside under those filmy shorts that made Ruben's eyes too heavy to raise.

Cachondo.

He brushed his teeth. Again and again, the blue pool and the blue shorts, and the glitter-spatter of diamond drips on the hot deck as Andy approached… step by step.

Gah. Uncomfortable and crazy, but Ruben knew better than to try and bottle it up and let it fester. Peach would have said that shame only puts the liquor in your hand.

Obviously Andy had started to symbolize something scary or important, something that needed attention, only he wasn't smart enough to put the pieces together yet. The first step was acknowledging this thing existed.

Whatever the next step was, he hoped he could take it.

CHAPTER SEVEN

HALOS TURN into nooses.

The second jet of semen hit his forehead and Ruben woke up shouting.

"*Goddamnit.*" He fumbled for the lamp. Another fucking wet dream. His third in a week. He could smell the salt, and taste a bit.

Bad enough to bust sauce in your own bed, but when you're sleeping on four-thousand dollar sheets that had to be hand ironed? He was covered in spooge and in two seconds the sheets would be too.

Worse, he remembered the dream that had tripped his trigger. And it had fuck-all to do with natural.

All week, he'd been blaming the sheets, their cotton softer than he was used to. Ever since he'd moved into Andy's apartment, he went to sleep drilling his thick stiffy into the silky slip of them. And about every third night, popping inside his boxers. What the hell was he supposed to do, wear a condom to bed?

More like he needed to stop sleeping.

In this dream, Ruben lay stretched out on the beach right where Twelfth Street hits Ocean Drive. He knew he was dreaming because in real life, he never went there. The locals knew it as a strip for queer tourists on the make... an army of young bucks juiced and shredded, stuffed into three hundred dollar bathing suits they ditched in the dunes.

But just now, this hot slice of dream sand in front of the Palace was miraculously noon-baked and gay-free.

Ruben lay spread-eagled with oily sweat sliding off his burnished brown skin into the sand. His dick and balls made a blunt mound under blue Lycra rowers, tight enough to ride up his crack under him. Stud meat grilling in the sun.

It had to be a dream because he wouldn't wear Lycra on a bet, and he could smell the haze of alcohol. Not beer or gin, but the clean sweet booze sweating out of him in the heat. His mouth felt too loose and sloppy to speak. His weak limbs tingled. Obviously in the dream he'd gotten plastered, and some sneaky homos had stripped him half-naked and staked him out like a sacrificial ram in the ocean glare.

With the strange certainty of dreams, Ruben knew he was late for something but couldn't get up. Had he overslept? Was he injured? Turning his head he realized his wrists were held by muscular hands sticking up out of the sugary sand. *The fuck?* Buried hands gripped his ankles too, and even with the oil and the sweat he couldn't wrench free or sit up. Ruben strained against the familiar hands, but they held fast. Too confused to call out.

What if someone sees?

His ass clenched, and the Lycra squeezing his privates felt a little too good. To his horror his thick foreskin slid back and his raw square knob punched past the waistband to kiss the air. The ticklish slip of the clenched fingers over his wrists and ankles gave him a funny feeling which he fought hard. His erection strained against his suit, dribbling sauce back into the sweat and oil. He needed to bust and go. He was so late already for... something.

What was I doing? All he could see was his boner glistening in the glare.

Worse, if he didn't get free in time, he was going to nut all over himself in burning daylight where anyone who bothered to look could watch his lust and shame. His shaft was granite and his balls an aching knot below. He'd never get loose in time.

Don't make me.

He tugged and flexed against those slick man hands.

"Se siente cachondo." Was Andy whispering in his ear or was he just remembering inside the dream? He could smell fresh bread and imagine lips against his neck. Andy's hushed-gravel voice. *"Caaa-chonnnn-doh."*

Whining with frustration, Ruben squirmed and arched with scorching grit stuck to his wet back. His slick asscheeks slid together, the sweat tickling, and his spine bowed up off that sand thrusting his dark cock like a pillar rising from his flexed muscle. His wrists and ankles pinned by pitiless hands while he fucked the air, fucked the scalding blue sky.

Don't make me. Don't make me. Don't—

"*Graawgh!*" On the imaginary Florida shore, he gave a strangled roar as he came. The sound and spatter woke him for real in Manhattan, panting in the penthouse, shouting into the air with Andy right overhead. *Sleeping, pray God.* Ruben had been plenty loud.

Loser. Globs of semen on his forehead, his chin, his left pec, and a jammy puddle at his navel trickling to the right. He remembered a dirty joke from junior high, about going to bed with a problem on his mind and waking up with the solution on his chest.

Before things got messier, Ruben grabbed tissues and mopped himself. He wadded them up and tossed them in the direction of the trash. His ragged breath and heart slowed to a jog and then a walk while he sucked in the starchy air. *Again.* He'd rinse the sheets and change them before the damn maid came.

He needed a woman in the worst way.

But I want him. He frowned. *I shouldn't but I do.*

He needed to get a fucking grip before something stupid happened. Andy Bauer had no interest in him.

Ruben opened the water on his nightstand and took a sip.

Just then, a wicked thirst for something stronger batted at Ruben, but he knew it for habit and laziness.

"HALT." He said it out loud, a warning. Medicinal booze had no place in his life. One of Peach's favorite slogans: *One is too many and a thousand is never enough.*

He'd popped his jollies 'cause his body needed it. The rush of lush endorphins only made him feel more insane; he rocked onto his feet and cracked his back, popped his neck.

To give himself something to do, he went to the john in the dark and tried to take a piss, then gave up. He opened the terrace door and wandered outside, glanced upstairs. At least Andy's lights were still off, so hopefully he hadn't heard Ruben's stupid shout.

To the west, the top of Central Park sprawled dark and fuzzy as moss. He remembered walking and running through it. Down on the thirty-third floor, the pool glimmered like a bright lozenge floating a quarter mile above the Park Avenue concrete.

How high was he? In his head he imagined his little brother's voice: "Too fucking high." Charles hated heights.

In Miami he'd have gone for a walk, taken a dip, climbed up to the roof to have a smoke, anything to clear his head. He couldn't do that in New York, especially in this foofy penthouse. His fingers itched to dial Peach for a sympathetic ear and stupid *West Side Story* quotes, but even if he did, he knew he couldn't tell her the truth about Andy. *No point.*

He rubbed his hard damp stomach absently and stared at the back door.

Gym. He'd go work out in the building gym long enough to wear himself out. He didn't even bother to go back to his room for sweats or a shirt. Fuck it: no one would be up at this hour. His sleep shorts covered up the naughty bits, anyway. He wasn't on duty till sunup. Who'd know? Instead of going back inside to the dumb bookshelf door, he hooked around to the service entrance by the spa on the north end of the terrace.

Ruben threw the dead bolt and tugged. A swoosh of dull, damp air from the back stairs met his face along with the smell of baked zucchini from the trash cans. The porter would come up in the service elevator to collect those before sunup.

Uncertain how loud the elevator would be or if it would alert the building's staff, Ruben opted for the stairs down to the thirty-third floor. The lit hallway led to the dark gym, and the wool carpet felt soft under his brown feet. Outside, the lonely swimming pool glowed bright blue through the glass. Watery reflections crawled over the ceiling like an antidote for the kinky sunbaked nightmare that had just made him squirt.

Maybe I need a dip.

No one would be up at this hour and the doormen knew him on sight. Ten bucks said the staff snuck up here with their kids on weekends when the whole building had decamped to swanky summer houses.

He grinned. When would he ever have a chance for a swim in a private pool, at midnight in midair? He'd soak long enough to clear the homo fantasies out of his head, and be back in bed in a half hour. No way could he sleep this keyed up.

Ruben stepped out of the toy gym into the dank June air. This high up, the only light came from the pool at his feet, which threw everything into hard silhouette.

Without second-guessing, he skinned out of his spermy shorts, the briny mess starting to cool against his thigh. At this god-awful hour, if any neighbors did see his brown ass swimming naked, he'd be a slippery shadow.

He plunged diagonally into the gleaming surface with a swoosh. Slicing through the lukewarm water, he reached the chalky bottom way too fast, and almost whacked his head against the pool's far wall and the wave machine vent. He stopped himself at the last minute with his outstretched hand and pushed off. Not really deep enough for diving, then. He hung suspended underwater for a moment, floating in the phosphorescent cube of tropical blue.

Ruben drifted to the surface. *Better.* Chlorinated water slapped against the tile as his waves doubled back. Kicking off the wall, Ruben swam slow laps. His body wasn't ripped and never had been. All his uncles had been the same kind of thick and solid, but he swam like a dolphin from growing up on the sea.

In the shallows, the pool lapped at his stiff nipples. The overcast sky was starless and the street below too distant to be anything but dim and quiet. Ruben knew he wasn't high enough to be swimming in the clouds, but it felt that way.

For the first time since he'd moved to this city, he felt right in his own skin. He scraped the wet from his face and his hair dripped.

Who lived like this? Ruben hung suspended in the middle of all this luxury he hadn't earned. His job was to protect and support the principal and keep the swag safe. He thought of the skinny armies of Upper East Side housewives: endlessly shopping-shopping-shopping so that their houses and wardrobes could best all the others. What did Andy say? Gladiatorial combat with a platinum AmEx.

Andy would be getting up in a couple hours for the opening of the markets in Europe.

Ruben twitched. All his buddy-buddy hero worship bullshit felt theoretical. He didn't *want* to know what two men did together. Well, he knew the basics, but Ruben had no interest in sleeping with some grizzled, hairy dude. Even if Andy wasn't grizzled or hairy, they were just buddies.

C'mon man. What if Andy had peeled those shorts off before inviting him in? What would he do if Andy turned up ready to splash around in the dark? If Andy snuck down right now to skinny-dip, would he have the guts to tell the truth like a good twelve-stepper?

He remembered the wet shorts plastered to Andy's perfect rear, the golden fluff on his calves, that goofy dimple.

Jesus.

As if Ruben had whistled for a blind dog, his cock hardened right up in the water. The head jutted almost rectangular in the snug foreskin that never slid all the way forward or back.

He wasn't gay. Andy worked out was all. Ruben could appreciate something well-made without needing to sing along to Beyoncé and hang around public restrooms with his fly open. Far as Ruben was concerned, it was a huge leap from admiring a nice ass to blowing your boss.

He shook his head, but no one had asked a question. A car shooshed by a couple hundred feet below, in whatever direction.

Even cupping his dick felt a little too good. Funny thing about a promise to yourself: only you know when you break it. He dropped his hand and reached for his boxers. Last thing he needed was some tenant seeing his crank because he was fighting a weird crush.

His sweaty wet dream had taken an edge off at least. Ruben had always squirted like a cracked hydrant. Big Colombian *huevos*, Marisa used to say. In the water-bent light his nutsack looked especially dark, snug against the oversized boxer legs he got from his pop's family. He always bought his shorts baggy so he could move in them.

After five minutes, his balls felt colder than the water and unpleasantly hollow, as though someone were crushing them in a vise. The aftershocks of blue balls; they emptied so fast they'd probably wracked themselves. The erection refused to flag.

Before his fingerprints pruned, Ruben decided he'd been out here long enough. He needed to catch a catnap at least because in another hour, Andy would be talking to his Belgians.

A sound made him look up at the dark wall of windows, aware of how naked he was. Nobody could be up at this hour, right?

Ruben debated slipping the shorts on underwater, but figured a pokey is a pokey. At least dry shorts wouldn't cling. He gripped the lip and pressed out of the pool, careful not to scrape the cockhead, because *ow*. The wetness had flattened his trimmed chest hair into whorls.

Conscious of the landscape lighting, he clambered quickly into the thin cotton. A breeze chilled the water on his dark skin and finally his erection faltered.

On the nearest umbrella table, a half-empty matchbook and a mashed pack of cigarettes lay, four left inside. *Thank you, Jesus.*

He wasn't a smoker, but he did love a smoke. And in the absence of healthy sex, it'd do him an unhealthy amount of good. He deserved some kind of treat for being a good boy. Peach's voice in his head muttered permission, *Halos can turn into nooses.*

Before he could talk himself out of it, he popped the match with his thumbnail and lit one. He sucked the acrid fumes into his lungs; the forbidden rush of nicotine came sweet and swift. He only let himself smoke half before he doused it in the pool and threw the wet butt in the trash.

Squirt. Swim. Smoke. Sleep. "Sweet."

Now at least he resembled a normal human being.

With a squeeze of guilt, he plucked the cigarette and matches from the table. *Fair game.* They'd be tossed by maintenance if he didn't rescue them.

Shivering, he ducked back inside, scooping up a towel from the cabinet. He scraped his torso with it quickly and wrapped it around his waist. His faded skin stank of chlorine. He tucked the borrowed cigarettes on the top of the cabinet for the next time he took a dip. *Just in case.*

Climbing the staircase warmed his muscles and, back upstairs, the apartment seemed as sleepy and still as it had twenty minutes ago. The stubborn tent in his towel guaranteed another dream if he wasn't careful. He needed a woman to take the pressure off. Time for his long-overdue night out or his laundry would start getting freaky.

Only when he passed through the living room did he see the lowball glass Andy must have left on the table. *Spying on me.*

No harm done, and no definite proof, but next time Ruben wanted to sneak down for a wee-hour dip, he needed to watch out for a witness.

CHAPTER EIGHT

"BUSINESS IS pleasure."

Ruben snorted from the other side of the limousine. "That's not how I heard it, boss."

Sunday night, nine-ish, and they were headed over to some titty bar on East Sixtieth Street.

"C'mon, Rube. In my experience, if you don't mix business with pleasure, you don't get much of either." Andy patted the limo seat. "I'm expected to entertain clients when they're in town."

"Like card tricks?" Ruben rolled his eyes.

"No. Well, not a lot." Andy grinned. "Strip clubs mostly. Broadway. Big games sometimes, but strippers are an easy sell for men and women. They come to Manhattan and want to get naughty. Throw cash around. I thought you might wanna come along for the jollies."

Ruben nodded. Steak and ladies sounded good to him.

He had never ridden in a stretch limo. Some kind of light-tube wrapped the ceiling, and one whole side of the car was taken up with an entertainment center: TV, stereo, and mini bar. Damn car was nicer than most houses he'd lived in and almost the size of his brother's walkup apartment. *Jesus.* If it had a urinal he could live in it.

Andy caught him scanning the plush interior and blew his floppy bangs off his forehead. "I know, right? So fucking tacky."

Ruben did not comment, and he kept his unsophisticated admiration to himself.

"Jaded has a contract with a car service and the stretch comes with their 'lube-the-rubes' package." Andy leaned back and patted the leather upholstery. "The muggles love it."

"Hell to parallel."

"No kidding." Andy winked. "But he never parks. We got him for the night. He'll circle the block if need be. Somebody spiked my tires once, but now we have combat tires installed. Idiots."

"Uh, great." Ruben stared at the blank partition wondering if the kid could hear them still, if anyone had checked his papers, if anyone but him saw the risks.

"At Hobson/Goldberg, we kept entertainment accounts at three clubs—" Andy glanced at him and then explained, "H/G was the boiler room I worked out of college before I set up Apex on my own." Andy glanced at him, up-down. "Mostly I go to Jaded now because it's close and they have a grill. The girls are smart."

"Oh." Meaning he'd fucked some of them. Ruben looked out the window as they crawled down Park.

Andy grinned impishly. "Don't tell me you never hit a strip joint."

"I didn't say that. I just wasn't expecting to do it with my boss."

The limo slowed in front of a big hotel with yellow bunting. A doorman opened the limo door, and a man and a woman climbed aboard the titty express. *Swell.*

"Ruben, meet the Lamptons. Elliot, Christy?" Andy shook his hand and bussed her cheek, then introduced Ruben as "My associate, Ruben Oso." And it did sound better than "my hired greaseball."

Fair enough. Hopefully no one would turn to him and talk about the stock market.

For a high roller, Elliot looked like a refrigerator in a conservative suit, bulldog head shaved bullet shiny and his knuckles scarred from some kind of manual labor. For all that, he acted shy. Like Ruben, he had resting thug face. He'd probably learned to *aw-shucks* his way through life to keep himself out of trouble.

Christy laughed loud. "He's all bark, I promise." She kissed her stocky husband with real affection. Even in her trim suit, she was a bombshell with a juicy bosom and a glossy tumble of mahogany hair. She wet her lips.

Elliot shrugged and nodded at Ruben, offering his hand to shake. Custom suit on a country boy. This guy knew what it felt like to have folks pick fights with your face.

The limo made a wide, unwieldy turn onto East Sixtieth and crept up the block, stopping in front of a glowing door and weather-beaten red carpet stripe lolling on the sidewalk like an old tongue. The driver helped Christy out and the men followed, Andy emerging last.

JADED, the sign said over the carpet and a pair of elaborate green doors about fifteen feet high. As they approached, Ruben could see that a single dragon was carved across both doors, scaly coils covering every square inch.

"Mr. Bauer!" The lanky bouncer at the front door obviously knew Andy and pumped his hand. His skin was black and his nose crooked and flattened by old fights. He stood seven feet tall easily.

Andy shook his hand. "Mamadou."

"They with you?" He looked down at his clipboard.

Andy nodded and palmed him a folded twenty. "Dinner then drinks."

Ruben stayed in place behind the Lamptons. He'd been a bouncer for long enough to read the signs. Andy came plenty and tipped even more.

"I gotcha." The bouncer grabbed the door and hauled half of the dragon open. The sign said "Open every day from noon & four a.m." *And* four?

Ruben had never made enough money to hang out in strip clubs. The girls paid attention to the big spenders, aka whales, who'd drop a couple grand in a night. Everything about Andy—the tips, the duds, the top-shelf liquor—identified him as a whale.

The hallway inside was dim, leading back to pulsing dance music, and a short run of stairs led up to a mezzanine restaurant called Raw. Again Andy tipped the hostess as she led them back to a private dining room. The menu seemed to be Pan-Asian.

Elliot laughed. "Tonight we get the tab, Bauer. That Dubai deal made us a helluva lot last quarter." He flapped his lapels, and Ruben caught sight of the shoulder holster and a gleam of gunmetal.

Why was a tourist wearing a concealed weapon to a titty bar? Did his wife and Andy know he was carrying?

Andy turned to the Lamptons. "You two wanted sushi? I ordered *nyotaimori*."

"Please." Elliot nodded eagerly at his wife. For all his folksiness, the linebacker frame seemed menacing now.

"Not for me." Ruben took a pass on the fish and ordered a rare Kobe steak the size of a futon. The blood would do him good.

Then a waiter rolled out a long platter with a naked girl spattered with colorful lumps. Her chestnut hair twisted in a shiny knot over a radiant girl-next-door mug.

Apparently, Andy had called ahead to order body sushi, which turned out to be raw fish served on a naked woman... as in, this poor chick was the actual serving tray. Ruben had a hard enough time eating raw seafood, but the thought of some desperate coed holding her breath while he jabbed her with chopsticks made him feel awful. His rare sirloin came about twenty minutes later.

Their naked platter's name was Heather, and Andy had requested her, because they joked about past parties and one funny banker from Brazil. To her credit, she seemed happy and relaxed, but through the entire meal Ruben wondered if she had kids and what she told her parents about her paycheck as a living dish. She kept teasing Ruben about trying some spicy tuna. He laughed, but didn't take the bait. "Does it get weird having people eat off you?"

"Hmm." She tipped her head. "Ticklish, yeah." Her tongue was pierced, and her lower lip was painted a hard brick red.

Andy toasted some contract, building a couple sky castles. Elliot beamed but waved off the promises, and Christy chimed in, "As long as the outcome is income, we're good."

After Andy and the Lamptons had eaten the rolls and strips from her shoulders and breasts, Heather propped herself up, proving herself knowledgeable about fish and food in general. Her boyfriend worked at a hedge fund that Andy knew. The money from this gig was putting her through dental school. She was so charming that Ruben forgot she was naked.

After dinner, Christy suggested they skip dessert and have drinks in the club with the dancers. Her eyes glittered with vodka and bravado. Elliot watched her with the predatory gleam he'd hidden before. Another shark, like Andy, and he hid it just as well.

They bid Heather farewell and made their way back downstairs toward the music.

The room was underlit with recessed teal neon, all the brightness focused on the brass pole and the black stage. The chairs were black leather with backs like deep horseshoes. As Andy led them across the chromed space, he tipped everyone, even before they'd had a chance to serve: doormen, maître d', bartenders, waitresses. He slid folded twenties to each hand he passed. When he caught Ruben staring, he shrugged. "Deductible."

Ruben raised his eyebrows and kept his yap shut. When you look like an idiot, your client looks like an idiot.

"Relax. It's just money, Rube: paper printed with presidents on it so we can take the stuff we want." He turned to the Lamptons. "Ruben is a fiscal conservative."

Ha ha.

The crowd nodded in spastic unison, eyes glued to the two redheads on the pole. The girls danced expertly, but their expressionless faces and slick skin turned them into matched dolls. Seemed likely that at some point Andy would just take out his plutonium card and buy them both.

Titty bars were the same all over. Walk through the door and you swam back into the same tank. A pecking order, sure, and the frills, but they were a big, baited aquarium designed to filter money out of lonely suckers swimming in the same dark water. *All business.*

Dancers in bright, stretchy gowns floated around the room like lazy fighting fish. Andy nodded to several, slipping them twenties as they passed. Obviously he spent plenty of nights camped out here. That explained the social life at least. The chicks he dated probably came here and got lap dances too, hard-faced VH1 girlfriends who made out with each other while you fed bills into their slots.

In Miami, Ruben had always been invisible in strip clubs; now the ladies scrutinized his clothes, his build, his skin, probably trying to make sense of him. Andy had turned him into a whale too. These ladies saw all the outward flags of a big spender.

Sitting in their VIP booth, Ruben felt powerful, relaxed, content in a way he'd forgotten was possible. *Presto!* Suddenly Ruben was fifteen, flush, and could have any girl he wanted. Suddenly, his cock was a two by four and his wallet fat with hundreds. *Change-O.*

Andy probably felt like this every minute of every day.

Based on the tipping, Elliott looked to be a serious ass man. The gun under his armpit made no more appearances, but Ruben kept spotting the bulge every time he lifted a fifty toward the ladies.

If nothing else, Manhattan made for some serious competition in Stripperland. No daydreaming in here. These ladies knew their shit and worked like hell, which made for a slick, satisfying vibe.

On his right, Andy raised his arm to signal someone. She waved at Ruben and looked happy to see him. If Andy had a spotlight on him then Ruben caught the spill. This must be what a quarterback's best friend feels like, so much pussy it splashes over the rim onto lecherous bystanders.

The Jaded girls were hot, for sure, but in that "grown in a lab" way that made Ruben feel ugly. All the hair was a weave, the eyes contacts, and their tits rock-hard implants with discreet dimpled scars. Most of the dancers were rocking stacked Lucite heels that hurt to look at. Even the makeup had evolved into an exaggerated uniform war paint that made them all look like cloned sisters in some satanic cock-mangling sorority.

Maybe the synthetic gear made them feel safer, armor that never came off, but sexy it wasn't.

Ruben preferred natural tits and hair he could touch. His favorite thing about sex was the nudity. Not the naughty bits, but the vulnerability that kept anyone from hiding from each other... exposing desire to each other and then doing something about it.

Jerking off had never appealed to him because it had none of the crazy give-take that got him off. Getting his dick wet felt fine, but if that was the bottom line then why didn't everyone just fuck prime rib? *No.* The best sex was more like picking a lock. You had to get right down in it together till the tumblers lined up. *Snick-snick-snick.* Make war and make peace.

The Lamptons made racy faces at each other. Christy seemed to dig the atmosphere even more than her husband, and they both knew how to spend cash. Maybe the gun was a Texas thing.

For some reason, the polished sleaze made Ruben feel superconscious of Andy's contradictions more than anything else. He seemed so wholesome and polite, surrounded by all the synthetic sex appeal. No way could he cut loose like this in public, descending from his apple-pie throne to slide in the muck with the commoners. A pulse ticked in his throat. His brow pinked and damp. Something about seeing his basic lusts laid bare hypnotized Ruben.

Just a guy.

All the money and bling didn't take away his humanity. He still needed to fuck and piss and sleep, even with his genius for numbers. He ate cereal and made bad jokes. He got lonely, scared, and stupid. For better and worse, he'd earned his life.

They were more alike than Ruben wanted to admit.

He signaled a cute waitress (real tits) for a sixteen-dollar Diet Coke. Maybe something was wrong with him after all. Here he was, pressed on all sides by some of the hottest tail on the East Coast, and all he wanted was to go for a jog and chat with his boss back at the Iris.

Ruben sighed. At least the music had a bass line. Frankly, most pop music sounded like it had been produced on a touch-tone phone. The DJ had mad skills, obviously. The transitions were seamless and the music veered clear of the generic humpa-thumpa he'd expected. Almost as good as some of the gay clubs in the Keys, and those mixes were off the hook. Coming from Miami, Ruben tended to be snobby about mixing. He had loved clubbing, back in the thirsty era when he had money and years to burn.

Ruben had expected Lampton to be the sort of flat-assed goober who got off on plastic titties while he looked down his nose. No reason, but the combination of his twang, wide-eyed enthusiasm, and the battered wedding band.

Zzzzzt. Wrong answer.

After the second round of Stoli Elit and a long, gross anecdote about the boarding school vice-principal he and Andy both hated, Lampton turned out to have a snappy sense of humor. They moved down to the stage so Christy could tuck bills into G-strings.

Ruben stared after them.

Bigshots in their own right, the pair of 'em, used to taking what they wanted. In the chair, Elliot's build seemed more massive, but if the ladies noticed, they didn't seem to mind. Everyone ignored the obvious bulge of the weapon under his armpit, so maybe that was normal. His crisp fifties kept plenty of attention on his wife even after she sat with him.

Andy caught Ruben looking. "You got yourself all ready to disapprove of the Texans and they shocked the shit out of you."

Did he mean the gun? "Guilty."

Andy raised his eyebrows. "We're not all uptight."

"I never said uptight." *Just thought it.*

"Relax, bud. You're off duty."

Andy sounded sincere, but Ruben knew he'd have a hard time relaxing in this kind of club. For once, the booze wasn't tempting even a little.

"You having a good time?"

Ruben nodded automatically before he actually answered the question to himself. Was he having a good time? *Yeah.* "Better than I'd expected." He could even admit to himself that the good time was Andy.

Andy smiled gently at him a beat longer than anyone should have. "You look tired, *Señor* Oso."

"Long day."

"Your boss works you too hard." A smile played on his lips.

Ruben shook his head. "Nah. I live off my investments."

"Wise man."

"Work is my hobby, staying sober is my job." He raised his drink at Andy.

A curvy girl with a mane of wavy auburn hair sauntered over to press her face against Andy's. Her fingernails were gunmetal and matched her thong.

"Trish… Delish." Andy grinned.

Trish was compact like a dancer, but her body was soft, even the obligatory boob job.

"Hey." Ruben nodded some kind of permission.

Andy smiled at her like she was making a joke. She probably knew him plenty. "This is my buddy Ruben Oso. Ven-Cap badass from Colombia."

The casual arrogance in Andy's voice gave Ruben that same snaky feeling he'd had the day they met, on the street and in Charles's office. This guy lied as easily as breathing. He was, at the end of the day, a salesman, slicker than spit on ice. Trouble was, the longer Ruben spent breathing his expensive air the more natural it all seemed. He was starting to want things he could never have.

"You boys wanna dance?"

Together. Ruben held his face steady, eyes on his boss.

A smile floated on Andy's thin lips. "Do we?" He looked to Ruben. "Well, I always wanna dance. And maybe Rube's too shy to ask."

She tipped her head at a wide run of stairs that ran up to the mezzanine. Blue neon cursive spelled out "Champagne."

Even though it was her job, it felt nice to have a hot lady flirting with him. Ruben was no pretty boy. Never had been. A lot of Hispanic guys had the slick caramel skin and soft eyes that stirred up all kinds of pussy pudding, but not him. He never admitted it out loud, but it made him an easy mark. Luckily he had no gold to dig.

"Nah. Here's fine." He looked at Ruben. "We don't wanna move, do we?"

The fuck? Ruben straightened. With an audience? His stomach clenched with rollercoaster jitters. Did Andy want him to watch him get off? Did he want to watch Ruben? Out here? Maybe this was just more bullshit show, part of the "buddies" ruse.

Trish huffed and rolled her eyes. "Bauer, you got some kinda nerve." She looked between them. "I swear."

Ruben started to shake his head.

Andy sold her with the dimple. "Please."

Trish gave in the same second Ruben did. Both of them there on Andy's dime. Andy Bauer had no fucking idea what it took to survive in the real world without parents who could bail you out of jail at a distance. Andy had never wanted something he couldn't afford. Never needed anything he didn't get. Never gone hungry in his life.

Tough shit, Oso.

Andy nudged Ruben, breathing Scotch in his face. "We'd both like a dance, if you're game."

"Game? I'm Monopoly, baby." She winked. "Roll those big dice."

Ruben shook his head. "No, I'm good." Again the sense he was being hauled up a long slow slope before the tracks plunged.

"Don't believe him." Andy laughed and she winked. He jerked a thumb at Ruben. "Bad to the boner, he is."

Rollercoaster was right. He couldn't stop it but he could buckle up and keep his hands inside the car.

Andy looked at her, but his flirty words were for Ruben. "We know how to share."

Ruben ground his teeth on his lust, guilt, and sarcasm. Irrational anger got mixed in there somehow. The muscle at his jawline flexed.

Whoomp crack. Whoomp ca-crack. The DJ bent the rhythm toward something funky and slower. Heavy bass boomed at the walls and floor. "I know this song," he muttered to no one.

Trish flipped her wavy hair back, and Andy spread his legs to give her room to work, pressing his hard thigh against Ruben's.

"*Nobody loves you like me….*" Bass shook the walls from a funky cover of the old Etta James song. Turned it into a raunchy R&B groove with a throbbing baseline under a woman spitting and growling out impossible promises in four-four time. "*Nobody, no-no-no.*"

Trish got right into that mess, straddling his right and Andy's left leg and sandwiching both limbs between her slick thighs. Her body twisted and flicked like a flag.

Whoomp-a crack. Whoomp ca-crack.

Trish undulated against them, grinding her pubic bone against their pressed thighs.

Andy gasped next to him, and Ruben tried to ignore the sound and the hard length of that muscle pressed against his. In his forty-one years, he'd never had a three-way. He'd always fantasized about two chicks, but for the first time he could see the appeal of sharing someone hungry with a buddy, the dirty camaraderie like drunken touch football in the mud.

Ruben's cock had risen into juicy iron. He felt manipulated and honest at the same time.

His tattered breathing flapped in his lungs and throat. His arms gripped the back of the banquette and he kept them locked there. Her grinding trapped the blunt, smeary head of his cock against his hairy belly in his fancy new suit. He was about three squeezes from dumping his sauce sitting next to his white-bread boss.

"*No. Body. Loves. You.*"

Maybe erections were contagious as yawns. Once you saw someone else's yours followed suit.

He ignored the pressure of her implants against his chest, because they creeped him out, but she smelled nice, and he hadn't boned up over a woman or gotten laid in long enough that he'd started to worry about himself. And he wasn't about to think about the dreams he'd been having or about Andy sitting next to him.

Not even the girl. She was hot, but to be honest the thing that pulled his trigger was Andy forced to watch him be a stud. Ruben didn't need to pay for it because he looked like the kinda guy this girl wanted to keep around: big, rough, scary. His tongue darted over his lip like a cautious animal.

"Like I do. Nobody-no-no."

A hand squeezed his upper leg with sharp, ticklish pressure all of two inches from his trapped rod. Andy's hand must have slipped off the arm of the chair and clamped on the first solid object, in this case Ruben's quadriceps. If he so much as slipped he'd grab a handful of leaky sausage.

Ruben coughed and turned his head to mutter, "Uh, boss."

"Yeah." Andy grimaced and released his grip. "Sorry."

Nuh-no. No. No-body.

Across the table Elliot was whooping it up and egging Trish on with raunchy glee. The clients had returned. Christy had a leg thrown over her husband's and was whispering at him while they watched.

All a show… a rollercoaster Andy wanted them to ride together in front of the Lamptons for whatever reason. The gun was a prop. If Andy Bauer wanted him to play up the good time they were having, it was the least he could do.

Ruben tried to focus on the girl-the girl-the girl, but Andy's side pressed against his right. His arm tensed and relaxed behind Ruben's neck in a slow pulse. One of them was a drowning man and the other would pull them both under.

He might not be into her, but obviously Andy & Co. loved the show he was putting on, so he played it up. Dragging his stubble over her skin and groaning at the sweet filth she lick-whispered into his ear.

"But if you don't choose / It's me you're gonna lose."

Even with his lap full of her ass, Ruben kept noticing the hard press of Andy's leg against his and the dull warmth of that loose arm behind his neck. Almost like college buddies or teammates. Locker room slap-n-tickle. For a moment, he pretended they were two financial whiz kids out on the town sharing sushi and body shots. Partners at the same firm. Brothers in the same frat. Colombia and Columbia, right? *Looker, leaper.*

His cock flexed on the edge, involuntary spasms that made Ruben hold his breath. He fought to keep his hips still and let Trish do the work.

A few inches to his right, Andy made a soft, strangled sound. His leg shook, knee bouncing as he rolled his head back to let the girl get closer, baring his throat and the underside of his square jaw. The hair at his temples soaked dark and cheeks flushed pink. He looked ready to blow too.

No-body's gonna love you. Not like me. Nobody's gonna want you. Not like me.

Andy whiteknuckled the back of the booth. The arm around Ruben's shoulder flexed hard, and Andy made a low strangled grunting sound in the back of his throat that he obviously couldn't control.

At that, Ruben stopped fighting and fell over the hot, slippery edge and blasted inside his shorts. Thick semen surge-surge-surged onto his belly in a scalding puddle so hot it felt like a severed artery.

Nobody loves you, baby.

He ground his molars hard and tried not to wheeze as cum slid back down to the base of his cock. His impatient load kept coming and coming, almost comical in its volume. Because it was hands-free, the contractions of the hard ridge behind his sack seemed slow and endless, keeping brutal time to the dubstep bassline as his balls turned themselves inside out with Andy beside him.

Not. Like. Me.

Ruben exhaled slowly, absurdly pleased with himself at cutting loose after so long. He wasn't an old man. If a guy couldn't blow a wad in a strip club he might as well go get himself buried.

But when his eyes could focus again and he turned to look, Andy's were closed, and he was chuckling low and stupidly nine inches away. Christy Lampton stood with a cocktail, grinning at him lazily, and Elliot had lipstick on his neck. He nodded drunkenly.

In their laps, Trish giggled and hiccupped, covering her mouth. The sound made Ruben smile, but his stomach knotted.

Either Andy was trying to get his homo fuck on or that had been some kind of performance for the Lamptons' benefit. Ruben couldn't tell which.

Fake badassery with Ruben costarring as a fake badass. Nothing to guard and no danger. Had Andy used him to entertain these clients? An imaginary slug crawled over his dick. Had Andy pimped him out so the Lamptons could feel powerful and perverse in the big bad city?

Andy whistled. "How do you do that?"

"Every man on earth wants a good girl who'll be bad just for him." Trish straightened and ran her hands down her lush body. She stroked Ruben's cheek. "And every woman wants a bad boy who'll be good just for her, huh?" With a flick of her weave, she was gone, peachy ass and all.

Andy's thigh flexed against his. "Well, that was neighborly."

Christy Lampton swayed and giggled. "Mmh."

"Nice woman." Ruben's voice came out rougher than expected.

Andy grinned. "She pays her taxes."

Elliot watched her cross the club, his eyes hot. "Pretty too."

"She loves couples. If you two don't have to be up in the morning."

"We certainly do not. Thanks, buddy." Elliot shook their hands and Christy bussed their cheeks before haring off in pursuit of Trish on the mezzanine. Lampton's gun was gone, at least.

Ruben tried to read Andy's face. "We good?"

"We've gotta table at Marquee if we want it. Hope booked us for bottle service." He glanced at Ruben. "Electro DJ. If you feel like dancing. We could pick up some company."

Ruben shifted in his seat and swallowed, superconscious of the starchy wad staining his pants. Unable to help himself, he clocked the matching load on Andy's inseam. "Usually, yeah. Hard to secure a space that big."

"Maybe not tonight." Andy didn't look down at Ruben's lap, which was as obvious as pointing and snickering.

Did Andy want to party with him? "Maybe."

As they stood, Andy gripped his shoulder hard, sending an electric pang down his right side and standing his hair on end. Ruben stared back, refusing to blink or react. *Fuck you.* He fought the urge to twist free or jerk the hand up into a half nelson or knee his dumb boss in the gut.

Just as suddenly, Andy let go and that side of his body went warm and soft as blood rushed to the muscles. Must be some kind of ninja pressure point. Mamadou appeared with the bill so Andy could scrawl on it and mutter something thankful.

Ruben rolled that shoulder. The tingle stayed.

They moved slowly, cautiously.

All the way back to the door, Andy passed out the twenties again like a greenback footpath that granted them passage. As subtly as he could, Ruben flexed the fingers on that hand, trying to get rid of the foamy tingle Andy left there. He tried to focus on the positive. Free dinner, nut busted, and he got to go home and sleep in a ten-thousand dollar bed he never had to make.

Andy blinked slowly. He'd gotten himself plastered again. He wasn't a drunk, but he definitely used alcohol inappropriately now and again.

Just because he drank didn't make him an alcoholic like Ruben. For some people, liquor made things easier. Not Ruben. As they stepped outside, he could hear Peach's menthol rasp: *You and me, we're drunks, kiddo. Instant assholes, just add booze.*

Not drinking sucked.

ON SIXTIETH, they waited awkwardly in the muggy night air for the limo to make the block and then climbed aboard in strained silence.

The wet spot in Ruben's pants had started to dry, leaving a patch of his pubes glued uncomfortably to his abdomen. The pungent smell of cum filled the backseat, starchy and sour, but that was probably paranoia. Of course if it wasn't his crazy load, it might be Andy's.

Gross. Or at least, he tried to think of it as gross, but his stomach refused to turn over, and the musky perfume turned him on a little.

His brother woulda joked about it and called it natural. Marisa woulda made him take a shower instantly. For his part, the relief was so strong he couldn't feel anything but grateful for the salty, soupy pong.

When they turned onto Park, Andy finally said, "Dude, this whole damn car smells like jism." He took a deep breath. "Or we do." He sniffed and laughed as he exhaled.

Ruben choke-laughed and nodded. The honesty felt like relief.

"Qué paja." Andy rested his conspiratorial gaze on Ruben again. "Jesus, was I backed up. Been too long by half."

Ruben looked away. "Yeah." *Tell me about it.*

The car stopped, and their driver hopped out to pop the door for them.

Ruben straightened and climbed out onto the sidewalk.

Andy did too. "You're a fucking wild man." He made it sound like a joke. "Not so straitlaced when we get you revved, huh?"

"Good thing I'm sober." Ruben led the way through the lobby.

"No doubt. Hunnerd percent." Andy giggled and closed his eyes, then snorted in wistful agreement. "You musta been wild when you boozed around." He punched the button for the penthouse.

"Not pretty, that's for sure."

Andy looked up. "Not like that, Ruben. I didn't—I meant you're fun is all. Not that you should get drunk. Fuck, that's not what I mean."

A long, uncomfortable silence puddled around them as the elevator climbed. Inside his head, Peach scolded him with slogans and urged him to make his exit like she was Jewish Jiminy Cricket.

When the door opened, Ruben turned toward his room.

"Don' have to go to bed."

"It's late. You're plastered. Probably a quart of Scotch."

"Sorry. Sorry. I'm sorry, man." Andy patted and shushed him. "Sober up. I gotta shower."

"Good idea."

Ruben didn't offer to help. That was something. And he did walk a few paces to the hall door. That was something else. But before he could escape, Andy shucked his suit right there. Balls naked, every smooth inch of him heavy with the same untanned Ken-doll muscle that Ruben had no business wanting. No shame or awkwardness. The plump, beige dangle of his dick drew Ruben's eyes and held them till he blinked to look away. "Whoa-kay, yeah. I'm gonna go to bed."

"Two secs. Two secs." Andy nodded at nothing and went into the bathroom. Something fell.

Ruben sat down on the perfect bed. He toed off his hot loafers and wiggled his toes. The quiet whisper of the shower jets pelting granite with water.

A yelp from the bathroom and a wet tumble.

Without thinking, Ruben stood. "Andy?"

A low mumble. "Fell. Fine."

Ruben's feet moved on autopilot.

Sure enough, Andy was on the shower floor, trying to raise himself. Wet and naked. His cock bounced half-hard against his thigh.

Be normal. Act normal.

Ignoring the spray on his suit, Ruben stepped into the shower and crouched to lift his boss. "C'mon."

"Idiot. Sorry," Andy whispered and let Ruben maneuver him out of the shower. "I'm getting you wet."

"Business expense." At least he wasn't wearing his shoes.

Andy stared at the floor. "M'okay." A cough.

"You need to rinse."

Nod.

"You manage on your own?"

Pause. "Mm-mmh." Headshake.

Ruben took off his wet jacket. His shirt was plastered against his skin. He was already sweating in the steamy room, but things were gonna get nuts if he wasn't careful. "I dunno."

"You know plenty." Shiver. "I shouldn't drink like this around you."

Ruben's front was already soaked, so he just put an arm around Andy's back and steered him into the shower, leaving the door open. "Stand." As if showering his naked boss was standard operating procedure.

Andy pressed his hands against the granite. The muscles of his back bunched and softened. A drop of water followed his spine to the impossible glossy curve of his high, square ass onto his hamstring, side of the knee, calf, ankle. Andy's legs flexed as his weight shifted. At the base of his spine, those insane dimples shifted.

Ruben swallowed. *Fast. Just go fast.* He took the shower head and tested the water with his hand. Twenty seconds tops. He directed the pelting spray at soapy skin, keeping his hands to himself. Whatever soap didn't come off could stay there tonight.

"Ungh." Andy grunted and rolled his head forward. "Good."

"You're drunk, boss." *Almost there.*

Andy nodded. "M'sorry." His mouth was open and water sheeted off his lips onto the floor.

Ruben's trousers were soaked and warm water skimmed down his legs underneath.

"So fucking good." Andy twisted to let the spray pound him.

Ruben was working toward a boner but couldn't stop himself. The combo of the Sears-dad face and moans of guttural pleasure did something funny to his insides. *All kinds of wrong.* "Let's get the shampoo out and we're done. Close your eyes."

Andy turned to face Ruben with his lids shut, his mouth loose, and his head tipped forward. *Trust.* His dick was half-stiff, which might have meant anything.

Ruben passed the spray over Andy's skull, and suds clopped to the stone floor. His hair splashed dark and flattened against his brow.

The hot water bounced between them, and Andy's balance was none too steady. Ruben didn't dare look down for fear he'd learn something irrevocable.

"Keep 'em closed." Ruben's wet pants did little to hide his thick erection, right under Andy's unseeing eyes. "Almost there. Almost."

Without thinking, Ruben reached down and scrubbed Andy's scalp, working the lather out of the thick, glossy hair. He felt the warp of the cowlick and smiled. He chased his fingers with the hot water, not caring when it sheeted off Andy's jaw onto his own trousers.

The sight of Andy pliant and naked, bent over Ruben's wet suit and hidden erection, was doing terrible things to his self-control. Time to go, but he couldn't make himself stop. His hands in Andy's hair got rougher than necessary.

Andy made no complaint, allowing himself to be manhandled. Straightening, Andy rested his hands on Ruben's shoulders, balancing himself. He faced Ruben but his eyes stayed shut and his mouth fell open. Water dripped from his open lips.

Nudge. Something firm bumped Ruben's quad through the wet wool and he stepped back, turned away. That had to be Andy's wood.

Abort! Abort!

Ruben fumbled and turned Andy's naked body away. For a moment, his hand gripped the hard curve of Andy's hip where it rose up to his perfect butt. "I think we're done."

"Okay." Andy's voice seemed quiet and unfazed behind him.

Ruben avoided looking at his boss and turned off the shower, then moved out into the bathroom to snatch at one of the big bath sheets.

Was Andy annoyed? Horny? Disgusted? Relieved? Queasy? Anyone's guess.

Ruben tossed the towel at him without letting himself look up. *Tricky, tricky.* "We good?"

"Ungh. Better. Thanks."

Ruben nodded without looking at his boss. "Fine." His hand, the one that had cupped Andy's muscular hip, still burned.

"Sorry about falling. Suit."

Ruben shook his head. "Nuh." Out of the corner of his eye, he could just detect the flicker of the towel scrubbing Andy's perfect skin. His wet suit felt chilly now, but fuck if he was gonna strip down here. He was already humiliated and terrified of his savage impulses. "I'm gonna.... Dry clothes."

"So fuckin' sorry, man." Andy wrapped the towel around himself and walked toward Ruben, the lump of his trapped erection square and center. He blinked.

Before he could close the distance, Ruben raised a hand and made his escape. "Night."

"Oh. G'night."

Ruben dripped his way through the bedroom and down the library stairs and into his quarters, shutting the door with a determined click. He peeled off the soaked clothes and draped them in the bathroom. The shirt stuck to his skin, so he had to peel slowly and when he was naked, his goosebumped skin felt clammy and dead. Only his dick hadn't gotten the message, stiff and hot inside his wet briefs.

He looked down at the hand. He flexed his fingers twice but he couldn't get rid of the memory of Andy's pale muscle still imprinted on his palm. To his horror, he caught himself raising the hand to his nose and inhaling as if the fresh bread scent would linger, as if it had mingled with his own musk, as if he hoped it had. The skin there seemed unnaturally warm, tattooed by the contact, maybe because he was paying attention to it. He leaned closer and the graze of his stubbled mouth on his own palm only made him imagine... things.

Cachondo.

Without questioning the impulse, he opened his mouth and licked his lifeline, a wide hot swipe of tongue over the memory of Andy's skin, but all he tasted was salt.

He shivered. The spit on his palm cooled. His clothes had gone cold and his mouth dry.

He climbed out of his soaked briefs and took his own shower, hot enough to scald his skin, but not enough to make his hand forget.

CHAPTER NINE

NO ONE should apologize for what they have to do.

To keep a lid on his inappropriate thoughts, Ruben started spot-testing the security systems and stopped sleeping. Four days after the Jaded excursion, Ruben woke up just after midnight.

More dreams, more questions, and a stiffy that wouldn't stop. He needed to get away, get his shit together. He just needed some oxygen, some distance, some perspective. The Iris felt like living in a casino. He couldn't keep track of the days because normal hours and regular habits went to shit. No clocks, free glitz, and hot-and-cold-running con jobs.

He called Peach and left a message, which didn't help much because he couldn't come clean about his feelings for Andy. He wanted to go *home*, but couldn't figure out where the hell that might be.

Truth was, he felt at home in this ridiculous building even though he had no claim on its space. But Charles's place was right uptown and empty.

Ruben glanced at the clock. *12:17.*

Andy was still asleep because his London conference call wouldn't start for three hours. Ruben told himself he'd be back before anyone knew he was gone. If he was gonna go, he didn't have much time.

Okay, but now.

Without showering again, he yanked on a pair of jeans he hadn't worn in weeks and a baseball cap and made sure his keys were in his pocket. "Hungry-angry-lonely-tired," he whispered to himself over and over like a mantra. "Hungry-angry-lonely-tired."

He reached Ninety-Fourth Street before he started to hail a cab and discovered he'd left his wallet in the penthouse.

No matter. He'd be back before he needed it.

His phone rang as he walked up Park. "Peach." He said her name as an anxious greeting. *Bad.* Everything he needed to share stuck in his throat.

"Oh kiddo," she muttered as she woke. "Talk to me."

He did, about everything but Andy, who was the only thing.

Neither of them mentioned the time, but she sounded grumpy and tired. "You're alone too much, Ruben."

"I'm never alone."

Annoyance made her sound older. "Up in that high-rise. Couch. Committing suicide on the installment plan. You're living in a cage, kiddo, and that's a problem for people like us. Isolation."

"I'm not. I'm going out with friends right now, actually. Dinner with my brother."

"Dinner. Now?" Rustle on the other end. "Maybe you need a sponsor up there. Could be, who knows?"

Ruben frowned, guilty. "I woke you up, didn't I?" The deserted streets made him feel like whispering.

"I'm too old to sleep." A wheezy cough. "Ruben, be straight with me. Is this a backslide? Are you drinking?"

"No! Peach, no. It's not booze or dope, it's—" *Andy.* "I'm not in trouble." A fucking lie.

"Are you trying to shit me, old as I am? Gimme some credit. Paranoid. Secretive. Outta control. It ain't the load that weighs us down, it's the way we carry it. Talk to me, kiddo."

"I'm lonely, is all. I don't need a new sponsor. I swear. I wish I knew how to pray."

"Ruben, trying to pray *is* praying." She sighed. "Breathe. Howzat Fourth Step coming?

He stopped at a red light as if the empty street were rush hour. "Listen, I'm almost there. Can I call you tomorrow?" As soon as he said it, he knew he wouldn't.

"Okay. Okay. Eat. Sleep. Work your Steps." Her voice pulled away from the phone to cough. "Ruben, I love you, God loves you, and there's fuck-all you can do about it. Okay?" She hung up.

Time bomb. Not much fuse left. How long before he blew?

The light changed and he flinched.

When Ruben crossed the street to his brother's apartment, the door and the staircase felt comically small. As he unlocked the door, he expected to find it empty but smelled mushrooms as soon as he went inside.

Shit.

Charles was cooking eggs for Daria in his boxers and an undershirt. His sweaty hair and cat-cream smile made it pretty clear what he'd been doing for the past hour or two.

"There he is." Charles pointed at him, grinning, like they'd made an appointment for midnight breakfast.

Ruben hesitated in the narrow kitchen doorway under a white plastic disc with a tiny red light. The salvaged carbon monoxide detector looked to be in perfect working order.

Charles followed his eyes. "Home improvement. Breathing easy now. Thanks for that, bro."

"Carlos?" Daria's hesitant voice floated down the hall. "Did you leave?"

"It's my brother." Charles jabbed lazily at the omelet pan.

"Didn't know you'd be here." Ruben glanced toward the dim living room, wishing he had somewhere else to go. "Sorry, man."

"Nah. Y'hungry?" He held up the spatula.

Ruben shook his head. He hadn't thought past getting here and sitting with himself. One shitty thing about this New York adventure, he didn't have any place where he was alone.

Daria stepped out wearing one of Charles's gigantic sweatshirts and a pair of girly pajama bottoms. She crossed her arms defensively over her big breasts. "Hey."

Ruben nodded bashfully. "I'm so sorry."

She smiled then and he knew it was okay. "We never come here because my place is so much nicer, but we went to a concert at the Ninety-Second Street Y and didn't want to go back to Queens."

Ruben nodded. His knuckles sweated. The thirst for a stiff drink, three fingers of anything that burned, grabbed his throat, and shook.

At the end of meetings, the chair always asked the group if anyone had a "burning desire." Meaning: was anyone in imminent danger of drinking as soon as they walked outside? If someone hadn't had a chance to share or be heard, that moment gave them a last chance to speak up. For the first time in his life, Ruben fully understood those words. *Burning desire.*

Charles and Daria being here was a blessing. Fuck knows what he would've done on his own. Shame made him blush in the hot hallway. "I just needed a break. Get away for a bit. Clear my head."

Daria nodded, patting Charles as he stirred the pan. "Air."

"Exactly."

Charles raised an eyebrow. "I thought that place had a deck and pool and all."

"It's a fortress. Surveillance and shit. You don't know."

Daria shrugged. "Sometimes you don't want anything between you and the sky."

Ruben nodded. He liked this girl. He hoped Charles treated her right.

Daria said, "When my parents moved here from Puerto Rico, everyone used to sit out in their windows all day long."

"*Fffnt*. Puerto Ricans," Charles said as if that explained everything.

"Hush." She punched his arm. "In San Juan no building was higher than two stories and they came to New York and suddenly everything was this stone tower with a view." She laughed and so they all did.

Ruben had a flash of his mom in the backyard picking tomatoes. Immigrants came to the States to get away from that other life they'd had, but most often they brought it with them, carried the past around forever. He did the same. And how much of Andy's razzle-dazzle was him trying to shake off the suburbs?

Ruben crossed his arms and squeezed himself. "I've been having trouble sleeping and I thought it'd be good to get out, go to a meeting." A lie, but an honorable one.

"But you're not drinking." Charles frowned.

"No."

Daria shook her head. "Carlos."

Ruben smiled at her. "He's right. I gotta be vigilant. 'There's no shortcut,' is what AA says. The elevator is broken; take the fucking Steps."

Humiliation didn't hang easily on him. The only time he'd felt real shame in his life had been right after the divorce, during his first meetings. AA kicked the stuffing out of you at first and forced you to salvage what you could from the rubble of your life. Even dropping out of boot, he'd thought only of the baby they'd lost, not the military oath of service he'd broken so casually.

Charles plated her eggs and stole a bite. "The check clears. He had a break-in but nothing happened, right?"

Daria side-eyed him and studied Ruben. "You gotta feeling. About that place."

He nodded. "I can't even explain it. I feel like all the pieces are there, but I don't know how to put them together. I'm too slow."

Charles shook a fork at him. "You searched the place? I dunno. Maybe answers. Maybe bugs. Paper trail."

Daria squinted at him kindly, mothering him. "Maybe you've been alone too much. Working too much. You need to meet people. Get around people who live right."

"I'd love that." Ruben meant it. "But Andy's got me living there. Bauer, I mean."

"He's gotta pool. He likes you. You should have a barbecue. Y'know? When you go back. Invite the whole building over for a cookout up here. Meet the neighbors."

"I don't think these are that kinda neighbors."

"Why?" She tilted her head. "You met 'em? All neighbors are the same, *papá*. Jus' people." She tickle-scratched his arm with her long pink nails. For once the invasion of his personal space didn't bug him. Just showed how far Andy had whittled away at his boundaries. He sighed.

How to explain what Andy made him feel, what this job was doing to him? He opened and shut his mouth. His loneliness strangled him like a python.

She looked at him with sympathy. "Oh, *papá*."

Charles laughed. "Cheer up. Life isn't everything."

"You want some eggs?" She offered her plate.

They smelled delicious, but Ruben shook his head. "I think you're right. I need air more than anything. I'm gonna walk back. I'll figure it out one way or another."

Daria wiped her hands and gave him a squishy hug. "You gonna be okay." A statement, not a question.

"Of course he is." Charles thumped him on the back.

"I gotta go babysit the boy who cried wolf."

She grinned. "I guess that's your answer, huh?"

"Why?"

Daria stared into his eyes, unblinking. "Because the boy ended up being right. There *were* wolves."

Ruben frowned.

She nodded like she knew. "And that boy was crying."

He thought about nothing else walking all thirty blocks in the dark with his hands jammed in his pockets. The "burning desire" had faded. His confusion had not.

Back at the apartment, he made it back to his room without incident. He set his alarm for four, figuring that while Andy was yelling at the

Brits he could snoop a little deeper than he had. Maybe he could access the surveillance equipment? The answers had to be here somewhere in the penthouse. His money was on Andy's private space. He told himself he was looking for clues to the threat, but in truth he needed to figure Andy out before he did something to embarrass them both.

There were *wolves.*

Snooping around Andy's personal shit for personal reasons was completely unethical, but he needed some indication of what Andy was thinking. Charles was right. He hadn't done a proper grid search; who knows what he'd find.

At quarter past four, he stood outside the office long enough to verify Andy was awake and inside, then crept up to the second floor and the master suite.

He hadn't been in here often and never alone. Like a lair, it was sweet with Andy's bakery scent.

He started with the obvious. The books on the shelf were a mix of business biographies and crappy thrillers, red and black paperbacks with a lot of stylized targets and silhouettes. The tiny DVD collection was action blockbusters and a Hitchcock box set. No surprises there.

Nothing under the bed at all, not a nickel or a shoe, which seemed bizarre. Ruben gave credit to the housekeeper.

The end table beside the bed contained a jumble of business cards, a strip of superthin Japanese condoms (*two missing*), and a pump dispenser of silicone lube (*Gun Oil*). Either Andy jerked off with grease, or else he just generally liked things slick when he got busy. The thought of Andy smacking one out on this bed over Ruben's made him skip a beat. There were no tissues, but maybe he wiped up with his shorts or a towel. Or maybe he just rubbed the hot load into his skin, while Ruben slept right below him.

Ruben flashed on Andy climbing out of the pool in wet shorts and the dream beach and just as quickly blinked the images away.

Cachondo.

He slammed the drawer closed.

The fuck was he doing anyway? This kind of addictive behavior didn't lead anywhere good. Should've left that first week. He'd tried.

A loud *whoomp-hummm* startled him. *Busted!* But no, just the compressor kicking on. Still, a good reminder that his clock was ticking.

Ruben saw bunched whiteness between the frame and the end table. A handkerchief? Boxers? He could only just reach it with his fingertips. Cotton twisted into a damp white cigar and a telltale briny scent. Ruben knew what it was before he reached down, and he picked the shorts up anyway.

Semen. Fresh enough to still be damp.

So Andy jerked off. So what? Most guys did.

Ruben licked his lips and a tightening in his pants told him he was on thin ice. His breath sounded loud and freaky in his ears. Without thinking, he opened his mouth to breathe more quietly. The cotton smelled like Andy and jizz, and any second Ruben was about to perpetrate some pervy shit that would land him in a tabloid.

Did these mean something? Surely he didn't leave wet shorts for the maid. Maybe Andy had frosted his boxer briefs and left them for Ruben to find?

Or maybe you're a sicko stalker.

He tucked the boxers back into place. His hands shook till he made fists. He'd been up here too long. He'd toss the closet and then head back down. Andy could wrap up his conference call any minute.

The closet was bigger than his brother's apartment. More suits than he'd ever seen outside of a department store, but that figured. *Thirty-six.* Thirteen pairs of dress shoes, two pairs of handmade sneakers, and a pair of crocodile cowboy boots that had never been worn, the soles glossy as nail polish.

On one side, a rack of gleaming ties, a tray of coiled belts, and a mesh basket of swimwear. A built-in cabinet housed socks, undershirts, and shorts folded in perfect sorted rows. A laundry basket in one corner held an undershirt, athletic socks, and a pair of sleep shorts still warm from being worn.

Ruben paused, the hamper lid raised, because until that moment he'd never realized just how much he'd thought about Andy's cock. It gave him a cold feeling in the hollow of his gut.

This is wrong. Snooping around the apartment like this had nothing to do with protecting Andy and everything to do with his own embarrassing impulses. He'd checked guys in the locker room, but never because he wanted them.

Inspecting the drawers, he lifted and lowered the socks, shirts, and briefs that hid... nothing.

Stuff had changed since he stopped boozing around, so maybe these feelings were jealousy of a life he couldn't afford. He'd never been a bigot, but fuck if he'd ever expected to obsess over some guy's hairy ass.

Except he knew Andy's wasn't; his ass was hard cream. And he wasn't some sissy boy with no gag reflex either. He didn't mesh with any experience Ruben had, which made the situation scarier.

There were *wolves.*

No surprises till Ruben went behind the hangers, where he found a small box of weed and rolling papers. Then some pretty intense porn in a shoebox on the second shelf: guy/girl stuff, mostly in the amateur or gonzo vein. *Street Heat. Bottled-Up Babes*. Nobody looked too glossy and made up. The women had real tits. The garish covers looked so out of place on Andy's carved wool rug that Ruben could almost believe they were borrowed, but for Andy's solitude. Underneath he found a couple thumbed issues of *Penthouse*.

So what? The porn didn't tell him anything special. There was one "bi" title, but that didn't necessarily mean anything these days. Some ladies loved that shit. There were a lot of swarthy dudes pictured, Hispanics and Italians with similar coloring to his, but then again, porn used plenty of working-class Latin lovers. That didn't mean Andy had a thing for *him*.

Bottom line: no way for him to know what Andy thought or felt unless he spilled.

Ruben lifted the box of DVDs down to check behind it and that's how he found the message. There, behind the box of porn, taped to the wall, a crisp calling card with three embossed words printed in Andy's square capitals:

"GOOD JOB, RUBE."

Cold dread made Ruben's hands shake as he replaced the porn. *Ha-ha, big joke.*

Andy had expected him to dig around, which made it okay, right? Except he figured Ruben didn't trust him, which wasn't. Andy had no idea that this intense curiosity had turned personal. All this embarrassing shit didn't embarrass Mr. Bauer in the least.

Ruben had found exactly what Andy had planted for him. Maybe the porn was a stupid prop. Maybe he'd left jizzed shorts as a gross guy joke? *Har har.* For the first time in weeks, Ruben felt as anxious as he had that first day. This entire job was bullshit. Fake conspiracies and danger that made everyone feel important. Andy was conning him and using him.

What difference did it make, really? Rich and poor fucked each other so much. He should be used to the friction between splendor and squalor by now. *The grass is always meaner.*

On autopilot, Ruben walked to the master bathroom to wash his hands though they didn't feel dirty.

Still shaky, he walked down the upstairs hall, deciding that he'd say nothing about finding the card or Andy's practical joke.

Water running in a sink below him. A cabinet closing. Knife sounds on the cutting board. Someone was cooking wee-hour breakfast in the kitchen.

Ashamed of himself, Ruben came down the spiral stair into the living room expecting to hear Andy's voice. Hell, he'd probably watched Ruben tossing the apartment the past hour on his surveillance cameras. The kitchen was a bubble of light.

Instantly, Ruben's irritation and shame melted.

Andy was humming to himself and bobbing to whatever music was playing through his iPod while he worked at the countertop, innocent and oblivious. The handsome face clean-shaven and flushed with pleasure. He'd finished shouting at the Londoners but hadn't changed or gotten dressed yet. He wore a shirt ripped open on both sides that left his muscular ribs exposed and a pair of those shorts that made Ruben's mouth go gummy.

Andy was dancing in the kitchen while he made some kind of sandwich, rocking out like a suburban dad who'd snuck into a Missy Elliot video: hip thrusting, shoulder popping, and head knocking as only a thirty-eight-year-old suburban white boy can.

Ruben grinned. The raw, goofy vulnerability made his chest go mushy and hot.

Part of him wanted to call out a hello, but he bit his tongue and stole warm eyefuls. He didn't want to startle Andy or squelch the sweet moment, so he stood and spied.

Andy sang along under his breath, off-key, dorky in the extreme but painfully endearing. Sexy as he looked, the implication of him dancing like that overpowered his good looks. He trusted Ruben to keep him safe and happy in this ridiculous glass box.

Ruben felt protective, almost defensive about the need to defend Andy against all threats. *Good job, Rube.* He was the wolf and Andy didn't know. Could never know.

How long could he afford to stand here spying before Andy spotted him? Would Andy even mind if he did?

Ruben kept silent as long as he dared.

He hated himself for snooping, but told himself he'd been doing his job. Maybe Andy would never know. Maybe the note had been a test. Maybe Andy had placed it there weeks ago before Ruben's feelings had gotten loose, before any of this. Maybe it hadn't been Andy at all.

Finally, Andy turned and saw and smiled right at him, a big blinding grin.

If you can't lie to yourself, who can you lie to?

CHAPTER TEN

WHEN YOU dance with a gorilla, it is the gorilla who decides when to stop.

After rummaging through Andy's things that morning, Ruben felt guilty enough to sit down and watch a movie. He kept to the other couch, obviously. He made appropriate noises and no comments about Andy's drinking. That evening, Andy fell asleep on the couch, only this time, Ruben roused him and steered him upstairs.

Not roommates, he kept reminding himself. The thought of Andy sleepy and vulnerable put some crazy ideas in his head, so he sat on the terrace wishing for a cigarette until his hidden stash called him down to the thirty-third floor.

As expected, the pool deck was empty at eleven o'clock. The teenagers from nineteen weren't out here killing a bottle of dad's gin. After all his night swims, Ruben knew this terrace had a couple fans in the building, but no night owls except him. Thirty-three floors down he heard the slop of traffic, distant and dull as the tide.

Ruben leaned out to look at Park Avenue, and the damp, airless heat slid over his skin. The Upper East Side really was an island within the island of Manhattan. A few cars nosed sluggishly through the empty streets. Midnight now and Park Avenue was dead. These uptighty-whities kept everything so damn quiet. Presumably some of the Haves were dining or fucking the neighbor's dog or whatever, but heaven forbid they make a peep after 10:00 p.m.

Ruben took another drag on the stolen cigarette, holding the smoke inside himself to churn around the truth.

You don't belong here, Oso.

He exhaled in a hot rush. The muggy air held the smoke around his face till he flapped his hand. He'd have to shower upstairs or his hair'd smell like nicotine and he'd never hear the end of it from the resident Boy Scout.

Andy was right, cigarettes were no better than booze. Another stupid addiction he'd let creep up on him. He needed to quit. Like he needed to find an apartment, get a checkup, meet a chick, and eat a green vegetable a couple times a year.

He needed to do all kindsa shit. *One fuckup at a time.* Worse, he wanted to quit smoking because Andy thought he should. Some lame part of himself craved that approval from a nice guy who had it all together. Not quite obsession, but intense admiration that he needed to hide.

Still, the smoking thing was an easy place to start. Ruben could imagine the little relieved smile it would squeeze out of Mr. Bauer, and he wanted it worse than he wanted another lungful. Sick.

Maybe that was the deal. His life sucked and Andy's didn't. Yeah. Maybe he'd fallen for the zip code and a lifestyle he'd never seen up close. Like men on TV, handmade suits and girls with perfect bodies falling over themselves to gag on his dark meat.

He didn't feel queer. He'd never messed around in school or anything. Some guys did. He knew a couple dudes who'd bent over and then gone on to get married and seed whole litters of kids.

This didn't feel like fooling around. Not halfway fooling.

Ruben sucked another lungful of smoke into himself and tried to imagine sharing some chick with Andy. Their dicks smashed together inside her while she went out of her skull. Just as fast he could see the lie. The imaginary girl didn't have a face, and the thing that got him boned up was the thought of Andy losing control and craning forward to kiss him hard and whisper to him in Spanish.

Something made him look up at Andy's floor. Not a sound or a light, but a hankering. Jesus. The only thing wrong was that Andy was farther away than he had been for weeks. The only danger he faced was Ruben copping a feel.

Days later, and Ruben's fingers could still remember the wet slip of Andy's hip as he came out of the shower. Ruben's palm remembered the firm handful of muscle and bone it had cupped for a heartbeat, then tasting his slick hand. Out of control.

He pulled at the cigarette again. A breeze shifted the muggy air and he wiped his damp chest absently. Playing cops and robbers and mooning over this guy wasn't gonna make his job any easier.

And if he was, y'know, that way, gay or whatever… 880 Park was no place to find out, fuck knows.

What scared him was the familiarity of the feeling. The nagging sense that his life was a gray, muffled dustbowl unless he turned one direction or the other. Just a different kind of addiction. Andy deserved better and Ruben deserved worse.

Standing in his baggy underwears on the thirty-third floor looking out toward the East River, Ruben tried to calculate how long he'd last before a hard dick or a stray word forced him into some horrifying trespass. He had plenty of experience with impending disaster.

He hadn't expected to like Andy Bauer, let alone respect him, admire him, and whatever the fuck else. He hadn't felt this way about anyone since, well, ever. Those frantic stabs of affection and anger worried him because they came so fast and felt so good. *Sweeter than bourbon.*

He sat down with his feet dangling in the glowing pool.

His feelings had gone way past envy or curiosity. Even with Raggedy Andy dreaming of dividends fifty feet over his head, the impulse to go back upstairs got his heart thumping. The obedience and adoration embarrassed him. This must be what dogs felt like when they heard a key in the lock. Living that close had gotten to him is all. He couldn't just chalk it up to loneliness, and the last thing he needed to do was put some nice guy at risk by queering out at the wrong moment.

The hairs on the back of his neck stood up and he glanced up, almost expecting Andy to be looking down from the terrace with a shameful crush of his own. *Homo and Juliet.* Wherefore art thou a bum?

Nothing. The penthouse was completely dark. His instincts playing tricks with him again. Most likely, Andy was smacking one out in his shower. All that wet pink skin and his mouth gasping at the floor while water sheeted off his lips.

Ruben's plump, drowsy cock nudged awake inside his boxers. He dropped his gaze to the glowing pool and the slip-slap of the water around his hairy calves.

He'd leave in the morning. For real, this time. Charlie could move some other talentless goon into Andy's life, and Ruben would find some nice girl with a round ass who'd help him get his head and dick on straight.

Pfff. A small sound made him turn his head. No one there. It had been a hushed impact, like a pillow on marble, but the pool deck was silent.

"The hell?"

Had he imagined it? He pulled his dark legs out of the phosphorescent water and rose slowly. The light caught and glittered on the deck at the shallow end of the pool.

A bull's-eye scatter of splintered glass.

Mindful of his wet feet, he circled to get a better look. A piece of long crystal stem gleamed in the seam between two slabs.

Before he crouched, he knew immediately what it was: one of Andy's fancy wine glasses from Prague.

He looked up again, craning and squinting up the sheer windows of the sleeping apartments to Andy's terrace. No light. No movement. No signs of life. The utter stillness chilled him. The wineglass must have fallen from the open rail, but if he expected Andy's face to be peering down at him, he was disappointed. The penthouse stayed silent as a coiled snake.

Gooseflesh puckered his torso. In his gut he knew: Andy wasn't alone up there.

Ruben's hairs stiffened, and he wiped his hands on his bare stomach. "In my shorts. In my fucking shorts." Why had that seemed like a fine idea? Sneaking out nearly naked for a smoke seemed so idiotic now. He hadn't been thinking straight. A cold fist squeezed his insides. Andy needed him.

He pivoted and jogged back inside. After the night sky, the uncanny gleam of the white hallways slammed into his eyes, making him blink. Like a rat in an expensive maze, he slipped quickly and quietly toward the hidden service elevator used by the building staff to perform repairs and collect garbage.

He pulled open the door beside the emergency stairs and jabbed the button. His balls shriveled. "Think." He had no weapon, no protection, no shoes. Ruben forced himself to take long slow breaths and hold his lungs full and empty at the top and bottom of the cycle. Tactical breathing, the army called it. Any more adrenaline in his bloodstream and he'd start to go blind and deaf.

The elevator cranked into life below him, lumbering upward. *Noisy.* The button needed to be held to keep the elevator traveling, so he held it hard with one damp finger. Ruben scanned the little vestibule for some kind of artillery; the only things on offer were empty trashcans and a huge extinguisher. *Hmm.*

The elevator stopped and its doors opened. The car was loaded with clear recycling bags.

Was there anything he could use? He shifted the piles of recycling inside in search of anything useful or deadly. *Slim pickings*: stacks of bundled newspaper and bags of shredded bills. On one wall, a folded ironing board being put out to pasture and a cardboard box of wine bottles. Then he saw the body. In one corner, a man in a crumpled uniform: the elderly porter's face cuddled hard by the heaps of clean garbage.

Barefoot on the cold metal, Ruben crouched beside him to check: a sluggish pulse. The poor guy was breathing, but out cold.

So much for exaggeration. Andy had tried to warn him, but Ruben had known better. Exactly like all the other times he'd known better even though he didn't know a thing. Like every other dumbass drunk, he never learned that he'd never learn.

No. This was on him. The elevator would be noisy and he couldn't risk the old man. The sweat on his skin felt chilly, but he went back to the stairs.

How could he help Andy? Right now he had a hill of paper and a few bottles. Maybe he could iron them to death. No time to waste thinking.

Ruben began climbing toward the deadly mess he'd made upstairs.

HE SWUNG the bookcase open, thanking Andy for this secret passage which had seemed so stupid on day one.

The library was dim, lit only by the screens on the wall. Hope's desk had been flung back and papers scattered over the floor, but no blood or fire that Ruben could see in the dull green light.

A low yelp from Andy on the other side of the apartment pushed him into motion.

So Andy was still conscious at least. Maybe they wanted information, and that meant they needed him undamaged. That was something to work with.

Ruben couldn't be sure how many there were, and right now it almost didn't matter.

He looked down at his damp boxers and bare feet. His best bet to send them packing was to invite a few more folks to the party. Still, if he just banged on pots and pans, they'd just come in here and kill him. He needed to make a racket big enough to alert the building staff, at least, and the NYPD if he got lucky.

His pants, his cell, and his firearm were in his room and no way could he reach the door except in full view. With the elevator so exposed, he couldn't run for help, and fuck if he was leaving Andy alone with them.

The terrace.

Ruben eased the glass door open and slid through carefully. Tiles cool under his feet, he hugged the shadowy corner and crept around the corner of his own room toward the bright windows. He couldn't even activate the digital shades to give himself cover.

A few feet away, through the white brick and glass, he could see the dim outlines of his clothes and his weapons, but he had no way to get at them.

For a moment Ruben wished for a carving knife or a crowbar, then scolded himself. Macho action-hero bullshit. In the real world, these animals would mow him down before he got close enough to do any damage. They wouldn't step up one at a time to get knocked down like Bruce Lee villains. All they needed to do was make enough holes in him before he could do likewise. Thugs weren't gonna attack in single file and fall politely to the side so he could scoop Andy into his arms.

Not that he actually intended to scoop anything. *Fuck you, Kevin Costner.*

Maybe he could toss a chair into the street and someone would come up to investigate. He glanced over the edge and saw the pool below. No chance he'd be able to throw anything far enough to reach Park Avenue. With his luck, he'd only kill some kid walking their dog and be gunned down before he could get himself arrested.

A bright trapezoid fell onto the terrace from the dining room windows.

Inside, the big table had been pushed to one side and Andy sat sagging in a dining chair, strapped to it and blindfolded with black duct tape. Two men faced the chair talking calmly. They were Anglo and thirtyish, not particularly big or scary looking. The skinny one had a walrus 'stache, and the stockier one leaned against the sideboard saying something muted by the triple-paned windows. *Chunk and Walrus rob a zillionaire.*

If Ruben crossed the terrace to flank them from the south, they'd see him in the glare from the lights. For all he knew, there were more upstairs headed his way with box cutters and a duffel bag. He started to tremble in the hot night air. *I know him.*

Walrus was the guy who'd swiped Andy's wallet on the day they'd met.

Who were these people? Not muggers. Not spies. For some reason, Ruben had expected the goons to be identifiable by their costumes: ugly gangbangers or mobsters in sharkskin suits or creepy Eurotrash with eye patches and a hairless cat. More Hollywood bullshit.

Chunk blinked at Andy as if waiting, then turned to snarl something at Walrus.

Andy struggled to shake his head, and his swollen lips moved. Walrus backhanded him, and bloody drool ran from Andy's chin.

The silent impact opened a searing hole inside Ruben, so hot and sharp that he thought at first he'd been shot. Andy could die in there while he stood out here in his shorts holding his dick. This job wasn't a game, but he'd been beaten anyways.

Even deaf outside, Ruben saw immediately what they were trying to do. They needed info, and Andy was stalling for time, but that would only work till they got impatient. If they could get him downstairs and into a trunk before the cops arrived, they'd exit through the garage, and Andy would disappear for good.

Chunk tipped Andy's chair back and dragged it a few inches, saying something unpleasant. Gory saliva ran out of Andy's nostril, off his chin, but he didn't whimper or respond. He looked brave. He looked handsome and terrified.

Keeping to the shadows, Ruben slipped back to the north door and entered the apartment in slow motion, hyperconscious of his bare feet and boxers, taking no chances.

Inside the library, Ruben flipped the panel to reveal a keypad and a screen that read MOTION DETECTED.

No shit, Sherlock.

All these systems featured some kind of silent panic switch that alerted the cops. Andy had shown him how to arm and disarm the system plenty of times, but beyond the basics he had no clue. Again Ruben cursed his laziness and complacency. He pawed the panel's buttons. A lot of fancy bullshit he didn't have time to figure out while seconds slid down the drain.

Andy muttered and grunted in the other room. A couple thudding hits and then something shattered. *No time.*

What had Andy said? "You know plenty."

Hardwired alarms tripped if the wires were cut, right? Without questioning the impulse, Ruben clawed the control panel off the wall with one tight hand, ripping it from the sheetrock so that it dangled on thin wires. *C'mon, NYPD.*

Instantly, all of the lights came on and a high *zeet-zeet-zeet* siren filled the apartment. The digital window shades began to strobe, clear-opaque-clear-opaque.

Time to move!

The dining room got quiet. Footsteps headed in his direction. He yanked a couple more wires loose for good measure and pressed his bare skin against the wall so they'd pass him without seeing him there. He had to get out to Andy.

Ruben tucked himself into the little tree alcove off the kitchen, careful not to disturb the leaves.

At the last second, the lanky thug turned and saw him and opened his mouth, showing crooked teeth.

Before he could make a sound, Ruben swung and his right fist connected hard; his left followed with an uppercut that lifted the guy off his feet. He crumpled like a deboned trout.

Ruben crouched. His knuckles throbbed and oozed blood but somehow didn't hurt. *Adrenaline.* He tried to calm his heart, tactical breathing: *four in, hold four, four out.*

A scraping sound from the living room, something heavy hauled across the floor.

He needed a weapon. Anything. A knife seemed silly, but maybe a club. He saw the red tube of a fire extinguisher and reached for it without thinking.

On the floor Walrus grunted and squirmed, but there was no time to waste. Ruben made tracks toward the living room and Andy. All that mattered was Andy being okay.

Ruben gripped the fire extinguisher in his sweaty left hand and crept forward in a rush, moving so fast along the hall he almost ran into the other asshole.

Chunk was dragging Andy strapped to the chair toward that service elevator. Andy sat still, his head lolling, and the goon was walking backward and cursing under his breath, so he didn't see Ruben's angry approach and had no chance to react till the last instant.

Ruben swung the extinguisher in a tight arc.

"Motherf—"

It connected with an ugly clang. Chunk lost his grip and fell back against the wall with a wet howl, his nose mashed sideways. Bloody spittle flecked Ruben's bare chest and ran down his mouth and chin.

Andy's chair dropped.

Ruben reached to catch it and missed. It slammed the floor hard, and a *whoof* of air escaped Andy's still face, far too quiet on the floor. He didn't groan or react. *Bad.*

The chunky goon spat dark red at the wall, along with a couple teeth as he scrambled away and toward the back stairs. "Ss'a mistake, man. Alla m'stake." He ran for it. "He didn't want trouble."

"Seriously?" Ruben followed him far enough to see Walrus inside the elevator as Chunk backed on, wary and defiant. Where were the cops?

"No trouble. Huh?" The unholstered gun stopped Ruben's feet because this wasn't a summer movie. *Never mind.* He backed away quickly.

The police would be coming. Everything was out of his hands except for Andy. He jogged back to the chair on its back.

Please don't be dead.

Andy hadn't moved on the floor. His shirt was split almost to his navel, half the buttons missing and one shoulder torn loose. Where the undershirt had pulled up, a large cluster of bruises had started to darken under his left nipple. Assholes had tried to break a rib.

Ruben crouched beside him. He put his ear to Andy's sternum. A sure heartbeat. And his chest moved slightly dragging air into him in shallow sips.

Breathing. Good place to start.

With shaking hands, Ruben peeled the tape free of Andy's bruised lips as carefully as he could. Instead of ripping out hair to get the tape off his eyes, he left the blindfold in place till last. "Shh. Easy there. Easy does it."

Andy's lips looked blue, or was that the halogen spill from the terrace?

Ruben rummaged in the drawer for a knife and cut Andy free of the chair one limb at a time, then slid him onto the floor as easily as he could manage.

"Shh. Shh." He hushed the silent room and realized he was trying to calm himself down.

Andy didn't respond.

Ruben leaned close to make sure the breath was real, and the heartbeat. He raised Andy's hands to touch them and they were warm, warm and softer than he'd expected. Everything was okay and Andy was safe now.

"Shhh." He traced and retraced the plump bow of that lip with his calloused finger, scraping the smooth-smooth skin.

Drop by drop the sizzling adrenaline drained out of Ruben, into whatever cold dark place that panic goes to hide. Queasy and ecstatic, he bent close to Andy, willing him to wake up. *C'mon.*

Andy exhaled and his skull rolled tentatively on the floor.

Relief flooded his chest. Without thinking he bent down in relief and joy and pressed their lips together and groaned at the impossible rightness of kissing Andy.

Oh.

He dragged their mouths against each other, feeling the grain of Andy's stubble under his lips and tongue. The fresh sweetness of his skin.

How could it feel so natural? Why had he fought this so long? He might never have another chance so he sure as fuck wasn't wasting this one. He held his breath and his pulse thundered in his ears.

Andy's breathing deepened, and his lips firmed under Ruben's for a moment as if he was swimming toward consciousness. For a sweet flash, Ruben's tongue slipped inside and touched Andy's. *Stop!*

Ashamed and aroused, he pulled back. The alarm had gone off, so someone had to be on their way, right?

He sat cross legged and kept vigil, afraid to leave Andy in case those fuckers returned. Ruben's right fingers crept under the oversquare jaw and onto his cheek. The pulse knocked against Ruben's thumb. *Good.*

His arms flexed involuntarily, wanting to hold Andy but knowing he had no right. *Pretend you're normal, Oso.* What would he have done a month ago? What would a professional do? What would a friend do?

He rocked to his feet and walked stiffly to the bar. He bent across it to snag a folded towel, blind to the bottles for once in his shitty life. He'd split his knuckles, but somehow he couldn't feel them. His heart still galloped as he walked back.

Andy groaned and stirred.

"Hey bud."

Andy's eyes focused and he smiled. "Rube." He laugh-coughed with some effort then winced. "Oh bud. Thank you. Thank God you're here." His eyes glittered feverishly as he went into shock.

"Easy, fella. You're okay."

"Naked." Wincing, Andy pushed up on his elbows and gave a couple slow blinks.

Ruben looked down at his damp boxers and bare torso. "Not exactly. I was—"

Andy barely nodded. Unspoken: the fact that he had been spying on Ruben naked in the pool again. Neither of them had been looking the right way.

"They're gone?" Andy searched Ruben's face for a few seconds.

Ruben nodded and wiped his smeary hands together, absurdly grateful that his boss had decided to fake amnesia. "I encouraged them in that direction."

Andy pulled himself to his feet and punched at the keypad. The alarm stopped short. "I thought I was a goner. You were downstairs." Now it had been said. They both knew that Ruben had been swimming, just as they both knew Andy had been watching.

Andy stumbled over to the wet bar and snagged a glass, filled it from a decanter. After pulling a pill bottle out of a drawer, he shook a tablet into his palm and then washed it down with the booze.

"You shouldn't use them to chill out." As if he didn't want to wrench the bottle free and down it in fiery gulps.

Andy grunted but didn't raise his eyes. He righted one of the chairs.

Ruben crossed his arms. "Do you know who they were?"

Andy wiped his face carefully and then shook his head. "Fast."

"You're bleeding." His heart turned over. *Some fucking bodyguard.*

Andy's head wobbled. The red ooze shone slick on his temple, and he dabbed at it carefully. "All at once. It's not like TV. I dunno. I think I expected everything to go slo-mo but it was like blinking. Balcony. Door. Swing. On my back. Jesus." A shudder convulsed his torso and he winced.

"Shh. Hey. Hey look at me."

Andy blinked and turned.

"Your eyes are all blown out. C'mere." Ruben reached toward him with a shaking hand. "You may be going into shock. I think you need a stitch or two."

"S'just a graze." Blood dripped from his jawline onto his pale chest.

"We don't know that." Ruben walked him back to the living room and the low couch.

Still dazed, Andy allowed himself to be sat. Another scarlet drop lengthened the thin stripe over his nipple.

"Let me check you out." His hand snuck out and held Andy's head in a soft cradle.

Eyes closed, Andy tipped his head back for Ruben to look. He was still sweating like a sprinter. Neither of them spoke for what seemed a long time while Ruben checked his head, neck, and shoulders with cautious fingers.

Ruben kept his hands under control and ran through what he could scrape up of his first aid training.

Andy swallowed and his larynx bobbed.

"Sorry." Smoothing Andy's hair back, Ruben inspected the brow more carefully. "Still bleeding." Ruben went to the dining room and took a crisp napkin off the table, handing it to Andy as he came back. "Pressure. Press hard."

Andy winced but obeyed. "They got my ribs pretty bad."

Ruben looked a question at him and Andy nodded, allowing Ruben to shift the torn shirt gently. The scraped bruise on Andy's ribcage had begun to darken to a dull rust, violet at the middle. The sight of Andy in pain and panic had turned his legs to pipe cleaners.

Andy sat so still he seemed to shimmer with his stiff nipples and his blown pupils.

"Deep breath." Ribs seemed sound but probably needed an X-ray. The blood had dried under his nose.

Andy sniffed and let out a shuddery breath. He looked about ready to barf.

Ruben expected him to ask for a Scotch, but Andy didn't. *Is that 'cause of me?*

What was he supposed to do now? Every part of him wanted to go to Andy and hold him, and no part of him knew what the reaction would be. If Andy had been a woman, he'd have postured and winced and let her lick his wounds.

Andy was anything but a woman.

Blood matted the left side of his hair and pooled in the collar of the shirt, a stained crescent in back like a diagram for a craft project: *cut along the dotted line*. Huddled against the cushions, he looked strong and stubborn and strictly male. He eyed Ruben's knuckles.

"You should box. I hope you broke his nose."

"I know I did." Ruben knew that sound well, the satisfying celery crunch of popping some motherfucker who wanted to hurt people he cared about. Growing up in Miami, he'd learned how to throw a punch that counted.

Somehow smashed and miserable Andy was the most beautiful thing he'd ever seen. An overwhelming urge to protect him, avenge him, claim him tore through him like warm whiskey.

And his mouth. *Jesus Christ his mouth, his mouth.* Ruben could still taste Andy, the sweet, sharp sting of his saliva… the sullen plumpness of his lower lip slipping through Ruben's teeth for one frozen moment.

Horrible thirst clawed at his throat. He fidgeted and paced, unable to rest anywhere.

I kissed a man, I kissed a man.

Unspeakable rage and loneliness made Ruben want to smash what remained of the sleek furniture, to punch himself in the face. What had he been thinking?

He hadn't thought, the whole time he'd lived up here in this ridiculous cage. He'd done his fake job and then the real feelings had slipped out. Maybe Andy would take pity and pretend nothing had happened.

I kissed him.

A jittery discomfort shook his hands and crushed his chest flat no matter where he stood. His terrible thirst clawed at him. *Just one drink would help.* In the still office behind him the computer fans whispered and rivers of financial gobbledygook rushed zigzag across the crooked plasma screens. He bargained with his past and his hope. All he needed was just one fucking drink to drown this impossible heat licking through him like gasoline alight.

I kissed Andy.

Ruben caught sight of himself in the dark windows looking out toward the black-curdled bowl of Central Park. In the glass, his eyes were haunted hollows. His jaw was clamped hard like he'd taken a gut punch that would make him piss blood. He pressed his hands against his reflection to stop the shaking, but neither of him could stand steady. His boxers had almost dried but the rest of him was slick with acrid, anxious sweat.

Ruben tried to slow his breathing down. Maybe Andy had been unconscious when he'd done it. *Please let him have been unconscious.* Who could he talk to? Peach? Charles? Marisa? A priest? He'd have called his new sponsor if he had one, but since he was a fucking genius there was no one to call.

"Oso?" Andy's low voice startled him.

Ruben looked over, squinting as if Andy were a klieg light that could blind him. *Here it comes.*

The voice sagged with wary tenderness. "You okay?"

"Sure." Ruben knew what was coming. "I'm not the one got beat." How this would go? He rocked on the balls of his feet, terrified and dripping in front of his boss, with sweat for once instead of pool water. His heart chug-a-lugged in his chest as it drove the adrenaline monster back into its wet, red cave. Another fuckup. Another pink slip. Another wasted chance.

Worse than getting beaten up, that's for damn sure.

He refused to leave Andy alone, but he did as much of a perimeter check as he could while keeping his boss in view.

Andy spoke in a low, calm voice, as if calming a rabid animal. "You did great. Hey. Rube, I'm fine. It's good." Blood scabbed his nostril and the socket of his left eye began to darken.

Ruben licked his dry lips and tasted brandy, and blood. His dick wobbled half-hard under his damp boxers, but who cared really. No secrets here anymore. *I'm a drunk and a queer.* "Sorry."

Andy rubbed his lips against each other. "C'mere."

Ruben lurched forward and smeared the sweat on his pounding chest with a numb hand.

Little by little he realized: the alarm had gone dead, but the cops hadn't shown. Why wasn't anyone banging down the door?

Andy laid his entire hand over the wadded napkin to hold it closer. He flinched, eyes enormous. "You really think I need stitches?" Even with the Dudley Do-Right jaw, he looked about seventeen.

"It's.... I'm gonna...." Ruben cradled his head with a careful hand. "We don't know. I'm no medic." He fought the urge to freak out. "Jesus. You scared the shit outta me. I still hoped you were paranoid."

"Shows what you know, Oso."

Ruben didn't laugh.

"I can call Dr. Bronstein in the morning." Andy's split mouth seemed gummy and slow.

Ruben knew exactly how it tasted.

Maybe the kiss would never come up. They'd both pretend to forget.

Where is everyone? Ruben's hands slowed and he straightened. "Why aren't the cops here? The doormen even."

"They're not coming." Andy spoke dismissively.

"Course they are, jackass. I tripped the alarm." He swallowed. "The cops are probably downstairs right now."

"No. I promise." Andy rubbed his upper arms. "That alarm doesn't alert the building or the NYPD." He didn't look like he was joking. "They don't even know anyone was here."

"Uhh." *Twilight Zone.*

"Those men were a warning, is all."

"You're saying those motherfuckers were just a couple dissatisfied *clients*?"

"We're fine." Andy lowered his hand before looking at him. "A disagreement, but it's done."

"Bauer, after all your paranoid bullshit, full-blown denial has set in? Was that some kind of felony-friendly negotiation technique you learned at Columbia?" Ruben grimaced like a maniac.

"They didn't have very much to say." Andy took another mouthful of liquor.

A lie.

Andy didn't know he had been outside watching, so Ruben nodded but said nothing. He didn't say anything about the unconscious porter in the service elevator. Things could've gone much worse. One thing he knew: Andy wasn't boxing with shadows.

"Bauer, those goons talked plenty. I saw them. I watched them grilling you. And they looked ready to pitch you off the balcony over something." The screwed-up thing was that Ruben cared too much to stop.

Andy looked haggard now. The rings under his eyes purpling under the clammy sweat. "Yeah. Uh. Yeah, I guess so."

"Good guess!" Ruben clenched his sweaty, sore hands over and over. Obviously he had failed to connect some dots. If Andy wasn't paranoid, if the threat was real, then he had no business guarding anyone. They needed real security, pronto, and Ruben needed to get Andy out of harm's way.

He swallowed. "We gotta call the police, Andy. We gotta file a report. This is serious."

"No!" Wide eyes. "No cops. I said no cops. I can't have folks in and out of here digging around. There'd be a record later."

"What are you ashamed of? I'm not gonna say anything. I work for you, remember."

Andy rinsed his face at the bar and dried with a linen napkin. The bruises on his temple and ribs had darkened. "Oso, I need to talk to you."

His heart sank. *About the kiss.*

"Ruben." Andy sat down and took a breath. He closed his eyes and opened them. "You made a serious mistake. About me, I mean. I haven't exactly been forthcoming but I let you believe—"

"Say it." Ruben braced himself for the shame and the dismissal. He'd admit it. He'd apologize. He'd take whatever Andy dished out because he'd taken advantage of a situation that was his fault. "Andy, those assholes were ready to—"

"You're right," Andy snarled, using the dickhead-executive tone he used on the phone with pushy clients. "They talked. We talked." The insistence made it sound like a lie. "Business. This was theater. They want to scare—"

"They did!" Ruben glared, irritated and protective and stupid as hell. "The porter was out cold downstairs. This isn't just you, man. They broke in. The building knows." He picked up the house phone.

"They haven't called up. They haven't knocked. And we keep them from calling the cops." Andy dug a few hundred dollar bills out of his wallet. The blood on his nostril had dried to sticky brown-black. Pellets of duct tape adhesive matted his hair.

Sick relief flooded Ruben. Part of him felt gratitude that they'd be ignoring the kiss, and part was queasy at the thought that his insane feelings would stay unspoken and unacknowledged after all. "Then we obviously need to call it in."

Andy's stare had gone brittle and cold as tin. A muscle ticked in his clamped jaw. His hand clamped on Ruben's wrist. "No! No, Ruben." Not scared, but embarrassed.

"They're the fucking bad guys. They left evidence out the ass. They broke in and assaulted you, man. Pretty fucking clear, there." Ruben held up the phone and dialed. *Nine, one—*

"Ruben, put the goddamn phone down!" Andy's voice snapped like a whip.

Startled, Ruben looked up. The dial tone from his hand seemed far away. "But why?"

"'Cause *I'm* the bad guy."

The dead silence slithered around them like a bathtub of slugs. "What?"

Andy's laugh was shaky, and he only looked up into Ruben's face after a few seconds.

"What the hell have you done, Bauer?"

Reaching out, Andy touched Ruben's lips briefly and came away with blood on his fingers. *Andy's blood.* "I could ask you the same."

CHAPTER ELEVEN

IF AT first you don't succeed, destroy all evidence that you tried.

I shouldn't have kissed him. I shouldn't have left him alone to go swimming. I shouldn't have ignored my gut from day one.

Ruben shook his head and looked at the floor, trying to figure out exactly how he'd let everything get away from him.

Andy paced in his bedroom, blotting his bloody face with a seven-hundred-dollar hand towel.

Ruben's lips still stung from the stolen kiss. "I should go."

When had he taken the first insane step? Letting his guard down with an employer? Not quitting in the limo when he'd first suspected his feelings? Taking the job against all his better instincts?

Rewind, rewind.

Keeping shit bottled up only gives your feelings a chance to ferment. The only thing that could have saved him from caring about Andy was never seeing him in the first place. If he had stayed in Florida? Stayed with his wife? Stayed a drunk? Regret was worthless.

"I shouldn't have done that. That was shitty."

"Done?" Andy opened his mouth to weigh in. "What?"

Ruben nodded to himself. Once he said the words, he could take the next step. Keeping a tight rein on his emotions had churned misery into disaster. "Kissed you." Ruben swallowed. Saying it aloud felt panicky and good.

"You did." He didn't sound angry, at least. Then again, he'd left the lights off.

"Mmph. Everything happened so fast. I didn't have a weapon and they were all over. But then you were okay and I kissed you without thinking."

Andy bobbed his head and blinked sheepishly. "About that...."

"I just—I got spooked and then I saw you safe—"

He grinned. "S'not a big deal, man."

"No. It is a big deal. It was a big deal." Ruben didn't let himself look away. "I shouldn't be here at all. I should've left the night of the museum."

"What museum?"

"When they attacked Hope." Ruben shook his head at the hallway carpet, where he stood just outside Andy's bedroom. "Even then I knew that I couldn't get hold of myself. Acting like a drunk and too stubborn to stop. Addicted. 'Cause it felt good, y'see? Idiot."

"Ruben, you're wrong."

"I swear it won't happen again."

Andy frowned. "Why?"

"I'm gonna leave. You're gonna hire someone who knows what the hell they're doing and keeps their private lives private."

"No."

"That wasn't a request. I'm telling you, man. I'm giving notice."

"No. Ruben, I trust you. That's what matters. Look, investment banking is a piranha tank. You decide who you think you can trust and you cross your fingers." Andy held up his hand and did just that.

Ruben frowned. "I don't understand. What is this?"

"S'complicated. Business."

"Bullshit, Andy!"

"This kind of wealth is always a motive." Andy waved an arm at the expensive wallpaper and the Kandinsky on the wall. "A lot of people would like me to drop dead for a lot of reasons."

"And for that, two hedge-fund assholes tied you to a chair and beat you? Because of your apartment? I knew one of them. He *mugged* you that first day."

"They are angry. For a good reason. Good enough." Andy shrugged. "I have a situation that needed handling. A—uh, y'now—client with some ugly friends who I screwed over."

"Are you saying what I think—?"

"Not the mob, or whatever. Like on TV? That mafia doesn't really exist anymore. Not like movies make it seem. No, he's a prep-school tight-ass like me."

Ruben's hands shook even when he crossed his arms and jammed his fists into his cold, sweaty armpits. He felt exposed in his boxers. "You know him." Not a question.

"None of this was supposed to happen." Andy pressed the heels of his hands over his eye sockets. "I fucked everything right up." He looked guilty.

Ruben got very still. "Some Wall Street ninja shit."

"H'yuh. He was displeased with the outcome, to say the least." Andy laughed, dry as dust.

"Legally, you mean." Ruben knew bullshit when he heard it.

"Sure. But in finance, legal gets pretty fucking ugly. Truly."

Ruben scowled. "Guilty is guilty. Prison is prison."

Andy flashed his Sears-dad grin. "White collar crime operates outside anything like law. Because the laws that get written protect us because we buy the politicians we need to keep doing business and we pay to keep the gray areas intact."

In Ruben's world crime was pretty straightforward. People were crooked, and when you got caught, you went down. "What are you saying, Andy?"

"I'm a hitman." The unblinking blue-gray eyes made a joke of the word. "A financial assassin. I mean, not Glocks and snipers or whatever, but I destroy people."

"For money."

"Of course for money. I'm not running a charity." Andy huffed. "Being a sociopath is expensive."

"You're not a sociopath, Andy."

"Maybe not. Well, not more than the average prep-school douchebag."

Ruben had misread everything. "He was your victim."

No response.

He couldn't wrap his head around it: Raggedy Andy the criminal mastermind.

"They're taking revenge." Ruben found himself pacing and forced himself to stop. "A small crime hiding a larger one."

Andy shrugged. "It's complicated. When you actually kill someone, they can't come back and kill you."

"Apparently not. Seems like all your metaphoric bullshit has gotten plenty literal, jackass."

"I'm not the villain here, exactly." Andy swallowed with effort. "These are bad people, you understand."

"So you have killed someone."

"Not like, in a coffin, but I've destroyed a couple lives metaphorically. To the point that life as they knew it became impossible."

"And you've done this kind of 'assassination' for exactly how long?"

"Fifteen years. First time happened almost by accident. A broker bankrupted my parents, and so I returned the favor. With dividends. I just took him down because I could. Then I saw the potential."

"That fucking people up is lucrative."

"No. Not like that. I only go after the assholes nobody can touch. Sleazy funds. Hell, I've lost more than they have."

"Because you can afford it." Ruben snorted. "What a prince."

Andy looked hurt. "Since the recession, things have gotten messier. Traders skate the edge and all the play money's gone. I may have... misjudged someone."

"Then this Apex shit has to stop. You could get killed. I could get killed."

"Not really. That was the beauty of it. Everything was aboveboard. Right out in the open with the SEC keeping score. Enough to keep me in custom shirts. I make most of my clients a lot of money."

"Until you don't, huh. Until you piss off some cokehead with anger management issues and no conscience." Ruben poked him in the chest. "You're not a sociopath, you're a suicide waiting to happen." His blood ran cold and thick in his veins. His skull throbbed like a tom-tom. "They beat you because you deserved to be beaten."

"I'm not a psycho. More like a vigilante for hire. Financial muscle."

Like you. Andy didn't say the words, but they hung there written in money and promises invisible to the naked eye.

"Yeah, right." Suddenly Ruben needed a drink. *Now.* For the first time in almost a year, the tender oblivion seemed worth all the hell it would cost him. *Halt.* "No sweat. Till you end up so, so paranoid you're carrying a gun to the john and taking one-eyed naps."

"Ruben, I never meant for you to get messed up in this part of my life. The whole point of executive protection was that once they saw you they'd back down."

"Fucking dangerous. When were you gonna tell me?"

"I did! I did tell you. I kept telling you. From day one I've been saying I was in danger. I told everyone who would listen. No one would believe me. Hell, I went and hired a bodyguard because I knew physical danger was possible."

Me. Ruben nodded. *He means me.*

"You screwed all that up." The scratches on Andy's face had stopped bleeding. He'd need ice for the shiner coming up. "You were supposed to be some ugly asshole who got hurt to prove a point."

"Great."

"That's not what—" Andy looked down. "I didn't know you, Ruben. I hadn't met you, and I went to Empire because I figured they were all thugs who could take a punch. Some ex-cop who'd get salary and bonus for a little roughhousing."

"Thanks. So I was supposed to be tied to a chair and beaten bloody?"

"No! To take a punch, to scare 'em off. I may have been a dick that first day, but then everything changed. Because of you." Andy hugged himself. "I liked you. More than I expected. Way." Blink. "So the plan went to shit because I refused to get you hurt. Everything changed."

Ruben walked to the windows and looked out over the dark city and the organic fuzz of Central Park.

"Say something," Andy whispered.

"Why didn't you tell me?"

"How? I didn't know anything at first. How could I? Apex was golden. You were gonna hang out, get paid, go home with a shiner and a thick wallet for sitting around. Looker and leaper. Real danger wasn't part of the deal."

"I was a dupe."

"You weren't anything! I hadn't met you, didn't know you, couldn't have known." Andy licked his bruised lips. "How I'd feel about you."

Silence.

Ruben grunted, his hair on end. "You watched me swim, man. Naked." The unspoken desire curled up between them like a drowsy tiger.

"You know I did." Andy flipped a hand at the room. "I made sure you knew. Left every kind of signal, so you could signal back. I mean, if y'wanted."

The animal was staked right out in the open where they both could see.

"But you never did till tonight." Andy sat down on the bed as if his legs wouldn't hold him. "I fucked up so many other things, and I didn't want you caught up in it. I just wanted you."

Ruben didn't move for fear he'd do something wrong to break the spell.

"Jeez. I never... I didn't know I could be attracted like that. You were so strong and good and clean. You've built this whole life out there with your two hands, and I was this rich wimp. I kept flying closer and closer. Windshield, bug. I couldn't stop. I wouldn't have if I could."

Ruben nodded. He paused in the doorway to Andy's room, not sure of his best next move.

The bodyguard in him knew he needed to secure the principal and phone for backup. The alcoholic in him wanted to drink a fifth of gin and catch a cab to JFK, just to ditch all this for the kind of fucked-upness he was used to handling. But the man in him needed to love Andy Bauer, and save him, and fuck him, and protect him, and wake up with him for the rest of their lives even if the world thought he was a disgusting homo. He cared so much that there was no room to care about what anyone else thought.

As if Andy had heard the smile, he turned.

For a few moments they watched each other, wary and happy.

Andy cocked his head and whispered, "C'mere."

"I can't." His voice sounded loud to his ears.

"Not to do… anything. Just come here, man." Andy scooted up till his back was braced on the headboard.

Ruben crossed the miles between the door and the bed and stopped at the edge of the mattress. Andy's biscuity sweetness seemed stronger here, probably embedded in the pillows by now. He sat down on the mattress, looking at the floor.

How could the power dynamic ever return to normal when it had never *been* normal?

Andy's hand touched his back. "S'no big deal."

"It is and you know it."

"Doesn't have to be." Andy's fingers rested warm and sturdy on his back. They didn't stroke or clutch at him. Then they were gone.

Ruben sat breathing, ashamed of how good the faint touch felt. His heart knocked uncomfortably and his throat tightened. His hands were shaking.

Andy wasn't just a theory or a paycheck. Improbably, hope sat propped up a yard away, smelling of warm bread, all that smooth skin fleeced with soft gold.

"I'm not making anything happen. Just chill out with me, man. Maybe we'll be able to sleep."

"Okay." Ruben swung his legs onto the bed. "Feels weird."

"Sitting in bed?"

"With my boss. Who's a dude. When we both know—"

"Stop."

Ruben grumbled. "I don't know what's supposed to happen."

"Let's take our time, huh. I didn't expect any of this."

Ruben scooted himself back across the cool sheets by inches. He expected Andy to touch him, to pat or squeeze him, but true to his word, he gave Ruben plenty of space.

My move.

His voice caught in his throat at first. "Ha—How's your head?"

"'Kay." Andy sounded anxious as well. "Stronger than I look."

Ruben chuckled. "Dumber too."

"The worst is my arms." He raised the right for inspection.

Ruben held it gingerly. Sure enough, he could see a broad welted stripe of raw skin. He didn't have any words that could be said aloud.

Andy sat rigid while Ruben inspected the mark with choked tenderness. *I'm crazy. I'm crazy.*

The air shimmered between them, all the bright, hard possibilities catching the light like terrifying glitter. One thing to imagine, quite another to give in or give up.

Ruben stopped stroking and just squeezed the muscular forearm. "You have a boner."

Andy raised his legs. "No."

Ruben raised his knees as well. "Wasn't a question. I got my own to deal with."

They sat side by side that way, legs bent like bums on a stoop.

Finally, Andy yawned. "I think… I may try to sack out. That okay?" He yawned again, and ended on a smiling sigh. "Feels good to have you here. Closer."

Ruben nodded. "Me too. I mean, yeah. That's good." *I'm crazy about him.*

Andy leaned in and for once Ruben didn't feel like he needed to pull back. The fresh-baked warmth of Andy settled his heart. "Ruben? Uh. Thanks."

Ruben rolled over, bringing him another four inches closer. His knee grazed Andy's solid leg. "Thank you, man. I'm…." He put a hand on Andy's abdomen and they both flinched at the contact.

"Ah." Hot under his hand, Andy's tight belly thumped with his pulse. His stiff wood was about seven inches south and trapped inside boxers.

Ruben kept his fingers still, conscious of every faint hair on the silky skin.

Any second they were gonna cross that line.

They blinked at each other and looked at each other. In a way the room was as quiet as Central Park under the trees, the two of them keeping pace and slippery with sweat in the green light.

His erection didn't help matters here. He shifted onto his stomach, where his hard-on lay trapped under his belly, hot as a fresh-fired pistol and so stiff that pressing it flat hurt. The bread smell was stronger with his face buried in Andy's duvet, even facing away.

Before anything crazy happened, Ruben lifted his hand and stuck it between his pillow and the mattress. "Sorry."

"G'night, Rube. It's gonna be okay. We're gonna be okay. You watch."

"What happens?" Meaning the Apex hitman thing and them both. Ruben looked at the wall for safety. No luck.

"We go out. Out-out."

"Like a date." That sounded excellent, actually. Crazy, stupid, and dangerous. But fun. "Maybe dinner? Hang out. Cigar."

Andy lit up at that. "Yeah. We're gonna date. I'm gonna date the hell out of you."

Ruben tried and failed to hide his nerves, apparently.

Andy shook his head gently. "Nothing's different, Rube. Not really." He rolled toward Ruben and brought his knees up, hiding the straining bulge in his boxer's folds.

Not that Ruben was watching or anything. "Plenty's different."

Andy uncrossed his arms, his blue-gray gaze gentle. "First step."

Ruben laughed and sat up again. A strange wave of lust and hope made him feel wobbly. Maybe everything was okay. At the very least, he had a chance to find out what he felt about Andy Bauer.

Andy exhaled and squinted. "Nice to meet you, Ruben. I'm Andy." He held out a hand.

Ruben took it and shook it. *See? Simple.* "Same." He didn't let go of the strong hand.

Andy squeezed his fingers. "So far so good." He leaned closer, until his heat bounced off Ruben's chest. "I like you a lot."

Ruben frowned. "Yeah? I wish I was smarter or richer or younger, but I'm not." Facing Andy put them exactly eye to eye.

"I don't. I don't wish anything."

Ruben swallowed, superconscious of his nearly dry boxers and all his other bare parts. Powerless and nowhere to hide.

Andy swayed closer, closer, as if asking permission.

Ruben gave a small nod and Andy erased the space between them. The lips pressed to Ruben's were firm and sweet. The faint stubble grazed his.

A man. I'm kissing a man.

Andy whimpered and wrapped one hot arm around his bare back, mashing their fronts together, boner to boner, which felt even better. A little too good, actually—

Ruben broke free, hyperventilating. "Okay. Okay-okay. Hang on."

They stared at each other, chests rising and falling like they'd sprinted at each other. Ruben's lips buzzed like they'd been burnt.

Andy's cool eyes glittered wickedly. He wiped his wet mouth. "Sorry. I been wondering about that myself."

Ruben nodded, dumb with lust. His rigid cock tented his damp boxers till he held it back against him with a hand. *I don't care if he's crooked, long as he's not straight.*

"Now I know."

Slowly, Ruben leaned in, leaned in, leaned—

Brrrrp. The house phone trilled—the front desk calling.

Someone must have heard the ruckus. Someone may have called the cops. Someone was gonna come back and finish the job.

Their eyes met and wrestled in midair. Lies and secrecy led nowhere good.

Ruben shook his head, but Andy was already moving toward the handset.

"Yello?" Andy sounded breathless. "No, no. We're good. Nah, nothing like that. They just got carried away." Even battered, he began to take control, and the calm mastery crept back into his voice. "My security's here."

Says you. Ruben had the oddest sense of standing on a ledge a half mile above Park Avenue, no wings and no way down. The pitch black only made it easier for him to imagine jumping toward the lights like a dumb animal. He knew what a mistake felt like. He knew what needed to happen. He knew what Andy wanted and had no idea what it would cost either of them.

Sure enough, as Andy talked to his doorman he ambled back toward the bed and stroked Ruben's hair. The firm pressure of his fingers made Ruben close his eyes in treacherous pleasure. Then he was hanging up and back on the bed.

"Think you can sleep?"

Ruben was worried, exhausted, and so happy his heart wouldn't stop chugging in his chest. He nodded before he found his voice. "Y-yeah. If you think it's okay"

"I trust you."

Ruben snorted. "If I have a wet dream, you're in big trouble."

Andy laughed. "I'm a gambler."

"No shit." A few minutes later, Ruben got to watch him fall asleep. Ruben lay still and counted all his blessings stretched out on the bed beside him.

Ruben felt too anxious to sleep and too excited to care. The stakes had gotten too high. Blind and stupid didn't begin to cover it, to stick around fighting shadows that fought back. If AA had taught him anything, to take any kind of step, you had to put your foot down.

Ruben knew this was a mistake. *Money. Revenge. Blackmail. Kidnapping. Assault.*

The first thing, the best thing he could do was hail a cab to JFK right now and fly his ass back to Miami and stay in the drunk tank for a week.

The last thing he needed was to stay in this fancy cage throwing pebbles at dragons.

The worst thing would be to give in to his lust and Andy's smile.

Only one thing kept him from doing the right thing.

Stupid heart.

CHAPTER TWELVE

NO BATTLE plan survives first contact with the enemy.

Ruben's eyes were still closed, but he could feel Andy's warm weight on the mattress a foot away. It couldn't be more than five o'clock in the morning, but he felt wide awake stretched out on the Pratesi sheets. He'd slept with Andy.

In his bed. In his arms.

They'd curled together so naturally. They'd shared this crazy bed without any disasters. Sexual crisis averted. They could take their time, figure things out like adults.

He had every intention of behaving himself, of sliding out and sneaking down to his room to shower and dress, but he took a breath of their blended scent, his own familiar musty scent spread over Andy's fresh-baked sweetness. After being single so long and getting sober, the dozy closeness felt sharper than he remembered. And though it felt sexy to touch Andy like this, no freaky kink-outs had occurred that sent either of them scurrying for cover. He just wanted to look at Andy a little and then he'd go.

He turned over onto his side. Without him making the conscious decision, his hand closed over Andy's stiffness through the boxers. He didn't pull it, but he couldn't help exploring. He gave it slow, rhythmic squeezes from blunt crown to scratchy base, weighing the heft and the heat of it.

Andy's breathing didn't change, but his cock went from hard to rigid. One long vein swelled into an urgent pulsing seam up its side. The head seemed especially sensitive.

Mouth dry, Ruben plucked at the underside, feeling sneaky and exhilarated at his own boldness at stealing pleasure from someone so unexpected, so beautiful. His heart thudded with a terrible certainty he refused to analyze.

Andy's breathing shifted, and his trim hips shifted slightly against the clasp of Ruben's arm, the press of his abdomen.

Ruben stroked the hard ridge of Andy's knob, but lightly, lightly in the ring of his thumb and index finger. He used the inside of his rough knuckle to pet the damp swell there, and Andy's erection lost all flexibility.

Andy squirmed a little in the dark. His head tipped on the pillow. He'd be awake any minute.

Thief.

Ruben kept his deep breaths steady and as quiet as he could. His broad boner had pushed above the waistband of his shorts, and he could feel the oily slip of his foreskin rolling back and forth, back and forth by millimeters. Holding Andy, touching Andy, wanting Andy felt so right he couldn't remember why he was supposed to want anything else.

Andy's hushed voice startled him. "Oso. You woke up."

In the light spill from the street, Ruben could see shapes, and at certain angles a little color. He didn't want Andy to turn on the light yet. The dark felt safe, sexy. Any second that lamp would snap on, and they'd have to be sensible.

Andy shifted onto his back, and in tandem, Ruben rolled onto his side, resting one leg over Andy's, stopping him from reaching for the nightstand.

Andy's breath caught.

Line crossed. Ruben left his leg there, letting them both get used to the contact. It felt so good that he just tried to keep his breath steady and enjoy the hard body trapped under his thigh. Maybe they'd simply fall asleep. *Right.*

Andy exhaled and fell still.

Their muscle and bone settled together by degrees, their bodies shifting subtly to accommodate each other. The fused strength, weight, and friction felt too right to put a price on. For the first time in his life, Ruben understood exactly what greed meant: a need so painful that it made the cost irrelevant, any price tag nonsensical. And not knowing the price, Ruben had no plan. Whatever came next, he'd take it and pay for it.

"Too warm?"

Andy grunted in the negative, breathing faster. "Not so far." His head was cradled by the down pillow about eight inches away.

Ruben closed his eyes and then realized that the broad helmet of his cock was snugged against Andy's hip. Lying together felt so perfect he hadn't noticed at first.

Andy had. He didn't speak, but his heart was going like anything. He began to sweat, and his glute flexed once under the jabbing pressure.

Ruben could feel the dampness against his boxers as his foreskin rolled back. His exposed knob was always hypersensitive to the lightest contact.

Andy sounded nervous. "Is that—?"

Ruben whispered. "Yeah." Grunt.

Andy inhaled sharply. Even in the dark, he had looked tan against the white sheets, but now Ruben's dark hand turned that skin to ivory. Andy's erection jerked twice inside his shorts.

Over and over Ruben closed and opened his fingers lightly, stroking Andy's abdomen with the broad tips as if digging deeper into dry sand.

Shaky breath. "Rube."

Andy's hot skin made him an offer that led somewhere he couldn't imagine properly. Heaven help him, he couldn't say no to it.

Ruben glanced down at the tented shorts, silhouetted by the light from outside. "You got a similar problem, boss." He rested his palm on Andy's stomach very carefully.

Ruben rocked his hips back, and his foreskin slid forward again, dulling the intense, wet pleasure. "S'okay."

Andy swallowed.

Part of him wanted to turn the lights on, so he could watch, and part was happy they were still hidden from each other. "I'm touching you, is all. Does that tickle?"

"Mmh-uh. No. But it's extremely, uhh, sensitive. *Jesus*."

"Tell me about it." Ruben pushed his ridge back against Andy's haunch. His damp skin pulled back, and his cock head burned with slithery pressure. The blunt snout squashed itself against firm muscle and liked it just fine.

"Ruben." Andy's voice lowered. "You're gonna make me pop like that."

"No way."

A sharp intake of breath in the dark. "Yeah. Way."

"Just petting your stomach."

"And humping my butt cheek with your knob." He chuckled.

The raw words made Ruben tense. His balls actually tightened a bit, and his shaft lost whatever flex had remained. "Filthy bastard."

"Says the big hombre painting me with cocksnot." Andy scooted up an inch, his ass flexing momentarily under Ruben's erection.

Ruben was leaking in earnest now. The fabric was smeary between their skin. He scooted closer. "Uh huh."

"For some kind of hands-free happy ending." Andy looked down helplessly.

Ruben's knee grazed the underside of Andy's balls. "Feels okay though."

"Yuh. Uh. Rube." He hissed through his teeth. His heartbeat seemed concentrated in his ribs, right against Ruben's.

Ruben squirmed in until his stubbled chin grazed Andy's throat, and the floppy hair was crushed against his forehead. Ruben's ragged breathing heated the trapped air there. "Nice."

"Rube, I… God. Ruben, wait. I thought—"

He knew he should slow down, but to stop Andy's protests he opened his mouth and closed his teeth over the cord of Andy's throat, tasting the salty muscle. *Line crossed.*

Andy arched. "Ah! Agh!" His rigid flesh bumped Ruben's elbow as he ground the bulge behind his balls against Ruben's knee, and Andy skinned awkwardly out of his shorts, working them down his legs, then dragged off Ruben's.

Good. Ruben scooted closer still, almost on top now, his cock so hard that the foreskin no longer covered the cap drilling into Andy's thigh no matter how hard he thrust.

Andy groaned under his weight and rocked their hips together until their erections made clumsy, delicious contact. His powerful arms closed around Ruben's back and squeezed.

Ruben stayed still as possible. Afraid to go further, but not willing to retreat. He laved Andy's throat with his broad tongue, dragging his rough stubble across Andy's.

"Zzh. Plea—" Andy wheezed and jerked under him as if electrocuted.

Ruben turned his head with deliberate languor. "What?" Millimeter by twitching millimeter he learned that this double sandpaper scour turned all Andy's entreaties into shocked, spitty moans.

Andy twitched and gasped at the air. His downy forearms slipped over Ruben's waist and ribs, struggling for purchase until they lay on their sides and finally Ruben ended up on his back looking up at Andy with their dorks jammed together at an angle. "Oso." He stroked Ruben's chest.

"'Sup." Ruben wiped his wet mouth. He could feel his precum drizzling and gliding between them.

Andy looked down. The glitter of his eyes went dark. "Uhh."

"What? No one can see."

"I know. I want to. God, Ruben. What you feel like." Using both hands, he encircled their erections, squeezing them together. Ruben's extra skin slipped easily between them. "I don't know how."

"This is okay, huh? Like that. Just to see. We don't need the light to find out."

"I know. I just want to look at all of you, man. In my bed and ready. I want to see you." Andy's soft voice sounded ragged, but he kept milking their cocks with steady, sleazy pressure.

But before Andy could trigger the lights or hit the lamp, Ruben rolled across him and crushed their mouths together, pushing his tongue into Andy's wet mouth. Even more light felt like too much, too fast. *Baby steps.*

Andy sighed under his weight, and his arm wrapped around Ruben's back. He pressed their cheeks together. Sandpaper. He licked Ruben's earlobe and chewed lightly at it.

Ruben almost blacked out. His ears had always been his weak spot. Touching, licking, biting… all sent him over the edge. Made him crazy. His breath came fast and frantic. His hands hovered, shaking, over Andy's back. Where to put them? His eyes widened, and finally he pulled Andy's skull closer. "That. That. Oh my God."

Totally different being this close to a man. Different everything.

First Ruben had known too little, and now he knew too much.

Andy pulled back slowly. "Good to know." In the dark his smile was a shifting shadow and his eyes barely a twinkle.

Going slow made it better and worse. He didn't feel out of control, but he could feel the slow, inevitable ratcheting of tension like a car climbing-climbing to the top of a rollercoaster, flirting with the plunge. Only without seatbelts.

Andy's body strained against his, short circuiting his brain. His rough fingers pulled Andy closer. Even in the dark, the clean, strong angles of him felt right in Ruben's arms. His cock was granite. The raw slip of his foreskin drilled his knob into Andy's abdominal ridges.

"Rube, I can't. I'm—"

"Unph." Ruben growled and covered Andy's lips with his own and made a sound of relief and assent. *Give it all up, gimme everything.* His heels pushed into the creamy sheets and drove their hips together with urgent finality. Ruben strained and struggled against Andy's perfect flesh, out of control and under Andy's power. "I can't take—" He pushed his hand below Andy's waist, cupping one round cheek and dragging Andy against his front. With nowhere to go, their hard cocks knocked together with electrifying pressure. They pushed toward each other, trying to eliminate the space that separated them.

Ruben growled and held Andy's mouth against his, tasting the sweet slide of his tongue. He ran one hand down Andy's spine until two fingers brushed the top of his crack.

At that, Andy's mouth closed on his throat and up to his ears again. Sucking and biting at him with slobbery ferocity. For once all of Andy's polish and reserve had melted away, exposing the male animal underneath.

Andy ran a light hand over his haunch.

Ruben stiffened and rolled away, trying to seem casual about it. What if Andy wanted to fuck him? They were two guys; guys fuck things. He hadn't considered that wrinkle. He wet his lips and focused on not freaking.

Ruben felt like a jerk for thinking it, but he couldn't change who he was. He wanted Andy, and maybe one day it wouldn't seem scary, but he was old enough to know how he was wired.

Pushing Ruben's legs apart, Andy knelt between them, panting and frantic. He poked at Ruben's hole, hard enough that the fingertip went in for a second.

Whoa, there. Ruben's ass felt exposed, and stupid nerves got hold of him. "Easy, Wonder Bread." He sat forward. He hadn't expected it, and though it hadn't hurt, it had felt weird as hell. "I'm full up on firsts tonight."

"Sorry." Andy paused and retracted his hand. The gold fluff on his forearms caught the dim light. He shook his head. "Not that. I wanna—" A quick kiss. A hand brushed across Ruben's chest hair. "I didn't mean to freak you out, Oso."

"You didn't. I mean it." Ruben nodded. "You surprised me. I'm not freaked. Maybe later. Okay?" The words felt like a lie. He knew he was a shitbag for stalling like that; he couldn't imagine ever letting anyone inside him like that, but then again a month ago he couldn't have imagined lying next to his boss smeared with their precum. *Sleeping dogs lie.* "I don't think I can. Do too much. Right now, I mean. Sorry."

"No." Still breathing hard, Andy hesitated a moment before smiling. "Let's see how it goes, huh?" If he was disappointed he hid it well.

Ruben could still feel the odd hollow spike of sensation of the tip inside him, which had to be imaginary. He put his own hand down there. He'd never felt his butt before. Never thought of that part of his body as something sensitive or shareable. Covering the hole with his cupped fingers seemed childish, somehow especially with everything they'd done already. "It didn't feel bad."

"But it didn't feel good, either." Andy blinked, contrite. "There aren't rules, man."

"I'm not—Andy, you surprised me is all. It's my butt, y'know." Did he? Ruben took a shaking breath. *Fooling around, fooling around.* Only his cock didn't know the difference.

"Hard to know where the boundaries are." Andy crossed his arms tightly. "You seem to like mine. And lord knows I liked the stuff you did." He cough-snorted.

"Just need a breather. This is—" *Too weird.* Ruben gripped Andy's hard flesh apologetically and the crown bulged in his palm.

Andy nodded. "I don't have all that much experience with butt stuff. I got the feeling you dug it."

Ruben glanced down at the jut of muscle, and the light down between those high cheeks. "Mmh." He nodded.

"You can touch me, man. If you want. 'Cause I do." Andy swallowed. "Want to. Want you to." He bent one knee and slid it higher as if offering his muscular ass.

"I can't help myself. That fuckin' skin. I just—"

Andy shook his head and frowned to himself.

Ruben wavered between lust and panic. "I'm an asshole."

Andy rested his brow against the side of Ruben's skull a moment. "No, Oso. What you are is a good man with bad manners." He rolled their heads together. "Thank Christ."

"Next time."

"Don't care. Not a little, even. I'm so glad you're finally in my bed." Another kiss, sucking at Ruben's lower lip and then the ear again.

Jesus.

Ruben groaned and squirmed but exposed himself to the delirious assault. "Bauer, I haven't made out since I was about thirteen."

Andy rocked back and shook his head slowly. "Fuckin' shame, that." His hair was in his eyes.

Ruben pushed it back, smoothing it. "We're not kids anymore."

"No kidding." Andy squeezed their dicks together in his hand. "You're practically middle-aged."

"Fuck you. Forty-one is not middle-aged. I'm not that much older than you. What, two years?"

"And a half. Those are two very important years, I'll have you know."

"I'm not your daddy." Ruben felt freaky saying it. And that freakiness made being in bed like this feel even freakier.

"Stop. Hey." Andy punched him in the side. "I'm not in this bed because of Sigmund Freud."

"Good. Ow." Ruben rubbed the ribs. "That was uncalled for."

They were both nervous then. Good.

Andy shifted to his side. "I didn't mean to jump you. You got me worked up."

Ruben tilted his head to look at the eyes glittering at him. "Couldn't sleep."

"Not true. You slept hard." Andy coughed and shifted. "I saw you."

"Yeah?" Ruben propped his head on a hand and squinted skeptically. "You watched me?"

"Of course I did. I like watching you. No new information."

True enough.

Andy murmured to himself, a thinking sound.

Lying on his back, Ruben felt exposed and relaxed both. He rubbed his stomach, painfully aware of his wee-hour wood and the sexual frustration that had made the past month so excruciating. "Did I do anything interesting I should know about?"

"Plenty." Andy bent one knee and scratched his tousled hair, unleashing the cowlick that always made Ruben grin.

Ruben could just make out the stiff lump under the sheet. His own erection kept that from being embarrassing. His mouth had gone dry and, for a few heartbeats, he tried to swallow. When he managed to speak, his voice came out as a rasp. "And you?"

"Yeah?"

"Did you do anything interesting?" Ruben asked. "That I should know about?"

Andy shook his tangled head. "Just looked my fill while I had the chance."

Ruben knew they were both waiting for permission, but from who, he couldn't say. "Awful polite."

Andy cleared his throat. "It's only—I love watching you do anything. Handsome."

"Shut up."

"But sleeping, your defenses come down and I can see all of you."

"Yeah. Uhh. That's creepy." But he grinned at the notion of Andy liking his blunt mug.

"I don't mean like that. It's.... You aren't hiding. No posing. Just you without a wall."

"Or a skin." Ruben rolled his eyes.

Andy laughed. "Okay. Yeah. I guess." He nudged Ruben's chest. "But you're always gonna be stronger than me. When you're sleeping is the only time I feel like I have a chance to watch over you, protect you."

Ruben didn't reply. Couldn't have if he wanted. His eyes pricked and he felt about five years old. Not once had he ever enjoyed someone watching him like that or thought they would. Never in his life had he wanted to be protected. With Marisa, he'd known what he was supposed to do because he'd spent his whole life practicing: job, wife, kids.

Now, he'd wandered off the path without any kind of map or advice. After all, they were both men. Two guys with two lives. And no matter what anyone pretended, none of this was simply experimenting, or getting off or even blowing off kinky steam.

Everything felt different.

Ruben had always figured queers were wired wrong, that being a homosexual was like being a lefty or color-blind. *Just... wrong.* Only, he hadn't rewired anything, and the rightness had overwhelmed him. He was still a drunk and a screw-up who missed his family and wanted a beer. These feelings seemed like the opposite of color-blindness. Whatever color shone in Andy had been invisible to him until he finally saw, and no amount of explaining would ever make anyone else understand what felt so obvious now.

Andy sat back. "Sorry."

"For what?" Ruben looked up and realized Andy had taken his silence for distaste. This time he reached for the lamp, clicking it on. The sudden brightness made them both squint. "Why would you be sorry?" Without stopping to question, he twisted and pressed their lips together.

Andy inhaled sharply, and then his mouth softened.

"Don't you ever apologize for being sexy. Or smart. Or kind. Not to me, at least. Deal?"

"Yes sir." And that was that.

No lynch mobs. No catastrophes. No personality transplants. Apparently, they were still just two people who dug each other. He could hang out with Andy without needing to wax his chest or binge-watch Beyoncé concerts.

His anxiety had next to nothing to do with what they were doing, and everything to do with other times and other places: What would the guys back home think? How did gays get treated when they wandered into the wrong parts of Hialeah? When would his brother stop giving him shit?

Someone would find out. Ruben knew that lying and hiding turned everything to poison. Being a drunk had taught him that. As two guys together, they'd catch hell, but New York had to be easier than North Dakota, right? Maybe on the six o'clock news they'd raise some eyebrows. But in the twenty-first century, who cared? People had way bigger alligators to wrestle.

Andy patted his chest playfully.

Ruben squinted, asking a silent question.

"Not a race. Yeah?" Andy shook his head and put a hand in Ruben's hair, not scratching but a lazy stroke. His eyes closed and he exhaled.

Ruben swallowed, unaccountably nervous. *Don't ask questions.* "Okay, then." His hand still covered Andy's erection protectively.

"I haven't felt this rested in… fuck. I dunno." Andy stretched against him and his cock brushed Ruben's grip to punch the sheet. "You gave me a huge boner."

"You musta been dreaming."

Andy nodded. "No kidding." He stroked the back of Ruben's head and gripped his neck.

Ruben rolled further onto his side, notching his stiffness into the meaty curve of that perfect ass.

"Two boners, more like." A grin.

"I watched you. I always watch you."

Andy tipped his head to look. "Yeah? I love that." He closed his eyes and smiled at the ceiling. "Sexy fucker. I love you keeping an eye on me."

"Yeah?"

"You have no idea. Getting caught." A slow blush washed from his collarbone up to his scalp. "Someone watching me. It…." He took hold of his own erection and squeezed it purple. The lazy vein looked thick as a pencil along its length. "Always has. I can't explain."

Ruben nodded, turned on by the feverish sparkle in Andy's eyes. "Keeping an eye on you is no kinda problem for me, Mr. Bauer. You're under fucking surveillance now. I don't know how to stop. Jesus. I don't wanna know."

For a moment, Andy shone.

Ruben blinked but the sight remained, as if Andy had begun to glow and the room around him had dimmed.

"You changed everything, y'know." Andy swallowed. Every part of him fell still except for the pulse in his throat and his erection. His gaze searched the ceiling for something.

"I never been with a guy before."

"I have. In boarding school a couple times. Once with my college roommate. Not like this."

A sudden swell of stupid, irrational jealousy swept through Ruben like hot bleach, and he kept his mouth shut. "Ah."

"Not like us, I said. Not feelings. Not trust." A sigh. "Not you."

"Good." Embarrassing that Andy had read his mind so easily. "You scare me sometimes, but in a good way I think."

Andy turned his head and pressed a kiss on the seam where Ruben's arm and chest met. "Gracias, Señor Oso."

Ruben loved hearing the language on Andy's lips. "You white boys." He rolled his eyes.

Andy frowned. "What's that mean?"

"It means…." What did it mean? He closed his fist around Andy's morning wood and pressed his own close. "I'm fucking glad to be in your bed, boss. Now I can keep an eye on you properly."

Andy laughed till Ruben joined in.

Andy sighed. "You wanna go on a date? With me? Out, I mean."

"We go out all the fucking time."

"I don't mean work. I mean—"

Ruben grinned. Because he wasn't just hired muscle, some jailhouse, boot camp fuck for the kinky rich boy. "You mean courting."

"Yeah." Andy ducked his head shyly. "Yeah. Like that."

"Of course I do. How do you say sexy?" Ruben stroked Andy's rib. "*Guapo.*"

Andy's eyes focused. "Stop it. You're *guapo*. Dark. Thick. Built."

"Classy, then. Charming." Ruben kneaded the relaxed muscles gently, milking really great sighs out of Andy. "Dashing."

"Oh, yeah. Great. Thanks. Fetch a fucking Disney princess."

"In Spanish. C'mon." He stroked the flank. "I dunno. Well-bred." He ran a rough hand over Andy's flank. "Put together. Stylish. Whatsa Spanish for that?"

Andy thought a moment. "*Pintón.*" He stroked Ruben's leg. "It's a little old school. But… yeah. Pintón."

"Pent-un?"

"Ón. On the second syllable. Like "own" but shorter. Pintón."

"Pinton." He couldn't make it sound right.

Andy licked his lower lip. "Hit the second syllable. *Pinto* is slang for convict. Marked. Or dick, if you're in Brazil."

"Oh, sorry. You're not a dick. Or a convict."

"That's what they all say." Andy laughed. "At first."

Ruben bent to kiss the faint veins in his wrist. "Eres muy pintón, Señor Bauer."

Andy's face lit up. "Thanks." Chest poke. "Quick study."

"Great teacher."

Somehow they were stretched out together, half-naked, without Ruben feeling terrified. The banked lust simmering between them felt like a promise or a prayer. He wanted Andy like crazy, but he had nothing to prove and nowhere to run.

Without second-guessing, Ruben reached out to stroke Andy's face and scalp. "I'd know this color anywhere."

Andy snorted. "You're crazy."

"Ash-brown. What would you call it?"

"I dunno, mousy beige? My mother always says my hair is nothing-colored. Not blond, not brown."

"Then she didn't look very hard." Ruben finger-combed the glossy length away from their faces. "It's not nothing. It's not like anything." He stroked the silk, rubbing the strands between his rough fingers.

Andy arched and flexed and sighed.

"I finally got to touch you." Ruben petted his forearm fuzz. "I used to be obsessed with this."

"My arm?"

"This." Ruben plucked at the springy fluff. "The way it caught the light. And your skin."

"Because my skin is whiter?" Andy brushed his hand over Ruben's knuckles.

"Nah. It's softer or something. Crazy smooth. I can't explain it. Like the smoothness is under the surface. In the muscle."

"I think that's fat you're talking about, my man. Or sweat."

Ruben shook his head. "But in certain places it's close to the surface. Here." He traced the cool underside of Andy's forearm and then pressed his lips to it. "Here." Andy's ribs. "And here." The nape of Andy's neck.

"You're giving me another boner."

"Tough." Ruben dragged his knuckles over the ridge of collarbone, the swell of his upper pec. "I never felt skin like yours. Not ever in my life."

"Bull." But Andy held his breath. His voice was respectful and hushed. "I think you may be biased, *Señor* Oso."

"No kidding."

Andy grinned. His erection lifted from his belly. "Thanks all the same."

Ruben squeezed it. "See, the softness is *just* inside, out of sight, but so close I can tell it's hidden there. Whatever you are." He inhaled behind Andy's ear: fresh-baked Bauer. "A secret you have to keep."

"Hey."

"Besides, isn't that what sex is? I mean when we aren't just getting off. Outside and inside get mixed up. All the other stuff gets stuck in there too, not just the meat but ideas, mistakes, feelings. Inside the bottle. Trapped like carbonation." His calloused fingers tugged arrhythmically at Andy's hardness. "The fizz."

"You keep yanking, I'll show you carbonation." Andy shifted onto his side, the blue-gray eyes half-lidded as he slid closer to press his firm lips against Ruben's. If he wanted to play, Ruben could play along.

Ruben snuck his tongue out just enough to taste the inside of Andy's mouth, then lay back with a satisfied sigh. "No, jerk. It's between the inside and the outside, but stuck in the middle of both, where they crisscross." He let go and patted Andy's stomach, wishing he knew the right words. "So it can't ever be either. It's only between. Which is how people hurt each other so much. Never mind. I'm too dumb to explain."

"You're not." Andy sighed. "I know exactly." He sounded convincing at least.

All the same Ruben recognized the feeling, though he couldn't give a name to it. That tender point of willing surrender where trespassing was required and crime paid plenty. "Only between."

Andy shifted and laid his head on Ruben's chest, sounding horny and drowsy. "If you say so."

Ruben idly stroked the glossy hair, letting ash-brown silk slip though his rough fingers over and over. "I do."

"Then I do too."

CHAPTER THIRTEEN

SEX RELIEVES tension. Love causes it.

Ruben barely got a wink but didn't get out of bed, so horny his skin hurt and his penis drilled itself raw under him. He kept expecting Andy to give him permission, but nothing doing. He knew he didn't have to ask, but he didn't know how to. Not like that.

Far from it.

Saturday morning, they slept in, mainly because Andy wouldn't get out of bed and made sure Ruben stayed put.

And so Ruben stayed put, terrified he might miss some sign of permission. He liked the fooling around, but the constant cocktease was turning his balls into molten pulp that hurt every time he moved. Weren't two guys s'posedta just fuck when they wanted? Wasn't that part of the gay deal?

When he got up to hit the john, the ache in his nuts made him actively queasy. *The spirit is weak but the flesh is willing.* He wrapped a hand around it and gave a careful squeeze. Too hard to piss, he thumped the head of his dick, once-twice, till the sting lowered him to half-mast.

He flushed and stepped into Andy's multihead shower, feeling trapped and exposed at the same time. His erection went nowhere in the shower, just bobbed, comical and relentless, while he fought the nausea of not knowing what came next and wishing Andy would magically appear to suck the suffering out of his aching spout... and praying he wouldn't.

The naked freedom terrified him. Intimacy with Andy felt like walking across a frozen lake. Nowhere to hide, everyone watching, and any second—*crack*—you'd plunge into the churning, choking blackness. The sense of impending doom hung over everything they did together.

He was drunk on it and knew better. He recalled the feeling from his bad old days when he'd guzzle down well drinks, wondering who'd pay the tab, who'd land the first punch, who'd toss him into traffic, who'd call the cops.

With every swallow of sweet poison, the bottle got emptier. *Drink faster.*

Ruben got out of the shower to find Andy holding a vinyl garment bag.

"Whatsamatter, Rube?" Andy's goofy grin snapped him out of the funk he was circling.

Andy wouldn't tell him where they were going, but he was definitely keyed up for some reason. He'd sent Hope home at two in the afternoon and told Ruben to tux up.

Ruben squinted at him. "The fuck are you up to, Bauer?"

Andy answered with a smile and a slow blink, like that was an answer. "Hurry up." His dimple exaggerated the filthy undertone.

Ruben unzipped the bag. "Black tie?"

"Fraternity." Andy squinted at the clothes and then at him, weighing something.

Snort. "We're going to a frat party?"

Andy laughed. "Sorta. The tuxes are kind of a joke now, but it's tradition."

Wobbly headshake. He couldn't wake up today.

Andy nodded at him appreciatively. "I say frat, but that's kinda bullshit 'cause it's coed and nothing like a frat-frat."

Ruben nodded like that meant something. All he knew about fraternities came from shitty comedies and porn: kegs and jocks and spanking. "So this is your fraternity, like from college."

"Well, technically it's a literary society, only that's a crock. Secret society, ditto. Saint A's about as secret as a boob job." Andy scowled. "These days they're trying to be a secret society like Skull & Bones."

"Sounds like moneybags bullshit to me." Ruben pulled on the pants and sat on the bed to pull on socks.

"Pretty much."

Ruben stopped. "If you can't stand them, why are we going?"

"Business. I still have three or four big clients through Saint A's." Andy dropped his gaze to the floor as if the rug was the most fascinating thing he'd ever seen.

"I have to say this, huh? This seems pretty unsafe, considering two homicidal idiots just broke in. You might recall." Ruben could hear the plea in his voice and hated it.

Andy didn't seem to care one way or another. He tossed the garment bag on the mussed bed. "Rube, it's done. I'm telling you. The whole thing has been a bluff. You scared 'em off, and they're off screwing with some other sad jerk."

Ruben sat up and scowled at that. He disagreed, obviously. Then again maybe he was hanging on to the original paranoia. "The fuck can you say that?"

"Look, there's risk. My whole job is calculating risk, but you've changed the board. Everything's different. All this time they saw me as this evil stick figure they could snap."

"If the threat is real, fucking deal with it." He was still unsure just how much Hope knew about Andy's sideline. He lowered his voice to an urgent whisper. "Don't lie to yourself. What makes you think these assholes would simply give up? In my experience—"

"In your experience people have balls. These guys don't. They got nothing. Why are you getting so upset?"

"Andy, they came into your house. They tried to take you."

"Only they didn't. Enough, okay?" Andy smiled and bumped shoulders. "¡Basta ya!"

"I'm not qualified." Ruben frowned and gripped Andy's bicep. "You need to get a team in here. I been saying this from day one."

Andy didn't reply. He just looked down at Ruben's rough fingers until they let go.

"Sorry."

"No. I appreciate it. But it's been handled." And with that Andy dropped the subject so hard it dented the floor.

For the first time, they dressed together, to go out together. It was like a date. Ruben hated himself for feeling excited, but hated Andy more for keeping him so off-balance.

Ruben took the time to reshave the sides and back of his scalp, keeping the wide mohawk clean. Mainly because he loved the way Andy traced the skin when they were alone, like he was writing music with his fingertips. Gelled into place, the haircut made the tuxedo look like a dire warning. He scowled and beamed at the mirror just to gauge the effect.

Head-to-toe, the impression was *crooked kingpin*.

Somewhere along the way, Andy had changed more than his clothes. "Jeez."

Behind him Andy entered damp and handsome in a pair of slacks, scraping his hard nipples with a towel. He bit Ruben's shoulder.

Ruben smiled absently, staring past him at their coffee-cream contrast in the mirror.

"Chop-chop, big top." Andy swatted him on the butt, and they grinned at each other like conspirators. Which they were. The grin died on Ruben's face but stayed banked and bright in his belly.

Whatever happened, whoever they met, however they made it home, they were gonna fuck tonight if it killed him. Or it actually *might* kill him. Only self-preservation. What was he waiting for, or Andy? Permission? A sign? As much as he liked the chase, he didn't want this to turn into another game. His grunting instincts demanded flesh. Nerves were one thing, but Andy lived to avoid trouble, which left them filling up on flirtation like a bag of chips.

Eying his sore boner apologetically, Ruben folded it into a pair of boxer briefs stretchy enough to keep it trapped against his belly.

He squirmed into the tux and walked stiffly back to the living room. The patio door was open.

Andy was standing on the terrace in black tie with a glass in his hand, staring over the gray city. Curdled clouds hung low, refusing to release the summer storm they held captive. All around him, the sky wanted to rain.

Ruben took advantage of the chance to spy on Andy, pausing in the open door and opening his mouth to keep his breath silent.

Silhouetted against the muzzy horizon, Andy's tuxedo and slicked hair turned him into a glossy black lever, as if with a pull Ruben could crack the sky open and release glitter onto the city.

Andy was right. Chunk and Walrus had vanished. Ruben could almost believe that the shadowy perps had tucked tail and run. He'd beaten the shit out of them, and they'd balked. Inept as he was, he'd done some good at least.

Andy took a sip and looked down at the pool below or at the street, maybe. *How does he even want me?*

Ruben exhaled in pleasure and gratitude, a near-sigh he couldn't control.

Andy heard him and turned. "Goddamn." His obvious pleasure untied some knot in Ruben's chest. "You sure clean up good, *Señor* Oso."

Ruben bobbed his head, embarrassed by the compliment, which reminded him: not only did he feel like a fraud, he was a fraud. Still, Andy's intense pleasure washed most of the anxiety away. "Good."

"Mmh." Andy shifted close to Ruben and patted his chest. "I need to make a quick call and we'll go-go-go."

"I'm gonna—I'll go down and get the car moving." Ruben grinned. He needed to sweep the town car, and he should've done it earlier instead of lying trapped under his boss in that bed. *Sleeping dogs, sleeping dogs.* "Gentlemen." He nodded at the doormen as he passed, wondering how much they suspected about his comings and goings with Andy.

The vehicle idled out in front, so he wasted no time. Hi to the driver. Tailpipe. Mirror sweep. Hood and block. *All clear.*

Just for form he flipped the interior to kill time, wishing he had come down with Andy. Together. Unsafe, but then, he wasn't just a bodyguard now, right? They were… something.

He climbed out of the Daimler and leaned against it casually, the metal hot through the tux. He'd kill for a cigarette, but then Andy would kill him. *Bad deal.* He scanned the lobby through the glass, conscious of the cameras and eyes on him, wanting to greet Andy like something other than his employer.

There. The elevators opened and spat Andy out.

He trotted anxiously out the entrance, looking like a billion dollars in crisp, new bills. Soon as he caught sight of Ruben, his face relaxed. "Sorry," he called out and nodded. "Sorry. Got stuck."

Ruben nodded and smiled back. *I gotcha, boss.* He shifted his weight off the car.

As he straightened, the world wobbled. Only Andy seemed steady and that was right too. Waiting for the driver to open the door, they stood close. Their hands brushed and their arms bumped, muscular under the black sleeves, like they needed to send a coded message in plain sight. *Morse code for lovers.* Ruben glanced up at the cameras. Part of him loved getting away with something forbidden that felt so good, knowing that no one knew. All these uptight goobers who tried and failed to sort life into boxes.

Their Israeli driver popped the doors, and they slid inside the sleek cocoon of the car as the door *choonked* shut.

Ruben stroked the leather. He loved feeling so in control and out of control in a way that scared and exhilarated him. For two seconds, he imagined a life together without price tags or plans. The two of them in black tie, going anywhere, everywhere, fucking in the Daimler, and giving the finger to the rules and the rest of the world.

I double-dog dare you.

Ten minutes later, they'd passed through the park and coasted by rows of older buildings in not-so-great shape.

"The upper Upper West Side." Andy tapped the window. "Which used to be part of Spanish Harlem."

Where Charles lives? Ruben still couldn't figure the geography out. "The hell are you taking us?"

"Columbia. Well, near-ish." Andy rolled his eyes and looked out the window as they turned uptown onto Riverside Drive. "Dancing for a disease. Well, without the dancing. This is a fundraiser at Saint Anthony's."

"The frat's in a church?" Did Andy sneak off to Mass on Sunday mornings?

Andy shook his head with a smile. "Saint A's. In the Greek system, it's technically Delta Psi, only no one calls it that. Columbia's the oldest chapter."

Whatever that meant. "Uh, great."

Andy grimaced. "Pretty awful, actually. Most people call it Saint Assholes."

Ruben chuckled.

"When you pledged Saint A's, they made you buy a first-class ticket to Hong Kong and burn it." Andy didn't look like he was joking.

"Why?"

"To prove you can afford to be a member."

Ruben shook his head. "You know some depressing folks, Bauer."

"When we were in school, everybody thought we were cokeheads. Or queer. Or racists. Or all of the above. At least it was coed."

"So you were a… frat boy." Ruben made it suggestive.

"Yeah. No! Not like that. Look, we aren't all spanking and fucking each other."

Smug smile. "So you say."

Andy shrugged and crossed his ankles. "I know a couple of the right-wingers messed around, but mostly we were all just trying to get through school and get laid without pissing off our families."

"I bet you looked nice in your blazer. Poster boy."

"Sorta. We were kids. The fuck did we know about anything?" He looked past the window at nothing. "Of course none of them knew I was an impostor. I was the only guy who had a chin."

To lighten the mood, Ruben nudged him and smiled.

The town car glided to a stop among other expensive vehicles, triple-parked on a wide street running east-west—116th according to a sign.

The driver started to get out, but Andy pressed the intercom button. "No need, Eli. Too many of these assholes to bother. Just hole up with your phone on. We'll be out in an hour."

Eli nodded and Ruben emerged onto the car-crowded street in front of what looked like a miniature bank with a balcony. The five-story building was narrow, faced with white stone below and red brick above. Scrolled carvings supported the window ledges, and up near the roof was a little triangle like a Greek temple over a medallion with letters that looked like a triangle and a trident.

"Delta Psi. And we know why." Andy climbed out of the backseat right behind him, straightening so close that his crotch brushed Ruben's backside.

Ruben moved to the side quickly while Andy eyed the façade with amusement.

Behind them, their car pulled away. On the sidewalk, a cluster of white people in formalwear drifted toward a short run of stone stairs leading to an iron and stone gate on the left. Inside, more stairs leading up to a front door. *Security? Pretension?* No one had spotted Andy or Ruben yet.

Andy whispered, "There's supposed to be a secret pool. A chef. A cleaning slave. Orgies. Hazing with a greased broomstick. "

"And...?"

Chuckle. "None of the above. Well, not exactly. There's some weirdness. Mostly it's suburban rich kids who want to party together off campus somewhere they can control the invitations." Andy led the way up through the gate and up the stairs to the entry. A chorus of "Heys" and "Bauer" rose up as he stepped into the lights, but Andy stuck to Ruben like a burr.

As they picked their way through the foyer, Andy touched his arm and leaned in noticeably, careless of Ruben's personal space. Maybe it looked like he was scolding a business partner or maybe they looked like obvious homo fuck buddies. *Hard call.* And not his to make, but it gave him a funny feeling in his gut.

Andy slid past the other guests quickly, avoiding handshakes and nodding hello until he fought his way to a parlor wall hung with awards and photos of past classes.

To Ruben, the whole crowd looked like the assholes who only flew into Florida at Christmas on their way to Nevis or St. Barths: white people with gray faces and black AmExes. Maybe they envied each other, but nobody seemed to like each other very much.

"You like these people?" Ruben eyed the black-tie crowd skeptically.

"I know them." He winked. "Not the same thing. Everything sparkles, but once you get close you notice the sparkles are rough scales."

Intellectually Ruben understood that these folks were powerful. The suits were expensive and the conversations muted. At the end of the day, all he saw was a roomful of sullen idiots busy frisking each other with their eyes. "You're supposed to come with an escort."

"I've got an escort." Andy eyed him playfully.

Ruben thought of the silent security gorillas hovering at the curtains and stealing dessert from the caterers. "You know what I mean."

Cater-waiters passed through the tuxes and cocktail dresses with booze and finger food. At the room's margins, Ruben spotted five or six bulky ex-cops in three-hundred-dollar suits… and spotted them spotting him. Logically they were here to do the same job, but Ruben was still undercover and kept pretending to himself that this was a date. Not just a job, for him.

Andy misread his confused silence. "Yeah. Exactly. Pretty dire."

Ruben muttered, "Tell me why we came to this thing again?"

"S'good for business." Andy stopped to scan the room, standing too close again. And not noticing. *Again.* "My mom wanted me to join. And my stepfucker too. Worked out fine, though."

A couple of the other well-oiled party guests had started to move in their direction.

Ruben looked up at the room. No one had noticed yet, but for both their sakes, he made some space between them. Before anything intimate had happened between them, the accidental flirtation had been odd; now it seemed like kicking a bear.

Andy didn't notice. "They have money. Most of them anyway."

"How much money?"

"What'd Onassis say? If you can count it you haven't got any." Andy surveyed the beige crowd. "When my father's parents were alive, there were only nine buildings where these people could live. Three on Park Avenue. Four on Fifth, one on Sutton Place and another at Gracie Square. That's a small genetic pool. Suitable for wading only." He kept scanning the crowd's faces.

Who is he looking for? Ruben leaned in. "All these people are members or brothers or whatever."

"Well, it's coed. And with spouses and whatnot. But they're part of our whole inbred tribe. I still pull a lot of deals out of St. Assholes."

Something in his expression made Ruben pause. "What kinda deals?"

"Ven-Cap. We're all members, so they trust me to take care of them and vice versa. My stepfucker hates it. Plus, they can all afford losses. When I have real work to do, they make great window dressing."

Ruben scowled. That sounded like more shady shit, and they both knew it.

Andy lowered his voice. "Oso, I'm not gonna start again. Apex, I mean. Not till everything blows over and we're safe. I give you my word."

Ruben sighed, wishing the hour was up. Not a date—nothing like a date, aside from Andy dressing him up and taking him out. Keeping track of Andy's schemes in public was like trying to force fifty cats to march in a parade.

Andy signaled one of the cater-waiters and ordered a Scotch. He gave Ruben a brief guilty look, which Ruben answered with an invisible nod. It wouldn't bother him, and it might keep Andy more biddable as the night wore on.

Ruben grinned and coughed; the idea of Andy with his inhibitions lowered sounded just fine. A crappy impulse, but an honest one.

Before Andy could turn back to him, a trio of middle-aged women swooped in between them to grill Andy about a museum gala he'd skipped.

Ruben tuned them out and checked his watch. Fifty-two minutes to go. This place sucked and a party it was not.

A reedy man with a snide laugh joined the group around Andy. "Marlon. Stanz," he said, making his name into two separate words. "And I know secrets about this so-and-so. Apex, my ass." He squeezed the back of Andy's neck and shook his head till Ruben wanted to break his fingers.

Two other guys drifted over, and another lady, until Andy was the jelly in a douchebag donut.

Little by little, Andy came to life in front of the whole mob, joking and charming them with his punch-me smile. Demolition by dimple. A killer in his element.

Ruben's phone buzzed in his pocket, but he purposefully did not answer. He saw that Peach had left a message, wondering why she hadn't heard from him in so long. He felt guilty, but not guilty enough to call back just this second. How would he explain what had happened without it sounding crazy and dangerous?

Ruben snagged a seltzer—"With lime, please."—and nursed it slowly. Andy got tugged toward a group on the sofa. Playing the part of colleague still, Ruben didn't stand with the other bodyguards, but he aped them. Meter's running: the goons kept an eye on their various principals and checked out the more beddable broads that drifted by.

Bored and ignored, Ruben did the same. Resting his eyes on the one or two women who didn't seem as antiseptic. A tedious half hour later, a creaky old geezer drifted by with a real bombshell on his arm. He musta been a fratboy in the 1930s. He leaned over to say something to his... wife? Mistress? A juicy woman with a meaty ass, dark hair, who sounded like she grew up listening to Yankees in art galleries. She probably could stand to lose about twenty, but she wore it well. Ruben wasn't attracted, but he checked her out of habit.

She checked him back.

And just as he looked away, Ruben caught Andy's eye. Was Andy jealous? The idea seemed bizarre.

Andy ambled toward him, trying to seem aimless but obviously intent. He'd had another drink or two, and his eyes were soft with Scotch. Reaching Ruben, he nodded hello. Ruben nodded back. Soldiers on the field.

Do I reassure him? Do I need to? Ruben consciously refused to look back at the bombshell. What was Andy doing over here when he should be working the room?

Andy swallowed. "You good?"

"Sure. You?"

"These stiffs. I dunno. Charity boards. Half these people can't even keep track of the disease they're fundraising against." He drained his glass. "I shouldn't care."

"But you do." Ruben glanced at the room again. *What are you doing over here?*

"Mmph." Andy looked back at the juicy woman. "Y'know, we could share a chick. If you wanted." Andy looked at the table, not at him.

"What?" Where had that come from?

"You might. Want to." First indication that Andy didn't have any idea what he wanted.

Ruben didn't look away, conscious that they were doing this in a crowded, hostile room. Had he been unclear? He scrunched up his scary face, superconscious of the roomful of stodges. "Why?"

"To cut loose together." Andy's bright eyes searched his. A dimpled grin, but the nerves simmered just under the surface. "I know this all looks like bullshit to you. We could go back to Jaded once we're done here. Or Marquee. Lemme take you out. Wanna? I mean, would you dig that?"

Would he? Sure, Ruben still checked out attractive women, but this thing with Andy didn't feel like anything he'd ever done in bed with anyone.

"Ruben?"

Nightclubs and strippers. Andy didn't actually, truly, seriously want to go do any of those things with Ruben, but he could offer them and they sounded like the options he gave to clients. *Tread carefully.*

"Hey." Ruben whispered forcefully. "Hey! Bauer, I am not looking for the exit here."

"No—"

Lowering his voice again, Ruben said, "Or whatever you think. I'm not like a lion in a zoo. You don't gotta throw live meat at me to keep me from jumping the fence. I'm here 'cause I wanna be. You better be here 'cause you wanna be. That's the deal."

"Okay. Sorry."

"Andy?" Ruben stood closer than he should have, but the hallway was dark and this mattered more. He glanced at the juicy chick for confirmation and back. "Are you jealous?"

"Yeah." The hushed word slipped out. "Stupid."

Ruben whispered, "C'mere, boss." He did a perimeter check; no one was paying any attention.

But instead of following, Andy let Ruben steer him from behind down the hall and past the kitchens to a small powder room. "What are we doing?"

Without answering, Ruben opened the door for him and pushed him into the dim room. He followed and closed the door without turning on the light. A green night-light above the sink made more shadows than anything. "Mr. Bauer, you have something on your jacket."

"Wha—?"

"Me." Pressing close, Ruben kissed him and pushed his tongue inside the surprised mouth. He ignored the tang of secondhand whiskey.

Andy backed into the tiled wall and grunted. His square face looked open, exposed, blind with some raw hunger he couldn't control.

Addiction. Subtraction.

After another moment, Ruben pulled back. "We clear?"

Andy nodded. "I love that." His lips were wet and his bowtie crooked.

Ruben straightened it and stroked his chest through the pleated shirt.

"You're a gentleman, but you're not gentle." Andy gave him a soft peck on the corner of his mouth.

Thank God for adrenaline. *Enabling rash impulses since the dawn of opposable thumbs.* Historically, the exact same caveman routine had gotten Ruben in plenty of trouble, but this was a unique situation. "I'm not interested in anyone or anything else. Dig?"

"Yes, sir." Andy squeezed his half-hard junk, milking it lightly through the pants and breathing hard. "I sure do."

Ruben hesitated. He'd only wanted to reassure Andy, not fuck in a frathouse bathroom.

Party sounds outside the door. The danger of getting caught, the fact that his boss, a man, was kneading his dick, gave him a freaky charge. His heart stuttered between them, and he tried to control the slow panting with tactical breathing as if he was in danger.

He *was* in danger.

Andy unzipped Ruben's pants and fumbled his big hand inside.

Ruben muttered, "No. Easy. Hey. *Hsssst.*"

Now? Here?

Andy gripped his cock and tugged, once, twice, and then an easy, lazy jerk that stood his hair on end.

Ruben batted his hands away and closed his trousers. "Stop. Now. Stop that, man. I'm gonna go back out there. You gimme ten seconds before you come out to schmooze. We'll finish this later." Stepping back he adjusted his arced bulge so that it lay at a less conspicuous angle. "Jesus."

"Amen." Andy snickered behind him as the door closed.

Ruben gave himself thirty heartbeats of measured inhale-exhale before he ventured back into combat. He stayed at a fifteen-foot perimeter, just close enough to monitor Andy's safety. *His job.* Giving the bar and any single ladies a wide berth, he stuck to the walls with the other goons and watched Andy glad-hand the whole room, passing out compliments and business cards in all directions.

Horny and off-kilter, Ruben tried to put the pieces together in his head.

Andy wanted to get caught, loved being watched. Shocking the prudes felt perfect because he felt like an impostor. *Clan of the Cave Bear.* What had he said? Caveman with an AmEx.

Ruben was thrilled to stay a dirty secret because he wasn't in any hurry to explain shit to his brother, but still a niggling doubt chewed at him. Dirty secrets got scrubbed away.

He shook his head at no one, feeling stupid and smart both. Andy's games put them in all kinds of danger, and somehow Ruben's emotions had made him an accomplice, roped him into riding shotgun next to a self-confessed sociopath with an exhibitionistic streak.

Without thinking his eyes met Andy's directly, scorching the air.

Andy crooked a lazy grin at him. Fellow conspirators. The batshit part of Ruben liked having a shared secret at this party full of stiffs who stood around comparing labels and pedigrees. Squillions of dollars and no sense.

"Marlon. Stanz." held court near Ruben, telling a long, gossipy anecdote about his daughter's boarding school and Andy's mother that made the listeners nod and scan the room for an escape hatch. He certainly didn't mind pissing people off, this Marlon person who groped everyone like a pimp.

Around quarter to ten, Ruben got stuck behind two women arguing about whether daffodils have a scent and something called deadheading. He avoided their eyes and tried to sneak back to Andy's perimeter.

Every so often assholes would actually flirt back at Andy, try to sidle up to him to fuck or fleece him, but Ruben realized he didn't care and had no fear. Nothing would get through him. He wasn't jealous, even, or nervous. Nobody was gonna replace him. Whoever tried could never need Andy the same way, never protect him, never reach him the way Ruben did and always would.

Bad. This is bad, man.

Sure enough, at 9:59, Andy appeared beside him and hooked an arm over his shoulders. *Bros.* "Let's blow, man." He said the words right into Ruben's ear, lips brushing.

Ruben swallowed, nodded, and hooked it before his boner could make an appearance. He led the way out the door and down the stairs clearing a path with his bull's-eye scowl. It was raining outside.

Andy kept mum at least and followed close behind, until he actually put his hands on Ruben's shoulder and trailed him like a tipsy horse-drawn carriage all the way back to the car and the curb.

Ruben's boner crested into an obscene mound right as they hit the street. "Let's go, boss."

Gross people, shit party, but if nothing else, all that oblivious attention inside his fraternity had pushed Andy to his absolute limit. He couldn't get at Ruben fast enough, and the frantic lust knew no boundaries.

Their car pulled up, and Andy pressed against him from behind, breath on his nape, and reached around to open the door. *Help.* His erection notched into the hollow of Ruben's flexed buttock. Right in the street, under the lamps.

A cough: Marlon Stanz on the steps like a sentry, watching them leave with dead alligator eyes. He gave a little jerky salute that Ruben ignored until Marlon turned to go back inside. What had he seen?

As the door swung open, Ruben decided to *forget* to grid check the Daimler before they left. Gossip worried him, and Stanz catching them, but Andy was right; there was no danger anymore. At least, not from outside.

Lazy? Stupid? Sure. But fucking impossible when he was about to dump his sauce in a three-thousand-dollar tux in front of a fancy frathouse.

Inside the town car, Andy put up the partition immediately. His erection filled a fold at the crotch of his tux.

"Wait a sec. Huh? Andy, one second."

He grabbed Ruben's cock and kneaded it.

"Agh. Easy, man." His cockhead bulged sticky inside his briefs. He could feel the slick crackle as his foreskin slid back. "What if someone saw us?"

"I don't care. Let me have it." Andy had never come at him so directly.

"Jesus." He glanced front at the privacy partition.

Andy pulled at his shirt.

"Easy."

Studs popped and scattered across the car's upholstery.

Irritated and horny, Ruben pulled their chests together, scrubbing his skin against Andy's clothes. *Nothing else matters.*

Andy slid to the floor of the limo. His exhibitionistic streak continued, but at least this wouldn't get them arrested. Pray God the chauffeur wasn't eavesdropping on the intercom.

"C'mon."

Eyes on Ruben's, Andy fumbled at the belt and unbuckled it. He pressed his lips against Ruben and unzipped the fly. He pushed his hand inside, putting sharp pressure on Ruben's confined balls.

"Ow. Hey." Ruben pulled back.

"Sorry. Sorry." Andy kissed his navel lightly and ran a finger under the elastic at Ruben's waist. "So fuckin' thick." His thumb scraped across Ruben's juicy crown. "So fuckin' wet." His fingertip dragged through stickiness.

Ruben gripped himself and squeezed to expose the head completely. The musky scent of crotch and precum filled the backseat. Honey dribbled over his spread fly.

Andy grunted. "Don't waste it. Don't jerk it."

If you insist. Ruben cocked his head. "I got any say in this?"

"No." Andy grinned. "This is strictly between me and your cock." He dropped his clean-cut face into Ruben's lap, pressing his face against Ruben's upper thigh. He angled the boner toward him and kissed the wet end. "Sweet."

A fluttery pride settled over Ruben's ribcage. He'd never been wanted like this, even with chicks. He'd never felt this kind of danger and chemistry. "You're crazy," he whispered with tenderness.

"I know." Andy licked the precum. "Nuts." Licked those too.

He took a handful of Andy's thick hair and shook his skull.

Andy closed his eyes and took a deep breath at Ruben's skin. "You did something to me."

"Andy." They were pulling up to the Iris, and Ruben's pants were down. "Stop. Andy!" He raised his ass to pull up his pants and buckle them shut.

Andy blinked and squinted, swaying on his knees. "Sorry."

"No. I'm sorry. We just don't want anyone—"

And then the door opened. The young driver held the door while they clambered out into harder rain.

Andy draped an arm over Ruben's shoulders. He saluted the underwear-model doormen but didn't pause. "Boys." The smile skittered over his dimple like a dare.

Ruben didn't bother to close his shirt, but held the jacket closed all the way to the elevator. "You're nuts," he whispered out of the side of his mouth.

"Your nuts." And Andy took hold of them, before the elevator had even closed.

Ruben jabbed at the PH button and braced himself in the corner. "Cameras."

"I don't care." Andy pressed against him, rubbing his face under Ruben's jaw and grinding their boners together. "I wish we coulda fucked in the middle of Saint Anthony's. In front of all the stale pale males." He grinned.

"You don't mean that."

"Hunnerd percent. Hell, they wish they could even see how you look right now." He licked Ruben's stiff nipple and sucked it hard. "Spoiled."

"If I am, it's your fault."

The door opened right as Andy shook his head no or yes. "You do something t'me." He stepped into the penthouse and headed outside without pause, right into the storm. "Rain's done."

"No, it's not!" Ruben called after him. "Stop. You're soaked."

Staccato rain on the terrace, the sheets of water pelting the tiles hot as fresh blood. Night or not, the sky had gone dim gray as if the clouds wouldn't let go of the lightning.

Andy went and he followed. The drops fell so hard they bounced off their shoulders and soaked the jackets.

Andy mouthed his throat, sending small spikes of ticklish electricity through Ruben. He lipped Ruben's ear, breathing hard and wet with the rain.

"You hungry, boss?" Ruben ran a dark hand over Andy's head and then tipped the panting face up so he could see.

"Not your boss." Another kiss. Andy's mouth tasted sweet and pulpy as a split mango.

"You tell me what to do."

Andy's reply was hoarse. "Yeah. But you don't listen."

"Mmph." Ruben wheezed a laugh as he fumbled with buttons. "Only when you're being stupid."

Slow rain pelted and crept between their pressed bodies. Ruben sighed and his eyes drifted shut.

The summer storm churned in the sky around them. Humidity made it even harder to breathe and the air glittered. The rain made silvery halos around the street lamps.

Ruben exhaled, dizzy and impatient. "Rain's making me sweat."

"I know. Feels great." Andy dropped his head forward and let the wetness run from his floppy hair onto Ruben's legs.

Ruben ran a rough hand over the wet jacket and wide shoulders.

Andy rocked his head to one side so he could look up. "You have a fatty." He squeezed it, but let his hand drop. "Fucking crowbar."

Their faces slid together, and it took Ruben a moment to realize that, rather than relenting, the downpour had broken loose in earnest. "Clothes."

Andy shook his head lazily. His hands cupped the side of Ruben's face and brushed their mouths together. "If you're worried, take 'em off. About them, I do not care." He ran a slick arm behind his back and squeezed their tuxedoed torsos together. Pulling the collar back, he bit and sucked at Ruben's shoulder. "S'just money."

Ruben yanked the shirttails out of his pants and tugged at the belt buckle.

A low grind of thunder cracked the sky. Bowling in heaven. If there was lightning in answer he didn't see it. Instead, the glowing clouds seemed to devour the city's light and noise, leaving the terrace dark and muffled. They had to find each other by feel.

Blind.

"Jesus." Ruben's breath labored in his chest. *Finally, finally.* What did clothes or water matter?

Coming together like this outdoors felt natural, inevitable. Not two men but starving animals in the hot scarves of water falling from the sky.

Andy panted. "I don't care. I don't care." Water ran from his open lips and dripped from his chin. His tiny nipples showed through the transparent undershirt. "I don't care."

Ruben swallowed hard. Andy's frank hunger made him feel invincible. The rain began to pelt them, and Ruben didn't budge. Clumsy hands as he popped the buttons to get the shirt open. Everything soaking wet and translucent. He unzipped the dripping trousers that clung to his legs.

The clouds swelled with hidden lightning but it refused to strike.

"I don't care. I don't care." Andy whispered and rubbed his face against Ruben's chest and throat. He peeled Ruben's sopping shirt back. The wet cling felt as though Andy were skinning him to get at the pleasure hidden inside. "I don't care."

Liar.

Ruben stopped struggling and clasped Andy's head roughly. He tipped it for a better angle to suck at the glossy lower lip. "I'm right here. Huh?"

"You are. Thank God."

Ruben blinked the water out of his eyes, panting and squirming under the assault on his nerves. His nipples were hard. His clothes made slurping noises as his movements pulled them away from his flesh. He shrugged out of the jacket finally and let it fall to the ground.

Andy wiped his face and ran a hand over Ruben's chest. "Fuck."

The water slid over them both, lukewarm and sluggish. Ruben groaned and let Andy control his movements.

No two women screwed the same, but this was something else entirely. A different set of possible intersections. What scared him most was that the difference felt sexy, exciting, irrevocable. He was learning a new language that opened scary doors in him.

Ruben licked the inside of Andy's mouth and gave himself up to the hypnotic intensity.

Andy sagged close. "I don't care."

I do. Jesus, but I do. Ruben blinked the drops out of his lashes and tipped his head back so the rain could pelt his face.

Andy sank to his knees. His tux was soaked shiny and the hair plastered to his skull. When he looked up, his soft eyes seemed huge.

Ruben looked down. "You want that big thing?" His erection made a wide ridge under the zipper. Not fully stiff yet, but firm, fat, and about two licks away from urgency.

Blink. Eyes half-lidded, Andy leaned forward, open mouthed and grunting, to rub against Ruben's concealed meat as if marking it with scent or memorizing it with his face. Andy fumbled at his own waistband and pushed his trousers open. His pubes showed dark and dick pale through his boxers.

"Smartass." Ruben pulled him to his feet roughly. Holding Andy's arm high, he licked up the ribcage and into the armpit, chewing and sucking until Andy fought free.

He panted in the sultry soggy air, so close to the clouds that they muffled the city below. All he could hear was the sounds they made against each other.

More determined now, Andy pushed his fingers under Ruben's balls to rub at his taint then further back to stroke the hidden opening.

Ruben sighed raggedly but didn't fight it. For once he didn't tighten up, didn't flinch. He hooked a leg around Andy's and grunted. The hot slip of the water made everything hypnotic, unreal. What did it matter who put what where while they melted together in the summer rain?

Sensitive, his skin was, and Andy knew exactly how to tease the little muscle and coax the nerves awake. Back-forth, back-forth, Andy rubbed across the little muscle and sucked at Ruben's mouth as if he owned it.

"Go." Ruben tipped his hips and pushed down on the tip. His only fear was that giving in would make him seem weak and wreck Andy's illusions about him. "Do it."

Andy leaned back to peer through the wet dark. Ruben nodded. Permission had nothing to do with it. He wanted to cross that line more than Andy did.

Andy groaned and sank one thick digit into Ruben. The rain didn't make it much easier.

Ruben didn't fight the freaky burn and tried to focus on Andy's filthy muttering and the dizzying sense of being violated by someone as ruthless and ruined as him. Suddenly Andy passed over something that splintered his senses. "Oh. Oh fuck." He kissed Andy hard, grunting with the freaky pleasure and trying to catch it again. Their chests slid and scrubbed together.

Andy mumbled and ground his cock into Ruben's leg. Obviously he wanted inside, and Ruben felt guilty for not giving in. Duh. He was a guy.

That must be part of the deal with two guys, who put what where. He set aside his nerves and tried to get the finger to hit that place again.

Ruben gave a hoarse yelp and shuddered, bracing his hands on the warm wet marble of Andy's pectorals. *A man. He's a man.*

Andy was seducing him, manhandling him, dismantling him, and he was doing the same right back. For once in his life, Ruben wasn't in control, and the thought made him feel drunk in the best way.

Never in his life had he made love so recklessly, reaching into someone while they reached back into him. This wasn't getting off, but getting *in* or getting *to* each other. A gleaming bridge over acid and alligators. Their bodies knotted together surely, but something else besides: a terrible, bright knowing that made him feel broken and mended at the same moment.

I never knew.

Maybe they really could have anything. All they had to do was want it together, build it together one kiss at a time. That seemed right, natural, obvious. Give and take with nobody keeping an account.

He opened his mouth and stuck out his tongue in undisguised enjoyment. "Filthy fucker."

Andy nodded.

Ruben raised a hand and wiped the wetness off Andy's brow, pushing his hair back and cupping the back of his skull. "Wanna go inside?"

Andy relaxed into the grip and let him hold the weight, rolling his neck lazily. He whispered, "I don't care." Then his mouth closed over Ruben's entire ear, tongue-swabbing it with a seashell roar that made Ruben's heart climb into his throat.

"Ah. *Ah!* Ugh-fuck." His legs shook and he stopped seeing anything.

Andy chewed the lobe lightly and asked, "Yeah?"

"Jerk."

Andy grinned and whispered in his ear. "I've been paying attention. See?" He licked Ruben's lobe and tugged gently at it with his teeth.

Ruben choked and his legs buckled. He would've fallen to his knees, but Andy caught his elbows and lowered them both to the terrace tile.

Their smooth sinew flexed in tandem. He'd known Andy was strong, but not what it would feel like to be strong *with* him.

Ruben had expected sex, but this had turned into something scarier. Andy seemed to be investigating his entire body, almost ignoring his naughty bits in favor of his vulnerabilities.

Both naked under the flashing sky, hot rain sliding over them and their erections jousting between them. *Finally.* They'd made it here at last.

"I don't care." Andy whispered and blinked close, his eyes colorless in the dark. Unaccountably, he laced their hands together and held their mutual fists at his flexing hips. Their knotted knuckles grazed Andy's perfect, perfect ass.

Ruben panted and leaned their foreheads together while the rain slid down their faces. "You're crazy."

Andy nodded, watching his eyes.

"We both are." He smiled.

A kiss. "I hope so."

CHAPTER FOURTEEN

CRAFT LOVES clothes but truth lives naked.

They jostled and laughed their way back inside. Andy led the way to his dark room upstairs, woozy and wild, shivering in the air conditioning. Ruben grabbed a towel and made Andy stand while he dried them both.

Andy sighed. "Rough."

"Too rough?"

Andy shook his head. The room was lit only by the sallow glow from the terrace and the lightning glow in the clouds.

"Better?"

"So much. C'mere man." Andy wrapped his hand around Ruben's cock and tugged.

Ruben's breath caught. "Uh huh." He pushed Andy, knocking him onto the bed. Andy rolled onto his belly to crawl toward the pillows, but Ruben held his legs and pinned him down. "Where d'you think you're going? No escape."

Andy grunted. Squirming under Ruben's weight, he ground his erection into the mattress. He bent his knee to give Ruben access. "You're spoiling me."

Ruben kneaded the muscle, and Andy's thighs tightened under his hands.

In some way, making love in shadow felt like a dream. Honesty for ostriches.

Ruben opened his jaws and bit down on Andy's inner thigh. He tapped Andy's butthole with his thumb. The tight knot of muscle was hot and dry.

"Yeah. Yeah." Andy started to lift up. His balls, draped over the cock, pushed back between his legs under Ruben's mouth and the drizzle of saliva.

God help me, I want to.

As Andy got harder, his taint rose to a hard mound. A trail of faint fuzz led beneath.

Ruben reached under Andy and pulled his stiffening cock back. If his flattened boner got too uncomfortable, Andy could push up on all fours, which sounded just fine as far as he was concerned.

Andy's swollen cockhead had darkened with the trapped pressure. A dot of precum the size of a quarter marked the sheets.

In the dark Ruben could just make out Andy's body against the white bed. Hiding? Begging? Sure. Not being able to see clearly made it easier for both of them.

If no one saw him steal his pleasure, was he a thief?

Without thinking, before he could stop the impulse, Ruben ducked and licked the underside of the firm helmet, long and slow. The raw salty-sweet taste exploded in his mouth. His nose nudged Andy's hot nutsack.

Andy whisper-laughed. His arms were folded and drawn up under his chest. His face lifted a moment, but he said nothing. He looked nervous as hell. A tic flickered across his clamped jawline.

Ruben still tasted brine on his lips. He wanted more but didn't have the guts to actually suck Andy's dick. *Yet.* At least he could admit that Andy's frank horniness turned him on.

He dug his rough chin into Andy's trench.

Andy hissed and arched his back, lifting them both off the sheet until his knees were under him. Freed, his cock sprang forward and smacked his stomach.

Ruben kissed one smooth cheek and raised his head. "Too much?"

A little headshake. Andy's eyes looked wet. He was panting through an open loose mouth. "Nuhh."

Ruben circled the swollen cock and balls, letting them slide over his palm, then spread Andy's butt to expose the trench. Curious, he pressed the tight opening with his thumb.

"Hsss." Andy jerked. "I don't know if I'm—"

Ruben kneaded the muscular ass and dragged his cheek down the back of Andy's thick thigh, scraping the light skin. When he reached the swell of muscle behind his knee he dug in with his chin.

"Oh muh—"Andy's voice was choked. "What are you doing down there?"

"Why?" Ruben lifted up and licked the slight rise, then sucked at the skin. His stubble scraped Andy's inner thighs.

I wanna taste him.

It was only polite. He'd eaten ladies out since he was in eighth grade. As his brother always said, "Fastest way to pick the softest lock." He didn't see that much difference, a couple inches down. His rough hands spread the cheeks, exposing the tiny opening hidden there.

Before he could think it through or psych himself out, Ruben dragged his tongue up the smooth trench, across the tiny hole.

"*Whhuuh!*" Back arching, Andy choked and barked at the same time. "Ruben?"

"I can't stop it." He gave a low chuckle. "I tried to contain myself but I escaped."

"*Hffft. Muh*—Hang on. You're gonna make me—Easy! What the hell, Ruben?" Andy flipped onto his back and he tried to sit up. His forearms dropped across Ruben's skull, and then he twisted away. A low light clicked on.

"Don't." Ruben squeezed his arm and stroked the golden fluff there.

Andy turned back to him. "I wanna see. Let me see you."

Ruben shook his head. "I don't need it. I can see you without it. I see you everywhere, anyway."

In the dark, his eyes couldn't deceive him.

A wet, open-mouthed kiss and Ruben turned the lights off again, blinded by the blackness till his eyes adjusted again.

In the dark they were the same color.

"I can see you now. Leave 'em off. Let me see you like this." Ruben ran rough hands over the smooth skin, kneading and tugging and mapping Andy's creamy muscle in the shadows.

In the dark, he could trust his instincts and his emotions.

Naked together in those crazy sheets, they finally met each other without any walls or hiding places left.

Andy slid down his body, rubbing his face against Ruben like an animal marking territory. After drying off, his fresh-baked scent was faint. "Can I suck it?"

"You can—" Ruben's voice came out broken and husky. "You can do anything you want to me," he said and hoped that was true.

Without any preamble, Andy pulled his hard dick forward and then closed his mouth on the end.

Not questioning the impulse, Ruben found his fingers scratching Andy's scalp quickly.... *Good boss.*

Andy groaned and choked on the intruder.

Ruben reached down, running his fingers over Andy's face and square jaw, tracing them lightly as Andy gagged and slobbered over Ruben's meat. *Eat that dick.*

Gradually, Ruben's foreskin worked itself back without any help from Andy. The stiffness and the wet pressure gripping him allowed the silky membrane to retract gradually and naturally until his square knob drilled into Andy's throat.

Andy choked. "Sorry." He coughed and wiped his wet mouth. His predatory hunger had taken a new form.

"I'm sorry. I shouldn't be so rough."

Apparently Andy disagreed. He pushed himself back down onto Ruben's hardness until he coughed and choked again.

"Careful, man. I'm not really built for that." Ruben shrugged. "Wide and flat. Foreskin's sensitive. When I was a kid, someone at the beach called me a dogdick because of it. I popped him in the eye, and he never did it again. After that I always kept it skinned back behind the head in the locker room."

Andy did just that. Pulling it at an angle that felt strange and rough.

Ruben's cock didn't mind at all.

Andy milked it again, forcing a blob of moisture out and then smearing it onto the head with his thumb.

Ruben grunted.

"Too much."

Headshake. "Nowhere near."

Andy milked the dark foreskin again, obviously fascinated by the way it hugged the hardness. Another drop of precum. He swiped it with his thumb, brought it to his mouth, and sucked the drop off with an impish grin.

"Ungh." Ruben shook his head at the sight of Andy enjoying his juice so openly. "There's more. Plenty."

"I bet." Andy squeezed Ruben's erection and licked underneath again, tasting it.

Easier in the dark, definitely. *Baby steps.*

He rocked back and dropped his head toward Andy's knees. He reached for Andy's boner and let it slip easily between his fingers, petting the stiffness and polishing the cap. "Gimme a sec." Not committing, but getting a handle on things.

Andy groaned and sucked the head of his cock back into his mouth.

Ruben bent and licked the underside as he had before, using his tongue to dig for that salty tang, then closing his mouth over it.

Andy sat up. "Teeth, man."

"Sorry." *Learning curve.* He opened his mouth wide and let Andy sink into his face. Exactly what it felt like. Andy pushing inside of him until it punched something in his throat that made him cough. He pulled off and satisfied himself with long, wet licks that made Andy's dick stiffen and jerk in his fist. Andy's fresh scent was strongest here.

Down below, Andy was sucking hard at him, letting Ruben's knob soak until it choked him.

Ruben sucked on Andy's sack gently. And licked the satiny slope of his thighs again until they fell open. Taking two handfuls of Andy's backside, he pressed closer. Ruben rolled his face against Andy's buttery muscle, pushing down past the thigh to the crack beyond, smearing his own saliva across his cheek.

Ruben's breath hitched in his throat, and his hands shook with undirected tension. That strange smoothness in Andy's flesh was making him crazy, making him frantic.

Andy whimpered and gagged and then pulled off his dick entirely. "Aw, Ruben…." he whispered. His hard shaft throbbed and bumped damp against Ruben's collarbone.

But Ruben had no intention of stopping. He drilled into the slick iris and chewed at the surrounding skin, pulling it wider with his fingers. He massaged the heavy hamstrings and that meaty, perfect jock ass with his hands, gripping and squeezing the glutes hard enough to leave marks while his mouth made mush out of Andy's hole.

"Ruben… Rube! *Ohmyfuck—*"

Ruben's tongue slipped inside, right inside, and Andy arched hard, rising up onto his knees with a surprised yelp. "Ruh—!"

"'Cause you're dirtier than I am, aren't you?" Ruben grunted and licked again, a fat swipe of his tongue over Andy's taint. "All your apple-pie crap is for show. Fucking frat. Black-tie bullshit."

Andy grunted.

"You're a fucking pig. Right? Beautiful pig." Ruben inhaled his scent and bit at his thigh. Reaching for the lube, he pumped too much into his hand and worked it inside, one silky fingerful at a time. He fed grease into Andy's entrance, then smeared the extra across his crown. Part of him wanted to turn on the lights so he could see, but the other part of him had no trouble staying hidden, out of sight and going out of his mind.

A low chuckle drifted down to him. "Busted."

Andy didn't feel anything like a woman. Everything about him seemed male, from the swells of muscle to the faint hairs dusting them to the square hands that clutched at Ruben with a serious grip. Just 'cause men and women shared some bits, a dude was simply a different animal. Even sprawled on his back, Andy exuded strength. He'd submitted to Ruben's lust by choice. Somehow a coiled danger snaked between them. Not violence, but the real possibility of being overpowered, of rules broken. Scary and exhilarating.

"C'mon, fucker."

Ruben panted and laughed. "Yeah?" For once in his life he didn't have to curb his desire or his roughness. Andy could take it. Andy could take anything he could dish out and wanted to give it right back. Both of them strong enough for anything.

Andy growled and arched his back, riding Ruben's erection with his own.

Ruben's grip left wide handprints on Andy's flawless skin. Was he being too rough?

Andy clawed at him, mashing their torsos together and scraping his fuzz against Ruben's chest hard enough to leave a mark.

Apparently not.

Andy shuddered and grinned. Apparently barbarian sex suited him just fine. The push-pull of rough fucking didn't scare him in the least. He was as strong as Ruben.

Without thinking he swatted at Andy's face and laughed. Andy laughed back and arched up, expanding his ribs, as he closed his mouth over Ruben's ear.

Ruben froze. The sloshy suction, the seashell roar of Andy licking at him there, deprived him of his senses, and he stopped worrying about anyone getting hurt. Something inside him gave way, a restraint he'd never acknowledged during sex. Andy took anything he could dish out and more. Ruben had been with kinky women, rough women, crazy women, always holding back.

Andy ground back harder and shivered under his hand. Anyone who said that fucking a guy was the same as a chick obviously spoke from zero experience. A man was something else entirely.

"Give it up." Ruben pushed inside.

Andy's eyes widened sharply, then relaxed as the width breached him.

Ruben paused, then asked a question with his eyes that Andy answered with a positive grunt and a nod. "Let me stick my fat dick in you, huh?"

Another inch. Ruben ran a hand over those small nipples, so different than a woman's. He kept watching Andy's face, trying to gauge his reactions.

Andy squirmed his hips closer and his stomach tightened. "*Yuh.*"

He pushed inexorably into the spit-wet constriction. "I don't wanna hurt you."

"No. Shh." Andy licked his lips and gasped again. "You won't. Agh!"

"Hold on." Ruben blinked.

"No. It's not hurt. It's... I dunno. Weird. Hard. Great." His greasy boner had softened.

Ruben worked a little further inside the greasy muscle, inch by punishing inch. "Don't fight me. Give all that up." He'd never felt anything so tight around his cock. "You want all of it." Telling, not asking.

Andy swallowed and opened his mouth wide to gasp. "Go. Go." His skin had gone slippery with sweat. He panted and stretched his mouth wide at something happening inside of him. "Jesus, are you in there. Oh Rube. Fuck." His eyes glittered with tears.

Ruben nodded. Planted deep, his cock felt as if it had been welded into place. "One sec." Uncontrollably, his hips drove a millimeter deeper.

"Agh." Andy smiled. "You okay?"

Ruben nodded again. "Scared."

"Don't be. Huh?" Andy ran his hands over Ruben's face, touching him carefully. "Try me. Do it."

Ruben braced his hands against the underside of Andy's hamstrings and slid out a bit. Gingerly he pushed back.

Andy grunted and nodded encouragement. "Yuh."

Ruben pulled out a little further and slid back home.

"Unph." Andy's eyes rolled back. "Again." Spit shone on his cheek.

Braver, Ruben slid his thickness about halfway out and then drilled it straight back inside, mashing his pubic bone close until their hips socketed together.

Andy smiled. "You see?"

Ruben repeated the stroke, *in-out*, then held again.

"C'mon." Andy clawed at his back, but even the scratches felt delicious, marking him as Andy's property. Stud bull.

Ruben curled closer to him, rubbing their rough faces together, and skewered him again. *In-out.* He cupped Andy against his chest. "Good?"

A sigh. "Ungh. That." Andy hunched back and grappled with him. He muttered something inaudible.

Ruben pulled back a mite and then bent his knees for a better angle to cram his full fat length into the strangling heat. "You're taking my dick so good." Anyone who said assfucking was unnatural obviously hadn't done it.

Andy panted and his ass squeezed the full thick length. His fingers stroked at Ruben's tight, hairy sack and then snuck around most of his broad back to pull them closer together.

"I'm finally fucking you. God." They fit together like something broken and mended.

"I know. *Grah*. You're nailing me, man." Andy flexed and bucked under his churning hips. "The hell?" His cock regained a lazy stiffness. His lanky muscles bunched, and his breath became a low rumble. His floppy hair was a sweaty tangle, and his stubble tickled Ruben's unshaven throat. Hair and spit and a lazy power always on the verge of breaking loose.

"Yeah, man. Yeah." Andy urged and nodded, then nodded again and licked his lips feverishly. "Yeah."

Ruben held his breath. "Look at me. Don't look away." A soft, salty kiss while his hips hammered relentlessly.

Andy squinted but did exactly that, staring back with a hazy, rolling pleasure that melted Ruben. He whispered under his breath and rocked his head drunkenly.

Ruben leaned forward to hear Andy's mumbling litany… something in Spanish. He pressed his thumb to the corner of Andy's stretched lips.

Andy turned his head and sucked the wide pad into his mouth.

Ruben's erection stiffened into a brutal spike. Point of no return if he didn't get a hold of himself. How long had they been fucking? Already his balls ached and his skin prickled with blind appetite. He needed to cool off before he lost control. He wanted to make it good for Andy, to take Andy all the way over the edge before he got his. Pride? Fear? Before the warning flashes could trip his trigger, he pulled himself free and sat back on his heels. His erection bobbed damp and dark between them.

"Yeah? You like my big thing busting you open?" Playing for time, Ruben tucked his finger into the greasy slot. The light fuzz was smeared with lube and the hole loose to the touch. He'd fucked it wide open and feeling the proof made his dick ache. Without asking permission he lunged forward and drove his full length back into Andy hard enough to make them both call out.

Andy's half-lidded eyes looked stunned and stupid, drunk on whatever raunchy miracle was happening inside of him.

"That good? Filthy fucker. You can't stop me."

Andy's voice shook with the pounding. "Duh-on't wanna." He gasped, and his eyes flashed with fear, but he looked plenty pleased with the prospect.

"Stuck. You're not going any-fucking-where." He chewed on Andy's wet hair and sucked the tangy sweat out of it. "Right where you are, you belong."

Andy's cock slid against his belly and hip, occasionally squashed by the collisions. His blue-gray eyes barely open, his pink tongue licking and licking again nervously at his lips.

"Nailed down. Huh?"

Andy nodded. "Juh." His eyes shut, and his mouth opened to gasp at some sensation. He winced and panted.

Ruben's hard thrusts punctuated the words. "You corrupted me. And now you gotta take. Every fucking inch."

Andy nodded slightly. His mouth was open and drool fell from his lips to the sheet.

Ruben wanted to mark him, paint him with scent and seed. *Pintón.* "I'm gonna put all my sauce right in you."

Andy nodded.

"All my fucking juice. In there, man."

Andy reached down and felt the junction where the meat went into him. "Jesus." His eyes got wide.

Ruben fell forward over Andy and scrubbed their sweaty chests together, drilling into him with ruthless precision.

"Jesus, Ruben. You're gonna make me go just like that."

Ruben nodded, his own climax boiling inside him. "Wanna wait."

"No. No, man. I can't." Andy's light eyes were wide and feverish. His boner rode the ridge under Ruben's navel, hunching against the slick, furry abs.

Too good. Too soon. But Ruben couldn't even pull all the way out. He snaked one arm around Andy's back and pulled him closer for better leverage.

At that, Andy's heels hooked behind him at the small of his back and raw instinct took over. The clutching, sucking heat bloomed around his hardness and Andy's lips and teeth tugged at his earlobe till Ruben thought he'd lose his mind.

"Do it. Do it." Andy whispered into his ear. "*Dame tu leche.*" Whatever it meant sounded filthy on Andy's lips.

"*Rnngh-mmph!*" Before he could stop himself, he roared in relief and his orgasm exploded out of him in a glittering river. His hips pushed hard against Andy's, and his arm squeezed the firm, slippery flesh against him while his pleasure crashed over them both and sloshed to a stop.

Andy chuckled, a low, whispery sound of genuine amusement. "Well, alright then."

"You didn't cum?" Ruben frowned, embarrassed at his short fuse. "Oh man."

Andy looked sheepish. "Only 'cause I was hanging on for dear life." He milked his erection again and dragged the head across Ruben's pubes. "Fuck."

He took hold of Andy's erection and gave it a stroke. "What can I do?" Ruben started to soften and moved to pull free.

Andy grabbed at his elbow. "Wait."

Ruben stopped.

Andy didn't. "Don't move. Can you leave it inside?" He sounded shy now, as if embarrassed by his own request.

Ruben nodded and left his spongy dick half-in, half-out of the tight warmth.

Squinting, Andy tightened his grip on Ruben's arms and pushed his hips back, driving himself onto Ruben's erect flesh. When he touched bottom, he closed his eyes and fell back against the wadded pillows. Under Ruben's clenched hand, Andy's heart slowed, slowed, and his ass clenched a few times around Ruben's softening erection.

Ruben flinched at the squirmy bliss of it, and in the milking pressure his semiboner didn't fade.

Andy licked his lips and opened his light eyes. He grinned and his ass clamped down again.

"Hey!"

"Too much?"

Ruben nodded, then shook his head. "Dunno. Ticklish."

"Hang on. *Unnph.*" His butt flexed again. "I can feel you in there."

Ruben chuckled and raised his eyebrows.

"No. Fuck you." Andy softened. "I mean. It feels good having all of you pressed inside."

Ruben raised an eyebrow. "For real?"

"Prostate." Andy exhaled and ground down with his hips. "Among other things." Smile.

Ruben grunted and squeezed his ribcage. His boner pulsed. He gave an experimental thrust.

"Jesus, man. Can you go again?"

"I dunno. Probably." For whatever reason, not jerking off or big nuts, Ruben could usually go twice without a break. He had no interest in pulling away, but wasn't sure how much Andy actually wanted.

Andy wriggled, working his way up toward the headboard, and his muscles milked Ruben hard.

Ruben flinched. "Hssst! Easy!" His cock rested half-inside.

Andy smiled lazily, and then his eyes widened in surprise when Ruben didn't slide free. "Fuck."

Ruben pressed back into the heat of his own semen. Andy's ass had stopped fighting him and, without permission or doubt, Ruben began to thrust again into the scorching wetness, tapping and then hammering at the walls of another climax. Just like that, he could feel how possible it was.

Andy's eyes widened in fear or disbelief. "God, Ruben. *Gahhd.*"

"Can you take it?" His pace didn't slack, yanking loose and driving home. "D'ya want it? All of it?"

A nod.

Ruben swallowed. He punched at the satiny opening in short frantic strokes, chasing his orgasm pitilessly.

Andy pulled his legs back and groaned. "I dunno. I dunno." His forehead creased. He swallowed and tugged at his hard, pale cock with fierce focus. Eyes on Ruben, he nodded brokenly.

Ruben took it for permission to plunder the greasy heat, pulling the muscular thighs around his waist.

"C'mon." Andy bared his teeth and whimpered low in his throat, a ragged, needy sound.

"Huh? Huh?" Ruben demanded a wordless response from Andy's perfect flesh, pounding in short jabs against that knotted spot that made Andy jerk and shudder.

Andy's lids closed as his mouth fell open in a wordless scream. His slick hole clamped around the drilling flesh, and between them his shaft spat hot syrup. Andy hissed through his clenched teeth in agonized relief. "*Hff. Hssff.* Ah! *Hsss—hff.*"

Ruben's eyes squeezed shut, and he curled over, planting his stiff meat deep as it would go while the jizz busted out to join the first round. Andy's load slid between their torsos and inside as well. Ruben caught himself licking a wide path up Andy's throat and putting his tongue inside that mouth so they could share the fresh taste of him.

Andy sucked at his tongue with lazy hunger until Ruben finally pulled free and rolled off him, groaning happily.

They lay side by side, catching their respective breaths.

Ruben frowned at the ceiling, as baffled as a virgin but acutely proud of himself.

A couple years into his marriage, the sex with Marisa had begun to seem like a construction crew hauling steel beams up the face of a high-rise. "A little to the right, slower now. Steady… steady. Careful of the bump." Pleasant, but precarious.

This was something else entirely. The raw, unfettered aggression and tenderness had demolished all the walls he'd carefully erected around his ugliest appetites. Andy's impatient hunger and his own obsession had broken him faster than a quart of gin. This much pleasure scared him, perhaps because he'd never felt this happy and free without a bottle in his hand.

Lying there naked in the dark next to his boss, he knew that for a lie. What made him panicky wasn't the crazy sex, but the crazier feelings. Fucking time bomb, this was.

Then, like a cold cobweb the size of a bedsheet, the full weirdness settled over Ruben in the dark.

I fucked a guy.

Andy had thrown a loose arm over his chest, which started to feel like an iron girder pinning him in place. Ruben wanted to run, to puke, to punch someone. A drink! That'd help. He could almost taste the burning slip that would fuzz out all his jagged edges. Medicinal purposes.

Didn't Andy feel freaked out? What did he expect? What did a cock in your ass do to your psyche? What would he do if Andy were a chick? Grab a shower? Have a cigarette? Duck out before things got too intense or too honest?

"Hey." Andy tilted his head on the mattress. "Oso."

Ruben grunted but didn't move. He knew that he didn't want a drink. He wanted to run away. The drink was always an excuse to run.

"Where'd you go?" Andy kept his arm in place, closing his fingers over Ruben's ribs. "You still with me?"

Ruben flinched, suddenly more ticklish than he'd ever been in his life. Any second he'd burst out of his skin.

"Don't freak out." Andy's jovial tone masked something else. "Hey." He propped himself up on an elbow and the rib fingers stopped. "It's just us, okay. Oso?"

"Us. Yeah." Ruben nodded, aware of his smeary, chilled skin and the trickle of semen on his inner thigh. *And we fucked. And you're a man. And what does that make—?*

"Hey!" Andy sat up for real, and his voice hardened. "Look at me. My name is Andy, and we just had sex. Superior sex, for the record." He tried to laugh. "I have beard burn for the first time in my life. Now I know why my girlfriends bitched."

Ruben stayed very still, counting his breaths, willing himself to stay in one place. His pulse cantered, and the hair on his head felt like a cellphone tower in a strike zone. "Sorry. About the beard."

"No. That's not what I meant." Andy chuckled and coughed. "Just… I'm on the verge of freaking out too. So don't."

"You are?" His entire skin felt bruised and burnt.

Andy nodded. "Broken every commandment. My family would disown me. A bunch of my relatives would kick me out of a moving car. But… it didn't feel wrong or stupid." Shrug. "It felt natural."

Ruben shrugged back. *No kidding.*

"Dirty in the best way. Like breathing. It wasn't like a chick at all." Andy measured him with his eyes.

"Well, thanks." He cupped his wet balls.

"I just meant it was great. We were great." Pause. "Weren't we?"

Ruben tried to speak but couldn't until he cleared his dry throat. "Yeah."

"You were so gentle. But rough. I dunno. I can't explain. You fucked the hell out of me and I loved it." A matter of fact grin.

Ruben could have nodded but didn't. Instead, he asked quietly, "Are you okay?"

"Mmph. Now? Yeah. At first not so much, but then *wham*."

"Sorry." Ruben grimaced.

"Don't be."

"Everything sort of happened, and you asked. No way could I say no to you begging like that. Not after…." To the victor the spoils, only they'd both won.

Andy reached over and tugged at Ruben's ribs, pulling him across. "C'mere."

The smooth muscle felt like heaven under Ruben. Their chest hair scrubbed between them. *Weird, sexy, right.*

"I just squirted to my eyebrows and I wanna go again." Andy wiped his cheek again.

"Yeah?" A little smile bent Ruben's mouth. "You talking Spanish does something crazy to me, I think. Sick."

"Relax. We're okay. No one died. No lightning."

"Speak for yourself."

Andy chuckled. "No electrocution and divine judgment, then." He pulled his face back. "We're here. You and me."

"Did I hurt you?"

"Uh, yeah? No?" Andy wiped his wet face and scratched his wet scalp until his cowlick sprang loose. "I don't know how I lasted."

"I lost control there at the end." Ruben nudged him. "I gotta problem with losing control."

"What you've got is a weapon of ass destruction. Jesus." He cupped his balls.

"Sorry, boss." Ruben blushed in the dark. "But good. Right?"

Andy lay back gingerly. "It was perfect."

A little of the weight on Ruben's shoulders evaporated. "Be careful what you wish for." His swollen dick still felt hot and sore from the delicious friction they'd built between them. He smiled and shifted to get up.

Andy didn't move off him. "What?"

"Gonna rinse off."

"No." He smiled with casual finality. "I like you here, just like that."
Ruben snuffled with undisguised pleasure and stopped fighting to keep it
inside himself. His heart had slowed to a slow walk, and he started to feel
dozy and dopey when he felt a low rumble under him.

"Umm. We forgot something." Andy plucked the wrapper on the
nightstand. "Stupid."

"Condom. Oh man! I'm not—I didn't—"

"S'okay. I know you didn't. My fault as much as yours. I wasn't
exactly taking my time."

Ruben's heart seized, and then he saw Andy dabbing at the semen on
his inner thighs. "There's no danger. None. I'm clean. I'd never have done
anything without protection if—"

"Same. But we're grown-ups. We both know better. You've fucked
people. I've fucked people."

"Not dudes." The truth was, Ruben had screwed plenty of women
without protection. "Some bodyguard I am."

"Not like you can knock me up, but it definitely—" Andy reached
down to his butt as if checking things out. "I dunno, you hit my buzzer
pretty fucking hard with that thing." Ruben's dick, he meant.

"And, uh, felt pretty incredible to feel you. Y'know? Just you, without
the latex." Ruben blushed and grunted.

AIDS had always been someone else's problem. *Until it isn't.* A sizzle
of dread reminded him that HIV affected guys who slept with guys. Like
him, now. "I'm sorry. I didn't think."

"Ditto. Stupid and horny." Andy swallowed and grinned like the devil.
"But next time we'll be smarter."

Ruben blinked. He'd said next time, like it was gonna happen again.
Just having the possibility on the table between them terrified and excited
Ruben. Gift-wrapped dynamite. Part of him wanted to dismantle it, and the
other part wanted to strike a big hard match.

Before his boner reacted to the thought, he rolled over onto his belly.
No way Andy could see it in the dark, but his roving hands could still grab
hold of incriminating evidence.

"Definitely more intense without a rubber on you. Geez." Andy flexed
his buttocks. "I feel like you pumped a pint of jizz inside me."

A big grin. "Tell me about it." If he was supposed to feel guilty, he was
failing miserably. "How do you say jizz?"

Andy knew what he meant and what he wanted to hear. "Leche. Paja.
Lefa." He tasted the words with a sexy smile.

"Mmngh." Ruben cupped one warm cheek. "You're gonna teach
me, *pintón.*"

"Gladly." He stretched. "Jesus, Rube. So goddamned good."

"Yeah?"

Some corner of him knew that Andy liked to imagine he was a scary thug. Like he pretended Andy was a Park Avenue prince to do with as he pleased. *Brute and suit.* The fantasy tripped their triggers, even if it was a lie. Sexy make-believe like dirty talk and kinky lingerie. No real harm done to anyone. They both knew better.

"I should rinse off, get rid of it, but I don't wanna go."

"Good." Ruben fingered his wet crack. "It'll give me something to dream about." He loved feeling his seed on Andy's smooth skin. The pearly wad glazing the fresh-baked warmth of him, marking him as Ruben's property.

They slept.

At one point, Ruben woke up to piss, and managed to rise without disturbing Andy. He drank a glass of water staring out the terrace window. The storm had melted into a friendly summer shower.

"Hey." Andy's muzzy voice.

He could barely see Andy in the dark, just the silhouette against the gray-black sheen of the window. His ribcage rose and fell. Andy's scent and the warm slide of his heavy calves. The square hands folded against his skin like sleeping birds.

"Rube?"

And then he was back in bed, whispering against the smooth skin. "I'm right here." He pressed himself against Andy and prayed he wasn't having another embarrassing dream.

Sometime in the late morning, Ruben woke up chilly and alone, and heard Andy on the phone in the hall or down in the office, but before he could rouse himself to investigate, Andy returned, hair damp, and crawled back under the sheets and curled against Ruben's back, wrapping one arm across his sternum.

Ruben managed to wake up before noon, enjoying the lazy, dozy, dizzy feeling of sharing Andy's bed and the mingling of their body heat. His eyes had adapted to the dim room, and the mattress was a jumble of bedding and downy muscle. Down at the end, one strong foot had worked its way free of the duvet. Andy's toes twitched, which made Ruben smile for no good reason. *Even kajillionaires dream.*

Ruben didn't roll over because the sweet pressure of Andy's arm thrown over his ribcage felt too good to disturb.

About twenty minutes later, Andy's even breathing became a low happy groan, and he woke up smiling. The first thing he did was blink at Ruben, and then his whole handsome face lit up.

And Ruben knew.

I love him.

He didn't say it, but he knew it in his bones and balls, sure as sunrise.

Andy sounded sleepy and sweet. "S'too early."

Ruben shook his head and smile. "Nah."

They did make it to the tub and (eventually) the shower Sunday afternoon, where they discovered that blowjobs on tile made for easy cleanup. And that someone strong enough to give back as good as he got could fuck for hours and nap and do it again. And again, as it happened.

That was something else Ruben learned. A man did to you what he wanted done back.

If he's a shark, at least he's my shark.

Given free rein, Andy showed no shame about his intense appetites and no personal boundaries about sharing them.

Ruben realized that Andy really did love to make out like a horny teenager until he was dribbling cocksnot all over himself… and that fooling around didn't have to turn into a greasy poke every time. And hour by hour, the strangeness and obsession gave way to rushing intensity, like they had to race against some cloudy clock that hung above the penthouse. Draining off a month of sexual tension left Ruben boneless and brainless.

Ruben came so many times by ten o'clock Sunday his balls felt like fried marbles, and even after an oily, languorous fuck in the hot tub, Andy could only get two squirts out of him.

"I give!" Ruben shouted, and Christ knows he had, though the mind-bending sex was only part of it.

Andy laughed and used the dollop of semen to jerk himself off again.

Ruben felt safe, and Andy slept deeply pillowed against his chest, slept for four or five hours at a time, which seemed a miracle. He tried to call Peach twice, but got no answer and left cryptic, happy messages.

For once the whole day seemed to spool out before them. Ruben needed to tell someone, but had no one to tell.

Having sated his lust on Andy's strong, willing body, Ruben expected to calm down, but if anything the permission made it worse. He could barely stand more than a yard from Andy without biting him and marking him. Pushing fingers inside to feel the slickness and dropping to his knees to suckle at the hard flesh till he drained the pleasure out of Andy into himself.

Andy was no better. Any pretense at personal boundaries vanished. Now that they'd done the deed, often and well, Andy did as he pleased, jerking Ruben off while they watched a basketball game and then using Ruben's fingers up his ass while he finished himself.

"Needed that." Andy mopped up the load with Ruben's boxers. "You have no idea how much I've been jerking off the past month. Actually you probably do."

"No. No, man. I didn't—"

"Oh." Andy's face fell. "I figured with the swimming and the workouts you'd been letting off steam. Well, damn."

"I don't jerk off."

Andy laughed at him. Then stopped.

"Seriously. I don't do that." Ruben knotted his fingers. "It should mean something. Sex."

Andy nodded silently, and swallowed. "Gotta take care of that, then."

Maybe he shouldn't have said that. *But I did.* "Doesn't it hurt?" Ruben asked, brushing three fingers against the hot dry skin of his hole.

"Jerking off?"

Ruben chuckled. "No, idiot. Your butthole."

"Yeah. No." Andy slid down to the floor and put his chin on Ruben's leg.

Ruben remembered the dizzy feeling of Andy pushing his button in the rain last night. Scary and delicious.

"Not to be gross, man, but it's designed to, uh, open."

Ruben realized what he meant and made a face.

"Nature, *cariño.*" Andy kissed his leg. "But no. It feels good-strange. More strange at first, but it's you inside me. Together. Like you said. All mixed up like carbonation. And boy does it make us pop." When they fucked Andy's loads had hit the walls.

"No joke."

"But that's just the sex. I mean. You're not…. You're the best man I've ever met. Person, actually."

"Likewise, mister." Ruben could almost imagine letting Andy be inside him like that, even if it hurt. It was his ass, after all. Hell, half the time it felt like Andy had already moved into his ribcage. *Maybe nothing's impossible.* He laughed.

"What?" Andy's blue-gray eyes shone in confusion.

"Not one thing, *pintón.*"

Andy crawled onto the sofa and pulled Ruben against his chest.

Strange to feel cradled. Ruben had always been so much bigger than his women.

"Hey." Andy kissed the back of his head. "Está bien?"

"So good. *Muy, muy bien.*" He turned his face to Andy's and planted a kiss that felt exactly like an unbreakable promise.

CHAPTER FIFTEEN

WHEN YOU'VE got a hammer in your hand, everything looks like a nail.

That next two weeks flew. During the days, Ruben went back to being a bodyguard, but after Hope and the rest of the employees left, they were together and the job stopped.

Getting away with something together made them both reckless. Andy stopped invading his personal space and began colonizing it. By mutual, silent agreement, they slept in the master bedroom, doing their best to peel the paint. Ruben used his own room as a staging area before the rest of the staff showed up. *The actual staff*, he had to remind himself. He didn't like to think of himself as an employee, although on some literal level he still was.

When they were showering on Thursday morning, Andy paused soaping Ruben's chest. Out of nowhere, he said, "I think you need to tell your brother." Silence. "About… well, this."

Ruben inhaled and exhaled carefully, unsure how to answer.

Andy leaned back against the shower's slate wall. "Sex."

"I haven't told him anything about anything. Us or the other. Y'know, the business part. Your hitman deal."

"Thank you for that, but this is different." Andy grabbed a towel as he stepped out.

"…'cause you asked. But I should. Part of it at least, because he can help." Ruben exhaled. "My brother is a good guy."

"And I'm a bad guy. Problem there."

"Hey, no. But I'm supposed to be your bodyguard."

Andy blinked. "I feel safe. I am safe."

Ruben killed the water and dried his hair roughly. "It's not. I mean, none of this is safe."

"He needs to have some kind of idea that we're in this together. He's your family." Andy looked out the bathroom window and frowned, but said nothing. Whatever he was looking at wasn't in the room with them. His family? His friends? His business?

"Bauer, will you stop being a jackass? I don't wanna step wrong here."

Andy bumped his leg. "You don't have to get graphic, but I think he needs to know."

Ruben shrugged. "I know you don't care what your family thinks, but I do. I screw up a lot. We talk every day. He asks how I'm doing, and I feel like I'm lying to him."

"He's also your employer."

Ruben nodded.

Andy frowned. "Even more reason to spill the beans, then. Conflict of interest. New intel."

"I'm afraid to talk to him." Ruben bunched his lips and sighed. "I'm already such a fuckup to him, but he gives a shit about me and I give a shit about you."

"You do?" Andy met his eyes on the big vanity mirror.

"I just have to figure out a good time." *How about never?* Ruben folded his arms. "Charles is less uptight than I am."

"Thank fuck." He shoved at Ruben's skull playfully.

"Hey!"

Andy looked serious. "None of my business really."

"He's gonna freak." Ruben picked at his pants.

Andy turned off the sink without looking up. "How much?"

"What?" Did he mean money? "I'm not blackmailing you, asshole."

"No. I mean how can you tell him about what's gone on? That I'm a criminal mastermind. That we're sharing a bed. That we're butthole buddies."

"Not details!" A whoosh of laughter. "The truth to start. Just that I… whatever… like you, care about you."

For the first time since they'd started talking, Andy blinked hard, turned his back to the mirror, and looked back at him, properly. "Okay."

Ruben waited. All the feelings he'd bottled up threatened to spill out of him onto the marble separating them. His tongue moved clumsily in his mouth, too thick to speak truth. "I do, y'know."

Andy nodded. "Me too."

Another language I never learned to speak. Maybe Andy could teach him that one too.

Andy leaned and licked the rim of Ruben's ear, ending the debate and rendering him incapable of speech or sense. After, they dropped the subject, but Ruben knew it was only a matter of time before he had to come clean. *A complete moral inventory.*

THE NEXT day he called Peach again, feeling guilty for the weeks they hadn't spoken, but certain she'd be pleased for him. Telling his brother seemed impossible, but Peach might understand better. It rang and rang, but he refused to hang up this time. He hadn't been to a meeting in how long?

Finally someone answered, a young woman who sounded distracted. "I'm sorry, she can't come to the phone. Jeez."

"Peach is an old friend." *Anonymity.* He didn't know what they knew about her alcoholism.

"I'm so sorry. She's gone." A shaky inhale.

"Can I leave a message, then? Can you make sure she gets it?"

"I'm sorry. No, sir. She's *gone*. She passed away on Tuesday."

Ice in his veins. She said more words, but Ruben didn't hear most of them. Someone hung up.

Peach's cancer had returned to claim her.

He sat down on the guest bed… queasy, freezing, and alone.

Peach Horowitz had been a lifeline through Ruben's divorce, a seventy-eight-year-old Jew from New Jersey who loved showtunes and bulldogs. She had been a tough old bird, saving his life with Camels and black coffee on her deck at all hours of the night, AA slogans at the ready.

The first time he'd met her, she'd bought him a cup of coffee after a meeting and covered his fists with her arthritic hands. "Kiddo, we can't get you into Heaven, but we can let you outta Hell." She always and only told the truth.

Ruben felt like a heel: he hadn't called since things had gotten crazy, telling himself he didn't want to bug her. He'd never come clean about Andy, and now he never could. He hadn't wanted to shock her or hurt her feelings. Just like he'd made excuses that kept him from going to meetings.

Fucking drunk, fucking idiot.

"Lighten up," she growled in his head in a haze of smoke and bright prints. "Analysis is paralysis."

He needed to find another sponsor in the city ASAP. Then again, maybe a sponsor didn't matter as much after a year. He hadn't taken a drink in so long. He wasn't drinking, so maybe he didn't need AA anymore, right? To be honest, he'd gotten weary of all the Higher Power business. Couldn't he be strong?

He had his brother and this job and this man. Andy had changed so much for him. Maybe he'd kicked the alcoholism enough to leave it down in Florida. *Cured.* Long as he stayed on the wagon, he had nothing to worry about. Peach dying gave him a graceful exit. Bone-cold comfort.

Maybe the hitman and the drunk had both retired. Maybe the bad guy was good for him after all. Maybe Peach could be his Higher Power.

Ruben grunted in disgust. AA called that a geographic, the stupid idea that your problems were strictly regional and you could move away from them. He knew that his baggage went everywhere he did, but this time it hadn't somehow.

For some reason, he didn't tell Andy about her death, mainly because he felt so ashamed about avoiding her at the end. Andy seemed to sense something, but he didn't pry.

Ruben went to no meetings, and his Fourth Step stopped dead. Moral inventory was beyond him.

Then on Wednesday, Ruben watched as Marlon Stanz, the snide pindick from the Saint A's bash, showed for an appointment that tripped every one of his warning bells. No warning. No eye contact. Andy laughing too loud and serving up a family platter of his white-bread, minivan routine, all jaw and dimples with the eyes twinkling like coins at the bottom of a mall fountain. And then an hour behind closed doors with Ruben invited to wait outside like a Doberman on a chain.

The hell was Andy up to? But Ruben knew. Apex assassination, had to be.

He told himself he was paranoid. Peach's passing had left him raw and irritable. He brushed it off as misplaced jealousy of their fratboy affection. He pretended the jerk might be a real friend reaching out to Andy after many years.

But he knew. And as soon as the office door opened, Ruben stood in the living room and drifted back down the hall toward their chummy voices. Still no eye contact, and Andy spoke in a low, conspiratorial voice that made the smug fucker chuckle.

Andy moved things across to the living room, then drinks on the terrace.

Guilty, grouchy, Ruben used the stairs to traverse the apartment over their heads like an angel without wings.

Ears open, he descended into the library and located it, hidden where any fool would find it.

In a locked briefcase under a stack of airplane magazines, Ruben found a week-old Apex prospectus that stank to high heaven, far as he could tell: shell companies, a run-down factory in Shenzhen, and a pair of accounts in the Grand Cayman. Marlon right there on the list of investors, and Lampton too. Without bothering to close the door, he read all eleven pages of it. "Motherfucker."

Andy planned to keep Apex going. So much for sensible. Ruben should have known better. Andy was used to getting what he wanted and paying for triage.

Exposure. Andy had left him evidence so he'd wise up.

Unless he was jumping to conclusions? No.

Ruben paused at the door and then trailed after them casually. He was still supposed to be a houseguest visiting from Colombia, right? In public, he was still a wheeler-dealer colleague investing with Andy. He wasn't invisible, but neither of them looked back in his direction. *Liars for hire.*

Was Marlon a friend or a target? Hell, maybe he'd orchestrated the attacks himself, and this was a bribe. No way for Ruben to know.

Andy's hand stayed on the small of the man's back, steering this weedy asshole out. Just as they reached the foyer, Andy caught Ruben's eye as he leaned over to press the down button. He winked. The shark fin broke the surface of the water.

Just like that, Ruben knew: Andy the hitman was still in business.

He could see the brick wall at the end of this particular freeway. Andy would never let up on the gas because it wasn't in his nature.

"Halt." Ruben gave himself the order out loud. *Hungry. Angry. Lonely. Tired.* All true, even though he didn't wanta drink. He wanted something worse.

Without telling anyone, Ruben left by the back.

Halt, he kept telling himself in the service elevator, riding down with piles of trash. *Halt, halt* while his feet moved underneath him.

He went to the park and stared at the sky till the sun gave up. His phone rang a couple of times, and text messages made it buzz in his breast pocket, but he knew who it was and didn't bother to respond. What could he say that wouldn't be a mistake? Couldn't call Peach or his brother. No one really. Even going to a meeting sounded like a Band-Aid on a head wound.

How many lives had Andy ruined? He thought of the lady at the museum benefit, throwing her champagne and snarling with her tit out. Remembered Andy sneering at his parents and his prep school while he slathered charm and crisp bills over bystanders. *Bait.* The angry faces on the street. If any part of Andy was ugly, that was it, the bruise on the wormy apple.

Ruben could never stop him, then. He had to admit he was powerless. *Let go or be dragged.* And until Andy could admit it, he'd keep going until he hit bottom, just like a drunk.

When Ruben walked back to the Iris, the evening had crept up on him, and the car service traffic was inching down Fifth Avenue toward expensive dinners. He felt entombed up here, and the last thing he wanted was to climb back into his glass prison.

Everyone thinks of changing the world, but no one thinks of changing himself.

Stalling for time, for a plan, he stopped on the thirty-third floor for a swim. He stripped to his boxers, not caring who saw, and swam laps till his arms and legs burned and his skin was pruney beige. Dawdling, he let himself air-dry in one of the deck chairs and smoked the last crushed cigarette from the stolen pack, holding the fumes inside him until he got light-headed. A sound above him made him look up. Sure enough, a familiar silhouette stood at the edge. Andy was awake, watching him swim for the first time in a week.

Finally, around eleven o'clock, when he couldn't sit there in his jockeys anymore, he shrugged back into his rumpled black suit and climbed the back stairs to the library. He stopped at the desk long enough to pick the lock on the briefcase again. The glossy prospectus made him feel like a dupe and a dope. *Walk away.* Analysis is paralysis.

Finally, he swiped the damning evidence, hoping to sneak into his room and skip a confrontation but still spoiling for a fight.

Andy's silhouette blocked the little dogleg hall to the guest room. "The fuck is going on, Rube?" A smile in his voice.

Ruben swiveled and walked out the library doors onto the terrace, the Apex prospectus rolled into a tight tube. He just needed some air if they were going to duke this out sober.

He waited until Andy came out onto the deck and nuzzled his neck before he let fly. "When were you gonna come clean?"

Andy stiffened. His breathing stilled. "What d'ya mean? Where you been all day?"

Slow nod. "You wanna get yourself killed."

His lips closed against Ruben's skin, and he pulled back. "What did you see?"

"He's a target, right? Stanz. You're gonna take that fucker out with your black market tycoon-fu." He crossed his arms and stepped back, annoyed at the paternal rumble coming out of himself.

"I didn't say that."

"You didn't have to, Andy. I know you." Ruben brandished the Apex report. He slapped the pages against his thigh.

"You read it?"

Ruben rolled his eyes. "What should I do, lick the info off the pages? Yes, I fucking read it. I'm not illiterate. You're gonna bankrupt him." He squeezed Andy's arm to take the sting out of the accusation.

Andy held up his hands, sloshing his drink. Scotch, rocks. "This is different."

"From what is it different? Looks like the exact same shady BS got you into this mess in the first place. Or else he's in on the deal."

Andy's fingers dripped whiskey. "Yeah. Look. Sorry. I should've—"

"Told the truth? Used your brain? Learned your lesson?"

Andy sighed. "D: all of the above. But this one's different. Personal."

"I don't care. You want revenge? Great. If they're crooks, then turn 'em in."

"Well, fuck." Andy dry-chuckled. "This isn't like before. Well, not full-on assassination. But he's a real piece of work, that one. Abusive. Conservative. Politically connected. His company just poisoned three thousand acres of groundwater and he's gonna get off—"

"I didn't move in here to find more bullets to dodge."

"Nah." A tight sip.

"This shit is dangerous. Stupid and dangerous. You know better, Bauer."

"No, Rube."

"Don't call me that. You're cranking this hitman bullshit back up with me on the premises. You tried to sneak it past me because you knew it was stupid and dangerous."

Andy frowned and looked at the tile, chin tucked against his chest. "I'm sorry."

"No, you're not. You're busted. That's not the same thing. I'm a drunk, remember. I know all about strategic apologies. Talk to me."

"He's a monster. His partners protect him. You think any of the partners give a shit? They stay on those boards out of boredom."

"And what are you, Deadly Do-Right riding to the rescue? You're dumb enough to think you're safe now because I scared a couple toughs before they could throw you off the balcony? *This* fucking balcony." His voice had gotten loud, and he dropped it abruptly at the end.

Andy squinted suddenly. "I never said I'd stop."

"You never said you'd be stupid, either. I can't believe you'd put yourself in that kind of danger again, for nothing. For kicks." Betrayal squeezed his guts. "Go ahead, hitman. Make some more enemies you can't handle. Good choice."

"You're wrong."

Ruben frowned and shook his head as if trying to unfog his eyes. "You're a *criminal* and you used me as a decoy. We almost get killed. And you wanna stay in business so they can take another swing at you."

"No."

"Then what, Andy? You don't need the money. You don't want the headache. You don't even care about these assholes. I'm standing here asking you to let it go. To stop testing the rules and breaking the law just so they can come bust you for good."

The dent between Andy's eyebrows deepened, but his eyes looked sad and sorry. "I don't want that, either."

"You don't need to get caught. I've caught you, okay?" *Please, Andy.* And for a moment, one glittering second, Ruben thought he'd saved them, protected them from the oily blackness churning beneath their feet, everyone and everything that would keep them apart and trapped in solitary confinement.

The lights inside lit Andy, left him a silhouette against the window. Better that his face stayed hidden. The windows and stone perspired in the muggy air.

Andy peered at the minnows of ice swimming in his Scotch. "I'm not brushing you off."

"Right."

"I'm listening, but I disagree, Ruben. We're both part of this. Together. You want me to just nod my head like a robot? I disagree because I know what I'm doing. I think you're wrong."

"Of course you do. You warned me. *You're* the bad guy." Ruben fake-grinned.

Andy shook his head. "Ruben, I don't want you to be a target."

"Yes, you do! You *hired* me to be a fucking target."

"That's not fair. We're not in any danger, huh? We're happy."

"Now you tell me," Ruben scoffed.

"You asked!"

"Don't put this on me. You tried to con me. You hooked a whopper and dragged him up here, and you thought I wouldn't notice. Hitman." He threw the prospectus. It flapped to Andy's bare feet.

"And I don't need you stomping around like Guardzilla anymore." Andy took a deep, double swallow of the gasoline in his glass and revved back up. "So I have to clear things through you now?" He put his glass on the ledge.

Over his shoulder the park at night became a woolly black shadow.

Ruben pressed. "You're used to buying things, hiring solutions. No price tags 'cause they don't factor. You want to install me, the new thing: a spic dick with the combat grip and Kevlar brain. You think I'm an idiot because I'll never make this kinda dough, and I'll never belong in this place." He swept an arm at the terrace and teak furniture and the zillion-dollar penthouse inside. A resigned shrug. "True. So I guess it's all true."

Andy flailed, boxing the air. "It's a test! Some moments in life, you spend your whole life preparing for." He looked around them, not seeing much. "None of us are perfect. Me least of all. But I know when something is worth the risk."

"That's the thing, Andy. You keep an invisible ledger in your head. Crazy fucking tally of everything everyone owes you and vice versa."

Slow headshake. "I don't—"

"Which is why you like paying for shit. You never have to owe anyone. Long as your wallet's open, the IOUs only flow one way."

"Until someone does something, offers something that doesn't cost money." Andy raised his eyes, hopeful and hesitant.

What did he want Ruben to say? Which lie was he supposed to tell to cover both their asses? Ruben ignored the swallow of Scotch balanced on the ledge.

Andy eyed him for a long moment. "Scared." An exasperated smile. "You're terrified and I'm terrified."

"Yeah? What am I afraid of?"

Andy shrugged. "Nothing. Everything! I'm afraid too. Whatever this... is, is worth being scared."

"The price."

"We both gotta pay it. And I'm paying. I want to. You changed everything, Ruben."

"For the record, Bauer, you got no problems money *can* solve." Ruben stopped talking so fast his teeth clacked together.

"Ruben, it's not zero sum... like, all the happiness gets used up before you get your fucking slice. We have a chance. Together. Look at me, will you. I'm telling you the truth."

"You think I'm blind? I've watched you! Sucking them all in, a Boy Scout's face with a hitman's heart. I should be fucking scared."

"But you're not scared: you're *scary*. It's your party trick." Andy gave a knowing chin-jerk.

"In Miami the guys used to tell each other, 'Don't stick your dick in crazy.' There's my trouble. We fucked just enough that the crazy came off on me."

"We're not in any danger. You said so yourself, and the problem has been neutralized because it wasn't a real problem to start with. Look at us. We're so good together, man. Can't you just enjoy that?"

Ruben chuckled without pleasure. "Spoiled rotten. Nothing touches you up here. You don't even know what's down there." He pointed past Andy's glass at the streets below. "I gotta go."

"Why?" Andy goggled, as if Ruben had announced he was going to jump off the ledge and grab a pizza on the way down.

"Just some air. Space. I'm not thinking straight." Ruben walked away before they both tossed out more regret bait.

Andy followed anyways, apparently determined to fuck things up. "Wrong. You had a plan. You came in and rubbed my defenses into rubble."

Leave me alone.

Ruben went inside, through the dark library, and down the unlit hall to the living room, trying to escape. Through the giant windows, the city glittered black and endless in all directions.

Andy's wary silence pressed against his back like a curtain.

If they could cool off, they could go back to being good together. *Lying and pretending.* Again the certainty that Andy made him act like an addict. Ruben rubbed his eyes, wishing he could go to a meeting or a bar or anything else than this booby-trapped glass box. *And I'm the booby that's trapped.*

Peach always said, *Just accept, don't expect.* True. Ruben had spent so much time projecting his assumptions onto the world that he forgot what reality looked like. A brief, cold spear of missing her pierced him. *Homesick.* Right then, staring out the glass over the mountaintops of Manhattan, he'd have given anything to hear her croak out a showtune while she wagged a knobby finger at his scowl. Andy didn't even know she was dead.

A crack in front of him and a damp rush of night air.

Andy opened the living room's double-wide doors and stepped inside cradling his half-empty glass of poison. Sweat stained his pits and the button-V at his chest, the pale blue soaked there. He must've walked around the terrace to head things off. His paranoid scrutiny drifted over Ruben's face like woozy spiders.

Ruben counted his breaths. How long had he sat on that bench today? Why hadn't he gone to a meeting when he had a chance? *Stupid.* "Andy, I don't want to work for you anymore."

Andy frowned. His voice went rough. "Stop it. Don't make this about money."

"Who said anything about money? I said work." Ruben pressed his lips against his teeth, searching for the sane way to defuse the fight before it got ugly between them. Before everyone started telling the truth all the fuck over this penthouse. "I'm not a hitman or a banker, or a liar or any of the other shit you've decided to be. You're not, either, but them's the breaks, I guess."

"You're doing this because you *want* to be here. You do. With me. But you're ashamed."

Ruben frowned. "I'm not ashamed of anything."

Andy laughed. "Right. Which is why we only touch in the dark. Why you won't turn the lights on or open the blinds."

"I've been trying to protect you, jackass."

"Me? Really? From who? Light bulbs? Oso, you hide from everything. You keep everything bottled up. Your whole life you've been hunkering down in these bolt-holes while the world happened around you. Keeping yourself in a cage so your hope never gets loose and embarrasses you."

"Fuck you."

"Well, here we are, man, the whole goddamn world outside your bottle. I'm right here inviting you to come be in it with me." Andy extended his hand, but Ruben didn't take it.

"I don't need your help." A lie, and he knew it.

"I need yours." Andy paused.

"Stop lying to me." He'd known that first day: *Nobody can be as honest as this guy looks.*

"I don't get why you're so flipped out, Rube." Andy held up his hands in defeat. "Look, Marlon's still solvent. Nothing has happened to that douchebag. I haven't done anything. I can pull the plug before he's plugged. If you tell me no, I won't."

"Andy, I don't believe you." And that was it. Everything. The boy cried wolf because there were wolves. *The boy cried.* Ruben wiped his nose. Oh well. He'd ruin this thing he had with Andy too, like anything he ever touched or cared about.

Congrats, Oso! You've won... a new low bar!

The trajectory of his latest failure painted itself so plainly that his disappointment almost felt like relief. Fucking up was his real expertise; it belonged under special skills on his resume. "You're going to get yourself killed. You want me to watch you get killed. To prove something to your shitty family."

"No. No, Ruben." Panic now. "You have nothing to prove."

"You think you do. It's like you're walking backwards. You can't even see what's in front of you 'cause you can't stop watching what you left. You want to be exposed and shamed and drag them all down with you." Ruben blinked. "And I'm part of that too. Looker, leaper. The dumb thug you fuck for kicks to rub it in their face. Bought and paid for." He slapped at the tailored suit and the three-hundred-dollar tie.

Andy froze, pinned by the words and obviously upset. "Wait a minute. I never asked you to do anything crooked. I spent a month keeping my nose clean to protect you."

"Revenge for growing up rich."

Andy raised the glass, sloshing to the last bit of whiskey, and all his ice gone. "More like the horrible realization that being 'most likely' to do anything is a fucking curse, and that everyone is waiting nearby to help you into the mud."

"Worst part, you think people saying mean shit to you in suburbia is the same thing brown kids get. Boo-hoo, you didn't get a supermodel handjob when you went skiing in Aspen. Spoiled."

The tic in Andy's forehead firmed into a prominent vein. His jaw clamped into two ugly knots at each side of his scowl. He swayed on his feet by the spiral staircase leading up.

Run. Go now. Leave now. Ruben pressed his feet into the floor so the impulse didn't take over.

"You know the price of everything and the value of nothing." Andy's bleary voice sliced like a sword.

"Jesus. Go ahead. Bait the cavemen, genius. Kill 'em all." Ruben spat back at him. "Spend the rest of your life fucking your friends over, drinking for company, paying for sex."

"Fuck you." He swallowed that last mouthful of Scotch like it was worms and Drano. *Medicinal reasons.*

Ruben shook his head, but the thought stayed. "I need to leave. Now."

Andy didn't like that. "Where're you gonna go?"

"Nowhere. Away. A walk. Cool off." A meeting, he should have said, but even that seemed impossible right now.

"It's ninety degrees outside. Have a—" Andy stopped the words before he said anything stupid. "We should eat. I just need a refill." Andy tipped the glass back and emptied it down his throat, larynx bobbing.

Just then the living room felt too harsh, the recessed lights blazing as if Andy's off-stage adversary had set them to broil.

Ruben tried to claim the glass. "I think you've had plenty."

Andy wasn't having it. "Plenty of nothing. I'm not a drunk, Mr. Oso. I don't have to watch myself."

"The fuck did you say to me?" Ruben straightened. "What exactly did you just say?"

"That was outta line."

"All of this is out of line."

Andy put the glass down on a tread of the spiral staircase. "Wait—"

"I never shoulda moved into this place, *pintón*. Taken this job."

"Ruben."

Ruben wavered, not sure which step to take. "I never shoulda left Florida. Fucking brother. Fucking Hawaiian shirts." He shook Andy's hands off him. "Fuck you, Richie Rich."

At the bar, Ruben dropped a handful of ice into a fresh glass and scooped up the decanter. For whatever reason, the smell made him feel like puking, but still he wanted that poison in his belly and blood.

HALT, said Peach from her grave—and she was right.

"Stop it." Andy took hold of his arm again. "Enough."

Ruben raised the glass and toasted Andy's felt-soft eyes, now wide with worry and anger. He brought the glass to his face, but instead of drinking it, he inhaled, filling his lungs with the peppery fumes. Saliva swamped his mouth as the drunk woke up in him and staggered toward the light.

"You're not that person, Ruben. This isn't who you are." Andy pleading.

"Really? I used to think this was the worst addiction, but I was wrong." Blink. Inhale again. "I was wrong. Everything is wrong."

"Ruben, this is not my fault."

Match, meet fuse.

"No." Ruben stared through the alcohol at him. "The fault is all mine." He lowered the glass and inhaled again as he bumped the rim against his dry lower lip, still swollen from the scrape of Andy's stubble.

If he tipped it an inch, he could take the swallow. "Well, I quit."

"A year, a year, Ruben. You've been sober for a year."

"You don't even know what that means."

"You're right. I'm sorry. I want to know." Andy swallowed hard on nothing. "Ruben, talk to me and we'll figure this out, huh? You and me." His eyes glittered, wet.

Ruben scowled at the liquor, his jaw wobbling with a grief that froze his blood. *A born loser fighting fate.* Maybe that was the mistake: he'd wasted a whole year, squandered all the booze and blackouts he coulda had. He'd missed out on all those emergency room visits and drunk tanks where someone else woulda cleaned up his messes for him. What was he thinking?

"Ruben, stop." Andy grabbed at the glass. Scotch sloshed over their knuckles and splashed the clear bear skull box.

"I already quit. You can't make me do anything."

"I love you." Andy took the glass and Ruben let him.

"Me too." Backing away, Ruben shook his head and exhaled in a sad nonlaugh. "Which makes no fucking difference to anything."

I have to leave or I'll cry or I'll hit him or I'll lose control and he'll see exactly what I am: an open drain that leads into a sewer.

"I mean it." Andy's face broke, the gleaming stare shaken. "All of you. Every part. We're so lucky."

"Not me. Speak for yourself." Ruben dragged himself to the foyer and pressed the only available button: Down.

Andy pleaded silently, a tic in his handsome, gee-whiz jaw.

"I guess that's why I'm thirsty. I was born empty." Ruben's teeth chattered, and he wiped his mouth to hide it, wishing he was dead or drunk in Miami. Same difference. His gaze roamed over Andy, trying to memorize him standing there crumbling beside the bear skull.

So this is what it feels like to commit suicide.

"Do you know how lucky we are, Oso? Do you know how happy I am to have found you?"

"I know plenty." Ruben stepped onto the elevator without turning, without looking back. *Sodom and Gomorrah.* He didn't need any more salt to rub in his wounds. "I know what you do… to me."

Andy moved forward to block the doors from closing automatically. "No. No you don't. You're terrified of being happy. Ruben!"

"Stop." He couldn't look Andy in the face. "Sorry, man." The delayed elevator squawked in frustration. "I'm sorry for everything."

I'll never see him again. All he saw was a world full of poison, rows of bottles waiting to drown whatever this feeling was.

Andy took a shuddering breath and wiped his mouth. "Ruben, you said, you said. All your steps should take you somewhere. Talk to me. Put your foot down."

Ruben shut his eyes so he wouldn't see and get stuck with the memory. "No. Please. Have the last fucking word. You obviously need it more than I do."

Then the doors closed behind him, unseen, on Andy Bauer, unseen, and he descended blind in the gleaming, seamless box all the way back down into the dirt.

CHAPTER SIXTEEN

NOTHING'S SO bad that a drink won't make it worse.

Ruben woke up on the filthy tiles of the Port Authority bus terminal with a mouth full of decomposing mice and a head like an infected molar.

He hadn't had a blackout or a hangover in, well, a year come to think of it. Funny too, how in all the no-drinking he'd developed complete amnesia about the ruinous downside of sleeping in a gutter, and this time he'd done it without the booze.

Score one for AA.

At least he made it to the bus station john before he yacked. He tried not to leave anything horrific behind for the maintenance crew. He stumbled out into the blinding light and waved down a gypsy cab. "Hundred and Ninth. East side. Off Lex."

He hoped he had money to pay but couldn't bring himself to check. He pressed his pounding skull into the shitty upholstery without opening his eyes.

Stroke of luck: he had fifty-seven bucks in his wallet, so the driver didn't have to kill him.

Second stroke, his keys were still at the bottom of his pocket, and he didn't puke on the stairs. He did, however, have to pause on the fourth floor landing so his stomach didn't come out of his nostrils.

His first indication that something was wrong sat in the hall flicking its tail on the doormat: his brother's tortoiseshell tabby, pawing at the apartment.

"How did you get...." He stopped when he saw the yellow police tape stretched across the door. "Out?"

The cat stood and arched as Ruben reached the end of the hallway, then stalked around itself in an irritated circle, mewing to be let inside the crime scene.

How had they found this apartment? Nothing connected Andy to this place.

Gouges at the locks and door frame painted a pretty clear picture. He hadn't slept here in three weeks, and Charles was at his girlfriend's, so who knew when it had happened or been reported?

Without stopping to think or check inside, Ruben scooped up the cat, jogged downstairs, and hailed a yellow cab. Holding the freaked animal on his lap, he dialed his brother's phone. No answer.

The detector. He'd installed the rescued CO unit from the penthouse in his brother's place. He needed to warn someone.

On a hunch he went to Daria's place. She buzzed him up way too fast to be safe, but when he got upstairs she was crying and panicky. She took the cat without question before Ruben asked, "Have you seen him?"

"Office." She spoke into the cat's motley fur. "They hit the office."

Ruben nodded, but his feet were already in motion.

Another taxi. His brother's phone still went to voice mail. He wanted to call Peach, but no phone reached that far.

The afterlife has the worst cell reception.

He kicked himself for not finding a new sponsor when he needed one so badly. At this hour, the traffic alternated between caterpillar crawls and breakneck progress, making Ruben straight-up nauseated by the time he paid the twenty-dollar fare and emerged onto the curb in front of Empire Security.

Ruben climbed the creaking stairs, wishing for the hundredth time that he had some kind of weapon. Some bodyguard.

The bright nail salon looked empty: a couple girls gossiping at the back. As he passed they turned to eye him suspiciously. Whatever had happened wasn't any secret in the building.

Empire Security had been disemboweled with a crowbar, the guts of its little office exposed to view. The hollow door had been split and pushed in, cracking the rickety frame. Inside, the receptionist's area had been pulverized into a jumble of papers, splintered electronics, and cracked particle board. One of the chairs was stuck in the sheetrock wall near the ceiling.

Ruben tried to close the door, but only the lower hinge was still attached. "Oh." He propped it shut.

"Rube." Charles's weary voice came from the little inner office. "Yeah. Not so good."

Ruben leaned and saw him back there. Charles sat in the wreckage with the stunned annoyance of a dropped infant. Today's shirt was tangerine, short-sleeved and covered in dolphins. He had a black eye and his fingers were taped.

Ruben waited. "I called."

"My cellphone's dead. It's in here somewhere, busted, and I need to get a replacement, but I been too busy getting assaulted."

"You're okay?" Ruben pointed at the purple eye.

Charles chuckled with grim finality. "Not so bad. You kept saying there was something weird about Bauer."

"Andy didn't do this." *Did he?* Ruben hated himself for even thinking it.

"Someone did. Someone wants to have a messy conversation with that asshole."

Carefully as he could, Ruben picked his way across the rubble. Andy might be in serious danger. He hated himself for worrying. For a lot of things.

"S'my fault. I saw the money is all. You warned me, but I kept thinking you were paranoid. Divorce. Drinking. I figured at this point, your instincts were shot. I didn't pay attention." Charles opened and shut his mouth, sad fish.

"What are you talking about?"

"They're not amateurs, these guys, I can tell you that. And not any kind of figment of Bauer's imagination." Charles pointed at his swollen eye socket.

He'd left Andy alone. *Asshole.* He had to get—

"And for some fucking reason, they are really not fans of yours, big brother. You did some damn thing to yank their rope all right. They were very clear on that point. Adamant, even."

Ruben whispered, "I fucked up."

Charles squinted. "They took your file, Rube. Your whole life. I got everything in there. Birth certificate. Marriage shit. Medical records. Taxes. I kept 'em in case of... trouble, y'know."

"I know." Ruben had always been sloppy about paperwork and that file was probably the last coherent record of his life on the planet. He didn't blame Charles for trying to take care of him. He had to get back to the penthouse. *Idiot.* Andy could be hurt or worse.

"S'my fault. Some security company. Didn't see shit. Crappy insurance. Fake cameras. Only reason they didn't do worse was one of the limo drivers came by for his check and got stuck being a good Samaritan." Charles raised his chin toward the window. "Poor chump's in the hospital." His hands were shaking.

Ruben took a step toward him. "This isn't your fault. I knew better. I knew the whole goddamn time. Eyes open. I could see it, and I walked right off the cliff." He saw the question forming in his brother's eyes. "Not booze. God, the booze would be simpler. No. Different. Nothing."

"Well, not nothing, exactly." Charles opened his arms at the mess. "What do you know?"

"I tried to leave him. I mean. I woulda quit last week. In June, even. I tried. But then they attacked his assistant, so I moved in." He leaned back against the wall, his shoes slipping on the scattered bullshit papers covering the floor. One cane back chair sat tilted in front of the desk, missing a leg. "I tried and I fucked up."

"You shoulda left! You promised me you'd bail before things went to shit." Charles probably thought he wanted the truth.

Oh jeez. "I know. That's what I'm saying. It hadn't gone to shit."

"You knew that these guys were serious. That Bauer wasn't imagining everything, and you stayed on, solo? What kind of asshole are you?"

Ruben's face heated and his eyes welled up, but hot as it was, who could tell? He loved Andy and he had split. Like a jerk. Like a drunk. He pressed his fingers to the lids like he could push the stinging tears back inside his head.

Charles glowered. "I trusted you."

"So did he." Why was he standing here at all?

"He! He who? You mean Bauer? What the fuck you screwing 'round in, Ruben?" Charles said his name in a baffled squawk.

He'd done the one thing to Andy he'd promised he wouldn't, abandoning him the second things got sticky. *I care about him.* "I hadta make a decision. I..." He swallowed and gripped the back of the three-legged chair hard enough it creaked. Peach in his head, *Truth, kiddo.* "Made a promise that I needed to keep because even if I did it for the wrong reason, it was the right thing and I knew it. I knew I had to even if it meant keeping a secret. From you, even."

"Since when?"

"Since I been with Andy." Done. "As in, Bauer and I were together."

"He hired you."

"No. More than the gig, is what I mean." Gulp. Still, he swung the hammer and drove the nail deep. "Personal."

A snaky silence coiled around the two brothers and squeezed.

"Meaning what, Ruben? What do you mean 'together'?"

Please God.

Ruben inhaled, holding the deep breath. Andy's flannel eyes filled the inside of his head till the words landed soft and low. "He's important to me. Still."

"Rube." Charles bit down on that like a wormy apple. "What in hell are you telling me?"

"The truth." *Stand there and take it.*

"Together. You are. Like what? Like making out? C'mon! You let Bauer get with you? On you?" Charles made a manic face and smacked papers off the desk that fluttered to the floor. "A guy."

"Don't start."

"Me, don't start!" An arc of spit hit the tilted desk, and the whites of his eyes gleamed. "Like Richie Rich porks you in the ass, and you like it?"

Ruben scowled. To his credit, he left the remains of the three-legged chair he was holding on the floor and didn't beat his brother with it.

"That dude pays you."

"He doesn't pay me for anything but the job." Frown.

"Hidden cameras and shit. He's been watching you, taping you. Some *maricón!*" Charles spat the Spanish for "faggot."

Ruben's heart tightened into a cold stone fist. A muscle ticked in his cheek, and a scowl welded itself onto his skull.

Charles stepped back and his eyes widened. He held up his hands.

"You forget, Carlos." He let the threat in his words swing free. "I don't *habla español.*"

"I'm sorry I said that. That was uncalled for."

"I'm not talking about protecting him. And I care about him more than—"

"Don't." Charles eyed him doubtfully.

"Anything you say about him, you can say about me. Dig?"

Both brothers ate the muggy air for a few moments, looking at each other but probably not seeing much they recognized. The quiet only made the entire mess look worse, a nauseous snapshot of his future.

Charles broke it first. "Are you and he…?"

All the possible words boiled between them: queer, stupid, crazy, fucking, doomed, angry, lovers, happy, scared, ridiculous, trapped, impossible, serious, still together?

Still together.

Ruben nodded longer than he should have. "I dunno. Yeah. Sure. Whatever the rest of that sentence is, the answer is yes." He crossed his arms and stared at his brother.

"Jesus. Jesus Christ, Ruben." Charles exhaled and swallowed. "Okay. Okay. I gotta sit down but I'm already sitting down."

Ruben frowned but nodded. "Whatever you wanna say, go the fuck ahead, because at this point, I don't have much waste-able time."

Charles stretched his lips into a freaked-out trout mouth. "So, uh… who's the, um, *girl*? When you… y'know…." Grimace. "Fuck."

"No one is the goddamned girl! We're not girls, Chucky. That's the point." The anger felt good, actually, felt like focus. He could see everything so clearly, with his situation magnified to tactical precision. *Still together.*

"All that surveillance." Charles rocked forward and then back, as if he was sitting on a cactus. "Andy fucking Bauer. Even his name sounds queer. Sorry-sorry."

"He's not what we thought."

"Obviously."

"Fuck you."

"I don't mean *that*. Well, no: yes, I do mean that, but obviously he was in some kinda serious actual danger when he sauntered in and hired us. Is what I meant to mean." Charles frowned and sat back, resting his palms on his dolphin gut. "You follow?"

"He—" Ruben tried to find a way to keep telling the truth that wouldn't mess him up. "—matters to me. And these people came after him. They hurt him. I plan to do something about that. Something not strictly legal."

As much as Ruben had dreaded facing his brother, telling the truth, just speaking the words aloud felt like someone had lifted an anvil out of his splintered ribcage.

"You shoulda said something. I get why you, y'know, didn't, but still." Charles looked at the floor and rubbed his eyes. "That was shitty. This is shitty. Jesus Christ, Rube."

"Charles, I'm not drinking. The feelings scare the crap outta me. The, uh, gay stuff even more. I made a mistake, but I'm not fucking up here. I didn't know. I found something good, someone real."

"Even now, huh? You're sure." Charles cast a baleful gaze over the remains of his company and took a shaky breath. "You're sure this is good? That he is."

"Yes." Ruben shook his head. "It was. Is. And so help me it's gonna be." Did he mean that? He blinked and tried to remember what had made him feel certain enough to predict his own future. He had to get to the Iris.

"And?"

"Andy is in real trouble."

"What kinda trouble?"

Keep telling the truth. Put a foot down.

Ruben lowered his voice and his gaze to the floor. "Get arrested trouble."

"As in *you* get arrested?"

Headshake. Ruben wanted to be gone, now. "He did some stupid things. Money things. But I can fix it, I think."

"So? Ruben, are you sure you should? 'Cause over here sitting on my fat ass, it sounds like all kinds of craziness has been going on with you as a stooge. While some banker takes you for a ride. Talk to the cops."

"We can't have cops digging in this business."

"What are you talking about? You're not a superspy! The cops came twice this morning. Two separate visits. They're coming back tomorrow. This is a crime scene, *papá*."

"Your apartment too. I came from there. Sorry. I took your cat to Daria's."

"Thank God. I don't have anything at my place anyways." Charles shook his head. "Rube, the cops are all over this already. They're asking."

"Then I gotta go back before they try to get me on the record." Ruben looked hard at him. "Listen, you need to have one of your guys check my carbon monoxide detector. Okay? The detector I installed, Charles. Like, now." A jerky nod.

Charles started to stand, looking too curious to be safe. "The what? Why?"

"Because I'm a fucking fool." Sad smile. "Thanks, little brother."

"Wait—"

But Ruben didn't given him a chance to say anything reasonable before taking the stairs two at a time back down to the street. He had to get back to the Iris before Andy did anything crazy. He didn't know if these assholes were watching, but from this point every wrong move put them both in actual, physical danger.

Down on Fifty-Ninth, Ruben walked right out into traffic with his arm up. *Like a born New Yorker.* He could almost hear Andy's voice in his head. As soon as the taxi stopped, he told him to head up West End and cut across at Seventy-Ninth. He didn't want to have to fight the crosstown traffic, and going through the Park would save the most minutes. The car bounced and rocked as it rocketed uptown, hitting the lights in seamless sequence.

He picked up the phone to call, but realized that if Andy didn't want to stop fighting a call might start some horrible ball rolling. He couldn't call Hope. Better to barge in and take control of the situation with his bare hands before anyone got sneaky or clever.

At Park Avenue, he paid his ridiculous fare and hopped out, slamming the taxi door in his haste. The breeze had picked up, and wind-tears slid down his cheeks. He jogged through the lobby with a nod at the doormen. They all knew him now. He jabbed for the elevator and stepped inside the paneled cube.

Ruben pressed for the penthouse to close the doors to prevent any other residents from joining him. As it climbed, he rocked side to side and jabbed the button.

Except for the digital numbers flicking by overhead, the silent elevator still gave him the feeling that he wasn't rising, that he hadn't left the lobby at all, that he was trapped inside a stationary box. He tried to imagine Andy's face the moment he walked into the penthouse. Surprise? Pity? Anger? Relief? He might punch Ruben, kiss him, curse him, thank him, throw him out... anything.

Still together. Ruben wiped his mouth with a shaking hand.

He would walk in and apologize.

For what?

He would admit that he was scared and stupid and Andy was right.

He wasn't.

No, he'd say that he'd told Carlos about them being together, and everything would be okay because they weren't alone.

We are.

Ruben nodded to himself anyways. "Still." A drunk can get dry and a hitman can retire. *Compromise.* They'd pay the money back with interest, and the psychos could go back to terrorizing other innocent criminals—

Then the silent doors slid open and the first thing he saw was blood on the floor.

CHAPTER SEVENTEEN

NOBODY TRIPS over a mountain.

Scarlet drips made a Morse-code trail which arced toward the library, and then there on the wall: a bloody handprint.

"Andy!" Ruben jogged past the dining room, the kitchen, begging the silence to prove him wrong. The walls were dented in three places. Slashed paintings. Broken china crunched underfoot. Hard dark scuffs marred the hallway floor where something heavy had been dragged.

The library had been tossed like a paper salad.

Books and files all over the floor. Filing cabinet tipped over and its contents smeared in a crumpled stripe. Two of the screens were cracked and hung by their cables. The door to the terrace hung wide open, leaving the air inside hot, damp, and still.

Where was the alarm?

"Andy?" Quieter now, afraid of what he'd find. Without thinking Ruben grabbed the rail and pulled himself upstairs. A shaky nausea dragged at his limbs, weakening him with each step. The sultry stillness made him feel worse than he already did, which seemed impossible. "C'mon, Bauer.

Don't be a dick." Up here the quiet air was hotter and the beds were all made. The electricity wasn't out everywhere, but at the breaker three circuits had been thrown.

He went downstairs through the library and found marks he could follow.

Ruben's bed had been stripped bare, for some reason. A lamp knocked to the floor, but there was no other damage to the room. They must have caught him sleeping in this room. In Ruben's room.

Alone.

"My—" He wiped his mouth with a shaky hand. "Fucking Christ." Guilt washed over him.

Andy had warned him, but as usual Ruben had ignored everyone's advice because he knew best, because he was such a genius. After all, his perfect life spoke for itself.

In the hall he found one of the pillows wadded against the baseboard. A shredded sheet, stained with more blood, stretched in tatters down the hall. Impromptu restraints. He crawled forward, following the trail.

They'd wrapped Andy in the bedding to immobilize him and dragged him out of the building like a sack of laundry.

Beaten? Unconscious? Probably. *Jesus.*

Ruben stopped. The drunk in him wanted to crawl back into a bottle. The bodyguard needed to notify the cops. The man who loved Andy was gonna scream or puke or punch holes in the walls until he thought of his brother's warning and laughed, without feeling an ounce of relief.

He'd rowed his leaky boat out into deep water.

Ruben's mind raced as he squatted for a closer look. Scrapes and smears on the plaster walls and hardwood floor. Andy'd struggled, maybe? Or woken up and gotten an arm loose. He forced himself to take steady breaths. Pictures crooked, one fallen with its glass shattered. A quarter million in damage easy. Tallying the damage kept him from adding to it.

With every move he was wrecking evidence, but what choice did he have? The gory handprint, whether Andy's or someone else's, was the last clear mark before the upstairs service elevator.

Think.

Ruben couldn't involve the cops or the feds. Charles had already taken a big hit he didn't deserve. Andy flew solo, and professional courtesy was thin on the ground. For a woozy second, Ruben considered calling his ex-wife in Florida, but to what purpose? A week ago he could have reached out to his sponsor, but Peach was gone and he'd done jack to get a new sponsor up here. He'd blown off AA on top of everything. Thinking with his dick. Thinking like a dry drunk.

Sluggishly, he considered going to a meeting and then stopped. *S'not about you, asshole.* And then he knew:

"Hope."

Before he questioned the impulse, he dug out his cell phone and called Andy's assistant. She might not know what to do, but she'd know where to start and keep her mouth shut while they did it.

She picked up on the fourth ring. "Stanford."

"Ruben here." He took a breath. "We gotta serious situation."

Silence. The muttering behind her shifted. "Hold." The sounds where she was changed. "Hadta step outside. Situation?"

"How soon can you get here?"

"You're at the penthouse." Not a question.

"Mmh. And Andy is... *not.*" He didn't want to reveal anything else on the phone. How much did Hope know about Andy's stupid hitman sideline? "I'm not calling anyone."

"Ah. 'Kay. I'm there in twelve minutes." A sigh. "Oso, you cool?"

"No. No, it's.... Just get here." He punched END and went down to wait in front of the elevator like a sweaty trap spider. He wanted to catch her before she saw any of the mess, any of the blood.

For a moment, he remembered Andy ambushing him on that first day, barefoot and holding a drink Ruben couldn't take. *Jerk.*

True to her word, Hope turned up in just over ten minutes, wearing fancy sweats and a crease between her eyebrows.

As she stepped off the elevator, Ruben held up his hand. "Before you see, I need to know how much you know about everything."

"What is going on?" She looked wary and tried to walk around him.

"Andy's gone."

Her forehead crumpled but she didn't comment. She scanned the dim hall and crossed her arms tightly over her chest. "Did you hurt him?" Strained calm.

"No! Course not."

Hope peered warily into the hallway, eyeing the crime scene. "Where the fuck is he? Ruben?"

Ruben shifted back and said, "I have no idea. And if *you* have no idea, then Andy is in deep shit."

She stopped at the blood. "Jesus. His?"

"I think."

"You weren't here when it happened." Her gaze flicked around the walls.

"We had a fight. Personal, not professional." With luck she wouldn't press him on that. "And not physical. Last night. I left."

"Lord." Hope inched down the hall, pausing to take in the red spatter. When she got to the handprint, she hugged herself. "Lord. And why aren't we calling the NYPD?"

Ruben met her eyes. Thin ice here. "We can't. Andy wouldn't… doesn't want them here."

Slow turn, slow question. "Why?"

"This isn't a robbery, Hope."

"You don't know that. Money at this scale? Whole apartment is an enlarged motive with a universal adapter. Everybody wants to rob him." Beat. "He's done something."

How much could he trust her? "He's made some, uhh, questionable decisions."

Side-eye from Hope. "That's what trading is, Oso. *Questionable*. Risk money to make more. Mostly someone else's. Andy hasn't done anything illegal. I'd know. I see his trades. I take his calls."

Maybe he could give her enough to figure it out without betraying Andy's confidence. "Not illegal, say…."

"*Hffft*. Andy isn't a criminal. Or not more than any other investment banker." Hope squinted, cold and savvy. "How much do you know about finance?"

"Are you shitting me? I dunno. Nothing. Buy low, sell high?"

She crossed her arms. "Anytime someone makes money, someone else loses it. Anything that helps you predict the future better improves your odds. Only no one can predict the future, exactly. Unless you cheat."

"Well. Uh. What if Andy's participated in some iffy deals?"

"Finance is about margins. Boundaries." Hope stepped into the library and frowned at the mess. "The real dough is right up on the edge of what's right and wrong. But we don't steal."

"No, but say Andy had a grudge, wanted to inflict some justice." Ruben spread his fingers and let her do the math. "Is that possible?"

"With the SEC watching?" Hope sat at her desk. "If Andy wanted to retaliate, he'd have to protect himself, visibly." She looked up, the idea brightening her face as it took shape. "Unless he played to lose."

"Howzat?" Ruben blinked. As usual, Hope was gonna end up being the smartest person in the room. "Like a mistake?"

"An on-purpose. Collateral damage." She looked more curious than shocked. "Oh, that's good." Off his look, she added, "Occasionally people took heavy losses in Apex, but that's the law of the jungle. Most of these folks can afford it. Apex was high-risk for a reason." A secret grin.

Ruben spoke slowly. "He invests his own money to gain their trust and then walks them into a disaster he can survive."

She nodded. "But the victims can't. Well, think about it. Andy's not a bank. He follows laws, but he's fallible. Mistakes happen, right?"

"Sucks for them."

"Assassination by margin call." Hope rocked back and took a breath. "Only they're not *dead*-dead, just dead in the water. A financial hitman." She looked to him for confirmation.

Ruben blinked but didn't contradict her. He hadn't blabbed and she'd put it together. Now, at least he had an ally without feeling like he'd betrayed Andy again. "Maybe. He musta buried a couple big-time assholes in his time."

"Or not." She tapped a perfect plum nail on the glass desk. "Killing someone puts them out of their misery. This would feel way worse than murder, and riskier too. When you kill someone they don't stick around to return the favor. They want payback."

"Let's say you're right." He put his hands in his pockets, ready to beg. He tried to ignore the blood. "If all this is payback, this is someone with a grudge. I'm not saying it's crooked."

"But it is, and any fool would say the same."

He looked around at the wreckage. "No kidding."

Hope grimaced. "He tossed the missionaries right into a pot and started a fire under them. Cannibal stew."

Ruben sat back. "Until one of them gets antsy. Andy adds some salt." Meaning himself. Hiring Ruben had been a warning.

She eyed the mess. "Looks like one little missionary boiled over."

Sudden flash of Fifty-Ninth Street and a crowd grabbing at a tornado of hundreds. "He knew them." And right then, Ruben realized. He glanced down at his battered hands. "The mugging. He knew. He knew 'em."

She blinked. "Why do you say that?"

"Because they tried to abduct him three weeks later and he didn't want the cops." He paced, the pieces slowly floating together in his mind.

"Abduct?" Her eyebrows rose.

Ruben didn't have time to explain. "I beat the living shit out of them and they bolted. Andy knew who they worked for."

"I'm not following."

"Not strangers. I'm the only stranger. You see? Everyone else is a known quantity. The clients, the staff, social circle. He couldn't afford to have me recognize anyone."

A deep frown broke her face. "Jesus. He set you up. These guys musta given him no choice!"

"Hope, how do I find him?" He opened his arms to the disarray. "He needs your help. I do."

She looked toward the blood in the hallway.

Ruben opened his fists. "I shoulda been here with him."

"Maybe. But you weren't and Andy's a grownup. We should call the cops, Ruben. What you're talking about—"

"No. Please. Those goons weren't sent to kill him. They're more scared of jail time than he is. This is about the money. An IOU." Sweet, sharp certainty swelled up in him like uncorked champagne. "Someone wants a piece. A share." He turned to Hope and squeezed her hand, only half seeing her. "We can pay Andy's bill and walk out the door."

She shook her head slowly. "I knew he was nutty. I knew he had enemies. I knew he'd faced a couple nasty margin calls, but who hasn't?"

Ruben paid attention to the quiver in his liver. "Apex." *Predator.*

"What about it? Whole fund always made a tidy profit. Nothing flashy. Totally out of character for him, finance-wise."

Ruben nodded at the financial crawl on the cracked screens around the library. "We're looking for an Apex client in this up to his neck and hurting. Whatever the deal was, our guy lost plenty because Andy lost even more."

She nodded, righted the laptop, and started tapping. "Enough to risk violence? Wall Street and jail time don't exactly mix."

"So… a certain type of investor. Small fry with intentions in over their head. They want to seem scarier than they can be." Ruben circled the desk again.

"Wolf tickets. They're selling wolf tickets. Know what I mean?" She laughed hollowly.

"Yeah. Yeah, sure. Big talkers. Threats and ugly promises. 'Don't you know who I am?' types. For all their slick shit, they still act like Neanderthals." How many times had Andy griped about the blue bloods he'd grown up with? "Part of the tribe."

Except…the trouble had stopped until they'd turned up in tuxes at—

"Saint Anthony's." Hope finished his thought first. "He took you to show you off to the stiffs and rub their faces in it. He got cocky. Someone in Apex got the message."

"Maybe Andy wasn't paying attention to the right people."

Hope rolled her eyes. "His Apex guys are always the wrong people. Big jerks, stupid risks. Andy wouldn't let me play, ever. The deals looked so solid, and I had a couple bucks socked away. Andy never came out and said no, but he shut me out." She squinted and mock-laughed. "Was I pissed! Jeez, I thought I was gonna kill him. But, I think he was helping out his family."

His *Clan of the Cave Bear*. For a second Ruben could see Andy's guilty eyes a few inches in front of him at the Museum of Natural History by the Stone Age dioramas. "Fucking idiot." Ruben wiped his face roughly.

Hope turned.

"Cavemen. Plain sight. There's no revenge. That was just Andy's superspy Tom Clancy bullshit." He chuckled. Hope getting shut out, Andy brushing off the attacks, and spending like nothing had a price. "I wasn't paying attention to the right things. His *tribe*. He kept telling me not to trust him, but for the wrong reasons, 'cause he started to care. Sex and guilt. Booze and money. The guy stuff, the gay stuff. Jesus."

She crossed her arms tightly. "Ruben… Slow down."

Ruben counted off facts on his dirty fingers. "Look: all along Andy swore some crook wanted payback. Obviously bullshit, right? Only, someone kept muscling him. Made no sense, and he kept treating it like a game." Because it *had* been a game, to Andy.

Hope tipped her head back, gears turning. "So you're saying—"

Ruben nodded. "First I thought the danger was a lie, then I thought *he* was a liar." Andy had been trying to protect him and get clean, only some evil bastard wouldn't let him stop. "Hell, even after I knew the deal, *Andy* had me convinced he was a villain and all this was payback. Ego. So fucking arrogant." Some would-be hitman. "Taking him wasn't revenge… this was an audition, a valentine." *Be mine.*

"From a secret admirer." The light dawned and Hope blinked. "Andy just misread it. Andy wouldn't let this jackass play. So the person we're after has had no dealings with Andy or Apex or anything else. They *want* to come play with Apex. They want *in*."

Ruben rocked back and forth on his feet, "Someone he *didn't* ruin, who's known him twenty years, who can't afford to play in Apex. Small fry with a big chip on their shoulder." He closed his hand into a weak fist. "Wolf tickets. Whoever it was woulda had a lot to prove and a lot to lose."

"Okay. Okay." Hope's manicure rat-a-tatted on the keyboard. I can work with that."

"Listen." Ruben held up three fingers. "Top of my head, I can name three options: The Balenciaga woman from the museum. The Texas Lampton guy. And Marlon Stanz." It was a start, at least. Any of them made sense. "Plus, Andy tried to appease all of them publicly."

Hope raised her eyebrows.

"Exactly my thought. Since when does Andy worry about bothering bystanders?"

"Stanz is out. His wife invested." She typed on the laptop. "And Balenciaga chick—Andy told me what happened—is an ex. Andy knew the parents. Ugly breakup in grad school. Sorry if that's—" Hope looked uncomfortable.

"No. Course." He nodded. "Lampton?"

"Nah. He's a Ven-Cap bundler. He'd never put money in a fund. None of them in Apex."

Ruben scowled at his own stupidity. "But they fit. Relationships stretching back to college. Deep pockets.

"Then I got nothing. I'll let you get back to it." Stymied, Ruben looked over the puddles of paper. "I don't know how to help."

"With the files? Grab a trash can and shovel it all in. Those are just bullshit hard copies for the feds. We have digital backups running every four minutes. Actually, there's a big clue right there. Anyone serious and under fifty would expect stuff to be backed up to the cloud. These assholes are old school and dim."

"So why throw the room around?"

"Wolf tickets." She tapped her nose and pointed at Ruben. "Kiddie show, in case we call the cops. These yobs don't know better."

Ruben found a trash bag and stuffed armfuls of paper into it. Gradually he began to see parts of the floor and more evidence of a struggle.

His phone rang, his brother's number. "Yeah?"

"Weirdest thing." Charles sounded exasperated. "Who the hell do you know north of the city?"

"Nobody." Another wad of files stretched the plastic bag. He knelt to scrape more into a pile. "What happened now?"

"That carbon monoxide whatsit. That detector you bought for the apartment."

Well, salvaged. "What'd they find?" Ruben's hair stood on end.

"Someone bugged it. It's a fucking bug."

Ruben dropped the armful of paper. "It's what?"

"A bug, Rube. I cracked the case so I could see, and I know what a wire looks like. These *boludos* broke in and bugged our apartment." Ruben knew better. It had been bugged when Andy threw it out. *Andy knew.* "Emilio just pinged it and found a receiver up in Westchester. One-a my cops. So I guess they're loaded, these guys?"

He turned to Hope and covered the mouthpiece. "Where's Westchester?"

She looked up. "Above the Bronx." Like that meant anything to him.

Charles explained. "It's a suburb, above the top of Manhattan. Scarsdale, Dobb's Ferry. Ritzy. Mansions and all."

Ruben sighed. "Is he sure? Your cop, I mean."

"Rube, it's a fucking wire with a transmitter. Expensive, to hear him tell it. Several grand." Charles got muffled. A muttered conversation.

"Jesus Christ." Now Hope sat watching him. He explained: "Bug."
He had her full attention.

Charles said, "Look, I'm waiting for the cops and the adjuster, but I
wanted you to know." He hung up.

Ruben sat looking at his phone.

"Ruben?" Hope crossed her arms. "What kind of bug?"

"I don't know. It was in that CO detector Andy tossed. And we thought
he was acting nuts. What the fuck's in Westchester?"

"A lot of clients. I mean as in *a lot*. Andy knows half of Scarsdale. He
grew up there. Went off to boarding school with those guys. His dad's firm
was up there."

Again that quiver in his liver. Ruben pinched the bridge of his nose.
While they sat here baffled, Andy was trapped, bleeding and—

"Half his frat, even." She tapped a nail on the edge of the laptop. *Tick-
tick-tick-tick*. A manicured metronome. "Talk about assholes."

Ruben chewed his lip, thinking back to that grim party up near Columbia.
He scratched his head. "Joining a frat seems so unlike Andy at all."

Hope scoffed. "His family's idea. Back when Andy was still making
nice and working for the family fund. Tibbitt, the stepdad's name is."

Ruben nodded. "Fucking poser, according to him. Scarsdale. Total
Neanderthal."

Their eyes met. *Click.*

Ruben said, "*Clan of the*—"

"*Cave Bear.* We're both idiots." Hope nodded.

"A caveman valentine."

Her fingers clattered on the laptop keys and squinted at the rows. "No
deals. No investments at all. Not even with his mother's trust. Not even
friendly tips."

"You think his stepfather could get that desperate?"

"He's no kingpin. Middle-aged paper pusher from the suburbs.
Seriously. He sells insurance now."

"Since when? I thought he was a finance guy."

"He used to be, but he had to quit after Andy moved into the city. Ugly
bankruptcy. Now he plays with the mom's money and sells homeowner
policies: fire, flood, act of God. Tries to drag Andy into small potatoes,
mostly." She looked dubious. "He's a yutz."

"Then we have to go after him ourselves."

She looked askance. "We? I'm not some ninja."

"I mean no police."

"Then that leaves you." She shrugged. "Does that mean you're okay
with dangerous?" She looked serious.

A nod. "Yes. Yeah. Can you pull the stepfather's info, all of it?" Talk about a burning desire.

"Ruben, you don't wanna rush in, here." She scribbled on a piece of paper, folded it, and held it out to him like a tip.

"I'm not rushing."

"You got your reasons." Hope's eyes met his and drilled deep. "He's lucky he has you."

Ruben kept his yap shut. *Thinner ice.*

"Oso, lying makes both of us look silly, and I need to know how much he matters to you." She didn't look upset, she looked… ready. "You care about him."

"Well, yeah." He fished for the polite words to talk about his love life.

"Oh honey. For real? In New York City? This day and age?"

"Andy and I are—"

"Raging homosexicans. Yeah." She sniffed. "Please. I danced in a club three years. If it happens, I've seen it."

He clamped his mouth shut, trying not to feel ashamed.

She patted his arm. "None of my business where your grease goes. I'm a Christian, and a buncha them folks don't like it, but the hell do I care? He looked happy. You're happy. Better you than one of the debutantes circling his ass like pterodactyls."

So much for a closet.

"Lord, what men don't know is a lot."

"I'm not even—" Ruben shrugged, thoroughly discombobulated. "I gotta fix this, and I don't know what to expect."

Hope sighed. "Hun, look at me. We both know better. Expectations are nothing but resentments waiting to hatch. You sit on 'em long enough, you get pecked. You wanna fix this, then you gotta. How brave do you feel?"

He nodded. "I don't even know where to look."

She crossed her arms and exhaled. "Plus we don't even know what Tibbitt wants."

"Yeah we do. Andy humiliated him and now he wants Apex. He wants to take over."

Tibbitt wanted to be the hitman and Andy stood in the way.

"And what does he want Andy to do?" Hope looked anxious.

"Retire." Ruben took the paper and looked down at his clothes. "I need to change." And get a weapon, and some kind of plan. His autopilot kicked in.

Hope held up her hands. "Let's talk it through. Strategize. I don't think this is a good idea."

He was already in motion toward the foyer. His body knew where he needed to be.

"What?" Hope trailed after him. "You can't just go knock on the man's door."

Before he realized it, Ruben was in the elevator with his back against the wall.

"Oso, what are you gonna do?"

As the doors closed, he looked up and met her startled eyes. "Save him."

CHAPTER EIGHTEEN

BEWARE OF silence; a dog has to stop barking to bite.

The drive from Manhattan to Westchester had taken less than an hour.

Ruben drove without blinking in a car rented with cash, just in case, to a suburb of mansions.

To get the address, Charles had called in a favor with an ex-cop on his payroll. Just to confirm, he compared it to the paper Hope had given him. *Bingo.* A match.

The residence was leased, not owned, by Herbert Tibbitt of Scarsdale, New York. Aside from a citation for not shoveling the sidewalks in winter, the city had no record of any kind of criminal complaints.

Tibbitt was married to the former Cilla Bauer, Andy's mom… which made this joker his stepdad. Herb Tibbitt was the man who'd booted Andy out of the house and out of his father's brokerage. In two years, Tibbitt had run the firm into a ditch and started selling insurance with spotty results.

From there, the trail painted itself right through the Apex files.

Hope found a smatter of phone calls from Herb dating back to the New Year. Andy had said his mother had mentioned money problems at Christmas. Herb had tried to squeeze his stepson without luck.

At some point Tibbitt must have gotten proof of Andy's other activities, seen some blue-blood dickhead taken out or witnessed a strategic meltdown. A suspicious string of bankruptcies and foreclosures had led him right back to Apex and Andy's control of it. Obviously the shame of being rebuffed and near-bankruptcy had provoked Tibbitt's attacks.

And given Ruben a job.

He could only think of one reason why this son of a bitch would pay to install any kind of detector in Andy's penthouse, and it wasn't for auld lang syne. The installation order had come to the Iris maintenance staff by phone.

I-95 was empty at midnight, and Ruben kept his speed five over the limit all the way to Scarsdale.

Why does crappy music always sound better on a car radio?

He parked three blocks away and kept to the dark side of the street, the air hot as a kiln. Ruben knew better than to wear black, but the dark Columbia sweatshirt two sizes too big covered his Kevlar. He was packing a sweaty handful of zip ties and a holstered weapon he'd only fired at a range.

The neighborhood was a rolling panorama of *House Beautiful* covers: gently sloping lawns and sculpted trees behind gates and cameras. Range Rovers and sheepdogs. The kind of white-bread haven he'd dreamed of living in for his entire childhood.

Ruben avoided security lights, keenly aware of his dark skin. Not quite midnight, but every six-million-dollar house silent, only a few bluish glows from the computers and TVs of insomniacs and binge watchers.

He heard Peach in his head: *Trying to pray* is *praying.*

Tibbitt's spread was a prim two-story faux-Colonial set back on two acres at the top of a sloping drive. Rather than risk cameras, Ruben pressed right through the dense box hedges, breaking a few branches and emerging onto a landscaped lawn facing a glowing pool about fifty yards upslope.

Where would Tibbitt have stashed Andy? *Basement? Toolshed?*

Tibbitt had the run of the place and enough yard that the neighbors would never hear. The silent house glowed with careful uplighting, so he stuck to the zinnia beds and crept toward the back, aiming for the bluish gleam of the pool.

The house was so lit that the rest of the yard seemed velvety black by contrast. Even the pool house was dark and dead silent. *Why?*

Slow down. Ruben measured his breathing by his heart: four beats in, hold for four, four out, hold for four.

Tactical breathing and powdered eggs were all Ruben remembered from his brief stay in boot camp way back when.

In four, hold four, out four. His heart steadied and his feet followed.

Hugging the hedges, Ruben did a press-check on his brother's .45 to verify the first round was in the chamber. The slide was stiff.

Guns had never been his thing, even in the bad old days. He knew the basics, but he was a so-so shot and distrusted anything mechanical. Holding one while walking into a confrontation had him crapping his proverbial pants.

Only the thought of Andy inside, in pain, kept one foot in front of the last.

The firearm was for show. He had to get in and out before it became necessary. *Be smart.* Once he found Andy, he had to bail before he ended up fighting some ex-con with a face like knuckles.

For once in his life, he thanked God that he looked like a criminal. If he had to, he could bluff and bullshit their way to safety.

Coming up the long driveway, he moved slowly and silently for a perimeter check. No security cameras. No alarm system. Nothing hardwired to the mains. Strictly bozo.

He traced the electrical to the east side and dug the cutters out. Finally he got to use his executive protection course, and it was to commit a felony. Rescuing Andy wasn't exactly self-defense, but it felt like exactly that.

According to Charles and his cop, this house had no security system. *Time to find out.*

Ruben squeezed the cutters and the yard went dark.

One heartbeat, two heartbeats.

No siren. No exclamations or movement from inside. No rabid Rottweiler. Nobody home?

He peeked through a window: the house was a tomb.

Ruben glanced at his watch. He'd been here seven minutes. Time to pick up sticks. Ruben swung wide and walked the fence's perimeter.

A cough froze him, and he edged around the back of the house.

No sign of Andy yet, but someone was on the premises.

In the backyard under a fig tree, Chunk stood smoking a cigarette, looking at the pool.

Relief and joy and nausea. If the goon was here, then Andy probably was as well. If both goons were here, there'd be a fight too.

Ruben slowed and floated closer silently.

Chunk was wearing a two-hundred-dollar cop suit, and the ground under his feet was littered with butts. Smoking lounge for dummies. His bulbous nose looked worse for wear after its close encounter with Andy's fire extinguisher. Ruben wondered if he'd bothered to fix his teeth.

Ruben kept to the shadows and glided forward.

At the last possible minute, Chunk must've heard a twig or a gurgle, and he turned... but not soon enough.

Ruben wrapped one arm around his throat and squeezed. The lit cigarette arced into the grass.

He knew this trick from Miami bars. Cut off air supply for a few seconds and everybody went night-night. No alarms, no corpses. He'd grab Andy and split before he made any noise.

Ruben squeezed the stout neck harder, flexing his bicep, and the round face turned salmon pink.

Chunk spluttered and snotwhistled, but his hands were trapped and his eyes started to roll back.

Ruben closed his eyes and held firm. He didn't want to kill anyone, but some brain damage sounded fine.

The guy's knees went, and Ruben lowered him to the ground silently to pat him down.

No firearm. The wallet had a driver's license and a Visa, which meant both were fake and these guys were amateurs.

Ruben zip-tied the fat wrists and ankles and duct-taped his mouth to keep him on mute. He tipped the stocky body into the back hedge and prayed for spiders. *Big ones.*

"Phil?" A low whine across the yard as Walrus came out of the dark house, tugging at his mustache.

Ruben breathed. *In four, hold four, out four.*

Taking one last long sip of breath, Ruben rolled his shoulders and, for better or worse, put his foot in it. *Time to make the donuts.*

As Walrus stepped past his hiding place, Ruben emerged and set the screwdriver against the skinny spine.

Ruben wasn't a murderer, but he could certainly play one for an hour. After all, Andy had hired him to play a thug. Looking like a villain had a couple advantages.

Walrus blanched. "Sh—"

"No." The low word almost a grunt. Headshake and the screwdriver dug into the meat of the skinny man's back. "Not a word. Don't you say nothing."

Walrus choked and nodded. He smelled like spearmint.

Out four, hold four, in four. "No killing," Ruben muttered into the hot air as he yanked the zip tie tight around the bony wrists.

Still no sound from the dark house. The pool glowed beyond.

Now that the plan was in motion, Ruben felt almost lightheaded with relief. He muttered, "I came to do some maintenance, dipshit. Sound good?"

Inhale, exhale. Walrus nodded but didn't turn.

"Here's my offer: no bullshit, I'm gone in ten. You get frisky, I'm gonna install a fucking doorbell over your spine so people know you're a cunt." He pressed, trying to break the skin. "Ding dong."

The mouthful of crooked teeth opened in soundless pain until Ruben could eyeball the dodgy fillings on his back molars from the side. Walrus whisper-screamed, "Aggh!"

"See? If I don't miss, you get life as a vegetable. I do miss, you're dead meat." Ruben's grip on the screwdriver tightened and he drove the tip between the guy's vertebrae. "Deal?"

Walrus closed his eyes. His lower lip quivered wetly. "Mmh."

"Then nod." Ruben squared his stance and did his impression of an immovable object.

"Uh, I'm—"

"Quiet. I think my buddy needs a ride." Jab. Ruben twisted the screwdriver. "Huh? You think he needs a ride home?"

Walrus shook, and then the air went sharp with ammonia as he pissed himself. He nodded.

"All done, huh? I think we're going to go collect him, because it's past his bedtime. Move." Another jab, and now blood sprang at the tip, a slow ooze. "Oops."

Walrus stumbled forward on the dark patio toward the pool house.

Bingo.

So it *was* the pool house. Weird emotion churned inside him at the image of Andy in there, bound in the dark: relief and hope and panic.

Ruben growled, "Let's hope that Tibbitt and your fat friend don't get any dumber."

The mustached face turned in surprise. His zip-tied hands had gone chalky purple with trapped blood.

"You're..." Ruben advanced slowly, using the skinny body as a shield, "not exactly masterminds, *hombre*."

Tibbitt was nowhere to be seen.

Ruben prodded. "We knew."

No reaction.

"Andy's stepfucker and his bullshit partners trying a new investment strategy. The feds might get the wrong idea about you boys and ring your new bell." He shoved and Walrus stumbled forward. "Slowly."

Walrus stopped at the door, swaying. Somewhere a few houses over, a dog barked.

Reaching around him, Ruben turned the knob slowly and silently.

Walrus didn't move. A jab and he stumbled forward.

They moved into a small, dark sitting room. Loveseat and a chair. A coffee table piled with food boxes. A wide laptop on the counter was the only light source, and it cast violet light over the silent space.

This wasn't right.

Ruben opened his mouth to call for Andy but thought better of it. "Show me."

Walrus scuffed forward. His bound hands bumped Ruben's leg.

Ruben's grip was sweaty. "You fucking touch me again, jagoff, and I stick this in your fucking ear." He meant it.

The laptop screen showed a muted sitcom family clowning for cameras. A half-eaten sandwich was beside it. He'd been watching TV.

Where did they have Andy? Surely this little bungalow didn't have a basement or an attic.

Ruben's eyes adjusted, and now he saw the room's bare walls. Folding chairs, folding table. Everything last minute and temporary. No kinda plan.

Walrus had stopped at another small door. Maybe a closet or a bedroom? Did pool houses have beds?

Ruben reached for the handle, his internal klaxons blaring but time racing past. Every second wasted put Andy in more danger.

Walrus shifted sideways but stayed stone still under the point of the screwdriver. His face was slick with sweat in the bluish light.

Please don't be dead. Please don't be hurt.

Ruben's fingers closed on the metal knob, and his heart thundered as he turned and pushed, keeping the skinny goon in front to take fire.

The doorway was pitch black. Some kind of room. He spurred Walrus forward with the screwdriver. More blood now black in the half-light.

"Andy." The name slipped out in a hoarse whisper before Ruben could stop it.

A step. Another. Walrus stiffened in front of him.

Then the crackle of a Taser. Blue flickering light scalded the inside of Ruben's eyes, and lightning jolted his entire skeleton.

"Guh!" Ruben's vision grayed, and he landed hard on one elbow unable to catch himself. His muscles jerked and boiled.

Beside him, Walrus rolled to his feet, his mouth bloody from a bitten tongue.

The light came on. Another crackle made Ruben seize and scream as Walrus kicked his head.

The room faded, but not before Ruben managed to turn and see the kind face smiling down.

WHEN RUBEN heaved his eyelids open, his entire left side felt as if it had been crushed inside a sack. The bus station this morning had been ugly, but now his sternum throbbed, his mouth was crusty with dried blood, and he felt pretty confident that at least two of his fingers were broken.

In the dark, someone moved toward him. A fresh-bread kiss. The pain evaporated like spit on a griddle.

Andy.

"Ow." Ruben smiled in relief, resplitting his lip against Andy's and too happy to care. "Hey boss."

"Oh man." Andy looked not so bad, considering. His face was scuffed and scabby: black eye, dings, and dents. "Pretty ugly."

"Nuh uh." Another kiss. Why did that feel so good?

They were in some kind of basement space, too big to be under the pool house. A bare bulb on a chain and one dingy window high in the wall gave the only light in a room heaped with battered file boxes.

Andy leaned him into the light and gave him the once-over. "Well, we're in the soup, huh? I guess you met my stepdad." He wore clothes Ruben had never seen before: a faded sweatshirt and size-fifty khakis belted tight. They'd taken him naked.

That kind face. "The old guy."

Andy shook his head and squeezed his hand. "Thanks."

Ruben squirmed up so his back was propped against the wall. "For getting popped?"

"For saving me."

"Great job I'm doing so far."

Andy glanced at the door. "Better than you think, *cariño*. They're shitting kittens now."

"All I did was get a screwdriver dirty and dent his boot with my skull."

"But you found me. They're waiting for the cavalry. What kinda idiot would charge in without backup, right?"

"*No kidding.*" Ruben gave a dry, wheezing laugh. His ribs and face hurt where Walrus had kicked. "How long I been down here?" Someone had taped his broken fingers.

"Couple hours? I'm not even sure what day it is."

"Saturday when I showed up."

"Time flies when you're trying to stay out of prison." Andy dimpled.

Here it comes.

Ruben touched his face, which had been cleaned at some point.

"I tried to patch you up." Andy's eyes, soft and certain, glittered. "I can explain everything."

Ruben snorted. "Then you're a fucking genius,"

"I'm so sorry. Anyone else woulda left me to take my medicine."

Stupid. Ruben shrugged. *I'm a goner.* Before he started acting like a dumb drunk, he got serious.

"Andy, if I stay, you're going out of business."

"What?"

"What you've been doing is illegal. You've wrecked people, ruined lives. Maybe they deserved it, but you can't just hand this over to Tibbitt and walk away. Even he knows that."

Andy didn't balk. "Are you going to turn me in?"

"No. Jesus."

"Really." He looked surprised. "Why?"

"Because I can't let you get away that easily."

Now the smile, conspiratorial as hell.

Ruben eyed him. "Look, I'm not letting anyone lock you up, but I'm not gonna put in time with a crazy person. I have enough trouble keeping myself sane."

To his credit, Andy nodded.

"You're gonna pay your stepfather and get out. Retire."

"I can't."

"You can."

"Ruben, he doesn't want money. He wants—"

"Apex."

Surprise on Andy's face. "Yes. Yeah. Exactly. How did you know that?"

"I looked, man," Ruben spoke gently. "You're some bigshot and he's trapped out here. He catches you hunting big game, and he wants in. Yes?"

Andy nodded, mouth tight, cheeks pink.

"You know he's dangerous, and you stall him and shut him out. Things get ugly."

"Worse." Andy heaved a sigh. "Ruben, he's my father." Grimace. "Like, the actual donor of the actual sperm. Stepfucker."

"Jesus."

"It's why he hates me so much. And why my mother played diplomat my whole life. Every time I defended my dad—"

Frown. "Andy, none of that matters. Huh? How can you use it?" Ruben spread his hands wide. "Think."

"Well, he wants ownership. Legacy. All these years he's been trying to claim me for himself. Ugh." Andy grimaced. "That's his blind spot. He wants me to act like his son, to put him in charge."

"So do that. Right? What do you care? You can't leave your whole life hanging and cross your fingers that no one notices."

"My *father*, Ruben. She never said a word."

"Then I'd say you'd better use that card while it counts."

"And what? I pay him and give him Apex so my skeezy sperm donor can wreak havoc on anyone who ruffles his feathers?" Andy closed his mouth in a frown. "And then what?"

"You live." Ruben frowned and took Andy's hand. "I'm being serious, Bauer. Prudent and rational and all that shit you hate because I want you to not be dead or crippled. You broke it, we fix it."

Andy rubbed his face roughly. "Give up working? Investing? What am I gonna do?"

Ruben snapped. "Well, first up you're not going to end up in the fucking penitentiary getting gangbanged in the shower! Oh, and you won't get abducted and beaten by sociopathic relatives! Jesus, Andy!"

Andy raised his hands and shook his head apologetically. "Sorry. You're right. You're solving my problem."

"Trying to. If we can." Ruben spoke with gentle firmness. "People think getting sober means sitting in a church basement and shame-bragging about all the crazy shit you did drunk." Headshake. "Sober originally meant *serious*. Looking hard. Thinking about your choices and responsibilities. Standing up instead of lying there."

Andy's brow creased. "I cannot give that bastard what he wants."

"No, but you can make him pay for the privilege." Ruben sighed. "Look, I know only one way to fix a problem you can't control. Admit it. Ask for help. Make amends. Keep serious."

"You're twelve-stepping me?"

Eyebrows in the air, Ruben opened his mouth, closed it before he said anything ugly, and—

"And that solves everything."

"No, genius. Nothing solves *everything*. Nothing's ever totally over. Just... over there." Ruben held his breath and counted with his heart. "It's a step, Andy. Serious. One step."

Andy's shoulders fell. "Put my foot down. And then another foot. Walk away? This is my business, my mom, my family."

"Your loser stepdad who you've been fucking with since you were twenty. Revenge banking and pissing on him because you could."

"There's no skeletons in his fucking closet; there's a bag of bones, pile of bone dust. My mom. Dad. My career."

"As a trust-fund hitman. What a rush." Ruben's face throbbed in the hot stale air, so he knew better than to touch it. "Yeah. My nose bleeds for you."

Andy's eyebrows tightened and his mouth turned down. "Easy for—"

"Is it? Tell me how easy I got it." Ruben struggled to his feet. "You gotta stop assuming everyone is as stupid as you."

"That's not what I meant."

"Wait, I'm sorry, Bauer…." Ruben pointed. "You don't mind if I call you *stupid*, do you? Obviously not, since you keep being stupid every chance you get. Luckily for you I gotta lotta practice being a self-destructive idiot. You talk about it like an addict, and I say that *as a fucking addict*."

Andy nodded with grim finality. "Are you saying I don't have a choice?"

"No! You gotta choice. I gotta choice. He's gotta choice. All these goddamn choices. Yeah. Yeah. You get to choose. Sure!" Ruben waved his arms at the basement they were trapped in. "I'm making a suggestion, Andy. I'm suggesting it, the same way I'd suggest pulling the ripcord on a parachute because the concrete's about to say, 'What's up, motherfucker?'" He didn't get to shouting till the end.

Contrite swallow. "You have a point."

"No shit! So you're gonna *choose* to give him what he wants and walk away. This isn't a dick-measuring contest. Crazy people can't lose because they can't win. You give him whatever financial bullshit he wants and take your fucking lumps." But he squeezed Andy's hand. "Money. Family. Business. Whatever."

"This is gonna cost me way more than money."

"Good." Ruben scowled. "I mean it, Andy. Don't wanna stay alive? Great. I'll just kill you myself, and they can bury you under your mother's fig tree."

Andy stood beside him and squeezed back. "No, you won't, Rube. You protect me. You kick my ass. Make me smile. Hell, you know how to finish most my sentences."

"If I had my way, they'd all end with duct tape." But Ruben grinned then, so relieved to stand there joking that he could almost forget what was waiting upstairs.

"I think you care about me." Long, intense pause.

Ruben stayed perfectly still, conscious of Andy's fingers laced warm against his.

"We're gonna get out of here, and then I've got some extreme apologizing to do."

"Likewise, *pintón*."

"Unless we die."

Ruben shoved him. "Thanks."

Andy shrugged. "Well… life isn't everything."

The goofy Sears-dad laugh made Ruben's hair stand on end, and somehow, the poisonous guilt started to leach out of him as if draining out of his fingers and face onto the concrete with each drop of sweat. He didn't want a drink: he wanted a shower… with Andy.

Here they were trapped and bloody in a basement in Scarsdale, and he didn't want to be anywhere else. An honest man would've had the sense to look miserable.

Not Andy. Crooked son of a bitch did the bit where his mouth stayed still, but his eyes melted.

Ruben scowled. "Don't you hustle me, Bauer."

"I wasn't. Well, I wasn't *really*. Just, I like watching you take charge of my bullshit. Ownership. You're the looker, I'm the leaper, right?"

"I'm never gonna be able to trust you if you keep taking these stupid risks for no benefit. It's—"

"Investment." Andy nodded.

"I was gonna say important, but fine."

"I trust you, *Señor* Oso."

"You better, *pintón*, you know what's good for you." He took hold of Andy's thick hair right at the cowlick and shook his skull playfully. "I got enough to worry about. I'm serious."

"Same." Andy scanned his face. "I see you, y'know? You can't hide." Andy squinted. "Hangman's face with a hero's heart." He tapped Ruben's chest.

"Ow. Fuck off."

"That didn't hurt."

Blink. *True.*

Andy pressed his face into Ruben's throat and inhaled. "That's why it's called a moment of truth." A nod.

"I guess. We still gotta get out of this place."

Andy's eyes searched his, digging for something… a promise, an answer? "We will. I swear. *Serious.*" The word had become a secret code between them. Everything they needed: serious life, serious money, serious danger, serious trust, serious emotion. Andy stepped back and shifted toward the door.

"Wait…. Are you leaving?"

Andy frowned, looked down and then right at him. "I love you, Ruben Oso. Like nothing I ever knew in my whole worthless fake of a life."

You do? Ruben nodded, too dumbstruck to make words.

The early sunlight fell across them like a kiss on the cheek from God.

Andy pressed their foreheads together. "I been spoiled, stubborn, and stupid since I was a kid. I never… I never—" A careful kiss.

"Me either." Ruben swallowed, his mouth gluey. "Like the world's a tuxedo, and I'm a brown shoe. A sneaker." Andy shook his head, but Ruben shushed him. "I wanna tell the truth. You were right. Not about everything but about some of it. You know me, and I shouldn't-a left you like that. None of this woulda—"

"No, Rube."

"Look. I'm a lazy drunk. I've lied and stolen and cut corners. Only reason I'm *alive* is 'cause better people took pity on me. Family, my ex. I don't deserve anything, least of all a second chance." Swallow. "With us."

Andy wiped his eyes and his mouth and nodded at the floor. "Okay. Okay."

"Yeah?" Better than booze, that sweet flutter under his sternum. "Okay."

"Good." A dazzling salesman's smile and Andy wiped his hands on his baggy, bloodstained khakis. "That's that then."

"That's what?"

"We have a deal." Andy swept into motion.

The hell? Ruben made a face.

"Not you and me. Me and Tibbitt. My stepfucker. I'll never be rid of him, but I don't have to care. You're right. I don't need him. It doesn't matter to anyone that matters."

"Wait, what?"

Andy was already yanking through a wardrobe.

"You hungry? You need clothes."

"Slow down. Slow down."

He tossed a handmade dress shirt at Ruben. "My dad was bigger. That should fit."

"Uhh." His father's shirt. Ruben decided not to be weirded out by that.

"Sorry. It's dumb, but they won't let you in without a collar and a jacket."

"Bauer, what the fuck are you doing? Where are we going? I thought you were a prisoner."

"I have been. I was. But you fixed that, too, by charging in." Andy dropped to his knees and rifled through a drawer. "If I don't have to fight him, then we can walk away free and clear. No time to shower. Get dressed."

Ruben knew what his face had to look like. Blood and bruises and worse. "Andy, he tried to kill us."

"No. He tried to convince us. That—" He pointed at Ruben's body and face. "—was just a conversation. He's a crappy negotiator. We aren't prisoners. It's my mom's house."

"They attacked me."

"An intruder. With weapons. C'mon. And you look fucking scary."

My bull's-eye face. Ruben's fingers fumbled with the buttons, still fuzzy on Andy's plan but closing the cotton over his battered torso. "Then why are we in the basement?"

Andy laughed. "This is my room. Was. Or it's where I slept when I came home from boarding school. Privacy." Shrug. "I was fifteen. Place to jerk off and get high. Without having to listen to him fight with the air."

Ruben looked at the boxes piled everywhere.

"Storage now. I just...." He shook his head. "I brought you to my room because I didn't want you anywhere else."

Ruben touched his back. "He's not your dad, he's your enemy. Even if he— He didn't raise you. He's just a problem we're going to solve."

"Jacket should fit." Andy lifted a navy blazer out of the closet and eyed the tiny gold shield on its lapel. "His Columbia pin, even."

Ruben accepted the jacket numbly. "I thought you were in trouble."

"I was. I'd screwed up my mother's life, left her with Tibbitt when I knew better, and then poked the mangy bear for twenty years. I'm trapped in that goddamn penthouse spying on the city 'cause I'm too afraid to live in it. Then I'd lost you. I was—" Another headshake and a frown. "Over and out." He snapped on the overhead light.

Sure enough, posters on the wall and battered textbooks revealed themselves. A boy's room buried under junk.

"You hungry? C'mon." Andy flipped a keyring. "We're going to brunch."

Upstairs, they walked through a very plush suburban mansion. The rooms were dimly lit, but Andy knew the way.

"Are we stealing one of his cars?" Ruben shook his head, woozy still and struggling to keep up. "Jesus! What are you talking about?" He jammed the shirttails into his pants. "Stop. Stop!"

A garage with two Jags, a Range Rover, and a Mercedes convertible. A half million dollars in automotive arrogance lined up like candy in a rack. Andy pressed one of the keys on the ring, and lights glowed from the Mercedes. "Good choice."

Ruben's voice echoed inside the garage. "They took you! They trashed your place? Blood, Andy."

Andy opened the door, but waited. "That is my stepfucker's idea of a conversation. He wants to show me how *serious* he can be. I'm only here because I wouldn't give him Apex and let him terrorize everyone he hates. Now I can."

"How?"

"Well, not the way he wants it." Andy gave the barracuda grin and climbed inside. The motor purred to life. "Now I'm serious."

Ruben popped the door and did the same, sitting his sore body on the buttery leather. "Fuck but I love that."

Andy turned.

"That shark thing you do."

"Yeah?" Andy held out his hand.

Ruben took it. "Sexy as hell. You don't know."

As the garage opened, Andy inched the car back in the swift arc of an expert driver on familiar turf.

"I wish I could be that ruthless." Ruben laced their fingers.

Andy nosed up the driveway, his eyes on the road hard as porphyry. "Practice."

CHAPTER NINETEEN

ALL PRAYERS get answered. Most of the time, the answer is no.

Andy drove like the map was burnt into his brain, barely looking at the road. Twenty-four minutes later they pulled through gates that said Scarsdale Golf Club.

"I thought this was a country club."

"It's both. Same diff." Andy rolled his eyes. "Don't judge."

"Why stop now?" Ruben rolled his sleeves down. His bruises looked even worse against his dark skin. "Andy, I look like a convict." He glanced over. "And you look like something convicts use to clean the john."

True enough. Andy's black eye had hit that "oily rainbow" stage. Butterfly tape held an ugly tear on his forehead together up to where his hairline was matted with blood. His arm hair was gummy with tape and showed raw stripes where it had been ripped free.

Andy nodded at them. "Good, huh? We turn up with war wounds; my stepfather has to answer a lot of questions." He squeezed Ruben's hand, then downshifted into second as he approached the valet stand. "The worse we look, the better this goes."

Ruben drummed the door with his fingers, scowling.

"I'd ask you to punch me just to get things flowing again, but my face hurts too much."

"Stop. I'm not gonna hit you."

"We want to make a terrible impression."

Ruben chuckled. "Ow. It hurts to laugh. That Walrus asshole got my ribs good."

"With the mustache? Ernie. That was payback for the other night, I expect. You almost fractured his jaw a couple weeks back."

Ruben stopped talking. Andy knew their names. Of course he did, they worked for his stepfather. He'd known them all along. Even the mugging that first day, Andy had known.

Shrug. "Ernie's a claims adjuster. No genius, obviously."

They glided to a halt under a porte cochère.

On cue, a scrubbed teenager trotted out in a melon-pink knit shirt with a logo over his pec. As soon as Ruben climbed out, he stepped back. "Whoa, man." He scratched at his neck and eyed Ruben with uncloaked fascination. "Jeez—"

"We're here for brunch." Andy tossed the keys. "Bauer."

To his credit the kid caught them, almost without looking, but he eyed Andy's injuries. "Uhh. You guys need any, y'know umm, help?"

Andy smiled. "Just the car."

"Uhh, sure." The kid backed away from them all the way around the Mercedes. He didn't climb inside.

Ruben raised an eyebrow. "There a problem?"

The boy swallowed and scratched his neck again. "Nah." Nervous headshake. "It's…. You both look like a TV show, is all? Uhh. Have a great brunch."

The car pulled away.

Andy nudged Ruben and steered him toward the entrance. "Remember: if he pisses himself in the car, it's not our car." His eyes shone fever bright. Was he enjoying this? "Let's go make a deal."

Retaliation. Retirement. Relationship. How could Andy protect himself and his mom? Would he actually give up his business? And how did Ruben factor in?

The old man wanted into Apex so he could take out his enemies. Financial assassination. He wanted to use Andy as a weapon, a hitman. The only way to get Andy out was to make him radioactive.

They passed through a silent lobby. Some overfed white folks stood in clumps.

Andy veered left. "Clubhouse."

Ruben muttered, "What are you... what do you need me to do?"

"Look scary. Let him assume anything. Everything."

They'd reached a large sunlit dining room. Ruben scanned the space, not knowing what he was looking for. "Wolf tickets."

"You been talking to Hope, *Señor* Oso." Andy grinned and nodded. "That's the one: sell him some wolf tickets." He smoothed his ill-fitting blazer.

They walked into a sort of lounge overlooking the pool and the green, featuring a bar on one wall and a gigantic curved sideboard piled with meat, fruit, and a freestanding omelet station. A handful of middle-aged couples clustered at low tables around the room.

Ruben asked, "And what are you gonna do?"

"Win."

There. Andy focused on a man in his late sixties, shortish with a receding hairline, nursing a Bloody Mary alone.

He saw them and stood. "Andrew. You look terrible." Tibbitt perused Ruben's injuries without making eye contact.

"We came for brunch."

"You can't afford attention any more than I." His gaze flicked to the scatter of other grayish suburbanites.

"And to do some business. My partner." Andy turned. "Ruben Oso. From Colombia."

Tibbitt swallowed that. "They do business down there?" The older man regarded Ruben with the mercy of a polygraph. "Only things I know come from Colombia are emeralds and cocaine."

Ruben clenched his fists but kept his face still. "He's filthy rich. I'm just filthy."

"This club is filled with minorities who swear they're victims." Tibbitt exhaled.

Anger made Ruben's voice louder than necessary. "And prisons are bulging with numbskulls who swear they were framed."

Andy put a calm hand on his arm.

Tibbitt wiped his mouth with a napkin. "You shouldn't have come here with him. Your mother is outside."

Ruben ignored Andy and made the threat clear. "I'm not going anywhere, pops. Or else we're all going. I'd love to take a fire extinguisher to your face."

Three tables over, a young couple with a toddler looked up nervously.

"Jesus." Tibbitt looked ready to shit himself.

Andy patted his back. "Ruben. I got it." He held a chair for Ruben and then sat himself. After a long moment, Tibbitt sat stiffly.

Ruben breathed and watched the stream of pastel idiots migrating to and from the buffet loaded down with waffles and pineapple. *Keep it together.* This was Andy's show. None of his business.

The old man thought Ruben was just hired muscle. That was something. Long as he didn't know about their relationship, this stupid plan might work. He would let his resting thug face do the talking.

The old man tapped his glass and frowned at Ruben's lapel. "I'm to believe you two met at Columbia?"

Ruben didn't say anything, but Tibbitt took the silence for assent.

Tibbitt huffed. "Light is the glory of life. Life in the dark is misery, and rather death than life."

The fuck?

Andy answered casually. "He means the motto."

Ruben looked down at the pin.

Tibbitt frowned. "No one goes to church anymore."

Andy's tone stayed goofy and noncommittal. "Ruben does. He goes to church a couple times a week."

Ruben gave his best Aztec asshole, heavy-lidded, hawk-nose, shadowy glare. *Retaliation* would be his part in all this. Tibbitt took a swallow. "You must be a sinner."

"'Cause I'm brown? I'd lay off, *puto.*"

Andy coughed. "Look, uh, I don't want any more trouble, Herb." On cue, he went into his goofy, clueless routine. "The Apex Fund is only one part of—"

"Don't be such a pussy, Bauer." Ruben set the bait. "He's halfway to the pen."

Tibbitt muttered, "Mr. Oso, I don't take kindly—"

"You'll take what I give." Ruben scowled, kept his voice just low enough. "Kidnap. Assault. Attempted murder. Extortion." A drop of spit arced across the table. He bared his teeth. "Man, you're such a tool, they ought to sell you at Home Depot. I would like nothing more than to shove that chair up your ass sideways in front of all these nice people." He raised his chin at Andy. "He's the only reason I haven't, but he's the reason I will."

Tibbitt stared at the spittle as if it were a rattlesnake. "Another suitably juvenile bit of posturing."

"Try me." Ruben sat forward and growled now. *Time to play.* "You think we're joking? By the time the feds get to you, they're gonna need a wet vac to clean you off the wallpaper."

Nearby someone gasped, and dropped silverware clanked. The other diners had begun to eavesdrop.

Tibbitt swallowed and flushed a greasy salmon pink as if he'd shat his pants.

Andy hissed, "Oso."

Ruben spoke directly to the old man. "You got some balls." If nothing else, Ruben knew how to look like a criminal. "Mr. Tibbitt, I got enough legal problems without you adding to 'em."

"I'm willing to let you take a leadership role." Andy glanced at his stepfather. *So that's the play.* They'd appeal to Tibbitt's ego and prejudices and leave him holding the bag.

Ruben popped his neck. He could play this part. "You got no idea, *boludo.* If this is the bullshit way you people do business, I want out."

In the pause, Andy encouraged him, a slight nod.

"And if I'm out, then Andy's out. We're partners. Yeah?" He raised his eyebrows at Andy. "And playing around in this white-bread sewer feels like a waste of his talents. He's working with me now."

Tibbitt looked to his stepson. "What is he saying?"

Andy took his hand under the table and squeezed. Ruben flushed.

Tibbitt sighed. "You've been disrespectful, to me and to your mother. After all I taught you, all I've done."

"*¡Gilipollas!*" Ruben ladled contempt over them. Andy had only taught him a few curses. "The two of you dancing around. Fucking Wonder Bread pin dicks."

The brunch crowd gave him a few disapproving looks, but not enough to make Tibbitt take the bait. *Retaliation, retaliation.*

Exasperated, Ruben glared at Tibbitt and pounded the table with his fist till the silver jumped. "Hump his mom, cheat your partner, and trash his place. Please, can I play with Apex?" He snorted.

Andy sat straighter but didn't interfere.

Tibbitt seemed genuinely startled. "Andy, you let him talk to you like that?" So far so good.

"Sir." A teenage waiter stood by the table. "Is there a problem?" All of a hundred and thirty pounds and ready to piss his pants.

Ruben ignored him and glared at Tibbitt. "Did you see that on cable, jackass?"

Andy smiled at the waiter and made a joke of it. "Family dispute."

"He gave me…." Tibbitt's voice was level, considering. "No choice." His hands settled on the tablecloth. "I had a rough spell. I'm just trying to recoup some of my losses."

Ruben didn't sit back. "Tibbitt, you disrespect us again, and I'm going to make a fucking warning out of you, one slimy chunk at a time in front of all your neighbors here." He let his face finish the thought. *Aztec asshole.*

The old man swallowed.

Andy scolded and smiled. "Ruben, I don't think that's helpful." The waiter looked dubious till Tibbitt nodded. *All in good fun.*

"Let me be clear." Ruben thought of Andy's sharkiest moments and rested his dead gaze on the old man. "Apex no longer interests me." If he could sell this to Tibbitt, they'd be home free. "So it no longer interests him."

Tibbitt went for it. "It's the least you can do. Lord knows you can afford it."

Andy said, "I don't want my mother involved. This is between us, and she's no part of it."

Tibbitt exhaled. "Your mother trusts me to make the financial decisions." From his tone, he could have been talking about a golden retriever or a potted plant.

Ruben frowned. If someone spoke about his mother like that, he'd have hauled them out back, but his mother would beat him to it. What kind of family was this?

"What do you care where he invests his money?" Ruben turned.

Andy said quietly, "I don't want him bankrupting her." Ruben could see the rage simmering and the gears grinding.

Tibbitt shrugged. "Music to my ears. One less thing to explain."

Andy nodded, eyes narrowed. "Then here's my offer. I'll give you a fifty-fifty split, but I retain control of the company." And there was Andy's retirement. So far so good. "A silent-but-deadly partner. All holdings, accounts, and shares split. But the assets and the liabilities in your name alone. I don't want my mother at risk because of our business bullshit."

Poor Hope. Ruben hated the idea that she'd invested all that time, gotten her degree, and now Tibbitt had cut in line. She deserved better, but she also didn't need the crooked bullshit attached to her career. Andy was making a *serious* offer, and he knew why.

"We'll own Apex together," Andy finished.

Tibbitt's eyebrows floated toward his hairline. "What guarantee do I have?"

"My business with my most lucrative fund ever, and I'm giving you half of it, old man. What better guarantee can I offer?"

"How do I know you won't bring in some other greaseball thug to scare me off?" Tibbitt pursed his lips.

Andy kept his gaze directed at the floor. "I've known Ruben—"

"For about five weeks. Yes. Noted." A mortician's sniff of competent displeasure. "This is what comes of sending my bastard to prep school. Pretensions to justice and—" A sniff at Ruben. "Low-hanging fruit."

Ruben kept his face still.

"I wouldn't say that, *Herb*." Andy coughed. A dark smile as his shark fin broke the surface. "I didn't hire Ruben."

What?

Andy lifted their hands onto the table. Ruben let him, shock making him jittery.

Tibbitt huffed. "Andrew, we have business to—"

"And he certainly doesn't work for me. Hell, he doesn't even do what I tell him half the time." Andy smiled softly, teeth knife-bright. "Ruben and I are together. Whatever you want to say to me, you say to him."

Tibbitt slowed. He stared at their linked hands as if at rattlesnakes fucking. "You think you can scare me off? You can't embarrass me."

Andy snorted. "Understatement of the decade."

Ruben blinked slowly and raised his voice. "We're not the ones making a scene, Señor Tibbitt. We didn't injure ourselves. I don't even like brunch."

Silence.

"Don't be ridiculous."

Andy kissed Ruben. Right on the mouth in the middle of the Scarsdale Golf Club. Grabbed the back of his head and mashed their mouths together.

Ruben rolled with it and gave a show. As the kiss deepened, silverware clattered around them and some low comments. They had an audience now. Finally they pulled apart.

The horror on Tibbitt's face said plenty.

Andy sat back and licked his lip slowly. "Ruben is my boyfriend, *Herb*." He snuck a glance back at Ruben. "Well, I think he is."

Grin. "He is."

A circle of country clubbers now eavesdropped without apology.

The old man spluttered. "Not here."

"Uh, no. There are vile homos right here in Scarsdale, I can promise. In this room, even." Andy dropped a hand into Ruben's lap.

Ruben was too startled to protest, too pleased to be embarrassed. Instead he leaned back and gave Andy access. This was his show. "We can prove it to you. On the fucking table if you want."

Andy cupped Ruben's balls. "Wouldn't be the first time."

Tibbitt's face and neck turned the color of raw liver. "You're disgusting. Both of you."

"I'm so glad to hear it, *Herb*." Andy grinned, full dimple deployment. "Now that we're all in business together."

"Don't be preposterous." The old man looked ashen. He glanced round the room of suburbanites. "This will kill your mother." He looked out at the course again, anxious and morose.

"*This* will. Not you bankrupting her. Not you ruining my father's company. Not you kidnapping and assaulting us. Not you going to federal prison as a fraud and a coward." Andy crossed his arms. "Me being with a guy."

Ruben grinned. "A brown one, *vato*."

"Doesn't matter. You can't shake me. You'll only hurt your mother."

"No. She survived divorce, mah-jongg, and faking orgasms under you twice a year. She's indestructible."

Tibbitt raised his voice finally. "God—" Guests turned. His voice dropped to a low whisper as he held up his mobile phone. "Damn it, Andrew. All I have to do is dial the SEC."

"You're all *hiding* from me." A woman's hoarse voice cut the air in a broad mid-Atlantic saw, like Katharine Hepburn with a quart of bourbon in her. Then she caught Ruben's stare and revealed eyes the same blue-gray flannel he knew so well. This had to be—

"Mother." Andy turned.

"Andrew Bauer. Brunch at the club. There's pork in the treetops." She winked at Ruben as if he'd laughed along with her. Her accent and elocution made her sound as if she'd learned English abroad. She said nothing about their injuries or odd clothing. Maybe it was impolite to ask?

Cilla stopped and crossed her thin arms, a fragile, blowsy woman, her auburn hair shot with gray. "With a handsome stranger."

Andy sighed. "Hardly hiding."

His stepfather began to fidget and signaled a waitress for a refill. "And a vodka grapefruit for my wife."

"Well, I had no idea where to look." Cilla gave a lonely, frazzled smile. "I'm not clever like that."

"I bet you are, ma'am." Ruben blinked at her with genuine warmth.

"He called me 'ma'am,'" she said to her son, husband, and anyone else in earshot. "Are you Southern?"

"Florida."

"Ohh." She made that one syllable sound as though he'd announced he'd survived leukemia. "But you're in the city now." She giggled hoarsely until he nodded. Without a doubt, she was the source of Andy's goofy charm and his sense of fun.

On the other side of the table, Tibbitt eyed his wife with unfiltered contempt.

Ruben thought of his own mother changing a tire. Andy's mom had never had her hands in cold water. She didn't act like a snob at all. She acted like a prisoner. She resembled nothing so much as a bird with clipped wings, flapping in circles and staring at the sky.

Down in Florida, Ruben had sat in a hundred AA meetings with ladies like this: dutiful dolls who realized they'd sold themselves for pennies on the dollar. Ruben loved his parents, but he'd always felt separate. As if his invitation to their party had been lost in the mail. Cilla's ditzy intimacy made him feel like a fellow conspirator, part of the family.

She looked up at Ruben. "Who might this big fellow be?"

"Ruben Oso, ma'am." He took her fragile hand and squeezed lightly, winking to disguise his crook face.

"Greek. Or Egyptian. You have to be. Portuguese?"

He corrected her gently. "My family is Colombian."

The waitress returned with drinks. Cilla's had a salted rim.

"Mom." Andy took a breath. "Ruben is my boyfriend."

Long pause. She blinked at him and at the floor. She squeezed Ruben's fingers back, with light involuntary pressure.

"Really, Andrew." Tibbitt crossed his arms. "Cilla, we were talking business. I had no—"

She finally beamed up at Ruben, then her son. *Those eyes.* "But that's marvelous."

Andy blinked. "It is?"

Tibbitt glared at the other brunchers who were pretending not to watch. "This is not the place—"

Cilla touched her hair absently. "Oh honestly, Herbert. You'd think I'd been packed in cotton my entire life. I watch cable. I'm a big girl," said the woman who probably weighed a hundred and five pounds in a full gown.

Ruben grinned at Tibbitt, then at her. She finally let go of his hand, but only to pat his arm.

"Where did you meet?" Cilla sipped her Salty Dog carefully.

Andy asked, "You're not surprised?"

"Well, of course I'm surprised, Andrew. I had no idea you were... that way, but you work too much, and you've never been *serious* about your women. Any of them."

Ruben considered Tibbitt's purple face.

She scrunched her face at Ruben and blinked warmly. "Not *serious*, serious."

That word.

"Thanks." Andy hugged her and kissed the side of her stylish head. "Mom."

That warmth lit something in her. She patted Ruben's arm conspiratorially. "You're very sturdy, Mr. Oso. And so handsome."

"He is."

Cilla straightened her wedding ring. "And if you ended up like your… father, hiding in tax exile, I'd have felt such a failure." She glanced at her husband, unaware she was keeping a secret everyone knew.

Across the table, Tibbitt did a good impression of a gray trout choking on the air.

Andy sat back. "Herb is going into business with me, so I'll be seeing much more of you." Eyes on Tibbitt. "Both."

Tibbitt's weak smile felt better than a crisp hundred.

Ruben exhaled, finally and fully. Now brunch sounded excellent. He wanted to sit here and watch this asshole squirm in front of his neighbors for hours. He stroked the back of Andy's head, smoothing and teasing at the cowlick.

Cilla eyed the pair of them, pausing on their injuries. "Now, how did you get so mashed up the pair of you? Is that some kind of rough sex thing?"

Ruben's face heated.

Tibbitt closed his mouth in an ugly crumple.

"Honestly, Herb," She scoffed at him. "I'm not a child."

But Andy chuckled. "No, Mother. We've been out in the woods, got lost, separated. Couple mishaps finding our way home." The lie came smoothly off his lips. His predator eyes flicked to Herb, daring him to pipe up. "We found each other again."

"One of those survival weekends," Ruben offered. "We survived."

She beamed back. "Oh good. My son's up in that apartment too much."

"Amen."

Two skinny waiters returned to clear the plates and top up the drinks. The bill landed in front of Tibbitt. Cilla waved to a family with a baby.

Ruben muttered to Andy, "I love your mother."

Andy said, "Give her time."

"Hush, you." Cilla turned back, but she looked pleased at the teasing.

Herb glared with all the menace of a confused bath mat. His mouth opened and closed but nothing emerged.

Ruben understood perfectly. Andy's announcement had stolen the righteous victory from Tibbitt. At the very moment the old man would have raised a glass in the country club and crowed about the Apex partnership, he was forced to zip it.

If it hadn't been for you meddling kids.

Cilla stroked the rim of her glass. "You two had better play nice now."

"She's right." Andy swung cold eyes back in that direction. "Dad."

Tibbitt looked relieved. "Excellent. We'll speak tomorrow."

Cilla stood. "Oh, now...."

"Well, we didn't mean to crash, and we've got a meeting back in the city. Lawyers." Andy stood. "Don't get up."

Tibbitt did not.

Cilla did. She looped her arm through Ruben's. The pressure on his bruised ribs felt like fire, but he let her. "I suspect you're a treasure. I like him, Andrew."

"I do, too, Mom." Andrew's blue-felt eyes fell on them. "A whole lot."

"And you boys will come to dinner. Now that my son has finally zipped his pants." She rolled her eyes and whispered to Ruben. "Whoring around, I mean. He gets that from Royce. His father, I mean." A glance at Tibbitt. "Biological, you know. Promise you'll come."

Ruben squeezed back, almost following her logic. "Cross my heart. And you'll come to dinner too."

"Do you cook?"

"No, ma'am, but I make a mean reservation."

"My favorite." Cilla laughed like chandelier crystal knocking together.

Ruben made his way through the brunchers at an easy pace, happy to be stared at for once.

Andy's hand rested on his back with proprietary pressure. "Let 'em look."

Ruben laughed. "Poor bastards."

Outside they waited in happy silence, retrieved their stolen car, and drove home to break the bad news to Hope.

CHAPTER TWENTY

YOU ONLY live once. But if you do it right, once is plenty.

Ruben drove them back, five miles under the speed limit. This time of day on a summer weekend was dead, and they made it back to Park Avenue crazy fast. Ruben parked out front. As they passed the desk, Andy tossed the keys at the doormen.

A floppy-haired kid caught them. "Sir."

"Just park it in one of my spots." Andy hesitated long enough to explain. "A guy will come pick it up sometime this week."

Ruben went right to that elevator button. He needed to get off his feet, throw up, eat something—in whatever order came naturally.

Andy joined him as the doors opened, and they rode up in relieved silence.

Happily, Hope was waiting for them upstairs, and the police were not. She stood in the living room, looking out over the city.

"Well, hello, Ms. Stanford." Andy headed for the living room. "Some day off."

Ruben smiled at her and nodded. *We're okay.*

"Oh thank God. You don't know. What a day." She turned to Andy, her face hopeless. "I'm fired."

"What?"

"You're firing me. Are they putting us all in prison?" She vibrated with anxiety.

Ruben held out a hand. "What are you talking about?"

"Look at the pair of you. I'm gonna call the cops now."

"No!" Andy held up a hand. "Not necessary."

"Andy, you tell me what I gotta say and I'll say it. You been good to me." She straightened. "You know I will."

For a second, Ruben could see the ballerina in her, her long neck and the line of her proud jaw. "Apex."

"C'mere." Andy smiled gently. "C'mon. Jeez, I never should have dragged you through all this."

"No." She looked like a guitar string on the verge of breaking and curling.

"I'm out of business. That doesn't have to mean you are."

She blinked. "Bullshit."

Ruben shrugged. "What the man says."

"You're not fired. I'm retiring. Hang on." Andy trotted down the hall toward the office.

Ruben and Hope eyed each other.

She didn't move. "He okay?"

Ruben nodded.

"You?"

He shrugged, then smiled.

"Okay." She exhaled, as if she'd been holding her breath.

Sounds down the hall. A low curse. Ruben sat down at the dining room table, and after a couple of minutes, Hope did as well.

Andy's voice came back down the hall as he did. "Mr. Oso and I have negotiated a very fair settlement with the other party."

Hope waited.

He dropped a stack of pages between them on the table. "I'm giving you half of Apex. Fifty percent."

No reply. She turned to look at Ruben. "Is he shitting me?"

Surprised, Ruben shook his head.

Andy grinned. "Nope. Half the company. But there's a catch. A big, ugly one."

"Goddamn it." She kept managing not to cry. "I can't to go to prison. I've worked too damn—"

"Hope, look." Andy initialed the pages swiftly.

Ruben nodded. "This is the truth. He's telling the truth."

"But—" Andy signed the last page. "In exchange, you have a partner who's an asshole."

She choke-laughed. "No shit."

"Not me." He looked at Ruben. "Effective immediately, I'm retiring so we all don't go to prison. My boyfriend over there thought that seemed like the wise move."

Ruben raised his hand. "That would be me."

"Good." Hope shook her head. "But I'm not comfortable with this retirement."

Andy bent over the table to write a check. "I've made some rash decisions that compromised clients, and we're going to make good on those accounts. My stepfather will be your partner on paper. He has no say on the business. He will collect profit, but you have control."

Her eyebrows creased.

"Not like that." He offered her the pen. "He's a thief, but a stupid one. He'll have no authority."

She shook her head. "What if he's an asshole?"

"No 'if'." Ruben glowered. "He is, but you'll eat him alive. Second he steps outta line, you call the feds."

Andy nodded. "Nothing's free. You'll have working capital and your own offices. Hell, you can hire an assistant. From now on, this is just my home. Ours." He glanced at Ruben.

"Hope? You don't have to agree," Ruben said.

"I'm trying to stop." Andy's tone begged. "This is out of control and it's not fair to anyone."

Ruben sat down. "We're trying to unmake the mess is all. He's trying to make amends, get clean." His eyes held hers. Andy didn't know she was sober, and he wouldn't betray her trust. "This transfer is only a step. He'd become *powerless* over all this." That word came straight out of the *Big Book*, Step One.

She looked up. Message received.

"Powerless and stupid." Andy continued the thought. "Business. My family. I don't want to keep making the same mistakes."

She nodded. "I get that." Another nod. "Amends. But why give all this to me?"

"Because you earned it." Andy offered the pen. "Because I'm out of control. Because Oso asked."

"Oso's right." She smiled for the first time since they'd walked in. "What if I'm not ready to run a fund?"

Ruben snorted and made a face. "You already were."

"What if I fuck up?"

"Fix it." Andy grinned.

She shook her head at the table and the papers. "Andy, you scared the hell out of us."

He nodded.

Her phone made a chirping sound, but she didn't answer it. "I gotta go. My fiancé's parents already think I'm nuts."

"We gotta deal?"

"Bauer. Give it a rest with the pen." She exhaled. "You *know* I'm not signing that craziness here." Her eyes scanned the document for a moment. "I'm having it checked by every lawyer I know. And a priest, maybe."

Ruben laughed. Andy looked sad.

Hope patted his arm. "How the hell are you going to survive without someone keeping an eye on you?"

Ruben chuckled. "Covered."

She stood up. "If you're not my boss now, what are you?"

Andy paused. "Your friend."

"I can live with that." She looked up and shook his hand. "Deal." And then she picked up her Chloe bag and was gone.

Ruben turned to look at Andy a moment before he spoke. "Tibbitt. What if he hassles her?" Hope, he meant.

"He can't." Andy walked slowly toward the living room.

"No more financial hitman bullshit."

"No. No. This is more ninja."

"Andy." Was he serious? "The last thing we need."

"That's not what I meant," Andy agreed. "Not a hit job. Promise."

Ruben rolled his eyes, like his brother actually. "What, then?"

"Banking booby traps. And a landmine."

"Bauer...." Ruben glared.

"I swear. Long as my stepfucker watches his step and leaves us alone, then they'll be fine."

"And if he gets pushy."

"I left Hope an SEC nuke and a big red button to press. But the only way he'll run any risk is if he breaks laws to come after us."

"No more stupid bullshit. I'm watching you." Ruben grinned, but he meant it.

"Totally legal." Andy tapped the door. "I exposed a vulnerability. That doesn't mean I exploited it. I found a security risk."

"Which your stepfather'll take advantage of."

"Not if he's smart. It's flagged all the hell over." His square face lit up.

Ruben had been waiting to see that grin for so long that he actually sighed with relief. "And?"

"And the feds would come knocking in about fifteen minutes if he got stupid enough to breach the security."

"You booby-trapped Tibbitt."

Andy shrugged and stretched. "Well, it only works if he's a complete boob."

"Which he is. I rest my case."

"You come rest your case over here."

"I may be too beat up to fool around just now." Ruben gestured at himself. "Okay if I take a shower?"

"I, uh...." Andy's brow creased. "Of course, man. You don't ever have to ask."

Ruben went to his old room—the guest room—and peeled out of the musty clothes, revealing his gritty and bruised body to the mirror. He didn't need to go to the hospital, but the bruises on his ribcage looked like an Everglades sunset. He'd pay for that tomorrow.

He could only handle lukewarm water, but seeing the grime and blood swirl down the drain felt right. Whatever came next, at least he felt clean. Afterward, he pulled on jeans and didn't bother with a shirt. Too hot, too sore.

When he emerged, he didn't find Andy in the office or the kitchen or the living room, till he looked through the double-height windows. "I see you."

Andy sat on the terrace with his feet propped up on the ledge, handsome and tired under the July sky.

Ruben tugged open the door and, sure enough, found Andy relaxed, no shark left in him now.

Andy stood. "Well, hey." Tired blink.

"How's tricks?" Ruben nosed into the nape of his neck. "You're gonna get a sunburn."

"Before you say anything." Andy looked down at the street below and back. "I wanna say something."

"That can't be good."

"I'd like for you to stay here."

"Tonight?"

"For a start. For more. For good."

"Nah. I think you probably need some space for a while." Ruben shook his head. "And, uh, I think I've gotta get my ass to a meeting. Work my Steps right." Moral inventory. He'd need a sponsor.

"I want to be part of that. If you'll let me."

"I lied. All this. I lied to myself. My bullshit Fourth Step. Peach. I don't even know where to start."

"You take a step. We'll figure it out."

"I'm not… that's not how it works." Ruben sighed. "I'm not s'posedta even date for the first year in the program."

"But—" Andy looked back again. "But people get sober without leaving their families. I mean, AA doesn't make you break up."

"Of course not. I never should've let any of this happen. We shouldn't."

"Well, maybe not. Maybe that's so. But this isn't theoretical anymore, Rube. We're not just dating, are we?"

"I guess not."

"I mean, are we? You live here. I love you. I want you to get clean and be happy." Deep breath. "With me."

"You don't know that." Ruben didn't feel like he could control where this was headed.

"I do know. I'm being serious now. I know what your Steps are; I did my due diligence. And I say we're together. Do you agree?" The son of a bitch was negotiating their relationship.

Ruben fought the smile.

"And if you need me to move things or do things to take away temptation—"

Ruben filled his lungs with hot, wet oxygen, drowning in midair. "No, Andy. Look. Nobody gets sober living in luxe with a cool job and supermodels fucking you stupid. *Seriously.* I gotta do it in a bar, surrounded by friends who put the poison in your hands and beg you to kill yourself. I gotta put my foot down wherever I am. I gotta stand up because I refuse to lie down and *die*." Peach would've kicked his ass for talking like that. A lot of drunks used sobriety to wag their fingers at the world. Just another kind of control. Another way to sidestep your shitty life. One more excuse to be an inauthentic asshole. "I'm sorry."

"For what? You're right."

"Maybe I am, but if so it's accidental." Ruben moved to stand in front of him. "I'm a dry drunk trying to get sober. That's my shit. Has nothing to do with you. The life I wrecked is the one I was given. I got no right to lecture anybody. That's the point. Alcohol isn't an excuse. I've got no excuse for anything. No one does."

"You never lecture—"

Ruben held up a hand. "What I'm saying is, nothing is free. Not one thing. We get the life we pay for."

Andy shook his head.

"I don't mean money or accidents. I mean by standing up. Working hard. Taking lumps. Telling the truth." Ruben sniffed. "Serious."

"Put your foot down."

Ruben smiled and squeezed his hand. "Exactly. One step and then another. Peach used to say—" He smiled at the memory. Menthol smoke curling in his mind. "Sobriety isn't an excuse for being a dick."

Andy stood, watching him warily.

"I used to believe that money fixed shit. Wrong. I figured growing up with all this, having toys"—Ruben waved at the penthouse—"made things easier."

"Yeah, no."

"Well, I get that now. Duh. For all my price tag bullshit, I never thought about what it cost. Cost *you*, I mean. Changed you."

"Ruben, it's different now. I'm different."

"Nah. We're all exactly the same. We never change, really, down at the bone. We shed our skin, but we're still snakes underneath, all of us, always."

"Goddammit! Will you stop?" Andy pushed a hand into his hair and scratched his scalp roughly.

Ruben sighed, grabbing his nerve before it slithered back into hiding.

"I feel like you're about to say something horrible."

"I am." Ruben laughed and fell silent.

To his credit, Andy let him take the time he needed to look at the sky, to take that breath, to count his heartbeats and take one final step off this glass cliff to face the hard ground rushing at him.

"I love you, Andrew Bauer." Finally Ruben looked up.

Andy's jaw clenched. His blue-gray eyes looked enormous.

Ruben smiled, weak with relief. "Which has to be the weirdest, craziest, dumbest, smartest thing I ever did. I love you in a way that makes hard work easier. Makes bad choices clear. Makes me safe from myself. And that shit's not easy. It's sharp, like a serrated knife, and it hurts. You cut away everything that isn't me. But I'm not saying that to guilt you into anything or make a scene. I'm saying it because it's the truth and you deserve to hear it from me. Okay? I'm being *serious*."

Andy nodded, not a smile back exactly, but the dimple did its thing. "You oughtta punch me and beat tracks. Run for the hills. I'd say you're an idiot to care about me at all."

Ruben frowned. "Why?"

"I'm not what you think I am, Rube."

"Likewise, jerk. Who is? That's part of the deal, I think. Two people get so tangled up there's no pulling them apart."

"I don't want you to get hurt."

"Well, luckily *I* get to decide. It's my hurt. My heart. And I don't want it to stop."

Andy smiled. "Well, me either."

"You know what I mean." Ruben swallowed. "Loving you."

"Oh."

Silence.

Andy reached and laced their fingers. *Cream and coffee.*

Sun licked their limbs and, for the first time, they were touching in the light.

Ruben squinted at the sky, suddenly conscious of the street sounds and the breeze playing across his skin. "The whole world can see."

"Good." Andy sighed with undisguised contentment. "They should."

The penthouse floated above all the surrounding buildings. Ruben remembered Daria's relatives sitting in their windows and understood why architects called these buildings high-rises. He and Andy had climbed a mountain. *Safe.* Unless reporters swooped by in a helicopter, and if they did, who cared?

Not me.

Andy started to say something, but Ruben caught his eye and barely shook his head, asking for a chance to stand there together in the sun outside the glass walls.

He smiled up at the sky.

Andy squeezed his fingers. "Next step?"

"Steps, huh?" Nod. He missed Peach just then. "I think I've got more than a couple. It's gonna take a while to put my foot down."

Andy asked, "What about a job?"

Ruben looked at the penthouse around them. "Uh, I think you're okay on finances."

"I might get bored. Idle hands. Who knows what I might get up to in your absence?" Andy raised his hands, tickle-ready.

Ruben laughed and swatted at Andy's jabbing fingers. "Well, I mean to keep you out of trouble. You're good with accounts. My brother might need a bookkeeper."

"That's not half-bad." Andy laughed and then stopped. "Nine-to-five actually sounds fun."

"Only because you've never done it. And I need to find an apartment."

Andy didn't break. "I gotta place. Maybe you can crash."

"And burn." Hand on Andy's arm. Ruben squeezed and pulled. Face-to-face in the hot light.

Big grin. "Sounds great to me." He leaned forward, but let Ruben erase the space between their mouths. The kiss was solid and simple, with a puzzle-piece calm that made the world stop spinning.

Ruben broke first to whisper, "S'pose I'm gonna have to keep an eye on you, *pintón*."

"One eye." Andy grinned. "That all?"

"Hardly." Ruben knocked him back against the wall of glass, and raw pleasure skittered over Andy's face.

Andy spoke with undisguised contentment. "Help. Stop. Don't."

The sun touched their skin gently. Ruben took a deep breath and exhaled in happy relief.

"That was some sigh, sir. What seems to be the problem?"

"Gonna sound paranoid, Bauer, but I'm pretty sure I'm in terrible danger." The smile stretched Ruben's face.

Andy grinned back and leaned forward with lazy confidence. "Why?"

"Just a feeling." Ruben tapped his heart.

"Good." Andy stepped in, trapping his hand there. "I'll protect you."

DAMON SUEDE grew up out 'n' proud deep in the anus of right-wing America and escaped as soon as it was legal. He has lived all over, and along the way he's earned his crust as a model, a messenger, a promoter, a programmer, a sculptor, a singer, a stripper, a bookkeeper, a bartender, a techie, a teacher, a director... but writing has ever been his bread and butter. He has been happily partnered for over a decade with the most loving, handsome, shrewd, hilarious, noble man to walk this planet.

Damon is a proud member of the Romance Writers of America and the Rainbow Romance Writers. Though new to romance fiction, Damon has been writing for print, stage, and screen for two decades, which is both more and less glamorous than you might imagine. He's won some awards but counts his blessings more often: his amazing friends, his demented family, his beautiful husband, his loyal fans, and his silly, stern, seductive Muse who keeps whispering in his ear, year after year.

Damon would love to hear from you.... Get in touch with him at DamonSuede.com.

Also by Damon Suede

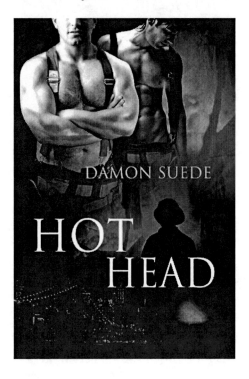

Where there's smoke, there's fire...

Since 9/11, Brooklyn firefighter Griff Muir has wrestled with impossible feelings for his best friend and partner at Ladder 181, Dante Anastagio. Unfortunately, Dante is strictly a ladies' man, and the FDNY isn't exactly gay-friendly. For ten years, Griff has hidden his heart in a half-life of public heroics and private anguish.

Griff's caution and Dante's cockiness make them an unbeatable team. To protect his buddy, there's nothing Griff wouldn't do... until a nearly bankrupt Dante proposes the worst possible solution: HotHead.com, a gay porn website where uniformed hunks get down and dirty. And Dante wants them to appear there—*together*. Griff may have to guard his heart and live out his darkest fantasies on camera. Can he rescue the man he loves without wrecking their careers, their families, or their friendship?

Available at
www.dreamspinnerpress.com

Also by Damon Suede

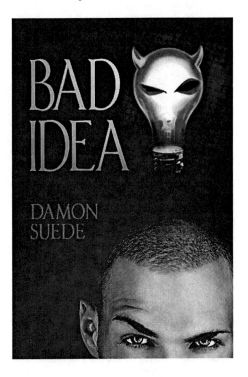

Bad Idea: Some mistakes are worth making.

Reclusive comic book artist Trip Spector spends his life doodling supersquare, straitlaced superheroes, hiding from his fans, and crushing on his unattainable boss until he meets the dork of his dreams. Silas Goolsby is a rowdy FX makeup creator with a loveless love life and a secret streak of geek who yearns for unlikely rescues and a truly creative partnership.

Against their better judgment, they fall victim to chemistry, and what starts as infatuation quickly grows tender and terrifying. With Silas's help, Trip gambles his heart and his art on a rotten plan: sketching out Scratch, a "very graphic novel" that will either make his name or wreck his career. But even a smash can't save their world if Trip retreats into his mild-mannered rut, leaving Silas to grapple with betrayal and emotions he can't escape.

What will it take for this dynamic duo to discover that heroes never play it safe?

Available at
www.dreamspinnerpress.com

Also by Damon Suede

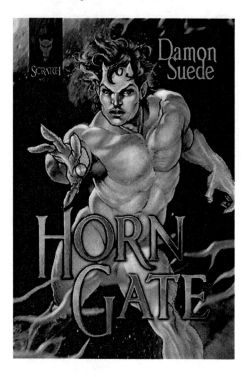

HORN GATE: Open at your own risk.

Librarian Isaac Stein spends his lumpy, lonely days restoring forgotten books, until the night he steals an invitation to a scandalous club steeped in sin. Descending into its bowels, he accidentally discovers Scratch, a wounded demon who feeds on lust.

Consorting with a mortal is a bad idea, but Scratch can't resist the man who knows how to open the portal that will free him and his kind. After centuries of possessing mortals, he finds himself longing to surrender.

To be together, Isaac and Scratch must flirt with damnation and escape an inhuman trafficking ring—and they have to open their hearts or they will never unlock the Horn Gate.

Available at
www.dreamspinnerpress.com

Also available in translation:

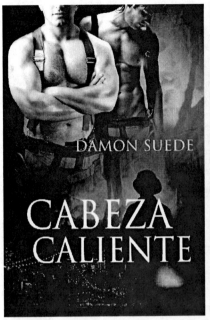

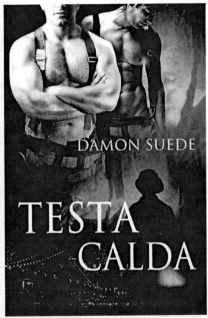

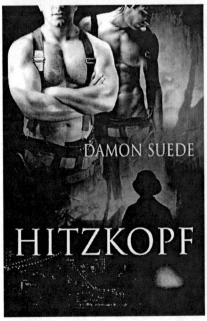

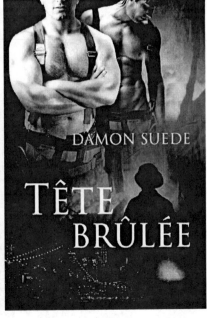

CPSIA information can be obtained
at www.ICGtesting.com
Printed in the USA
FFOW04n1854280218
45347659-46012FF